Praise for the first edition of *Lost Angels*
(formerly titled *As Above, So Below*)

"Fans of paranormal romance, urban fantasies, kick-ass fights, and some damn hot sex, check out *As Above, So Below!* "
— Dana Fredsti, author of the *Plague World* trilogy

"Beautiful, intoxicating and strange as only a relationship that spans heaven and hell can be, *As Above, So Below* is the most evocative and entertaining novel you're likely to read this year. Just keep a strong hold on your soul as you do so; you don't want to become a victim in the eternal war."
— John Everson, author of *Sacrificing Virgins*

"If you enjoy theology and the idea of angels and demons at war among us, you need to check this book out. You won't be disappointed."
— HorrorAddicts.net

"Aside from the framing of the war between Heaven and Hell through well-developed characters and a familiarity with theology, Rhoads and Thomas's depiction of temptation *make* this book. Sometimes the mix of horror fiction with romance and erotica in literature leans mainly toward horror, or pulls the primary attention of only one gender of reader. However, *As Above, So Below* is not that story. Any fan of erotic horror fiction, male or female, is going to have fun reading this one. *As Above, So Below* has a creative plot, vivid descriptive imagery, relentless temptation, graphic horror, and fiery, fun sex."
— Jeremy Price, *Up All Night Horror Fiction Review*

Praise for "The Angel's Lair" (the first chapter of *Lost Angels*)

"This is a story of high ideals and blazing intimacy. Very powerful stuff."
— David Niall Wilson, *Macabre Ink*

"Good story, done with an eye for gritty urban detail and sexual explicitness."
— Fright.com

Lost Angels: As Above, So Below, Book 1

Published by Automatism Press, San Francisco

Cover photograph by Carmen Masloski.
Cover design by Mason Jones.
Interior design by Automatism Press.

Photo of Loren Rhoads by R. Samuel Klatchko.

Previously published as As Above, So Below by Black Bed Sheet Books in 2014.

Paperback ISBN: 978-0-9636794-2-0

e-Book ISBN: 978-0-9636794-3-7

Loren's dedication:
For Mason and Dana, who saw us through it,
and Mart, who survived the aftermath.

Brian's dedication:
To Coop, Kozik, Angelina, Aria, Anton, & Charlize:
inspirations, all.
To Joz, who read every draft. To Dana, who abided.
Last but furthest from least, to Lo.

LOST ANGELS

AS ABOVE, SO BELOW: BOOK 1

LOREN RHOADS
&
BRIAN THOMAS

AUTOMATISM PRESS

SAN FRANCISCO

CHAPTER 1: THE ANGEL'S LAIR

Lorelei licked the last traces of soul from her lips, then smoothed the knee-length hobble dress over her thighs. The black lycra snuggled around her like a living creature. The barbed tip of her tail twitched as she scanned the dance club, seeking more prey.

Her violet eyes locked on the creature seated at the end of the zinc bar, dressed in a rumpled khaki trench coat. Through the smoke and flashing lights of the dance club, she saw him for what he was: an angel of melancholy. Hers. His wings weren't manifest, but the unmistakable glow of his halo enforced a margin of emptiness around him. Shoulders hunched over his glass, he was doing his best to ignore what was going on around the club. Clearly not having fun, which was a damned shame, considering that fun was what Lost Angels was all about. Lorelei wondered what it would take to put a smile on his face.

She patted hair over the nubs of her horns and adjusted the dress's zipper to be demure as could be, only the pale white column of her throat revealed. Once she'd made certain that the seams on her stockings were straight and her mortal glamour was flawless, she stepped out of the shadows. Let's see if this one could be won without a fight.

The angel ignored her when she leaned across the bar at his elbow, straining the Lycra dress just so. Lorelei waved the bartender over. "My usual," she shouted above the music, "and whatever he's drinking. On my tab."

When another Crown Royal appeared in front of him, the angel made no move toward it. Lorelei breathed into his ear, "Say thank you."

Vaguely in the bartender's direction, the angel repeated, "Thank you."

Lorelei touched her glass against the angel's, then downed a good mouthful of her drink. More Absolut than cranberry, just the way she liked it. However, the angel continued to ignore her, tense and miserable, wanting his whiskey but apparently afraid to touch it.

"Thank you, Lorelei," she prompted. She leaned against the angel, nestling his shoulder between her breasts. She reached around his waist to hold him close. He could escape her, certainly, if he wanted to cause a scene. She licked her lips, so close to his ear that he quivered at the sound. "What's your name, Angel?"

He sipped his drink before answering, "Aza."

There should be an 'el' on there somewhere. Amused by the dropped honorific, she echoed, "Just Aza?"

"Aza will do."

The nickname made him sound accessible. Not fallen yet, but unimaginably lonely. Lorelei asked, "Looking for company, Aza?"

The angel put his glass down very precisely on the bar. She was unprepared when his stormy green eyes turned to her. "Maybe I came looking for you, Lorelei."

The timbre of his voice shivered through her like lightning.

When she was sure of her composure, she purred, "Here I am, Angel." She planted a kiss between his blond eyebrows. Rather than strike out at her, as she expected, he drew a shuddering breath. Deep down in her hips, the succubus felt a connection made. Not fallen yet, but hers. Her lipstick looked like the mark of Cain on his ivory skin.

A mortal voice preempted her next move. "Hey, Lorelei, aren't you here with me?"

She ignored it. "Wanna go?" she asked the angel.

Aza swiveled on his barstool to regard Steve, the shady stockbroker, over her shoulder. Before Lorelei could figure out how to get the angel's attention back, the angel said, "I should," then drained his glass, and strode off.

Fucking Steve-o. Lorelei spun toward him, wrapped her fist in his Sean John sweater, and dragged him toward the dance floor. There she positioned herself so she could watch the angel thread his way through the crowd toward the exit. Pressing her haunches back against Steve, she let her hips find the rhythm of his lust. No challenge there.

The flavor of the angel lingered in her mouth. She closed her eyes, never losing the rhythm of the dance, and licked her lips, savoring. She tasted myrrh, beeswax, years of solitude. Cast out, but not fallen. She stared after the angel speculatively.

Her sister Floria glided across the dance floor, lithe and so golden that she burned in the strobe lights. Her scarlet dress barely grazed her thighs. Lorelei accepted the glass Floria offered. Her sister slithered up against her, straddled one of Lorelei's thighs, and mouthed in Steve's direction, "Ready to go?"

Steve took a half step backward, clearly blown away that these two hotties wanted to be with him. "All of us?" he shouted.

Lorelei sipped the Cosmopolitan and passed the glass over her shoulder to Steve. He gulped the rest of the drink. Lorelei barely caught him when he sagged. Floria let the glass hit the floor.

Still, she did help Lorelei get the mark out of the club. They arranged his hands on their bodies as if the party had already started. The mortal security guard stared after them, aroused but on duty. Floria flashed him a grin that helped his situation not in the least.

At the edge of the street, Lorelei dropped her purse. When she knelt to retrieve it, Floria bent down beside her. Steve reeled, uncertain how they'd vanished. He tottered off the curb into the path of a yellow cab. Brakes shrieked too late.

Floria calmly handed back a tube of blood-red lipstick. "Did I see you flirting with an angel?"

"Yeah. When was the last time you saw one who wasn't fallen in our clubs? He said he'd come looking for me."

"That's a scary thought."

"I don't think so." Lorelei licked her lips again. "Would you handle the Yupfuck? " She waved toward the body in the street.

"I'd rather do that than chase anything with feathers," Floria answered.

A crowd gathered, drawn by the blood. Someone demanded an ambulance. The cab driver was shouting, "What the fuck, man, what the fuck!" as Lorelei withdrew into the city shadows.

"Where have you gone, Aza my love?" she purred.

Her gaze searched downtown LA's sparkling high-rises, looming over the dance club. She was reasonably certain the angel wouldn't have gone there. Cast out of Heaven, dwelling miserably on the mortal plane: was he looking for a reason to fall? Lorelei hoped she could supply it. One of the enemy brought to heel ought to advance her far up the infernal ladder.

The faintest trace of his scent drifted down Temple Street. Lorelei unfurled her wings and let the angel's loneliness summon her.

The streets of the warehouse district looked as if a neutron bomb had gone off. On the buildings, graffiti swirled and screamed, naming names, making accusations. Lorelei flew low to the ground, glorying in the rush of air through her thin dress. She crossed the train tracks, then circled back. A block away, a tarnished white figure walked down the rusted steel rails, head down and hands in pockets.

She dropped to her feet and hid her wings and tail. She'd meet him as a mortal.

He didn't look up when she joined him. Lorelei matched his stride over the railroad ties and let the silence stand.

The angel nudged her with his elbow, offering a pint of Jack Daniel's. Whiskey burned pleasantly down her throat.

When she handed the bottle back, his gaze was appreciative. She resisted the urge to preen, appreciating him herself. She wanted to feel his soft blond hair between her fingers. She wanted to wash his deep-set green eyes with her tongue. She wanted to take those soft lips between her teeth and kiss him until she tasted bruises.

"Have you come to hear about Heaven?" he asked.

She smiled, slow and serious, and let firelight flicker in her eyes. "You're looking pretty earthbound to me, Aza. What do you know about Heaven anymore?"

"It lives in me. I never forget it." He knocked back a long swallow of whiskey.

Lorelei taunted, "I thought drinking was a sin."

"There's no prohibition against alcohol," he corrected. "Only drunkenness. It'll take more than this to get me drunk." He sucked down the rest of the whiskey. When he flung the bottle away, it shattered against a cinderblock warehouse with such force that it popped like a light bulb. Shards of glass shimmered off into the night. Aza looked more startled than the situation warranted. He halted in mid-step, suddenly supernatural.

To get his attention back to business, Lorelei asked, "Which do you prefer of the sins of the world?"

"I prefer the sinners."

Lorelei grinned at him, opening her arms to display the whole package. "This is your lucky night, Angel."

He cocked his head, half smiling. "It may well be."

Encouraged, she pressed her body against his, feeling solid flesh beneath the sharp corners of the trench coat's buckle.

He crushed her against his chest, holding her pinned so that she couldn't kiss him. "Bearing in mind I've seen actual Paradise, what do you think you can offer me?" he asked.

"Bliss," she whispered. "I can give you bliss."

"And the price?"

"Your fall."

"Too high." He lifted her off of him, set her carefully on a railroad tie so that she didn't stumble in her four-inch heels. "Kiss me and go."

"If I don't kiss you, can I stay?"

"Will you be in trouble if you let me go?"

"Let you go from what? We haven't struck any bargains yet."

He shrugged and started walking. She kept pace, but when he didn't answer, she reached out. To her surprise, the angel turned abruptly and

4

snatched up her hand. "My conditions..."

"Yes?"

"As long as I stay in mortal form, you do as well. Make no attempt to seduce me. Anything more than kissing, our truce is off."

She stared into his eyes, wondering how serious he was.

"I know how your kind are," he continued. "I know what your promises are worth. So don't promise me anything; simply understand."

The angel was older than dirt, she recognized. He'd seen the beginning of the world, the Wars in Heaven, the Fall, yet remained subservient. Here he was, trapped in the mortal realm and longing for Heaven.

"Kiss me, if that's all you want." She tipped her face to catch the distant streetlight.

Instead, he tugged her down a side-spur of the tracks. Weeds straggled up between the ties. Occasional rusting cans and an abandoned hammer made treacherous footing for a girl in heels. Lorelei watched her feet. Any injury to this mortal body was going to hurt unless she could guilt him into healing it for her. That might be a way to go, if she couldn't use typical avenues of seduction.

Against her hand, his skin was smooth as marble, the same temperature as the evening air.

They passed the homes of urban campers, walls constructed of tarps and shopping carts full of their belongings. Eyes followed their passage. A dog barked. Lorelei wondered what fear felt like. The angel owed her nothing. He'd set his conditions without discussion of extenuating circumstances. How far would he test her to see if she'd keep her word? How violent would he get if she overstepped his boundaries?

If he killed her, she hoped her sisters would shred the angel and rouge their lips with his blood. A gang of them could probably take him down. Even Floria might rise to the challenge.

Aza tugged a handful of keys from his coat pocket and unlocked a rolling metal door. Lorelei was curious to see an angel's lair. Perhaps he'd insisted she take mortal form for her own protection, to allow her to enter: possible, though doubtful. He'd accepted her company, but took no responsibility for her. Yet.

She followed him into the warehouse. When he rolled the door closed behind them, darkness crowded the building. She took a step simply to hear her heel ring against the cement. Long, narrow, the echoes said.

The angel grasped her elbow. She leaned against him for safety's sake. He didn't push her away. The building seemed to hold its breath.

Several paces in, he unlocked another door and eased her across the threshold.

With a rush of wind, a legion of candles burst into light. They clustered in knots on every flat surface. Creamy golden beeswax had pooled around their bases.

On the eastern wall, he'd built a shrine. Shards of mirror formed a starburst. A small casket hid his ritual implements from her gaze. Traces of myrrh lingered in the air.

In the corner lay a single futon on a frame made of loading pallets. The bed had neither sheets nor pillow, but a couple of blankets spilled over its foot. She wondered why he wasn't living in one of the better hotels downtown. The Biltmore was reputed to have several angels in residence, since its façade was inscribed with their names and images. What was Aza's story that he didn't rate a room there?

"Make yourself at home."

As the angel shrugged off his coat, Lorelei stole a glance, but saw no wings. Pity. It would have made a nice bit of show. She stepped out of her shoes and perched on the edge of the futon to rub her feet.

Aza hung his coat on a simple wire hanger behind the door. Beneath the coat, he wore a clean white button-down shirt, worn chinos, and boots that needed a shine. Did he always dress like Nondescript Man, or had he spiffed up to go out tonight?

Ignoring her, the angel knelt before his shrine, resting his hands on the casket.

Lorelei stretched out on the futon, feeling chilled, and pulled the blanket over her.

The angel got himself right with his Maker and came to lie beside her, also fully clothed. He didn't share the blanket.

"I'm cold," she said.

"Hold your hands out," he answered.

She pushed them out from under the covers, expecting him to rub them warm. Instead, he caught her wrists. In an unexpectedly swift movement, the angel swung his weight over her, pinning her beneath him, entangled in her shroud. As she struggled to claw at him, he snapped a metal cuff around one wrist. He dragged her toward the head of the futon, wound the handcuffs around a bare pipe there, and cuffed her other arm.

As she tested the strength of the handcuffs, the pipe, and her flesh, he draped the blanket over her. He stretched his legs out along hers, then laid his arm across her midriff.

"Sleep," he commanded.

Cursing him, she did.

6

She struggled awake, disoriented in the darkness. The angel's sweet breath tickled the top of her head. He lay against her, arm draped loosely over her waist.

She was sweltering under the blanket. Her thighs were humid above her stockings. Lorelei loathed sleeping in clothing.

Trying to get comfortable, she snuggled back against the angel. The movement forced the hem of her dress up so that she felt the fabric of his chinos against her bare thighs.

Just like that, he was no longer beside her. Instead, he sat on the far edge of the futon, gently phosphorescent in the darkness. He regarded her as if he'd just figured out that he didn't know what to do with her.

"I just woke up," she complained. "I'm cramped from lying in this one position. Maybe if I could curl up..."

He knelt beside the futon. His hand landed unerringly on her knee. Without tugging on the handcuffs or hurting her, Aza lifted her legs, blanket and all, and helped her to double up.

"Can I ask you another favor?" she wondered.

"You can ask."

"My stockings got all messed up when I wriggled around. They're pinching me."

He spoke light into several of the candles. "Don't move," he ordered.

When she nodded, he folded the blanket back over her thighs. The angel grasped the first crumpled stocking without touching her skin and slipped it down over her foot.

The rubber top of the second stocking had rolled downward, tightening just above her knee. She watched his face as he reached for it. Something avid flickered behind his eyes. Her tongue slipped out to wet her lips.

He plucked the stocking back with the index finger of his right hand.

Lorelei realized how tense her hips had gotten at the thought of his touch. Grinning, she watched him look for a place to put her stockings where they wouldn't contaminate his belongings. He settled for the pocket of his trench coat.

"What are you going to do with me?" she whispered.

"I don't know."

"I'd sleep better if I aroused you a little."

He barked out a short laugh. "I'll bet you would. So I have another condition." He returned to the bed and lay beside her again. Her hopes rose a little. Then he rested a cold steel blade against the warm side of her neck. "Just because we're in bed together, don't get the idea we're friends."

"Deal."

To his complete surprise, the succubus dropped back to sleep despite the knife at her throat. Those born in Hell must be accustomed to a certain level of peril.

As he folded the knife closed against the wall, he suspected that he should just kill her. He existed on sufferance as it was. It would be safer to kill her than to risk temptation...except that, asleep, she was as close to a state of innocence as her kind was likely to come.

Testing himself, he stroked silken chestnut hair back from her face, admiring the shape of her nose, the bow of her full lips. Without her violet eyes measuring his every movement, she seemed a completely different creature. Almost human.

He withdrew from the bed again. Lorelei sighed as sweetly as any mortal child, but did not stir.

Aza felt the coming dawn and knelt before his shrine to pray for guidance. She'd followed him here. Her half-hearted attempts to seduce him had seemed assured of their failure before she began. All the same, something about her touched his heart. She was barely more than a child, playing a game she couldn't possibly comprehend. He would have liked to think of her as a moth, drawn to his light. Unfortunately, he knew where that led for moths. He told himself not to pity her. How many souls had she attracted and destroyed?

The number came to him easily, more than he would have liked. It upset him enough that he had to get away from her. He tugged his coat off its hanger and left the room.

Just before dawn was the best time in the park. Aza drifted down near the statue of the Marquis de Lafayette, without paying much attention to the nondescript granite.

An old Mazda wagon was parked just off of Sixth Street. Its driver lined take-out cartons behind the luggage rails on the car's roof. Aza liked Noc for remembering vows made in the worst of times.

One by one, the homeless appeared from under benches or behind bushes, drawn by the scent of food. For many, this would be the only meal of the day. Even so, Aza joined the line, trusting that Noc had more than enough food.

Aza recalled waiting on the docks twenty-five years ago with the other Watchers. Noc's prayers reached him days in advance of the boat's arrival. Though unable to help the boat land, the angels catalogued the pleas from those packed onboard. Aza remembered Noc's plaintive offer to The Word: If the pot of brackish rice held out until his turn to eat, if it kept him alive, he would spend his life feeding others.

Aza recalled the dead-leather feel of Noc's skin when he'd pulled the man ashore. He tasted the man's hopeful desperation. By nightfall, the Cambodian was settled with a Chinese family in Van Nuys, assuming the place of their recently deceased uncle. Noc worked in the kitchen of that family's restaurant with missionary zeal.

In the decades since, Noc thrived in the city. Now he owned his own place. His profit margins could have been better, but his soul was unquestioned.

Noc tapped his nose. "Not alone this morning, friend?"

Chagrined, Aza shook his head. He must reek of the devil's perfume.

Noc stacked two cartons, more than enough, into a plastic bag and thrust it toward Aza. When the angel gripped Noc's hand, the restaurateur's face lit up. Then he returned to feeding the needy.

Aza wondered if a mortal could guess how much an angel appreciated the contact.

Something was scratching at the door. Lorelei moved to wipe the hair out of her face, but couldn't reach because of the damned handcuffs. She wondered if she had to keep her mortal form if rats attacked. Was this one of Aza's tests?

A pair of candles flickered on Aza's altar. Their reflections fidgeted in the broken mirror.

The whine of stressed metal set her teeth on edge. Something larger than a rat was forcing its way into the room. Who else lived in the warehouse? Was one of Aza's neighbors dropping by to see whom he'd chained to the bed this weekend?

"Awake?"

Her master's voice galvanized her. "Of course, my lord."

What was Asmodeus doing here? He never dropped by during her regular tricks.

Lorelei struggled to get her feet under her hips, to push herself into sitting up. With her arms immobilized by the handcuffs, the wriggling around completely disarrayed her clothing, rolling the hem of her dress up farther. She caught hold of the edge of the blanket and covered herself as much as possible. "Please, my lord, come in."

The door glided open. The demon in charge of LA lounged against the doorframe. Asmodeus fanned gray silk gloves in front of his face. "It stinks of piety in there."

"I'm doing what I can about that," Lorelei assured.

"Alone?" The demon studied the curve of her thighs beneath the ragged blanket, the way her hands were clasped to conceal the cuffs. "Quite a predicament: one of my pets named and bound by a minion of the Enemy. It pains me to see it."

He puffed out his breath. The candles went out. Asmodeus burned with a dark radiance.

"He'll fall," Lorelei promised. "He's shown me tenderness already."

"His kind lavish tenderness as a distractor technique," the demon sneered. "Perhaps it would be better to set one of the older girls on the case, someone with more experience. Maybe Yasmina…"

"I'm not going to need that bitch's help," Lorelei snapped.

"In mortal form, you're an easy mark for him," the demon taunted. "If your flesh dies alone with him, none of us will come to collect you." Asmodeus tilted his head as if scrutinizing her will.

Lorelei decided to change tacks. "He said he'd come to Lost Angels looking for me."

"Your sister reported as much."

Of course Floria had. Ever dutiful. "Then you know I'm the only one who can do this job."

"It's not enough that Azaziel fuck you," Asmodeus explained. "He's fucked mortal sluts before. Lust must drive all other desire from his heart."

"You know I'll do anything required of me."

"You'd better," the demon threatened casually. "Do you have any idea how rare it is for an angel to fall? Countries die easier deaths. If you begin this and fail…"

Lorelei put everything she had into being persuasive. "It will be my pleasure to do this task for your honor and the glory of Hell."

"That's what I was waiting to hear." With a mocking bow, Asmodeus pulled the door nearly closed.

She'd be damned if she would admit defeat, Lorelei told herself. Already Azaziel had asked for a kiss. Maybe she'd just give him one and see how he liked it.

The door slammed open. The beeswax candles blazed to life. Startled, Lorelei jerked her head backward. Impact jarred her skull, then red exploded across her vision. She'd forgotten how close she was to the wall.

"Did I scare you?" Azaziel asked.

"Half to death." Lorelei blinked back teardrops prickling her eyes.

He set a white plastic bag on the floor and slipped out of his trench coat. While his back was to her, he asked casually, "Who unlocked my door?"

No point in lying, she suspected. "Asmodeus."

Rather than getting upset, the angel showed an unexpected sense of humor. "The trouble with family is that some of them think they can drop by any time."

She laughed. It hurt her chest.

"He came to check on your progress?" Aza prompted.

"As if I've made any progress. He came to remind me that I'm on my own here." Lorelei held the angel's gaze. "Anything happens to this flesh, I'm formless."

"I intend to do something about that."

"Do you?"

The angel gave her an enigmatic smile as he sat on the edge of the futon. Lorelei frowned. Something warned her that the angel was about to adjust their arrangement again.

Then she smelled something so wonderful that she forgot all about business, overwhelmed by a wave of weakness. "Is that Chinese food in the bag?"

"Yes."

She rattled her chain against the pipe.

"Oh, no," he said. "I'll feed you."

"I'll behave," she promised.

"I'm sure," he answered easily. He reached into the shopping bag between his feet, broke open a paper envelope of chopsticks, and unfolded the first carryout box. "Mongolian Lamb. I love lamb, one of the first mortal foods I ever sampled. Shall we begin?" He deftly picked up a bite of lamb and a slice of scallion with his chopsticks. She turned her head away. Aza shrugged and fed himself. She watched the food travel from the box to his mouth. She closed her eyes to shut out the sight of his pleasure. Listening to him eat was worse, but she forced herself to endure it. Saliva flooded her mouth.

"Aren't you hungry?" he asked.

"I'm not a big fan of lamb."

"Let's see what else we've got, then."

He knelt in front of her and opened a second take-out box. Without identifying it, he held a bite out to her with the chopsticks. It looked like duck, smothered in Chinese five-spice powder. Hot, just the way she liked it. She chewed slowly, dragging the process out. She quite enjoyed having his constant attention.

"Accepting hospitality from an angel," he teased. "What are they going to say about this when you get home?"

She hung her head to gaze at him through the veil of her hair. As long as the outcome was good, Lorelei didn't much care what the others thought of her methods.

Despite appearances, she had options in this situation. Whenever she decided it was time for a fight, she could resume her true form. Aza was older and undoubtedly stronger than her, but nothing forced her to accept his "hospitality." That he offered it did seem a point in her favor.

She watched his face as he fed her. His eyes were as changeable as diffraction paper, sliding in color from palest blue through vivid green to a steely gray. She thought about licking them again, especially now that her tongue was hot with the Five Spices. She wanted to drink his tears.

When she shifted, the handcuff chain rattled. The angel grinned, enjoying her predicament immensely. Her confidence came rushing back. Not yet fallen, not yet hers, but the odds seemed to be improving.

She dropped her gaze so he wouldn't see the sparkle in her eyes. She waited until he touched the chopsticks to her lower lip, then darted forward, catching the bamboo sticks in her teeth. She bit down hard, snapping one. She spat it out onto the floor and grinned at him.

"Bored?" he asked.

"Yes," she hissed.

He scooped up a bite of duck and held it out to her with his fingers. She met his eyes again and opened her mouth.

He slipped the morsel of duck past her lips without touching her. She let him feed her by hand, not menacing him in the least. She waited for him to drop his guard. All living things eventually revealed their fatal flaw. The trick was to exploit his without revealing her own.

This felt like the longest she had ever gone without sex in her life. The fire inside made her edgy, but she had to be careful now. If she lunged at him, if she moved too fast in the wrong direction, this seduction could become suicide.

Aza began to toy with her. He held out a bite of duck and made her crane after it. She played that game for a while. Then she stuck out her tongue, mocking him. She caught his fingers with her lips, gently nuzzling the Chinese spices from his fingernails. When she felt him drawing back, she circled his fingers slowly with her tongue and raised her eyes to meet his.

His sigh was so deep it rattled his whole body. He set the takeout box onto the floor. "Stop that," he said in a deeper voice.

She formed her lips and tongue to be as soft and hot and wet as a man could want: an image to linger in his mind.

"I mean it."

He didn't yank his hand away, but she felt his arm tense. It was tempting to see if he'd hit her for giving him pleasure. Rather than push him, she leaned back and let him take his fingers from her mouth. The handcuff chain rattled.

"Come on, Angel. Show me a little mercy."

"I'll show you mercy," he threatened, looming over her suddenly. Lorelei whimpered—it wasn't entirely feigned—but there was nowhere to go to get away from him. The angel grasped her head in his palms and bent down over her. She felt his cool breath in her hair. His lips melted against her flushed forehead. Sweet angelic compassion washed over her.

Lorelei collapsed as if her limbs were unstrung. The lingering pain in her head vanished, but the kindness of his grace turned to terror in her chest. She tried to remember how to breathe. She thought he'd killed her.

"Fuck your compassion, Angel," she snarled weakly.

He laughed, the first truly amused laugh she'd heard from him. He stroked the hair from her face. "You're all right, Lorelei."

As he said it, it was true. She drew a deep, shuddering breath. "That was one hell of a kiss, Aza."

"Glad you liked it."

She dropped her gaze and put just the right amount of hesitation into her voice. "Can I have another one?"

When his lips brushed her cheekbone, she turned her face into his. Their lips met. A spark passed between them, magnified as it traveled. They both jumped. He pulled away just a fraction.

Lorelei yearned toward him. Weakness trembled in her muscles. Aza couldn't resist that. He supported her in his arms.

Using all her guile, Lorelei pressed her mouth into his. His compassion flowed into her again, but now that she was prepared, it didn't paralyze her. She felt it swirl down into her body, curling smoky tendrils around her heart.

Deep in her hips, though, was the unquenchable fire of who she was, the lust that drove her. Raising that power up the ladder of her spine, she focused it as finely as a laser into her kiss.

Something in the angel reacted to it. He held her so tightly that she wondered if she would break. She squirmed, rubbing her flank between his thighs.

The connection she'd made in the club tightened deep inside her. The knot of power refused to crack, declined to spill its energy through her limbs. Instead, the sensation lurked dangerously close to cramps. She had to do something to break the stalemate.

"I want you so badly," she whispered, "*Azazi-El.*"

Big mistake, calling him by his angelic title. She knew it instantly. The door slammed open as a whirlwind roared through the room. Half the candles snuffed out. The others guttered, throwing fierce shadows. Aza flung her away from him, snapping the handcuff chain. She hit the wall hard and collapsed, breathless, into the corner.

He towered over her in the wild light. She saw the shadow of his wings. He trembled, fighting the desire to tear her apart.

She remained in helpless mortal form. If she transformed now, he would kill her before she got off the bed. As hard as it was to do, Lorelei bowed her head. She feared to incite his hatred if she so much as looked at him.

Aza spoke an angelic oath that Lorelei didn't understand, then snatched his coat from its hanger. The wind followed him out the door, taking with it the last of the light.

CHAPTER 2: SANCTUARY

Lorelei crouched on the futon, unable to believe she'd escaped unscathed.

Of course, Aza was getting away.

Sighing, she stood up. The cement floor was icy beneath her bare feet. The wind had slammed the door shut behind the angel. She laid one hand on the doorknob. If she couldn't get out in human form, he meant for her to stay until he'd calmed down.

The door swung open in her hands, its bolt sheared off by Asmodeus's visit.

Lorelei peered out into the night-black warehouse. Once more the building echoed with silence. She was alone.

She resumed her own eyes first. The darkness resolved into a long narrow hallway. As she crossed it, her legs lengthened out painlessly. By the time she reached the roll-down door to the outside world, her arms had regained their strength. She clawed open the door, flung out her wings, and leapt upward into the morning sky.

The rush of wind against her flesh exhilarated her. She hadn't realized how emotionally captivity had affected her. Anger flooded into her. How dare he demand she remain in mortal flesh in his company?

She caught a thermal in her wings and soared upward. Where the hell had he gone? She scanned the skies around her, half-expecting him to drop toward her, pinions flashing.

She passed over a pool hall surrounded by a ring of police cars. The frantic red lights revolved silently. Whatever had happened was over. Two policemen lounged against the fender of their car, smoking cigarettes. Other men were busy inside the bar. Lorelei filled their minds with sudden desire—just because it amused her.

Aza would avoid all of that excitement. She peeled away toward downtown.

As Lorelei searched the alleys between the derelict movie palaces, she didn't worry about being seen. People reduced to living in these doorways saw angels and devils regularly, for all the good it did them. Despite the daylight, humans who didn't expect to wouldn't see her at all.

The tarnished white flash of Aza's presence caught her eye. He stood in mortal form in one of the alleys, consoling himself with more whiskey.

Lorelei smiled, cutting her lower lip on her sharp teeth. She swooped into an updraft to gain height for her attack. Then, folding her wings, she plummeted down at him. If lucky, she might break him by speed alone.

Aza looked up at her. The bottle dropped from his fist. His expression was joyous. For someone who had insisted she maintain mortal form, he certainly looked delighted with her now.

The connection inside her hips tugged. At the last moment of her attack, Lorelei resumed her mortal form. Helpless, she dropped the last few feet into his arms. Her weight knocked him back against the crumbling wall, but they didn't topple into the unsavory debris carpeting the alley. Pity.

Aza's lips found hers. She used to think Paradise would be an eternity of fucking. By the time Aza took his lips from hers, the kiss had made her reconsider.

"You broke your attack." He sounded genuinely surprised.

He eased her down until her bare feet touched the ground. Troubled, Lorelei dropped her gaze. If the situation had been reversed, the angel becoming helpless in the midst of an attack, she would have walked away to give him time to become more pliable, or maybe even put a dagger in his throat. She was no angel, of course. But being born of Hell, she had no soul to interest him in saving. Why had he stayed his hand, here and back in his cell? Something about her mortal form swayed him, something beyond comeliness, beyond personality: the appearance of weakness?

The realization made her frown. Just how weak did he assume she was?

"Why did you come to the club last night?" she demanded.

"Because you're exactly what I needed, Lorelei."

She liked the sound of that. She rose up on tiptoe to trace the tip of her tongue around the sweet curl of his ear. "What do you need me for, Angel?"

Aza thrust her away, holding her at arm's length. He lifted his free hand, three fingers extended. Then he grasped her neckline and tore the stretch fabric of her dress to her crotch. The lycra molded against her fleetingly as it slipped past. The angel dropped it to the alley floor.

"Now you're talking, Lover." Clad in nothing but the broken

handcuffs, Lorelei stretched, the better to show him she was entirely comfortable naked. "Shall I be your Lilith?" She cupped her right breast in her hand, stroking the dark flame of her sex with the other.

Aza studied her. Something very like desire flared in his eyes, before it melted into a regretful smile. He rested his palm against her sternum and said, "More like my Eve."

Shame hit her like a physical blow. All defiance, all pride evaporated from her as surely as human resolve did before Hell's flames. She saw herself as if for the first time, very naked before him, before the world, before...God?

She looked up at the angel uncomprehendingly. He helped her into his trench coat as one would dress a child: closing the buttons and cinching the belt around her waist. He even turned the cuffs back for her.

He took her hand and led her from the alley onto Broadway. Lorelei followed, struck dumb as she watched the filthy sidewalk pass beneath her bare white feet.

Behind them, a section of the alley wall wavered. First the cinderblocks were solid, then oily blackness swallowed them. Out of this darkness stepped Asmodeus, trailed by two fiends in the form of large men, angular to the point of being misshapen.

Probing the refuse with his ebony walking stick, Asmodeus picked his way through the alley. Near the passage's mouth, he halted. At his feet lay a crumple of shadow: Lorelei's cast-off dress. The demon gestured down toward it.

Recognizing its master, the dress stirred, lifting a sleeve flirtatiously. When it brushed his hand, the cloth hurried upward into his grasp.

The demon rolled the fabric between his fingertips. Lycra had definitely been one of his engineering staff's most useful inventions. He considered how tasty Lorelei had looked poured into this pinnacle of the art. What a shame the angel cast it away so maliciously.

Asmodeus raised the torn fabric to his face and breathed deep. Beneath the dark fragrance of Lorelei's musk—wound amongst it—was the scent of the angel's longing. He'd lain beside the succubus, kissed and caressed her, but his desire didn't end there.

Unsmiling, the demon prince crushed the dress in his fist and let it dissolve.

Lorelei became aware of muted feminine laughter behind the tinted windows of a slowly passing limousine. The sound made her realize the angel no longer held her hand. She found herself alone on a curb, arm extended, fingers curled around empty air.

He'd abandoned her.

Lunchtime traffic rushed by, heedless of her proximity. Balancing on her toes, Lorelei closed her eyes. The unpleasantness Azaziel had inflicted on her in the alley still eddied in her chest.

She thought of the creature she'd failed to seduce.

She thought of Asmodeus, who'd have no use for a bashful succubus.

She thought of the laughing temptress in the passing car, sharpening her claws in the wings.

A single step would destroy the body she wore. As she stepped off the curb, she heard footfalls behind her like the beating of wings. Aza eased her around and gathered her in his arms. Lorelei clutched him.

Before she was ready, he moved away with an apologetic sigh. He led her to a recessed doorway and knelt beside the figure huddled there. It was an underfed girl, seventeen at most. Her tortured hair might have been magenta once, now faded to the color of dull blood. She stared at the angel with glazed yellow eyes. The amateur tattoos on her doll-like hands implicated unsterilized needles.

Death had its own current, one that flowed outward in unmistakable patterns. The girl was unsaved, something Lorelei recognized even in her muddled state. Her mouth began to water. How sweet. Aza found her something to eat.

Someone whooped down the block. Lorelei twisted around to see a pair of harpies, camouflaged in dirty human forms. The blonde wore a mangy rabbit-fur coat over a cheap mauve leather miniskirt. The other, her shaven skull tattooed, was all dyke-y tough in Doc Martens and ripped fishnets. A ragged red warm-up jacket molded itself around her muscular arms. Standing by for their meal, Lorelei realized. The tattooed one flashed Lorelei a shit-eating grin while the blonde made a playful sign of the horns.

Too damn bad. She was a hell of a lot hungrier than those two.

Out of the corner of her eye, she saw the angel's head dip close to the girl's. The child inhaled sharply. Passing his lips over hers, Aza eased the girl's final convulsion.

Even from a block away, the harpies' snarls were audible. The girls dropped into fighting crouches. The blonde's peroxided hair fanned behind her.

Aza straightened from the dead girl. One of his hands rested just below his throat. He took three swift steps toward the harpies, tracing divine symbols in the air before him.

Shrieking with rage, the harpies' tore their jackets away to bare their breasts. Their feathered arms swelled into wings that pulled them skyward.

Lorelei knelt beside the corpse, but found her meal had vanished.

The angel returned to the body and sank down by it. He quickly unlaced the dead girl's boots and handed them to Lorelei.

"You're joking," she said.

"If those harpies attack, you'll want some sort of armor."

"If those harpies attack," Lorelei corrected, "what makes you dream I'll stand on your side? That was my breakfast you just gobbled up, Angel. I didn't even know your kind fed on the unsaved."

She put on the boots anyway, glad to have something between her tender feet and the pavement. Warmth lingered inside. She wriggled her toes, luxuriating.

Aza grasped Lorelei's arm and propelled her across the street during a lapse in traffic.

The blonde harpy dropped onto a mailbox in front of them. Her talons furrowed its enameled surface.

His eyes set hard on the harpy, Aza drew his left hand back. The inner three fingers pressed into a tight point. His right hand, however, spread protectively across his breast. Lorelei puzzled over that. What did he have hidden there?

A sharp whistle brought her attention back to the harpy. The blonde cocked her head toward Lorelei. "Oh, Sister!" she taunted. "What I won't do to be there when you get yours."

She bounded straight up between the high-rises into the lowering clouds.

Lorelei followed the angel's gaze around. Behind them, the tattooed harpy crouched atop a limo, conversing intently down through its open sunroof.

"Come on," Aza ordered, starting off anew.

He seemed determined to keep her around, so that was promising. They entered the border neighborhood on the far side of the Pasadena Freeway. The formerly thriving residential streets barely held their own against the encroaching city. The neighborhood had fallen by stages into decay. Corner markets had become liquor stores known as murder marts. Family homes had become boarded-up, graffiti-splashed crack houses. Lorelei knew devils who considered this landscape a work in progress, one on which they lavished artistic attention.

She hoped none of those devils were watching now. There was so much urban cancer in this so-called City of Angels that it was likely their attention would be elsewhere. What did it matter, anyway? The gossip had no doubt already started in Hell. Asmodeus was never one to let an amusing story go unrelated. She wondered if he'd thought it worthwhile to dispatch someone to defile Azaziel's lair.

She wished she'd thought to do it herself. Maybe, if she played her cards right, she'd still get a chance. Despite everything the creature had shown her—benevolence, charity, hints of desire—she had also glimpsed his other aspect. She recalled her vision of him before the candles had gone out: fierce, barely reined, almost savage. Aggression, passion, lust: one led to the next down the right road. Despite the danger to her, savagery could lead this angel straight to her feet, if she provoked him efficiently. Lorelei had never been one to step away from a dare.

"I'm getting cold." She rubbed her arms through the trench coat. "Can we go back to your place and see about warming me up?"

"No. Before I left, I spoke an abjuration. You left shortly thereafter, didn't you?"

"I didn't feel banished," Lorelei protested.

"You weren't," he said. "Only the temptation you represented."

Past tense, she noticed. Before she could comment, Aza stopped abruptly and took both of her hands in his. "At the risk of getting myself into any more trouble," he said, "you are incredibly beautiful, however you choose to appear."

She wasn't choosing to appear any special way, so whatever he was seeing was in the beholder's eye. Still, the compliment had a sincerity Lorelei had never heard before. She shivered as the spark leapt between them again. She had a sinking suspicion that he wouldn't be the only one in trouble before this was over. Refusing to relinquish his hands, she pressed her lips up against his. As long as the kiss lasted, she wouldn't have to think about anything else.

She felt the moth-wing flutter of the girl's soul against her teeth. Stumbling back, Lorelei stared at Aza.

The angel bit his lip self-consciously. "Sorry," he offered, a tinge of guilt in his voice. "Scared her."

"You almost lost her," Lorelei blustered. How was the angel holding on to the unsaved soul? "Of course, I can understand you might savor her. No matter how tainted the flesh might become, nothing matches the sweetness inside."

She rose onto the balls of her feet. Instinct commanded her to pounce, to steal the girl from his very kiss. That should amuse her prince.

Aza's hand flashed out, fingers splayed like talons over her skull. He compelled her to settle back. "If you're hungry, just say so."

Lorelei removed his hand from her head. Never taking her eyes from his, she stretched out her tongue to taste him. The feathery, electric hint of soul was replaced by the flavor of loneliness and myrrh.

With a smile, Aza disengaged his hand from hers. "You *are* hungry, aren't you?"

"I've changed aspects since I ate last. That always burns a lot of energy." She tugged on the trench coat's belt to snug the coat closer around her, in case he'd forgotten what was wrapped inside.

"Let's see what we can do."

They continued on, turning corners so regularly that Lorelei suspected he was deliberately trying to confuse her. What could possibly be at the center of the labyrinth? She licked her lips and played guessing games.

Aza stopped at a street vendor's cart. Lorelei brazenly studied the cart's owner. He was an old man, creased skin the color of weathered walnut under a snowfall of hair. When he acknowledged her, Lorelei gave him a knowing smile. After it registered that she was naked except for the borrowed trench coat and boots, the old guy's head snapped back toward the angel so fast Lorelei thought the man was going to give himself whiplash.

They might not know what you are, Lorelei thought, but when they see you with me, they guess what you're capable of. A few more days of hanging out with Aza and she might alienate every soul who'd ever looked up to him as an emblem of goodness.

Pulling her close, Aza reached unceremoniously into the neckline of the coat. His hand passed her breast as he felt for the inner pocket. When he withdrew, he held a small chamois pouch. Extracting silver coins with the dexterity of a magician, he rolled them across his knuckles into the metal can atop the cart.

Oh, Aza my boy, she thought, you have no idea how this looks, do you? She thought about tugging her stocking from his coat pocket like a magician's scarf, give the mark a glimpse of real magic.

Then Aza's hand was back inside the coat, lingering a moment, leaving a weight behind. Delicious warmth radiated against her breast.

"Fresh pupusas," he explained. "That should warm you up some."

He linked his arm through hers, pulling her forward once more. Lorelei turned to give the vendor a wink, but he was trundling away with the awkward cart as fast as possible. Lorelei struggled to keep the grin off her face.

Rounding one more corner, Aza leaned close to her ear. "This is going to be a first among firsts for you."

She glanced up the street. She had to squint, as the sun broke through the smog to silhouette the building ahead of them. Without a doubt, their destination.

A church.

"You can't be serious."

Reaching out to touch her face, he said, "There's nothing for you to fear."

"Easy for you to say!" she snarled, pushing away from him. "Walk with me to the Portal of Abandoned Hope and let's see how you fare."

Aza favored her with a smile of purest angelic condescension. "I may yet visit your home. Depending how our relationship progresses, you may not like the manner of my arrival."

She had a fleeting vision of Azaziel in the front ranks of some Heavenly horde, wings outstretched, armor shining with painful brilliance, brandishing some terrible instrument: just like the tales meant to put fearful resolve into young devils.

This time laughter burst out of her. "You think they'd follow you into Hell over little ol' me?"

The laughter cleared her mind—at last—of the nastiness he'd inflicted on her hours before. She saw now that the church doors were sealed shut. Sooty tendrils ghosted above the boarded-up windows, staining the adobe-yellow paint. Burned out and abandoned. She hoped Hell had had a hand in that.

Aza left her in order to survey the neat plywood bolted over the doors. Everything about him seemed relaxed now.

Lorelei realized he was giving her a chance to walk away. Maybe he didn't grasp this wouldn't be her first conquest in a desecrated church. It was a kick last time and that guy had been a mere mortal. She climbed the steps to lean against him. "Looks like the management has moved on."

"It never left," he announced decisively. "When we go in at the back, why don't you pretend I'm sneaking you in?"

"Whatever works for you, Angel."

In the back of the building hung a fire escape. Aza leapt gently upward to pull the ladder down for her, then gallantly gestured her up the steps.

She climbed through the window into a room that must have been an office once upon a time. It had been spiffed up, even painted recently. Most importantly, it had a real bed—box springs and a mattress, anyway—and nothing to which she could be chained.

Aza followed her through the window and pulled the ladder back up.

Lorelei examined the place. An unfinished fresco of angelic script scrawled across half of one wall. Pillar candles clustered together in knots on the scuffed floor. Another starburst pattern, like the one she'd seen in his cell, adorned the wall between the windows opposite the bed. This starburst was composed of fragments of stained glass. The windows themselves overlooked a potholed asphalt playground.

"Be it ever so humble…" Lorelei teased, implying that Heaven could no longer be considered his home.

Without a word, Aza indicated she should sit on the bed. He knelt at her feet, unlacing each boot with a deft flick of his fingers. Then he disappeared into another room. Lorelei heard water running. She hoped that indicated plumbing, not merely a garden hose strung in from outside.

"What are you up to?" Her voice echoed, surprisingly loud. She wrestled off the boots and cast the coat off too, for good measure.

Aza returned with a basin in his hands and a pair of what appeared to be towels draped over his arm. Setting the basin at her feet, he unfolded one of the "towels" to reveal a roughly woven shirt. "Arms up, please."

She complied, posing so that he could appreciate the contours of her body. The shirt he eased over her did divine things to her breasts. She shivered with pleasure as the large shirt slid over her torso, settling in her lap. She rubbed the fabric in her fingers, trying to name it. The thick material felt surprisingly soft.

"Ready to eat?"

Turning back the cuffs of the long sleeves, she said, "Like you can't imagine."

Aza handed her a still-warm pupusa, fragrant enough to focus her mind on solid food. Lorelei unwrapped the foil around it to discover a cornmeal patty. Inside was some kind of savory meat folded into shredded cabbage. She wolfed that one down and unwrapped the second, before she realized the angel hadn't joined her.

In fact, he sat on the floor at her feet, gazing up at her. Lorelei liked that more than she had anything all day.

After she checked her compact to make certain she didn't have anything stuck in her fangs, Yasmina let herself into the club. A gang of fiends lounged around the silent bar. None of them dared to look at her, which was the way she liked it.

"Is he here?" she demanded.

"Office," one of them grumbled.

Checking the books, no doubt. Yasmina slithered through the silent shadows toward the private parts of the club. She rapped gently on the closed door.

After a moment, one of the new succubi opened the door, wiping her mouth with the back of her hand. Yasmina spoke over her head. "I was hoping you were free for a cocktail, Master."

Asmodeus answered, "I have a few minutes." To the new girl, he said,

"Bring us a bottle of Châteauneuf-du-Pape '78."

Yasmina slipped into the office and closed the door in the face of the eavesdropping succubus. "I'd like to talk to you about Lorelei's new project."

"I expected you would. Don't imagine for a nanosecond that I'm taking Lorelei off the case."

Yasmina noticed that he didn't smile as he delivered his warning.

CHAPTER 3: INSPIRATION

Lorelei waved the second pupusa tantalizingly under the angel's nose. "Want some?"

"You eat it," Aza insisted. "You'll need your strength."

"Really?"

Tentatively, he reached out to massage her feet. Lorelei gobbled down the pupusa so she could pay closer attention. He worked the pad of his thumb in lovely firm crescents along the arches of her filthy feet. Smiling, she settled back to watch him get his hands dirty. Maybe, for her angel, it was all about slumming. Whatever. She hoped that the more she let him have his way, the more careless he would become.

He slid the basin forward and began to wash her feet. Aza worked carefully, lavishing attention on each toe and the spaces between. He paused occasionally to cup the water in his hands, allowing it to slip between his fingers and run gently over her skin. He made the process so gradual that the water felt neither cold nor particularly damp.

There seemed something more ritualistic than hedonistic in his actions. Lorelei was such a creature of the modern age that the strangest part of the procedure nearly escaped her attention: the water in the basin remained clean.

"Aza," she wondered lazily, "what's in that bowl?"

Without answering, he picked the basin up. Lorelei noted how reverently he carried it.

"You fucking blessed me, didn't you?" Startling fury flared from her body. Lorelei's skin burned to its natural scarlet color. Her wings tore through the fabric of the angel's shirt. She hadn't intended to manifest her true form. It just happened. She hadn't felt this level of horror in a long time.

With her infernal eyes, Lorelei perceived hints of the true angel hidden in Azaziel's mortal seeming: a blur of wings like stained glass shadows behind him, a silver-gold corona that cast his features into stark perfection. Returning to her true form violated their agreement, but the angel didn't seem to care. He was too busy fussing over that damn basin.

She flung herself after him. Clasping her hands together, she swung her arms like a club. Her strike sent the bowl flying. Holy water sheeted before it, slapping thickly against the frescoed wall. When the crockery followed, it broke into sections with a metallic clink.

Aza pulled her into his arms, holding her there with implacable strength.

"You could've taken the flesh off of me!" Lorelei shouted.

"Relax," Aza soothed. "Harming you is the last thing I intend. Besides, if you were going to burst into flame, it would have already happened."

He sealed his mouth over hers. A shock arced through her entire body as he pressed the kiss. A low thrum raced from his heart to hers. The kiss in the alleyway had been wonderful. This one menaced fate. Grinning in triumph, Lorelei wound her limbs around the angel and clutched his body against hers.

Without warning, Aza tore his lips away. In a jagged voice, he whispered words that returned her to mortal form.

This angel had *serious* control issues. Still, in the end, it didn't matter which of her aspects he fell for—mortal or infernal—as long as she was the one to ride him into the abyss. She pulled him nearer and captured his mouth again.

The angel breathed deep into her lungs. Lorelei felt the flutter of the girl's soul, unafraid now, pass into her, bolstered by Azaziel's angelic power.

Lorelei wanted to consume the soul, but it seemed to have soaked into her as if into a dry sponge. She gagged, trying to cough it out of her. Aza clamped his hand over her mouth.

A single word, spoken with ancient authority, ended her resistance. Her body became a stranger. For the first time, its palpable mass anchored her to the mortal plane. Her quivering legs refused to support her weight. She sagged helplessly into the angel's arms.

Aza laid her gently on the bed.

She found herself suddenly dependent on oxygen, gasping after it. Then she clasped her hands over her ears to block the terrifying wheezing.

Aza eased onto the bed, gazing at her apologetically. He cupped her cheek, but she cringed away, all too aware of his featherweight touch against the solidity of her flesh.

"Take it out of me," Lorelei begged. Her voice sounded frighteningly weak. "Please, Aza, I'll do anything you ask... Take it out of me and I'll go away. I won't bother you anymore."

"Calm down." It sounded more like an entreaty than an order. "This won't kill you."

Scrabbling away from him, Lorelei missed the edge of the bed and failed to stop. The fall knocked the breath out of her. It hurt.

By the time she managed to roll over, the angel bent over her, holding out his hand. "Please, Lorelei. I know this sounds horrible, but trust me. I really don't mean for you to be frightened. I *can* take the soul out of you now, but if I do, you'll have to go."

"Fine," she said, taking his hand.

He pulled her to her feet and sat her on the edge of the bed. As he retrieved a vial of oil, he asked, "What will you tell Asmodeus?"

Involuntarily, Lorelei shuddered. She hadn't thought that far ahead.

Aza moved some candles around her. Their lights were unnecessary in the daylight, but they seemed integral to whatever ritual he was preparing.

Asmodeus would be pissed. He hadn't been thrilled to have Lorelei attempt the angel's seduction in the first place. She'd slipped up when she bad-mouthed the prince's chief bitch. And if nothing else, Floria would certainly never let her live this down: the day Lorelei finally bit off more than she could chew.

"Are you sure I can't stay?" Lorelei asked.

"As long as you stay here, the girl stays where she is."

Apparently, he saw no room for debate.

"Can I have some time to think about it?"

"Why don't you sleep on it?"

She knew what was coming next, the same trick he used last time her will opposed his. He commanded her, "Sleep."

Lorelei looked positively childlike in her sleep, scarcely older than the runaway had been before her death. Aza slipped the tatters of his shirt off of the succubus. For the first time, he observed her nakedness without her preening and posturing. She failed to grasp—maybe it was too far outside her ken—that it wasn't her flesh that appealed to him.

When Aza tugged the bedclothes back and tucked her inside, her body had a human heft. Poor, pitiful creature. He was really going to have to take care of her now, see that she ate and bathed and learned to care for her flesh.

He caressed her shoulder—smooth, soft, perfect beneath his fingertips—pretending for a moment that she was his.

The other angels were going to hate this. He wondered what he would say in his defense.

When she awoke, something alien swam amongst her thoughts. Lorelei lay still, seeing unfamiliar faces, hearing voices she nearly recognized: the mortal girl's recollections. The child had been seventeen. She had a predictable incomprehension about not getting any older. She suffered a prickle of repentance, too. *Typical. Useless.* To all outward appearances, she was headed straight for Hell.

Something inside her flinched at the thought. Lorelei grinned. *Are you listening, little girl? Your body is going to wind up burned and dumped into an anonymous box at the county coroner's. The angel's given you to me. I'm the last friend you've got.*

The soul within her recoiled sickeningly.

Welcoming the nausea, Lorelei twisted the knife. *This angel is ripe to fall—with your help, little girl. Just think of all the degradations you'll get to experience on his way to Hell.*

The angel's lips touched hers. Lorelei jerked her eyes open to find Aza sitting a hand's-breadth away, only the bedclothes to divide them. A faraway streetlight vaguely illuminated the room. Lorelei tried to push the shadows back with her vision, to no avail. For it to get this dark, she'd been out a long time.

"Hello, Lover," she said, more cheerfully than she felt.

"So you know: with the soul inside you, I can hear your thoughts."

Lorelei caught her lower lip in her teeth, before turning it into a grin. "You won't have to imagine all the things I've got to tell her, then."

"She's ready for them now. We talked while you slept."

"So you've gotten her onboard for this special little three-way?" Lorelei tried again to manifest her infernal form, but it was futile. "Lucky me, getting to be your prisoner! Who'd have guessed angels got off on this sort of thing?"

Azaziel took hold of her right wrist and easily removed the broken handcuff.

"And the other?" She offered her left hand.

"When you leave me."

"What makes you think I'm going to leave you?"

"Before your nap, you were in a hurry to go."

"Before my nap, I hadn't thought how kinky it would be to damn a mortal soul at the same time as her guardian angel fell."

Shocked silence stretched between them. Out of concern he would overhear, Lorelei refused to think.

"Can I touch you?" Aza asked.

Lorelei answered skeptically, "What are your conditions?"

"Lie still and enjoy yourself."

She heard a brief—intriguing—sound of ripping cloth. Then his hands eased her into sitting up. Despite the darkness, he gathered her hair, tying it back with care. Was he subtly reminding her that, as a celestial being, he could see her under any conditions?

Lorelei's flesh shivered up into goosebumps. It was a new sensation, one she didn't enjoy.

Then his hands were on her shoulders, fingertips over her collarbone, thumbs pressing into the knotted muscles.

Lorelei leaned back into the pressure. The novelty of being touched in this state was undeniable. He had her at an unfair disadvantage, though. Of course it felt great. He could see things about her flesh, feel things about her reactions, that she could no longer sense herself.

For the first time in her life, Lorelei grasped a fraction of how it felt to be prey.

"This will be easier if you lie down," Aza told her as he guided back her to the mattress.

"What are you going to do to me?" Lorelei whispered hopefully.

He sat back away from her. Lorelei immediately regretted her honesty. She needed him to touch her. Only having his hands on her body made her feel like she wasn't in terrible danger.

After a moment, he asked, "What do you want?"

"Take this dead girl out of me."

"Soon, I promise."

She rolled over to face him, so that he would see she was serious. "Then do whatever it is you want to me, so I can get the hell out of here."

"So I have your permission?"

Lorelei could barely see the angel's expression in the darkness. She hoped she saw a smile, not something nastier.

"I'm asking the same deal you'd require of me, Lorelei, if you were trying to damn me: cooperation."

"So we're clear: I *am* trying to damn you, Aza. Welcome to the program in progress. No matter what you do to me, I'm still on the clock."

Aza's hand caressed her cheek. "Me too, dear."

Lorelei was surprised to hear that. "You gonna fuck my parasite into Heaven? How good *are* you in bed, Angel? You may have me locked in human form with a human soul inside me, but this is my place of business." She patted the mattress.

"So you're finally ready to make love with me?"

"It would be nicer for us both if you let me take my own form," Lorelei said, "but I can work with this if I have to." She pulled him down into a kiss. He allowed it, then something popped softly in the darkness.

Her nose twitched. She smelled something rich, too complex to sort out with her dulled human senses. It smelled too nice, almost holy.

As she wrestled her limbs from under of the bedclothes, Aza touched her lips with a fingertip. With a gasp, Lorelei dropped back to the bed. It was only a matter of inches, but it felt like ten stories. The oil burned with an intense cold that ramped up and up as if it would never stop. Lorelei wanted to scream, to protest, but found herself paralyzed.

The angel pulled the blankets away, leaving her naked before him. He touched more of the oil to her forehead, then to her sternum, each of her shoulders, and finally, to the hollow of her throat.

Taking her head in his hands, Aza placed his lips on hers and gently puffed inward. Her chest swelled. Something coalesced within her, gathering strength. The intense pressure choked her. The sensation had something to do with the human soul, but Lorelei could not imagine what.

Until the angel spoke again. "Ready, Ashleigh?"

Although terror jolted Lorelei, her body hardly twitched. Her lips formed words that she had no part of: "Are you sure it's...?"

"You heard her give me permission, right?"

Helpless rage flooded Lorelei. The warped fucker. He'd given her body into the possession of the dead girl.

The angel kissed her. Lorelei would have bitten him, spat his lips after him, struggled and fought with all her strength, but the angel's spell left her a spectator.

Unbidden, her hand went to Aza's cheek, touching it as if for the first time. To her immense despair, Lorelei felt only the surface of his flesh, not the mystical pulse of his being. This was worse than being blinded by darkness. No wonder mortals were so hungry for experiences of the flesh, for anything that could lift them beyond the isolation of their senses.

The angel stretched out beside her and took her into his arms. The thing he had hidden in the darkness was his nudity. His chest was bare against her breasts, his sex hard against her thigh. She couldn't enjoy it, however. The edge of her awareness halted abruptly at the surface of his skin. She plummeted into more intense solitude than she had ever imagined existed.

He stroked her body, exploring its curves and planes. Warmth and texture, pressure and moisture were no replacement for all the subtler pleasures she had lost. If she had been able, Lorelei would have sobbed.

Her body responded to the angel's caress: not with the practiced sensuality of a lifelong temptress, but with the yearning of a mortal girl. The child had no clue how to move to inflame the angel's lust, to say nothing of magnifying her own gratification.

Aza moved over her. At least the stupid child had enough sense to part her legs. *Finally!* Lorelei laughed to herself, recognizing its hysterical ring. She wondered if there was a name for this: fucking a ghost in succubus-flesh? Had the angel created an original sin? If only she could read his heart and know for certain what burned there was lust.

He took his time and entered her slowly, drawing out the moment of connection. He seemed to treasure the girl's every quiver, every sigh. The last thing he seemed to want was to hurt her. "I love you," the angel whispered.

Nestling her sweat-dampened brow against his throat, the girl whispered, "Bless you, Aza."

Lorelei gagged. *Bless?* With supreme effort, she tried to find words of her own, only to have the girl squander them in a round of feverish kisses.

The girl, at least, seemed to be building toward some sort of climax. That was familiar territory. Focusing her will to Ashleigh's desire, Lorelei drove want upon want, need upon need. As orgasm broke over them, the girl's grip faltered on her stolen flesh.

Lorelei swept forward into full possession of her senses. The angel held her tight in his arms, sighing gently against her neck. His breath was like a benediction. Lorelei turned her head to catch his lips. The kiss had an electricity of its own, locking them together.

Lorelei forgot who she was, what she was doing, what her purpose in creation was. All that mattered was this communion with the angel.

He broke the kiss and leaned back to study her face.

Grinning, she remembered her goal. Lorelei writhed beneath Aza, using everything she'd ever known or guessed to climb from one orgasm to the next, moaning in delight when she knew he'd sensed the change in her and—most importantly—did not draw away.

As she became certain Aza was nearing his own release, the room blazed with the morning sun glare of angelic rage.

A second angel.

It hovered at the foot of the bed, humanoid but with no pretense of humanity. Pale golden hair streamed behind her like light striking the ripples of a pond. The sword she held aloft was an ethereal razor of flame. *This* was the terrible angelic beauty against which Lorelei had closed her eyes in Aza's cell.

Aza tore himself away from the succubus and flung himself to his feet. Before Lorelei could cover herself, he yanked her up, bedclothes and all, to stand against him. Lorelei buried her face in his chest and clung to him.

A fierce exchange raged over her head in a divinely arcane tongue.

She waited to be skewered against her angel, to feel their blood mingling as she died. She waited for the floor to open beneath them, for succubus, angel, ghost, and all to be swallowed into Hell. She waited for Aza to thrust her aside and attack his sister with an angelic weapon of his own.

Instead, a thunderclap resolved into the slamming of a door as Aza's sister flounced out of the room.

"Drama queen," Lorelei remarked softly. "Her timing could have been better."

Using the same word as he had in his lair, Aza called fire to the candles around them.

"You must go," he said. He tilted Lorelei's face upward and kissed her as if she meant something to him. Then he whispered words she didn't comprehend. They hovered, burning, in her mind. She felt a shift in her personal gravity as the dead girl took control once more. Uncomfortable certainty grew in her: when dawn finally broke, it would be the girl-ghost who saw it.

Aza rummaged inside a trunk against the wall. He handed over a pair of blue jeans and a large red plaid flannel shirt. "These should fit."

Lorelei was glad to see he wasn't sending her out into the world in his coat and the dead girl's boots.

"Can I …" The girl faltered.

"There isn't much time, Ashleigh."

"Do I have a moment to wash?"

"There's a restroom through that door." He pointed. "Hurry."

Clutching the clothing, she scooped up one of the candles.

The door where the female angel made her exit grated open on warped hinges. It led to a space that was part anteroom, part landing. The stairway that should have descended below had been removed down to the last brick, board, and scrap of plaster.

Turning to her left, she located a bathroom, tiled in dingy yellow. The girl propped her candle on the ledge above the sink. Lorelei watched as Ashleigh took stock of the reflection in the mirror. The girl's expression was certainly good for Lorelei's vanity. She remembered the child's stick-thin body and skeletal face.

Ashleigh ran her fingertips across Lorelei's sensitive lips. The girl's eyes slid half closed as she mouthed the name of her guardian angel.

Shaking herself, she discovered that the sink worked, albeit only with cold water. Ashleigh rinsed her hands, splashed her face, and did the best she could to give herself a sponge bath without benefit of sponge or towel. She touched the rag Aza had tied over Lorelei's hair, but left it.

Lorelei wished she knew what was going on. Did the angel intend to leave her a prisoner inside her own body, trapped behind the ghost? She tried to communicate with the girl, but there might as well have been a wall between them. She caught no echo of the child's thoughts. In this latest twist in their symbiosis, Ashleigh could block her out completely.

Ashleigh swam into the big flannel shirt. Lorelei would have worn it as a dress, but the girl didn't seem so inclined. To Lorelei's satisfaction, though, Ashleigh paused, unable to ignore the womanly curves she was stuffing into Levis better suited to her old emaciated frame. Without comment, Ashleigh zipped the jeans up.

Lorelei wondered if Ashleigh asked herself why her angelic lover had a supply of women's clothing on hand. Using every ounce of will, she nudged the thought forward, hoping to elicit a reaction. Pushing the boundaries of this imprisonment was the only hope she had to transcend this bondage.

Ashleigh's gaze locked on the mirror. Lorelei saw a red glow burning at the back of her eyes, like a wolf's outside the campfire light. Ashleigh shoved away from the sink, face crumpled with fear.

A breath of wind carried voices. Picking up her candle, Ashleigh staggered over to the tiny window at the end of the room. A knot of adults conversed on the sidewalk outside the vacant playground's chain-link fence. Lorelei recognized them for angels. Apparently, so did the girl, who hurried back to her own guardian.

Aza handed over her boots. The girl held them up by their laces, letting them spin. Lorelei wondered what memories they elicited.

"It's time," Aza said. "Put them on. We must go."

Ashleigh sank onto the corner of the bed and quickly laced the boots up. The angel raised her to her feet, clutched her tight in his arms.

"Thank you, Ashleigh. I appreciate your cooperation. There was no time to reason with Lorelei."

When he spoke her name, the succubus felt as if a firm hand pressed the center of her back. For a heartbeat, she passed through Ashleigh's thoughts, parting them like smoke. Then, when Lorelei thought to stretch, her body complied. It was exquisite.

Azaziel took hold of her elbow and dragged her toward the doorway. "That stairwell leads past the sacristy at the back of the sanctuary. You're going to leave via the lower floor. You should be safe with me as we pass under the church."

"You're putting me out?" Lorelei set her feet and struggled to hold her ground. "Did your handmaiden realize that, once you'd had your fun, she'd be on the curb like yesterday's garbage?"

"Ashleigh knew. The terms of the agreement were hers."

"Mortals setting bargains with angels?" Lorelei hooked her thumb into the junction of his grip, digging the other nails into the smooth flesh of his hand. If only she could turn right now...

"Her entire life was one string of abuse, misuse, and emotional neglect." His voice panged with empathy.

"She lived her life, made her choices, and then tries to slink through Heaven's back door with the aid of the very flesh-besotted angel in whom I've invested my time and honor? You used me as her escape vessel, humiliating me in the eyes of Hell..." Lorelei trailed off, unable to force her outrage into words. Finally, she spat, "What was your bargain?"

"She agreed to help me, in return for a single night of unqualified love, given to her as the woman she will never grow to be."

"Help you what?" Lorelei demanded.

"Show you love."

"Love?" Lorelei shrieked. "Sex in which I am a paralyzed recipient, not an active participant, is not love. You bound me and raped me, as surely as if I'd been cuffed to your bed. You fucked me while telling a mortal girl you loved *her!* In what world would that demonstrate anything but contempt for me? I think you're confused about what the concept of love means. No wonder your God has turned from you. No wonder his angels watch your windows and disturb your trysts. Who is supposed to be in love with whom, Angel?"

The girl within her tried vainly to block these words, to blunt their intent.

Screw her.

Eyes alight with rage, Lorelei's words took on a momentum of their own. "It appears, Azaziel, that you are the only one who doesn't accept your place in hellfire with the honest pedophiles, sadists, and lechers."

She felt frozen fire on her fingertips. Glancing down, she was shocked to see her fingers slicked with Aza's golden blood. He wrested his hand from her grasp. Somehow, she'd managed to pierce his angelic flesh with her ineffective, girly fingernails. Angels must be a whole lot more fragile than she'd been taught to believe.

Moving swiftly, Aza pinned Lorelei's arms and propelled her toward the window. He slammed her against the edge of the sill hard enough to knock the breath from her. Gasping raggedly, Lorelei waited for the final push through the glass, for the pavement to swell toward her before it shattered her skull. Destruction of her flesh would render her formless and liberate the girl, leaving them defenseless before the angels outside.

Lorelei's hands clawed free. Trying to push herself back, she succeeded only in shoving the frame so hard the window broke. Long blades of glass curved outward.

Aza popped open his blessed oil. The scent surrounded her as she heard his quiet Latin invocation.

A fearful swelling filled her breast. Unable to help herself, Lorelei opened her mouth wide. The scream changed pitch until it became Ashleigh's voice, ranged back down to her own, then combined both.

Aza's own voice became a tortured whisper, urging the spirit to vacate the succubus.

An iridescent tunnel ringed her vision as she regained her infernal senses. Tears of purest blood welled as her eyes ached with the strain.

The sound of Aza's voice broke up in her hearing. With a childlike cry, Ashleigh struggled to flee.

The angels outside the playground took that as their cue. The blond bitch sprang to the top of the high fence, perching there to fling open terrible wings. With similar bounds, the other two took up positions and waited.

The pain inside Lorelei was tremendous, surpassing endurance. However, the soul was almost out of her. That was all that mattered now, even if it left her too weakened to escape the angels across the way. Aza would *have* to protect her. He owed her that.

The angel's incantation halted. So did Ashleigh's progress. *That* alarmed Lorelei worse than her imminent destruction.

The words in her ear took on a familiar cast. Aza spun her around, pressing his lips to hers. His thumb once more anointed her with oil.

Ashleigh's reentry was far faster than the process of being removed.

Her heartbeat faded, to be replaced by the sound of wings beating hard across the playground.

Aza stumbled away, dragging Lorelei after him. When he paused on the landing to shoulder the heavy door closed behind them, Lorelei glimpsed the blond angel perched on the windowsill, feral and elegant. She casually pushed a shard of glass inward to embed like a scimitar in the floor below. Lorelei's disappointment at not being released was tempered by the marrow-rotting fear that the angel inspired in her.

Aza indicated she climb onto his back.

"Why?" Lorelei screamed. "I was almost free!"

"They will kill you if they catch you," he said simply.

His feathery floor-length wings were not as enormous as they'd seemed in the half-light of his lair. Before his transformation was complete, Lorelei kicked him as hard as she was able at the junction between wing and spine.

Gasping, Aza pitched forward into the torn-out stairwell. Lorelei leapt astride his back, intending to ride the fluttering form to a painful landing in the darkness below.

The angel hardly had time to spread his wings to slow their fall before he snatched the railing of the landing below. As they jerked to a halt,

Lorelei climbed him like a cat. She dropped to a crouch outside the sacristy door.

Lorelei faced Aza as he struggled to get the railing under his elbows. One wing bent at a painful angle. The other drooped into the darkness below him. He gazed at her with puppy dog eyes.

Help him! Ashleigh pleaded. The thought was clear enough that it might've been Lorelei's own.

Lorelei grinned at the angel. As she brought her booted foot up, the girl screamed in her mind. It threw off her aim. Her foot went wide, hitting the rail next to Aza's elbow. Wood splintered as the railing gave way. The angel dropped with a cry.

How could you?

Lorelei shut the girl out. She had bigger problems right now: trapped in a church, pursued by angels, and help undoubtedly very far away. Luckily, she'd just knocked the nearest enemy a few yards closer to Hell. That suited her fine.

See if he's all right.

"He's immortal," Lorelei hissed. "I'm not."

I want out, I want out, I want out!

Lorelei didn't bother to answer that. The vestry doors were open. He'd anointed her, she reminded herself. She could pass through. Angels were gathering on the opposite side of the landing door above. No time for fear. Lorelei put her left fist to her lips and tasted Aza's blood. It tingled on her tongue, like licking a battery. She'd drawn angelic blood! That gave her the courage to step into the smoke-blackened sanctuary.

She hoped she'd read Aza's love for his mortal girl right and he'd do what was necessary to protect her.

CHAPTER 4: PENANCE

Damp chill like the heart of a cloud engulfed the succubus. Lorelei slammed the sacristy doors behind her and discovered they had no bolt. She spat onto her fingers and used the angel's blood to paint a Satanic ward. The cold intensified until her flesh shrank against her bones. The ward steamed. Tiny flames licked its outlines.

She heard the angels screaming at each other in the stairwell outside the door, Aza's voice among them. She'd lied to the girl, of course. Aza was immortal unless his brethren killed him. If that happened, she hoped Hell would send a force strong enough to claim his spirit.

Now, however, Aza's spirit was not her problem. She'd felt his strength and knew she couldn't stand against one angel, let alone four. Not in mortal form, certainly. As she'd hoped, Aza's protests bought her time to escape.

We can't leave him!

"If you think," Lorelei said aloud, "that being expelled from me by grace was painful, imagine what it would be like to have those angels rip you out by force."

She'd have to pass the altar, Lorelei realized. If only she could fly, she'd be beyond it in an instant.

The door behind her shuddered at the blow of a sword.

Maybe, if she just didn't look at the altar... Lorelei shielded her eyes with her hands and flung herself into the sanctuary.

Cold enveloped her, but there was no mind behind it, nothing to tempt. Lorelei fought forward, listening to the sword falling behind her like an ax. She'd seen only three of them, right? They wouldn't have posted a guard outside the church. They wouldn't expect her to escape this way...

She prayed to Asmodeus, aware that her master had promised to leave her to her fate. She'd failed. Azaziel wasn't well and truly damned. If he begged mercy, his brethren might grant it. He had something to bargain with: while he hadn't saved his succubus, he had warped her with Ashleigh's mortal spirit. That was a point for his side.

Her foot caught on something that flung her full length onto the floor. She pushed herself up and saw a wrought-iron candelabrum sprawled across the red carpet. Lorelei snatched the candelabrum up even as she heard the door behind her give way. She fled into the foyer at full speed, smashing the heavy iron against the boarded-up window. The plywood cracked and gave way. Lorelei flung the candelabra out the window and dove after it.

"Lorelei!"

Her head twitched toward the familiar feminine voice. Floria leaned out of the open door of a cab. In this devastated neighborhood, she sparkled as brightly as a ruby.

Lorelei tumbled down the church's steps. Floria slid over inside the cab to make room. As soon as she'd scrambled in, Floria commanded, "Go!"

Eager to be gone, the mortal driver pulled away from the curb with a screech. The door slammed beside Lorelei.

A shadow flowed over the roof of the cab, dropping the passenger compartment's temperature noticeably: another angel come to join the fray. It had been wise of Floria to find a mortal driver. As long as his soul held a possibility of redemption, he might serve as their talisman of safe passage.

Floria pointed at the angel's blood staining Lorelei's hand. "Fuck, doesn't that burn your skin?"

It didn't, not at all. That was enough to erode the fragile self-control Lorelei had left. Her eyes felt as if they were melting with tears. Floria turned away, too shocked to watch Lorelei cry.

Aza drew a shuddering breath. The chill of the floor crept into his aching bones. It hadn't been a dire fall, but he'd been caught off guard. There was no question why Lorelei ran: terror at Muriel's attack clouded her judgment. What troubled him was what to do about Ashleigh. If they caught the succubus, would the other angels bother with the formalities of liberation?

"She's gone." Muriel dropped down into the stairwell to land at Aza's shoulder. She jabbed her sword into the floor. Puffs of pulverized concrete rose with each touch of the blade. The naked weapon charged the air like unspent lightning. "Your whore and her sister have a human driver to ease their way."

"I'm sorry," Aza muttered. "I was trying to let the girl's spirit go when you pounced."

"So it's our fault that a succubus is now possessed by the unsaved child?"

Two more angels, Barbelo and Shebniel, dropped from the stairwell behind him, sniffing the air uneasily. Copper-skinned Shebniel knelt beside him, full of sorrow. "Why, Azaziel?" he murmured in funereal tones. "Why did you betray that poor girl?"

Aza shook his head, unable to find a denial that would ring true. He hadn't intentionally betrayed anything.

To face the informal tribunal arrayed before him, Aza drew himself to his knees. His wings dragged heavily, unbalancing his attempt. With a concerted effort, he withdrew them. Only then did Barbelo and Shebniel reach down to pull him the rest of the way to his feet, stepping aside when it seemed he could stand alone.

"So few Watchers of your generation did not fall, Azaziel," Muriel observed. "Perhaps you waited all that time for this particular harlot."

Before he could reply, Muriel pushed Aza around to face the wall. She snarled an instruction to the angels flanking him. Their implacable fingers seized his arms.

Barbelo's sweet-smelling breath caressed his cheek. She'd been drinking Manischewitz. Aza wondered if she had the bottle on her, whether he still merited a pull from it. Aza met his friend's dark eyes. At the transmigration of understanding, Barbelo smiled and said, "Forgive me, Brother." Her fingers penetrated just below the collar of Aza's trench coat. With a single brutal motion, she rent the garment, as well as shirt beneath it, to the small of Aza's back.

There was an intake of breath from the assembled angels. Aza wondered how ugly the bruise was where Lorelei kicked him. The area felt raw in the cool air of the basement.

Muriel's palm pressed hard against the bruise. A flare of agony purpled his vision.

When she withdrew her touch, his wings manifested. For the first time, it occurred to Aza that his compatriot had something other than a scourging in mind for him. He listened to the song of her drawn sword. Fear was theoretical to him. Then again, after having to leave Heaven, almost everything was. Except love. He didn't sense any of that from Muriel.

"Muriel, we're going to need him," Barbelo implored. "There are too few of us for the work as it is."

Muriel's sword thrummed steadily, close by his ear. The sharp edge rested against the spar of his folded wing.

Aza's heart froze. "Dear Father, please, no," he prayed, eyes closed tight, breathing in the dry mortar of the bricks against his cheek. He had no doubt that Muriel meant to lame him. In the unnumbered ages of her existence, she'd eliminated Pontiffs of the Holy Church when she judged them badly astray.

Shebniel's grip loosened on Aza's arm. "Muriel, *no*. This hasn't been ordered from on high!"

The angry angel at his back relented. Against his wing, the pressure of her blade eased.

The sound of wings proved a better interruption, Aza thought. Then he recognized to whom those wings belonged: Samael, harvester of souls. If Muriel had a close friend among the Hosts of Heaven, it was Samael.

"I don't even have to ask if this is true. I have only to see with my eyes and hear the name of this traitor to know he's had congress with a second woman." Samael's voice was a slap against Aza's ear. "He should be lost to us."

Samael's fingers closed like talons on the roots of Aza's wings. "Don't sully your blade, Sister. Let me tear them off."

Barbelo spoke up. "You don't have time for this. Every moment you're distracted, the foe uses against us. Leave him to us, Brother. Let us decide his fate."

Samael's hand left Aza's wing. Aza felt a rush of air at the back of his head and heard the clap of flesh upon flesh like a blow halted in mid-course. Aza closed his eyes in gratitude. Barbelo had stood up for him against an Angel of Death.

He heard an exasperated snarl and the rush of gathering wings. "Deal with him, then. But do it well, I pray you. What is left undone, I will see completed."

Shebniel gave a sigh of relief as Samael left, echoed by a cold sense of resolve in Muriel. Her sword-edge was back, keen against Aza's flesh. Thanks to Samael, Muriel had made up her mind.

Aza wondered if she'd take one wing or both. He wondered if they'd let her. He thought of the vanquished rebels after the fall. Once mutilated, they never fully healed. Often they resorted to hiding their deformities behind facades that concealed only to the direct gaze.

But he hadn't fallen. He could hope to escape after injury: with scars, to be sure, but with his divinity intact.

Unless he was about to fall. The thought alone made Aza's blood run cold. What if, despite what Barbelo believed, Samael and Muriel *were* acting on a higher directive? Either these angels had nothing to stop them—or the Almighty was trying to frighten him. That itself was too terrible to contemplate.

"Thy will be done," Aza decided aloud.

Nothing happened, as if the angels sensed the wrongness of this ad hoc punishment.

Aza looked at his tormentor. Silver tears of fury lined Muriel's bland face. The sight of her unhardened his heart.

"Can you have forgotten, Azaziel?" Disappointment tinged Muriel's musical voice. "We are supposed to be the Almighty's gift to each other, first and foremost. You could have talked to us. We would have helped you with these mortals and their temptations. Forswear this folly. Destroy the harlot that beguiled you. You have no more chances after this."

"I must save the gir—"

Muriel cut him off. "I asked your assent, not a bargain."

Aza turned his gaze sadly back to the wall.

To the assembled angels, Muriel said, "You harbor doubts about the punishment I would levy upon Azaziel."

Placing one palm against the edge of her sword, Muriel used her own flesh to force the weapon into his wing. The double-edged blade bit deeply on both sides. Aza felt the down, then muscle separate, giving way to a molten shock of sacred metal against bone. The sword ground to a halt with a muted squeak.

As quickly as the blade bit in, it was withdrawn. Its absence was as painful as the incision.

Unseen by Aza, his punisher slumped, her sword dipping to the floor. After holding out her sliced palm in demonstration of her personal sacrifice, Muriel forced her hand around the sword's grip. Rivulets of her blood traced the holy inscription on its gleaming surface. The dusty floor of the church swallowed the droplets, absorbing them without a trace.

Resolved, Muriel straightened, raising the sword until its hilt was level with her heart. All gazes but Aza's followed the point heavenward. Mouthing a silent invocation, Muriel slammed the hilt forward against the cut in his wing, once, twice, yet again. On the third strike, the muffled crack resonated at the core of every angel present.

The force of the blow drove Aza against the wall. He began an agonized slide to his knees, tears of pain and grief mingling with the blood left on the wall by his abraded cheek.

Before he slipped into darkness, it occurred to him that no matter what, he still had to find a way to help the two girls he had intended to save and for whom he was now suffering.

Lorelei's body still hummed from the angel's lovemaking. She could feel his weight atop her, his hips moving between her thighs. If only that damned warrior angel had given them another half an hour...

She wondered if her sobbing would ever stop. She wasn't sure if the tears were her own or little Ashleigh's. Either way, Lorelei suffered. Her lungs felt bruised. Floria offered a tissue with two fingers, but it soon became too sodden to be useful. At least she didn't have on any makeup to smear. That thought brought on a chuckle that ended in a hiccup. Lorelei rubbed the flannel shirtsleeve across her face. "Where are we going?"

"Tuan's."

"He won't mind?" Lorelei asked.

Floria frowned. "He wouldn't dare."

Tuan was Floria's current long-term project. He'd signed a contract after one spectacular weekend. Floria used him to run a gang of Vietnamese boys. They believed Floria was just Tuan's girlfriend, which was simplest for everybody. Lorelei envied their domesticity.

The cab pulled up in front of Tuan's building. The driver put his hand over the seat. He was missing his thumb. Floria leaned up so her breast brushed his maimed hand. She counted the money out slowly so that he couldn't pull away before she was finished rubbing against him.

Lorelei climbed out of the cab and turned her smile away. Luxury, she thought wistfully. A hot bath. A hard bed with satin sheets. Maybe Floria would even let her fuck Tuan. *Why* had she been slumming with the angel?

The thought flooded her eyes with tears again. Once more, she wasn't sure if they were hers or Ashleigh's.

Floria punched her code into the security box and yanked Lorelei into the building. Once they stood inside the elevator, Floria demanded, "What did he do to you?"

"Possessed me with a human." Lorelei had never envied them, never. Pitiful and mortal, so soon to age and die...

"He put a soul in you?" Floria gasped.

Lorelei nodded miserably.

"Why don't you eat it?"

"I can't. He did something with sacramental oils and holy water..."

Floria hissed and drew back. "Is *that* what that thing burning on your forehead is?"

Scrubbing her sleeve over it, Lorelei begged, "Help me!"

Always practical, Floria calculated what her help was worth. Lorelei had seen the expression too many times to mistake it.

"I don't think this has been done to devils before, do you?" Floria asked. "Still, there must be a way to get it out. An exorcism or something."

"We have to find out," Lorelei said. "We have to get her out of me and sacrifice her. In the meantime, I want to guarantee her damnation, angel's grace or not." She wiped her face again, pulled the rag from her hair. "Can I borrow Tuan?"

The elevator's doors opened on the hallway outside the penthouse. Floria favored Lorelei with a smile that cast a light of its own. "Of course you can borrow Tuan. You shower and I'll call him home. He was doing a delivery up to San Francisco last night, so it might take a while. You'll like the things I've been teaching him."

"I can't wait." Lorelei peeled the oversized shirt off and threw it toward the kitchen garbage.

"I've gotta run some errands," Floria continued. "You'll be okay here."

"Of course," Lorelei answered. She let herself into the bathroom and turned the shower as hot as it would go.

Ashleigh fretted about her angel. It horrified her that Lorelei had hurt him, first by drawing his blood, then by kicking him down the stairwell. The girl was working up a hatred of the succubus black and powerful enough to be nearly damning in its own right. Lorelei smiled and left her alone to stew.

She perched on the toilet lid to unlace the combat boots. She dropped first one, then the other, behind the commode. Lorelei peeled out of the jeans and threw them away too. She was free and the angel was no longer her problem. Maybe, if she asked prettily enough, her prince would assign Yasmina to him after all.

Trying one more time, Lorelei squinched her eyes tight and willed herself into infernal form. Nauseating weakness swept over her. She stumbled against the vanity.

The attempt got Ashleigh's attention. *You can't change as long as I'm in you, can you?*

Lorelei didn't answer. Looking at herself in the mirror, she could imagine the angel's blessed oil flaring on her forehead. Her eyes burned red with shame that Floria had seen it. *That* gossip would be a bitch to live down.

She stepped into the shower and immediately flung herself back out. Hellfire and brimstone, why was she so stupid? Her skin was bright pink where she'd practically scalded herself. Lorelei turned the hot down and the cold on before stepping back under the water, dreading what it would cost to get this soul out of her.

Aza lay in the dark, wings folded back against the wall as if to protect them. The doors across from him were closed, although not locked. The rebuke of his fellows held him as firmly as any chain.

The thick doors did little to muffle his brethren's voices: Muriel, still full of wounded rage; Barbelo, his advocate; and Yehudiah, the Heavenly accountant, smooth and calm as ever.

Rolling to his hands and knees, Aza eased himself upright. It would be best to face what was coming on his feet. With an excruciating effort, he drew in his wings.

His sundered coat lay heaped in the corner, with two of its horn buttons folded over one cuff. They looked like empty eye sockets above a slack-jawed mouth. With grim amusement, Aza recalled skinned prophets and flayed saints, the sort of things that happened when one stepped out of line in the old times. Perhaps this was a return to the ancient ways, with signs and portents everywhere.

Walking over gingerly, he stirred the pile with an outstretched toe until it became an unrecognizable mass. So much for portents.

A ribbon of darkness spilled from one pocket. Aza started to bend down, then—thinking the better of it—knelt. The phantom resolved into one of Lorelei's stockings. With all that had happened, he'd completely forgotten it.

He regarded it at arm's length, stirring in a draft like a shadow floating on the air. His nostrils twitched at the scent of her: not merely the wild promise of her perfume, but something baser, more electric. This insubstantial thing contained temptation enough: to hold it close, to breathe the proximity of her skin, the hint of her musk.

His sigh plucked at every raw nerve in his body. Why had he done this? He'd prayed for guidance, begging for clarity from a voice that he'd grown to find heartbreakingly indistinct. Everything had seemed to lead him to Lorelei…

The doors parted abruptly, revealing Barbelo. She wore a men's blazer, collar turned up and sleeves turned back. Alarmingly, something about her recalled Lorelei in his oversized trench coat. Barbelo carried a fresh shirt for him, to replace the one torn for his laming.

After closing the doors behind herself, Barbelo gestured at the wisp of silk in Aza's hand. "My advice is that you make that go away."

Aza wound it around his fingers before shoving it back into his coat pocket.

"Not what I meant." With one finger, Barbelo ripped the pocket along the seam and plucked out the offending lingerie. At a whisper from her, it disappeared into a tongue of flame.

"For the best," she reassured. "No mementos, no messy explanations."

Barbelo gestured for Aza to turn so she could inspect his back. "Not too bad, considering." Her tone became more critical. "But it hasn't properly closed yet and, without help from one of the higher orders, it's not likely to."

Aza wondered if that was part of his punishment: to forever bear an oozing wound on his back. "I suppose this means a bandage and two shirts from now on," he said, trying to crane his neck back for a look. He received a painful crick for his trouble.

"That won't be necessary." Barbelo blew cool, healing air across the skin, then guided Aza's fingertips to the injury. To his surprise, the skin had closed over the spot. Beneath it, everything felt cloven and loose, shifting in a way that made him ill.

"That'll be enough of that." Barbelo moved his hand away. "Keep touching it and you will find pain."

A soft, liquid sound within Barbelo's coat made Aza realize how thirsty he'd become.

Barbelo pulled out a pint of Manischewitz, cracked the seal, and offered the bottle. Aza tried not to down half the wine in a gulp.

Barbelo's grin lit the darkness. "I felt you wanting this earlier, but..."

"It wouldn't have been appropriate," Aza finished for her. The sweet wine made his tongue burn, but the liquid was a blessing.

Barbelo took an extra long pull herself. "In my estimation, it would have been more than justified. Not that anything could fortify a body to face that."

Handing the bottle back, she motioned for Aza to finish it.

"Come on. We have to go face the others." She took his hand and walked out beside him.

As Floria strode past the frosted glass doors, the bottle blonde receptionist's gaze traced the height of her hem. The woman's snot-green suit didn't complement the orange tone of her tan. In addition, her roots were showing. Her nose had been fixed, along with her cheekbones and jaw. Her face seemed an artificial composite of the more famous features in the framed headshots on the wall behind her.

"Tell Jequon I need a moment," Floria directed.

"Mr. Jequon," the receptionist corrected icily, "is in a meeting. Please have a seat."

Floria rose up on her tiptoes to lean over the high desk. She stabbed a finger down on the phone.

"Yes?" Jequon hissed.

Floria stared at the receptionist. The woman cleared her throat. "Mr. Jequon, there's a young lady here—"

Floria supplied her name.

"Don't keep her waiting," Jequon answered. "No telling what sort of havoc she might wreak out there."

Floria released the intercom button and gave the receptionist a smile that would melt steel. "I'll find my own way," Floria said, honey in her voice.

Jequon met her in the doorway to his office. He looked like a long slim man, dark as espresso, beautiful in an aquiline way. He put an abrupt end to the conversation on his cell phone just before Floria pounced. She had her tongue halfway down his throat—for the benefit of the gawking receptionist—before Jequon shouldered the door closed.

He carried her across the room to seat her on the edge of his large, empty glass desk. Floria kept her ankles crossed behind his thighs.

Making no effort to extricate himself, the fallen angel asked, "To whom do I owe the pleasure of your company, Floria?"

"The angel who molested my sister Lorelei."

"Molested?" One of Jequon's ebony eyebrows arched. "Which angel would that have been?"

"I expected you knew," Floria purred, twining her fingers in the exaggerated collar of his crimson blouse. "Didn't you set her up?"

Jequon laughed, a rich warm sound, and twisted back to release himself from Floria's legs. She held him a touch longer, for emphasis, before unhooking her ankles.

"Unfortunately, you girls are hands-off for me." Jequon circled the desk and sank into the thickly padded leather chair. "Both of you are exclusive to the boss, thanks to your various talents."

Floria turned to face him. "She reeks of piety, Jequon. In my house. In *my* house."

He grinned, revealing perfect even teeth, white as stars in the desert sky. "Put her to work, Floria. You're a smart girl. You'll find a way to rub the sanctity right off her."

As much as she wanted to slap the smug son of a bitch, Floria restrained herself. Hell and earth, she hated angels. If it were as easy as that, she wouldn't be here making nice with this fallen asshole.

She leaned across his desk, so she could be eye-level with him. She wanted him to understand the gravity of her visit. "Lorelei says this nameless angel put a soul in her. She can't eat it. It's possessing her."

Jequon rocked back in his chair and steepled his fingers together in front of his heart. "What exactly would you girls like me to do?"

"Lorelei wants an exorcist."

"That should be entertaining."

"I expect so," Floria agreed. "Don't you have someone on staff?"

Jequon shook his head. "Let me make a few phone calls. And in return…"

"What do *you* want, Jequon?"

"The angel's name, of course. If he's looking for company, I must be managing someone to suit his tastes."

The phone hummed on the desk. "Leave the name with my receptionist when you get it," Jequon directed, his hand already gliding toward the phone.

CHAPTER 5: CONSEQUENCES

It was late afternoon as Aza walked into the sanctuary, unsupported by Barbelo. Muriel and Shebniel perched in the high windowsills, joined by other local angels. As one, they looked down on the pair.

Muriel held up her hand. "We don't need him here for this."

Barbelo's smiled. "Azazi-El is one of us. He should be here."

Had Muriel's wings been manifest, no doubt they would have ruffled. Instead she wrinkled her nose at the hint of wine, reminding them how she felt about non-sacramental imbibing. "Nothing will be determined without quorum."

Aza disliked being talked around. Angelic protocol being what it was, he had a right to be spoken to directly. If nothing else, he outranked his self-appointed judge. Aza had been created a seraph. A Grigori and a Watcher, he'd been known to mortal-kind, revealed and recorded. Muriel, however, had been created among the numberless hosts who toiled unceasingly in the name of the Word. It was commonly known that she barely tolerated her posting to the mortal plane.

Gently drawing free of Barbelo's grasp, Aza stepped forward to address the other angels. Each became interested in the call of some soul passing outside or the play of dusty light falling from holes in the roof above. He wondered if they expected him to fall to his knees and humble himself further. The pain that slivered his back told him he'd done enough by bearing that punishment without complaint.

"I erred in my execution of Ashleigh's release to your custody." Erred was too light a phrase for it. He hesitated. The protocol of all this was unbearable. When had it become so difficult to speak to those he should know and love so well? Even now, a soul he had meant to rescue was somewhere in this sinful city, locked within devilish flesh. "I can get her back," he promised.

Muriel stepped off the sill, opening her wings to float down. Her immaculate white Reeboks never touched the soot-dusted floor. "Even when you had her, she was in doubt. Now she resides in damned flesh, bound for acts that will tip the balance irrevocably."

Aza shook his head. In his heart, he knew better. "She is—"

Muriel pressed her palm to his lips. "She is lost to you, Near-Fall. For survival's sake, you ought not to attempt to see the harlot unescorted again." When Muriel smiled, Aza knew she was thinking of Samael's promise. "Better to concern yourself with souls you might still aid."

Muriel's first function had been the eternal hymn, an ever-spun litany of praise and glorification of the Almighty. Compared to her natural realm of light and music, the mortal realm and all that dwelt in it— particularly in this devil-infested corner—seemed to contradict that song. In her heart, Muriel wanted all creatures she encountered to be worthy of the choir. To disappoint her once was to be marked as a discordant note, one that might need to be removed from the hymn of creation.

"I know Ashleigh's soul," Aza argued. "Its core is unsullied."

Muriel addressed the others who perched above. "Oh, he knows! Like he knew Roman, sworn to be redeemable. When I think what I had to do to resolve that!"

Aza watched the other angels exchange uncomfortable glances. Muriel, for all her zeal, remained oblivious to the fact that she continued to be posted to the city for the same sort of unorthodox behavior she accused the others of engaging in.

Roman was a young filmmaker Aza had lost, one who'd made a blasphemous masterpiece upon inspiration from an infernal muse. Afterward, Muriel lit the way to his home, allowing young mortals in thrall to Hell to dispense her justice upon Roman's friends, his young wife, and their unborn child.

That it had all come to pass so terribly—that Muriel had duped the fallen camp into helping her carry it out—should have been unthinkable. But angelic will, with its undreamable boundaries, was subordinate only to instruction by the Word. Such directives might not be felt for ages. Muriel was not one to wait. It made her reckless.

Turning his back on Muriel. Aza said wearily, "Take me away."

"I will, Brother."

Barbelo escorted Aza back through the damaged sanctuary. He froze in front of the sacristy door. Lorelei's ward, written in his blood, scorched the shattered wood. His heart sank at the sight. Then, conscious of Muriel's gaze on his back, Aza straightened as well as he could and stepped out onto the landing.

"That could've gone better," he supposed.

"Thy love become thy shield." Barbelo brushed her lips across Aza's cheek, imparting her own gift of courage and faith. Then she pressed him close to her for the ascent of the torn-out stairwell.

The sound of a key turning startled Lorelei awake. She sat up, swaying woozily. Nothing in the slanting afternoon light looked familiar until she saw the big screen TV against the opposite wall. She was at Tuan's, where Floria had left her. How long had she been out? The lost time was as frightening as anything else that had happened to her recently.

The boy stood in the doorway, dark eyes scowling, infuriated at having been called away from business. It was strange to see his anger but not to feel it. Damn, Lorelei thought, mortal limitations suck.

"You okay?" he demanded.

Lorelei nodded, stretching.

That warmed his expression. Tuan was a remarkably pretty boy, tall and slim and delicate like a dancer. His black hair stood straight up, glistening with gel. Lorelei warned herself not to lose an eye on it.

"Floria said you'd been kidnapped."

"I picked up a guy at the club the other night. He kept me chained to his bed." She twisted her arm to make the broken handcuff flash.

Tuan sat beside her on the sofa. He took her hand gently and looked at the steel. "I've got a key that'll fit that."

Take it off? She hadn't really considered it. Now that she did, she wasn't ready to part with the cuff. Aza said she could have it removed when she left him, but it symbolized... What, exactly? A reminder to stay away from angels, if nothing else. Lorelei would have to consider what it meant, later, when Ashleigh was not around to eavesdrop. "No," Lorelei surprised Tuan by saying. "I want to keep it for now. A souvenir of what I've been through."

"What do you want me to do then, Lorelei? You can't exactly go to the police."

"I know." She swung her leg over him. "Take me to bed, Tuan. I want to be with someone I know. Help me forget this trick."

To overcome his protests, she pressed her lips against his, parting them with her tongue.

He held her against him long enough that she was sure she was having the desired effect. Inside her, Ashleigh raged ineffectually. Nothing would stop Lorelei from getting what she wanted right now, maudlin thoughts about angels least of all.

Tuan pushed her back so he could breathe. "You're not makin' sense," he accused.

She nipped at his ear. "What do you mean?"

"You wanna forget this guy or not?" He caught the handcuff with one finger.

"I want someone to help me forget what he did to me." She stood up and dragged the boy toward the bedroom.

"Wait!" Tuan protested. "Where's Floria?"

Lorelei shrugged. "You need her permission? She doesn't ask yours."

That was enough inside knowledge about her sister to spark his pride. Lorelei watched him struggle with his possessiveness of Floria. Good, Lorelei thought. Even trapped in mortal form, she could still inspire jealousy.

Decision made, Tuan trailed her into his bedroom. His fingers raced hers for the buttons of his shirt.

Ashleigh babbled protests that Lorelei wasn't inclined to decipher. *Shut up!* she thought fiercely. *He can't hear you and I don't want to. You might like this. Even if you don't, you got yours.*

Tuan shucked off his 501s as Lorelei crawled onto the bed and started throwing pillows to the floor. Room to work. Tuan shoved her off balance and followed that with his full weight, pinning her to the down comforter. Lorelei struggled enough to incite him, pressing her hip up hard between his thighs as she twisted onto her back. Tuan forced his hand between her legs. Lorelei hadn't noticed how wet she'd gotten until she felt it on his fingers. "I want you so bad," she whispered into his ear.

Which was a lie. She didn't want the boy, or even the angel, just the act. She wanted to feel like her old self.

Unfortunately, this wasn't the way to accomplish it. As soon as he entered her, Lorelei plummeted again into the isolation of her flesh. All she could feel was the contact of their surfaces. His emotions, which she desperately needed to feed on, were hidden from her.

Tuan went rougher on her than he'd ever done before, pounding his hips down against hers hard enough to drive her breath away. One of the things Floria had been teaching him, no doubt. For the first time, Lorelei considered that there might be such a thing as too rough.

Something recoiled within her. Hopefully, that meant Ashleigh was paying attention.

Lorelei waited for the next shift in his balance and threw herself sideways, rolling atop him. She ground her hips down until he was as deep in her as he could go. Then she clenched herself hard around him, holding him frozen, as she fucked his mouth with her tongue. Tuan said something, but she swallowed the words.

Shoving her head down, she intentionally split her lip against his teeth. She sucked at the blood, then fed it to Tuan with her tongue. He swallowed it without protest.

She rewarded them both by surrendering to a shuddering, moaning orgasm that probably half-deafened the boy. Tuan took it as encouragement and quickened his pace.

Make sure you enjoy it now. The words, plaintive and certain, distracted her. *He won't live long. These gang kids never do.*

Shitfire. The little bitch was trying to play conscience. The time had come to put "Ashes" down once and for all. Lorelei pressed her lips to Tuan's collarbone. A vicious bite ought to shake both of them: a mouthful of blood to throw Ashleigh off, followed perhaps by an angry backhand from Tuan. It would hurt, sure, but the rage and confusion it inspired would be absolute tonic to Lorelei's chaotic nature.

Plus, if he got a taste for it, it would give Floria all new material to work with.

Her teeth were about to break the boy's skin when something struck her more harshly than the anticipated blow. The thought hadn't been Ashleigh's.

Furious, Lorelei bit him anyway. Tuan pulled away from her so fast that she would have lost him if he'd been any more coordinated. Lorelei clutched him with her limbs and slid back into place.

"What was that for?" he demanded.

"Hit me."

"You're out of your mind."

Without hesitation, she clamped down on his flesh again, working her teeth from side to side. Something crunched sickeningly against her bottom teeth. The pain must've been hot glass to Tuan. He froze. Then, with a hard inhalation, he yelled, sufficient to bring people running.

In a blur of motion, Tuan's hand pumped back and slammed in. Lorelei barely had time to throw Ashleigh's spirit forward to receive the blow. The succubus had been expecting a slap. Instead, Tuan delivered an openhanded strike with the heel of his hand. Catching her full in the chest, it exploded the breath from her in a brilliant white flash. That dissolved into a red-tinged world of agony that left Lorelei questioning her judgment.

Thrown back against the coverlet, Ashleigh wheezed. Tuan flung himself away, panting. The door slammed open, followed by two Vietnamese boys with drawn guns. They looked from Tuan—blood running down his chest—to Lorelei, gasping, on her back with knees still parted. Ashleigh would've curled into a ball and hid her furiously blushing face, but the pain wasn't fading.

Laughing, the boys tucked their guns back into their waistbands.

Floria drifted into the room, unconcerned. She traced her fingers through Tuan's blood, assessing the depth of the wound. "That'll need stitches."

"Crazy bitch!" Tuan shouted. "She fuckin' bit me!"

"What do you expect me to do about it? I can't put her out," Floria reasoned. "Not yet, anyway. I promise you she'll behave." Floria shot Ashleigh a look so venomous that the girl's blood iced. She wasn't sure if the glare was meant for her or for Lorelei.

"You will behave," Floria reiterated, "won't you, Sister?"

Ashleigh nodded mutely. Lorelei prompted her to lick the blood from her lips, but Ashleigh only shuddered. She whispered her angel's name.

Something yellow flared in Floria's eyes. She crossed the room in a stride, slapping Ashleigh hard enough to draw tears. "Be-*have*," she half sang, as if talking to a bad puppy. Her hand was drawn back, ready to hit even harder if needed.

The boys led Tuan from the bedroom, still chuckling. The last one out closed the door after them.

Floria coiled her hand in Lorelei's hair and yanked until Ashleigh met her gaze.

"Please don't hurt me," Ashleigh begged. "Lorelei bit him."

Floria's slow smile didn't warm her amber eyes. In a soft, cold voice, Floria said, "I can smell you, Soul. I don't know what that angel did to Lorelei, but I promise you will suffer torments you cannot begin to imagine if you invoke the Enemy here. Don't pray, don't call his name, don't even imagine his face—because if there's any trouble in my house, death will be the last good thing that happens to you. I *guarantee* you that."

Watching to make certain she was understood, Floria unwrapped her hand from Lorelei's hair. Her smile, as she left the room, was the most fearsome thing Ashleigh had ever seen. She shivered, then found she couldn't stop.

Ooh. Got on her bad side pretty quick. Lorelei laughed. *If we're gonna party together,* the succubus told Ashleigh, *you'll have to learn to take the pain with the pleasure.*

"I don't want to be here," Ashleigh whispered.

I know, Lorelei commiserated. She sounded almost sympathetic. *We have the angel to thank for this situation. But you're the one with the free will. You chose to come into me. You notice he didn't give me a choice.*

She gave the girl time to remember the negotiations just prior to their "lovemaking." Lorelei *had* told the angel to do whatever he wanted to her, Ashleigh recalled, but the succubus had clearly believed they were negotiating sex.

I hate to say it, Ashleigh, but he wasn't being totally straight with either of us, Lorelei confided.

"But he's an angel," Ashleigh protested.

That doesn't mean he has to tell the truth. It doesn't even mean he's working with divine blessing.

There was a long silence while Ashleigh considered whether angels could lie. Her next question surprised Lorelei. "Why did you bite Tuan?"

The succubus laughed again. *Because I wanted you to know where you stand in all this. You have no friends here. Your only hope is that Floria finds an exorcist. To survive until then, you're going to have to keep everyone happy. Including me.* She changed the subject. *Get up and dress.*

"You threw our clothes away."

Take something of Floria's.

Ashleigh's knees wobbled when she crawled off the bed. She reached out to steady herself on the bedstead. One hand gingerly touched the livid pink spot on her chest. The ache that met her fingertips made her whimper.

Hush, Lorelei soothed. *Of course, now that I'm stuck in mortal flesh, Tuan could've killed us, if he'd hit directly over my heart. But he didn't. Because however much Tuan gets off being with Floria, he's afraid of us. That ought to tell you something.*

Ashleigh tottered over to the mirrored closet door and rocked to a halt at the sight of the blood dried on her lips. Her gaze leapt around the room before landing on the box of tissues on the nightstand. She spat into a clean tissue and wiped her face. Her whole body trembled.

She'd thought fighting with Deion had been scary. She'd thought dying had been scary. Nothing prepared her for this.

Dress, Lorelei repeated. *It will make you feel less vulnerable.*

Ashleigh opened the mirrored closet and fingered the wild array of finery inside. Leather, velvet, spandex, lace: it was like a porn star's fantasy. There wasn't a single opaque blouse in the lot. Ashleigh pulled out a couple of dresses until she found one with a neckline high enough to cover the bruise on her chest.

She swam into the purple angora sweater dress and tugged it down over her behind. It was barely thigh length. How would she ever be able to sit down? *Keep those knees together in public,* Lorelei mocked.

Ashleigh closed the closet door to study herself in the mirror. The wispy angora molded itself over every curve, making Lorelei's body seem even more voluptuous than it had been nude. *Gonna need a thong,* Lorelei suggested, but Ashleigh shook her head. It was one thing to borrow a dress; she couldn't bring herself to peek into a succubus' underwear drawer.

The bedroom door opened and Tuan walked in. Apparently, since he was paying the rent, he didn't feel he needed to knock. Ashleigh shrank back against the wall. He glared at her as he swept his jeans up off the floor and stepped into them. Someone had taped a gauze patch over his collarbone.

Lorelei directed, *Make nice.*

"I'm really sorry," Ashleigh quavered.

"Should've thought of that before you started gnawing on me," he snapped. "I know what happens when the contract is up. You don't need to get started on me yet, Lorelei."

How could he know what they were? Ashleigh wondered. How could he know what they did? How could he live with them, serve them, and know where it would lead? He was just a boy, not much older than she had been. Ashleigh felt the angora beneath her fingers and saw the over-engineered Nikes Tuan was lacing onto his feet and understood how a street kid would crave just these things. They'd bought him with sex and clothing and a nice penthouse apartment. And now that he had everything he wanted and understood the price, he saw no way out.

Ashleigh saw no way out either and started to cry.

Tuan handed her a tissue. Ashleigh blinked up at him. He saw something in her eyes and knelt beside her. She crawled into his lap, mindful of her aching chest and his bitten shoulder. He held her, letting her cry. When she stopped to catch her breath, he asked, "That guy really fucked you up, huh?"

"Yeah." She sniffled. "Yeah, he did."

"Oh, brother," Floria carped from the doorway. "What a tableau. Don't tell me you've forgiven her already."

Tuan looked down at the girl in his arms. Ashleigh felt some kind of connection had been made between them.

Don't fool yourself, Lorelei said quickly. *It's me he's looking at. He doesn't know you exist.*

Floria crossed the room and hauled Lorelei out of the boy's lap. She surveyed the height of the angora dress's hem and hissed, "Nice," in a way that implied anything but. Ashleigh tugged the dress down. It wouldn't go far.

Watching them, Tuan got his back against the wall and pushed himself to his feet.

"Back to work for all of us," Floria ordered. She handed Tuan his cell phone. "The boss sent a car for you, Lorelei."

Cold panic flooded through Ashleigh. *You'd better let me take this*, Lorelei said. She accomplished the personality transfer easily enough. Aloud, she asked, "You have any shoes that will fit me, Sister?"

"You don't have time to try things on." Floria looked over her shoulder. In the doorway stood a pair of fiends, all slicked back hair and sunglasses, hulking physiques packed into Italian suits. Wow, Lorelei marveled. Did Asmodeus think she was going to run?

"How's my hair?" Lorelei asked.

Floria handed her a brush off the top of the dresser. "Fluff it up a little. And bite your lips."

Lorelei caught the sleeve of one of the fiends on her way out the door. "Come on, boys. We don't want to keep the boss waiting."

CHAPTER 6: MESSENGERS

Aza surveyed his room. He'd stripped the bed, resisting the urge to hold the sheets against his chest and see if he could detect the last traces of Lorelei's warmth. He'd collected the broken window glass and swept the floor. Still the other angels did not come for him.

He knelt painfully before the starburst on the wall, meditating wordlessly on a single candle flame. No response seemed forthcoming. What had come into his mind, then? Self-interest? He'd thought it was divine inspiration: to seek out a creature passionate enough to endure an eternal relationship.

"If what I've done is so wrong, why didn't you tell me?" he begged aloud. "Why didn't you stop me?"

"You know the answers to that," a voice said quietly behind him.

The archangel Rafael, resplendent in a brilliant white suit, reached down to help Aza to his feet. Grinning, he engulfed Aza in a bear hug. He smelled like sweet breezes and honey, like the sun-bathed meadows of Heaven.

Aza's eyes filled with tears of relief at the archangel's embrace.

"How's the wing?" Rafael asked.

Aza stepped back and rubbed his eyes dry. "Healing as much as can be hoped." He left the request unspoken.

"Much as I'd like, I can't do more for you yet," the archangel said. "Let's go join the others and we'll discuss the future."

When Lorelei and the fiends left the building, sunset painted the sky scarlet. A limo idled in front of the fire hydrant. The car's windows were smoked so dark that Lorelei couldn't see what was driving. One of her escorts opened the back door for her. The other got in on the far side.

Lorelei expected to find Asmodeus within. Instead, the back of the limo was vacant but for the three of them. As soon as the doors closed, the car pulled away. Both fiends slouched silently against their doors, not touching her. Lorelei frowned.

All right. Asmodeus hadn't come to meet her and hadn't asked Floria to bring her. This summons felt like being called onto the carpet. Guess Asmodeus really was serious about not leaving Aza unfallen. Still, she'd injured the angel. She'd gotten him in trouble with the other angels. Just because she'd momentarily retreated didn't mean she'd renounced the battle. And even if she didn't manage to damn Aza, all devils lost a victim occasionally. Even the great Yasmina.

The fiend on her left reached forward and slid open the bar. He pulled out an iced bottle, twisted the cap off in his meaty fist, and held the beer toward Lorelei. A man in a red devil suit, brandishing a pitchfork, grinned from the label.

"Aren't you joining me?" Lorelei asked.

The fiend smiled, revealing teeth filed to points. Lorelei felt the hair stand up on the nape of her neck: yet another unpleasant new sensation.

"Let me fix myself up first," she said, bending forward and stroking the hairbrush through her hair from the roots. She half-expected to feel a hand on her shoulder, hauling her upright, but they left her alone.

If the issue was Ashleigh, Lorelei was still toying with her. Maybe the girl wasn't guaranteed food for the fire yet, but Lorelei already had her questioning the angel's motives. In another day or two, she'd have the girl worked up to full-on despair. Why wasn't Asmodeus giving her the time she needed to work?

And anyway, so what if she had a soul inside her now? Floria would locate an exorcist and Ashleigh would be damned and everything would turn out fine.

Lorelei flipped her hair back and fluffed it.

"That's enough," the fiend on her right said. His voice sounded like stone grinding stone. "Who're you gonna impress?"

"Aren't I impressing you, Handsome?" she purred.

The reddish black skin of his square-planed face ended in a goatee. He looked her over from bare feet to lavender-blue eyes, but said nothing.

Ashleigh was being awfully quiet. Just as well, under the circumstances, but Lorelei caught herself missing the company.

Lorelei took the beer bottle and sipped the bitter brew inside. It tasted like wormwood. The icy bottle infected her hand with a chill that traveled up her arm and coiled around her heart. Was this what fear felt like? She didn't care for it.

Have you always been such a cheap date? Ashleigh asked.

Lorelei ignored her. She wondered how to get the fiends to put on some music. Instead, she asked, "Where are we going?"

Of course they didn't answer.

"How bad am I in trouble?"

"Just drink," the bearded one advised.

Yes, please, Ashleigh chimed in. *If not for you, do it for me. I could really use a postmortem buzz.*

Out of spite, Lorelei tipped her head back and sucked down the brew. When she opened her eyes, her head felt wobbly on her neck. The cabin of the car tilted slowly to the right. She shifted on the bench seat so she could lean her head on the shoulder of the fiend to her left. She let the bottle slip from her fingers. Her guards let it fall.

The liquor's hitting you hard because you haven't eaten anything, Ashleigh explained.

The last thing she'd wanted to eat was a certain junkie's ghost. Lorelei hoped the boss would have something more appetizing on hand.

She curled up and put her feet into the lap of the fiend on her right. He dropped one huge hand onto her knee, rubbing it with a calloused thumb. She closed her eyes.

Floria pulled her red Alfa into the Shell station. "I need to make a call," she announced.

"You can't use the cell?" Tuan answered.

The succubus narrowed her eyes and held her hand out for some change. Occasionally the boy forgot she wasn't required to explain herself. Tuan folded, as always, and dug into his jeans pocket with his good hand to find her two quarters.

Floria slid out of the car and stalked over to the pay phone. The trio of cholos at the gas pumps whistled appreciatively, which improved her mood a little. She fed Tuan's coins into the phone and dialed, expecting to get voice mail rather than the cookie-cutter receptionist.

"Jequon."

Surprised to find him answering his own phone, Floria mocked, "Working late?"

"You have that name for me, Floria?"

"Azaziel. The girl-ghost called him, but he hasn't come. Yet. Am I gonna need protection, Jequon?"

"No. Azaziel remains an angel on sufferance alone. This ought to be the transgression that undoes him."

"So Lorelei didn't fuck up as bad as it looks."

"You be the judge of that," Jequon teased. "I've found a potential exorcist, but the loan of him will cost a couple of your boys."

"What's a priest want with my boys?" Floria growled.

"They're not for him. They're the price of his loan, as I said. Think about it and call me back," Jequon said. "I need to pass Brother Aza's name around."

Before she could answer, Jequon disconnected her. Floria dropped the receiver into its cradle. Shit. Why should *she* have to pay to get her sister straightened out? Lorelei was going to owe her big time.

Lorelei's thoughts drifted. She found herself wandering in an enormous underground cavern. Two fiends walked behind her, barely visible in the dim red light. At first the path sprawled wide and smooth, then it sloped steeply downward. Lorelei's heart skipped joyfully. Home! They were taking her home. She hurried, eager to regain her true form and bask in the fires' warmth.

Small chips of obsidian littered the path. The pebbles sliced Lorelei's bare feet. Although she tried to pick her way, her tender feet were soon bleeding.

A fiend shoved her. "Don't keep him waiting."

Somehow, without moving, she stood in Asmodeus's audience chamber. She prostrated herself. The mosaic floor radiated heat, burning the cheek she laid against it.

Her prince sighed. "Can you imagine how displeased I am with you, Lorelei?"

"No, my lord." She didn't dare look up. Her sisters were whispering. She wished she understood their distorted words.

"Let me make myself clear."

The fiends hauled her to her knees. Lorelei wasn't surprised to find herself nude. Asmodeus stood before her, swinging a walking stick from one hand as regularly as a pendulum. The motion was hypnotic. "Let me see who you really are, my girl."

She allowed her flesh to melt, to conform itself to her spirit. The transformation felt exquisite, a freedom she craved more than sex. Before she'd been saddled with Ashes, there had been no demarcation between Lorelei's flesh and spirit; they were one and the same. Her appearance shifted with her thoughts or the expectations of her prey. For days now she'd held the same form, the one of the angel's liking. She hadn't realized how cramped her thoughts had gotten in consequence.

She flung her wings wide, glorying in the sensation. Throughout the room hissed a horrified intake of breath. "There," Asmodeus said. "You see?"

In place of her beautiful black bat wings, she had the white-feathered wings of an angel.

Asmodeus limped off into the shadows. "Destroy this abomination," he commanded.

Lorelei's world became a maelstrom of blood-spattered feathers as her sisters and the fiends ripped her apart. Galvanized by the pain, she jolted awake. Her heart pounded like a fist in her chest. Sweat slicked her body and she recognized her own scent: fear.

It's a dream, Ashleigh soothed. *Only a dream. A nightmare.*

I don't dream, Lorelei argued. *You need a soul to dream.*

Someone carried her in his arms. Lorelei smeared hair from her face with a clammy hand. Lights shone in the distance. The shifting darkness around her was vaguely illuminated by light reflected from the night sky. She heard sluggishly running water.

This was not at all where she expected to find herself. She'd thought the fiends would take her up to the house in Holmby Hills, the one with the incredible view, from which Asmodeus oversaw his operations in the mortal world.

She breathed deep the sulfurous odor of the fiend who carried her. The familiarity calmed her a little. He was the one who'd placed his hand on her knee. Lorelei slipped her arms around his neck and pulled herself against him, so that her breasts crushed against his suit coat. "Where we going, Daddy?"

He halted and shifted her weight so she'd have to put her feet down. Her bare toes encountered a broken chunk of concrete. He unwound her arms from his neck and pushed her away. Lorelei barely made out the reddened glow of his eyes.

"Turn around and cross the water," the other fiend ordered.

Her fiend encircled her hips with his hands and guided her around. He slapped her butt to start her moving. Lorelei wished she'd had a chance to ask his name. She might need a friend when this was over.

The air smelled green and faintly rotten, like an untended aquarium. She'd stepped in worse in Hell. Lorelei kept going.

Her foot encountered a tuft of grass. Its blades were soft and cool against the arch of her foot. Then her toes found the water. It was not as cold as she'd feared. She stepped forward into it, onto a piece of broken glass. The pain reminded her abruptly of her nightmare. Cursing softly, just to make herself feel better, she limped forward.

Where are we? Ashleigh demanded.

"The LA River."

Why did they let us go here?

"They haven't let us go." She squinted at the shadowy hulks waiting on the far side of the water. "They just can't cross running water."

She stepped down into a shin-deep pool. There the water traveled a little faster, tugging at her. She felt her blood coiling out from the gash in her foot, flowing away downstream. Lorelei paused to enjoy the sensation. It might be the last pleasure she felt.

Why don't you run? Ashleigh begged.

Lorelei laughed. The sound rang through the darkness like a rolling bottle. "I could run until the water or my strength gave out, then they'd tear us apart. Fiends are Hell's enforcers, Ashes. They're the ones who stick the pitchforks in. There's no escaping them."

This is the sort of place where people are brought to be executed, Ashleigh thought.

"I know."

I don't want to be torn apart by fiends.

"Me, neither."

Our Father, Ashleigh began, *who art in…*

To stop her, Lorelei flung herself face down, hoping to find water deep enough to drown in.

Instead, she fell against the greenery growing in the midst of the shallow river. Something caught her in the chest, pounding the bruise from Tuan's strike. The air huffed from her lungs. The pain silenced Ashleigh. Furious, Lorelei instructed the girl, "If you want to pray, you say: *'Father of Lies, accept my service…'* "

The girl whimpered.

"Floria wasn't kidding when she said death would be the last good thing that happens to you," Lorelei growled. Ashleigh didn't answer. "We haven't got much time, Ashleigh Johnson, so listen to me now. I am only a devil. The fiends are lower in Hell's hierarchy than I am, but they aren't subservient to me. We all serve our Prince, who is a true demon. He is older than the creation of this planet, as old as Aza, if not older. I can't begin to imagine the limits of his power. If we are to survive this meeting—at all—you must shut up and stay quiet. He will hear your thoughts, so you mustn't think of Aza or the Enemy or we will die in such agony that it will become legend. Do you understand?"

Ashleigh didn't say anything.

"Please, Ashes. Ashleigh. Child. I want to live. Please promise you'll give me that chance." Lorelei rested her forehead on a cold stone and begged. "Name your price."

The silence stretched out. Lorelei heard the fiends shifting restlessly at the water's edge.

"I can't wait, Ashleigh. I need your answer."

Protect Aza, the girl ordered.

Lorelei nodded. That was not unexpected. She got gingerly to her hands and knees. "I swear to do everything I can to protect your guardian angel," she said. "Promise me you'll think only about safe topics…" Lorelei considered the little she knew about the runaway girl. "Think about your grandma or your mortal boyfriend or something like that. Promise?"

I promise.

Lorelei crossed the rest of the water. As soon as she reached the river's edge, four strong hands grasped her arms. They hauled her up the incline to a storm drain.

She reached out with what remained of her infernal senses. The night around them was silent except for the sound of the water and the breathing of the fiends. Shadows congealed in the drain.

Lorelei wrapped her fists in the sodden angora dress and peeled it up over her head. She passed it to the fiend on her left. He laid it over his shoulder to keep his hands free. Lorelei stretched up onto her tiptoes, feeling the flow of her muscles over the bones. The night caressed her skin. She drew a long breath, then knelt and slipped her feet into the gap of the drain.

What are you doing? Ashleigh demanded.

Lorelei didn't answer.

They're going to kill us and leave your body here to rot!

Lorelei wriggled her legs through the opening. Her feet dangled into the drain. She'd never feared the dark before. Never feared death. Never thought of fear except as a curious sensation she might find erotic. If she'd never hosted a soul, she would never have felt so many things. She wouldn't have a name for the panic rending her breast now.

She stubbed her toe on the concrete wall of the drain and forced herself to focus on what she was doing. She slid her hips over the lip of the drain, adjusted her handhold, and pushed the rest of her weight backward into the darkness. She wondered how far the drop would be.

When she hung full-length down the wall of the drain, toes stretched downward into space, someone grabbed her. Hands rested on her calves, holding her hard enough that she understood that he expected her to kick. Actually, it hadn't occurred to her. She wiggled enough to make certain that he had her, then let go.

He lifted her down with a strength that implied her weight was nothing. Lorelei twisted in his arms and planted an awkward kiss on his scabbed cheek.

In the darkness, Asmodeus laughed.

As soon as her feet touched the sandy bottom of the drain, Lorelei prostrated herself. "Have you come to take me home, my lord?"

He placed his foot on the back of her neck, pressing her face against the backs of her hands. "I always liked you, Lorelei. You're one of the youngest girls to interest me in a long time. There seemed nothing you wouldn't dare."

He dragged his foot around beneath her throat and nudged her upward. With a small cough, Lorelei climbed uncertainly to her knees. Whatever else was in the drain with them yanked her to her feet, but she didn't raise her head.

Asmodeus caught her chin. The sharpened nails of his thumb and forefinger forced her mouth open. Lorelei closed her eyes as the demon looked down her throat. When he finished, he thrust her jaw up hard enough to clack her teeth together.

"Explain this to me, Lorelei: I can smell a soul in you, but I don't see it. All I see is you. I hear a childish voice mumbling to itself about boys and motorcycles. I smell terror as sweet as any mortal's. You are not the succubus I left chained to an angel's bed."

"No, my lord."

"You promised me that he would fall. Has this been accomplished?"

"No, my lord."

"Did you manage to provoke him to lust?"

Lorelei considered that. While Aza had created her as a creature of his desire, his lust had not consumed him. "No, my lord."

"How is this possible? If any angel were to fall, it should be Azaziel."

Ashleigh's spirit leapt at the name. Lorelei concentrated instead on the sound of Asmodeus's pacing around her, the slight drag of his lame leg, broken when he was cast from Heaven.

"You know him, my prince?"

Asmodeus chuckled. "After the expulsion from the Garden, Azaziel was set as a Watcher over mortals. Like the other Watchers, he took a mortal wife. Her name was Anah. She was meant to die when the Enemy flooded the Earth, but Azaziel carried her to another plane where she could sate his desires until her death."

Ashleigh quavered, *No way*.

"His disobedience of the Enemy is as great as any of the Fallen, yet he continues in the Enemy's service." Asmodeus traced a nail across her left nipple. Lorelei shuddered, grateful for the sensation. "You, my dear, are only the latest sweet young thing to tempt that pedophile's appetite."

That's bullshit! Ashleigh raved.

"Besotted little minx," Asmodeus chided. "Did you think you were the first?"

"She knows she was not, my lord," Lorelei said. "He gave her clothing from one of his earlier worshippers."

Asmodeus switched subjects. "This soul that possesses you, Lorelei: tell me about her."

"Ashleigh Johnson." Lorelei paused, mining Ashleigh's memories.

Mockingly, she ticked off the various facts like plot points in a bad after-school special: "She ran away from home, breaking her grandmother's heart. She lived in lust with a boy named Deion Gutierrez. She died in the street of septicemia and methamphetamine abuse. She knowingly possessed my body to fuck an angel."

"Yes, yes," Asmodeus said impatiently. "Have you made her any offers? Did she renounce the Enemy? Have you damned her?"

"No, my lord. The angel's grace..."

His walking stick cracked against the back of Lorelei's knees, dropping her onto the floor of the drain.

Metallic talons clicked close by. Lorelei smelled sour feathers. She didn't have to see the harpies to know which, in all of Hell's employ, would be here.

Her prince's voice floated down to her. "Damia and Keisha have already apprised me of the meaningless details of your little parasite."

Damia crouched next to Lorelei. "Hey, Sister. Just like I tol'ja, here we are again."

Keisha rapped her knuckles hard against Lorelei's skull. Those cheap Venice Beach biker rings hurt. "Hey, Ashes! Y'in there? Come out an' party!" Taking a double handful of Lorelei's hair, Keisha dragged her nose to nose. She stank of clove cigarettes, musty feathers, and fortified wine. "Bitch, stole our food."

"It's true, Master, and you know how hungry our work is," Damia simpered.

"You'll be compensated, by and by," the demon assured. "But you, Lorelei...Words cannot convey how deeply I am disappointed in you. You stood by as an angel took a soul cultivated by servants of mine, a soul that you've failed to damn. As you failed to topple my brother Azaziel from his ever-so-precarious perch. I see no further use for you."

Before the sentence quit echoing, the other creatures in the drain fell upon her. Claws pierced her back.

"Give me more time, my lord," Lorelei whimpered. "I might have fucked him into falling, if it hadn't been for that blond warrior bitch..."

"Wait," Asmodeus ordered calmly. The assault halted. Lorelei felt blood pulse, hot and slick, across her skin.

"Tell me," Asmodeus commanded. "Don't bore me with begging."

You promised! Ashleigh screamed.

So did you, Lorelei snapped.

She spat the words out as fast as she could. "I shifted Ashleigh's soul aside as he rode me. I know he felt the change, but he showed no sign of stopping. Then the bitch appeared with a flaming sword. I don't know what they said to each other, but he put us out soon after. He sent me into the world with Ashleigh along. His friends didn't seem thrilled by that. I heard a screaming match behind us as I fled."

Asmodeus must have gestured: the creatures surrounding her retreated. Lorelei heard the sound of claws on concrete as they crawled up and out of the storm drain.

CHAPTER 7: HIGHER POWERS

Angels leaned forward in the soot-stained pews, clustered in the aisles and perched on the window frames. Some were quietly rapt; others murmured joyously. All turned their faces to Rafael like flowers following the sun.

Rafael stood in front of the altar, arms outstretched, passing on Heaven's blessing. Even without wings or corona manifest, the archangel blazed with magnificence, holier than any of the assembled LA Host. Like the others, Aza felt acutely aware of how much his own glory had dimmed in his time away from Heaven.

The archangel dropped his arms and turned to him. "Muriel and Samael have asked that you be proclaimed Cursed of Heaven."

The pain in Aza's shoulder spread through his entire body. "How can they?"

"They've as much right to beseech the will of the Almighty as you do, my friend."

"More." Muriel stood on the railing of the choir loft at the back of the sanctuary. "Considering the way he's flaunted the Rule and Way of the Word, Cursed of both Heaven and Earth should he be."

Quietly, from her place in the third pew, Barbelo said, "Your view is not shared by all our assembly, Sister."

"How can it not be?" Muriel demanded. "I don't find as much mutability in the laws of the Creator as some here, as any spirit born of Heaven should agree."

Barbelo's smile was subtle. Among all the angels, she alone had been born. She alone had a mother and many fathers. It made Muriel her elder, but gave her no right to be insulting. Aza wondered if the slur had been intentional and why Muriel should resent his friend.

Barbelo met his gaze and accepted his sympathy.

Muriel hadn't finished, however. She sensed that she did not have the company's full attention. She leaned out farther than weight or balance permitted, canopying the angels below with her outstretched wings.

"In two nights of mischief, Azaziel imperiled not only his own standing in Heaven, but endangered all of us who work in this midden."

"What I have done was inspired by love," Aza said quietly, letting his words display their truth.

"Don't hide behind that. I came to this appalling place out of love and sacrifice, so please don't speak to me of love, except where the Almighty is concerned. There is more to our being than love."

"Have you said as much to the Word?" Aza asked. "Or do you keep silent on the faintest hope that nothing said will be nothing judged?"

A wave of anger swept through Muriel. It charged the dust around her to take flight, reflecting back the glow of her self-righteousness. "We are knowledge, truth, and justice, *Brother*."

Rafael chided her. "We are messengers of love to all creation."

"In spirit," Muriel blurted. At the sudden rustle of the congregation below, she amended quickly, "The Word does not require of us liaisons in the flesh."

Aza would have preferred to confess that to Rafael in private, but the archangel did not seem as shocked by it as the others of the LA Host.

Muriel continued. "If I had been allowed to follow my will, I would have killed the hellspawn last night and spared Azaziel any further temptation. Then none of us would have to retrieve the girl-child's soul."

"As I told you last night," Aza said, "Lorelei had accepted my hospitality, placing herself willingly under my protection. We ate together. How could I allow harm to come to her in my home?"

Rafael received this information with a calm nod.

Muriel refused to concede the point. "Don't twist the laws to fit your defense. You knew she was evil when you invited her in."

"We must know all things," Barbelo said in her unruffled voice. "Good and evil, above all else."

"Nothing requires that we court evil, embrace it." Muriel quivered, tears sparkling in her blond lashes. "How can he still be here among us?" she demanded. "How can he be unfallen?"

"What Azaziel has done was inspired by love," Rafael repeated. "Where strength of arms has failed us, perhaps love will tip the balance." He hopped up to sit on the altar and crossed his legs. "Let us talk no more of the succubus and her charge now. Their association must play out without our intervention. We must discuss our continuing work in this City. How many demons are arrayed against us here?"

The blood had cooled against Lorelei's skin before she found the nerve to speak. Her human eyes had adjusted to the gloom, she realized. She could see Asmodeus, at least vaguely. Shaggy fur curled above cloven hooves. She suspected he'd taken that form to frighten Ashleigh, but that meant he knew she'd be able to see him. Lorelei was weary of playing games with creatures older and wilier than herself.

Unable to tolerate the tension any longer, Lorelei asked, "I would do anything to be rid of this ghost, my lord."

"Would you?"

"Please, my lord, believe me. Will you free me from this possession?"

"How was it," he asked, "that the angel infused you with a soul?"

"He bathed me with holy water—"

Asmodeus interrupted her. "You allowed that?"

"My lord, I sat half-naked in his bed as he knelt at my feet. It shames me to admit it, but he laid the trap with such cunning that I had no indication that my seduction of him was not progressing as planned."

Asmodeus shook his head. "Seduced by an angel? Lorelei, how could you be so stupid?"

Ashleigh stirred at that. Lorelei wondered if the girl was tempted to come to her defense.

"I should have taken you off the case in the first place," Asmodeus continued. "An older girl would never have dropped her guard."

While her intention had never wavered, Lorelei *had* allowed herself to relax under the angel's ministrations. She'd never doubted that he would fall for her. That misguided pride burned inside her now. How *could* she have been so stupid? From the instant she broke her attack in the alley, Aza had controlled her.

"I had hoped that the more I submitted to his demands, the more I would seem to be the helpless mortal girl he desired. But he kept me disoriented and celibate through the daylight, bound by an agreement to remain in mortal appearance as long as I stayed with him…"

"Ah," the demon sighed.

"He breathed her into me. Before I could consume her, he said something…a single word…and I was trapped."

"Do you remember the word?"

Concentrating, Lorelei remembered her fury when she discovered how Aza had defiled her with the holy water. She remembered the sweet apology of his lips on hers, the warmth of his breath inside her lungs, the choking flutter as Ashleigh's soul flowed into her. The sudden sensation of her body's crushing weight. The discomfort as the soul soaked into her, then locked her into her flesh.

Her awkward resistance had been no impediment to the angel. He hugged her close, whispered something into her ear… She remembered his strong arms pinning her, the myrrh-like scent of him, the way her body heat had reflected from his chest—but the memory of the command had evaporated.

"Too bad," Asmodeus remarked.

It must have been angelic speech, Lorelei realized now. That tongue had once been taught in Hell, but Lorelei hadn't troubled to learn it. None of the young devils did. How often did any of them choose to engage the Enemy's minions directly?

Asmodeus took her shoulders in his hands and raised her to her feet. His grip lingered on the edge of pain. She could make out his beautiful face and his sharp black gaze. She breathed deep his scent, wild and dark, like crushed grapes and blood.

The quivering within her told her than Ashleigh was terrified. Lorelei herself no longer felt afraid. To be in her prince's arms was a rare honor. She wondered if the veneration she held for him was a kind of love.

"Ashleigh," the demon purred, "come tell me what you've done."

Lorelei slipped away from her senses as the girl was summoned.

The mortal girl trembled so violently she might have fallen if the demon hadn't supported her. "Cold?" he asked.

That wasn't the reason for her shivering, but she nodded anyway. A fiend stepped out of the shadows and shrugged out of his suit jacket. He was big and angular, designed for fucking things up. Ashleigh remembered what Lorelei had said about sticking the pitchforks in.

Asmodeus draped the borrowed jacket around her shoulders. It fell almost to her knees. "Just because my own servants choose to come naked before me, there's no reason for you to, child."

Say thank you, Lorelei prompted. Ashleigh couldn't find her voice.

"Your angel has done a very serious thing," the demon said. "You were meant to die, dear child, as do all mortal creatures. Neither damned nor blessed, your soul would have fed the harpies as your flesh did." She shuddered, but the demon continued in a slow, measured tone: "Your angel interrupted the natural order of the universe. It's not for us to judge him damned, but I imagine the Enemy will find some severe way of punishing his hubris."

Go on, tell my master how Aza talked you into this conspiracy, Lorelei prompted.

Asmodeus smiled. "He came as you lay dying and offered you an escape."

"It wasn't like that," Ashleigh blurted. "He offered…" Startled to hear her voice, she caught her lower lip in her teeth.

He rewarded her with one night of love as the woman she would never grow to be, Lorelei reported. *A woman in my flesh.*

"Both of you seduced by the same angel?" Asmodeus asked. "Perhaps I should petition to have him added to my staff."

Lorelei laughed in delight.

Asmodeus took her face in both hands and tipped it up to meet his gaze. "I won't hurt you, little girl." He followed the promise with a kiss of such ardor that Ashleigh felt lightheaded.

Asmodeus held her against him. The coarse fur on his legs tickled her skin. Ashleigh squeezed her knees together, but the demon made no attempt to force himself on her, other than the kiss.

Relax, Lorelei soothed. *He promised not to hurt you.*

The girl fought to keep her eyes open, but the demon stood so close he seemed to fill the world.

The metaphor amused Lorelei. The succubus pointed out the sensations of the silk lining of the fiend's jacket against her bare skin, the ache of her nipples swollen by the chill, the sensuous warmth of Asmodeus's fur against her thighs.

Her back throbbed where the devils' claws had pierced it, but between the demon's kiss and Lorelei's mischief, Ashleigh had trouble concentrating on the pain. She had to remember she had no friends here. She knew instinctively that if she gave in to them, if she surrendered to desire, she'd be lost.

Yet it was so *very* tempting. Wrapped in Aza's arms, Lorelei had hinted at secrets that she would gladly share, pleasures she could happily teach. It had been easy to ignore her while sheltered by the angel's love…

But where is he now? Lorelei asked. *Oh, Ashleigh, we deserve some fun, you and I. Just relax. Let Asmodeus show us a good time. He promised not to hurt you. What have you got to lose? You'll like it. I know you will. I know how wonderful this body can feel. Please, Ashleigh, please. You don't have to do anything but say yes.*

Asmodeus's soft lips explored her cheekbone. His breath smelled like cloves. He traced her throat with feathery kisses. Ashleigh felt her head loll backward. She forced her eyes open, trying to focus on the fiends standing guard nearby, watching with disinterest as their prince seduced her.

She wished she could go back to the time when she hadn't known angels and devils really existed, when people were only people and they might hurt you but it would stop when you died. If only she were dead now, really dead, gone forever, free of this place and Lorelei and her master and this blackness…

Asmodeus leaned away from her so she could see the smile curving his lips. "Tell me, little girl, is *that* what you really want? Freedom from Lorelei?"

Without hesitation, Ashleigh nodded.

"Even if it means oblivion?"

She swallowed hard. "Only if it means oblivion."

He actually grinned at that.

Lorelei kept ominously quiet. Ashleigh had expected her to protest, to push more strenuously for sex with her boss. The silence was Ashleigh's first clue that the trap she'd walked into was not the one she'd been expecting. She trembled.

"I don't want any of you to eat me, either," the girl protested. Was it too late to clarify?

Asmodeus released her. Ashleigh swayed, unable to find her balance. Her foot stung where Lorelei had stepped on the broken glass.

Pale orange flame ignited in Asmodeus's hand. He dropped it into a golden bowl supported by a waist-high tripod. Incense began to smolder, filling the damp air with heavy perfume. Ashleigh had only smelled the aroma once, at a party of Deion's, but she recognized it: opium.

The demon addressed the other creatures in the drain. "Leave us."

In answer, the fiends turned to leap, one at a time, at the lowest rung of the emergency ladder. They hauled themselves up without comment.

Asmodeus circled the drain, touching a forefinger to the wicks of red pillar candles. Ashleigh got her first real look at him. He didn't have goat legs at all, but wore black velvet trousers beneath a tunic of burgundy brocade. His skin shone the color of burnished mahogany beneath glossy black hair thick as fur. He made her think of Omar Sharif, her granny's favorite movie star.

Ashleigh looked upward to see a length of scaled tail slithering over the lip of the drain. It disappeared into the night above. She was alone with Asmodeus, Prince of Hell.

"What are you going to do?" Ashleigh quavered.

"Separate you from Lorelei," he answered, "and set you free."

"Will it hurt?"

"Probably."

"I wish you'd lied about that."

Asmodeus laughed. "Contrary to popular belief, we demons deal in truth. None of that 'we'll tell you later, after you're dead' crap the other side of the family likes to dish out. Life is painful. Death is a simple transition."

"And Hell?" Ashleigh wondered.

"We find it beautiful." He came back to her and caught her hand, pulling her into the center of the ring of candles. "You will have to take my word for it, however."

"Why?"

"Once I release you from Lorelei, I will ensure that you cease to exist. Since Lorelei failed to damn you, you will never see Hell. Or Heaven either, since your angel neglected to redeem you."

Asmodeus took the walking stick from where he'd tucked it under his arm. With its tip, he traced a ring around her in the debris on the floor of the drain.

"What will happen to Lorelei?"

Asmodeus shrugged. "Why should you care?"

I care, Lorelei told her. *Thanks for asking.*

The demon sketched runes that Ashleigh couldn't read. *The Satanic Alphabet*, Lorelei explained. *The circle will protect Asmodeus from being possessed by you and you from being consumed by him.*

What will happen to you? Ashleigh wondered.

I'm in trouble, Lorelei answered. *I didn't damn you—and you should've been easy—or Aza, who I shouldn't have approached in the first place. There'll be penalties, probably a demotion. I don't want to think about it now.*

You did your best, Ashleigh thought.

Lorelei sent her such a rush of affection that Ashleigh blushed.

"Be still, you two." Asmodeus stood before them, outside of the circle, and raised his walking stick. Topping it was a knob of ivory carved into a heap of writhing naked human forms. Tiny heads thrown back, their mouths grimaced in excruciating ecstasy. Chips of ruby flashed where their eyes should have been.

Asmodeus rotated the walking stick in his hands, making the rubies flash. Ashleigh's gaze locked onto them. She couldn't blink or glance away.

"Ashleigh Johnson, I call on you to come out of this succubus."

"How?" Ashleigh wondered.

Just let go, Lorelei said. *Let the sound of his voice draw you out.*

When Aza had spoken his summons, Ashleigh hadn't understood the words. She thought they'd been Latin only because Lorelei thought so. Those commands had propelled her as surely as if he'd shoved her from behind. Whatever Asmodeus was doing now was completely opposite. Ashleigh felt Lorelei's flesh growing heavier and heavier, as if turning to stone.

"Come out, Ashleigh. Let Lorelei face her fate alone."

Opium smoke wafted into her face and she breathed deep. It felt as if the last latch had abruptly been peeled back. Ashleigh had a sensation of rushing upward, like flying in a dream. The ceiling of the drain came up on her too fast. She jerked to a halt.

"No!" Lorelei moaned.

Ashleigh looked around wildly. Asmodeus stood below, inside the ring of red candles but outside the ring of runes. Still in human form, Lorelei's body lay crumpled on the floor of the drain. A shimmering silver ribbon trailed from the body up to Ashleigh's heart. She saw her own skinny legs and arms, transparent as a ghost's. Tangled around the umbilical ribbon that held her to Lorelei's flesh was a vine with poisonous-looking thorns.

At the end of the vine, Lorelei floated in her true form, supported by delicate black bat's wings. The voluptuous proportions of her body were further exaggerated. Her skin burned a deep and bloody red. She plucked desperately at the barbed vine with sharp black nails.

This was wrong, Ashleigh understood. Lorelei claimed there was no difference between her flesh and spirit, that they were the same. This ghost of Lorelei should not have been able to exist alongside the body below. Something had changed the succubus, broken her into parts.

Lorelei wrestled with the vine, piercing her hands on its spines. She didn't look up at Ashleigh. "My lord," the succubus begged, "please, I don't want to die."

Asmodeus gazed up at them in amusement. "So when you said you would do anything to be rid of this girl, you lied?"

Lorelei gave up on the umbilical vine. She swooped, shrieking, at Ashleigh. Transfixed, the girl watched the attack come. How could she get away, when they were so tangled together? Lorelei crashed into her, then through her, leaving a trail of embers flickering in Ashleigh's soul. The succubus whirled around to attack again, not realizing she was snarling things worse.

"Stop!" Ashleigh begged. "Just let me go."

Lorelei collapsed in on herself, dropping her head and crossing her arms over her breasts. "Whatever the angel did when he shoved you back into me," Lorelei groaned, "he knotted us together. It would take forever to unravel that. Inseparable."

"Oblivion," Asmodeus told Ashleigh, "is as easy as snapping the cord that binds you to this flesh."

"I don't want to die!" Lorelei moaned. "Ashleigh, please, I know you don't have any reason to help me. I know I've been mean to you. You know it's nothing personal; it's what I'm supposed to do. But look at me!" She flung her wings back and jabbed a talon toward the body on the floor. "Whatever Aza did to me, I'm flesh *and* spirit now. Two, not one. If you break your cord, you'll have your oblivion, sure. But unless we get untangled first, you'll break my cord too. And you know me, Ashleigh. You know I'll be damned to eternal torment. That I never had any choice in the matter. You will have damned me so you could sleep with an angel."

"You're pathetic," Ashleigh snapped. "You would've damned me without a second thought."

"I'm a succubus," Lorelei pointed out. "I was created to damn people."

"Shall I list Lorelei's damnable offenses?" Asmodeus offered. "She's had roughly a hundred and fifty years from the moment of her hatching to lead souls to torment. She spent much of that time as a succubus. Rarely did she fail to deliver at least a soul a week unto us. Some years, as I remember, were spectacularly prolific."

"That pleases you, right, Master? I worked hard to serve you."

"Not hard enough. Not when it counted."

Ashleigh stared at her. Lorelei gazed back, broken and scared. Tears of blood welled in the ghost-devil's eyes. She'd never felt fear until Ashleigh had been thrust on her. Never faced death, or damnation. In her way, Lorelei was more innocent that Ashleigh had felt in a long, long time. Against her better judgment, Ashleigh felt sorry for the succubus.

Ashleigh tugged experimentally on the cord and watched Lorelei flinch. "What other choice do I have?" Ashleigh demanded.

"Wait for Floria to find us an exorcist. It won't take long," Lorelei hoped desperately. "Then we can have a ceremony and get disentangled and you can go free."

"If I agree, you stop trying to damn me," Ashleigh said.

The succubus began to nod. A sharp shock hit them both. Ashleigh plummeted and vanished into the body, dragging Lorelei along behind. Asmodeus kicked aside the outer lines of the magic circle. Adrenaline screamed through Lorelei's veins.

Asmodeus twisted the knob atop his walking stick. As he strode toward them, he drew out a slim serrated blade. "Tell me why I should not kill you now," he demanded.

Lorelei struggled to get her legs under her. Terror had overwhelmed her to the point that she couldn't form words to beg for her life. She made a high-pitched wail. Even buried deep inside, Ashleigh wanted the sound to stop.

A male voice interrupted from overhead. "My prince?"

Asmodeus halted, rotating the blade to make it flash in the candlelight. "What is it, Jequon?"

"Muriel and Samael have requested that Azaziel be proclaimed Cursed of Heaven. The Archangel Rafael is in town to sort things out."

Lorelei collapsed back into the debris. Why Jequon had been spying on her angel? Why had he chosen this moment to come to her rescue? What would she owe him for this?

Asmodeus's blade touched her throat. Lorelei jumped. Holding herself still as stone, she peeled her eyes open.

"Do not forget what you are, Lorelei," the demon cautioned. "You serve me and you serve Hell. I will devour you myself before I allow

Heaven to have you."

She nodded.

In a rush of heat and flame, the candles snuffed out. Darkness flooded the drain. Asmodeus had gone.

CHAPTER 8: CONTRACTS

Lorelei lay listening to her heart pound.

Damned.

How many mortals had she sent to eternal torment? Somewhere in Hell labored a quill-carrying devil with a ledger book so big he had to walk across it to make entries, tallying the names of the damned and crediting the parties responsible. The Hellish statistics determined privileges devils might attain. Lorelei had done her job. Enjoyed it. Held friendly competitions with Floria and Conchita and other succubi of her generation. She had sent millions of souls—most of them Russian—to feed the fires back home. Chances were that every one of them would weigh against her soul when her own death came. She would be damned amongst her victims.

"It's not fair," she whimpered.

Life's not fair, Ashleigh snapped. *Shit, I was only seventeen and I knew that.*

"It was always fair before," Lorelei countered.

For you, maybe. What about all those people you damned?

"They had a choice," Lorelei answered. "No is as easy to say as yes. It's just not as much fun."

We're finding out right now how much fun 'yes' is, Ashleigh commented.

Lorelei curled up inside the fiend's jacket. Her head hurt too much to cry. "What am I going to do?" she asked hoarsely.

If you hadn't sold Aza out, we could've asked for his protection.

"You've got to be kidding, Ashes. Aza is the enemy."

Seems to me that he's the only person not trying to kill you.

"I think you're the only person not trying to kill me."

You have to warn him, Ashleigh pushed, *or his misery is going on your record, too.*

"Shut up!" Lorelei shouted. Her voice echoed in the empty storm drain. Chastened, she said, "It was him or me. If I hadn't said anything, I'd be dead now."

And I'd be free.

Lorelei curled herself tighter. Everything had gone *so* wrong, she could barely remember what her life used to be like. She scrunched her eyes closed against the darkness. Parties, she finally remembered. Sex, whenever she wanted it, with whomever she wanted. Nice clothes. Warm beds. Hot baths. Drinks on the house if she smiled at the bartenders. Asmodeus liked her, let her experiment. She'd toyed with her prey. Been happy.

If only that accursed angel hadn't come into Lost Angels. She remembered the hunch of his shoulders as he sat at the bar. She remembered his flavor on her tongue, how good he smelled. She should've walked straight past him like every other devil in the club. But she'd been foolish and cocky and his loneliness had been irresistible. She'd bet her happiness on him. In return, he'd damned her.

Maybe that had been his plan all along. He served the Enemy. He'd told her he was only doing his job. In fact, he would probably come at the first convenient moment to retrieve his little helper, now that they'd successfully ruined Lorelei.

Lorelei shook her head. Damning devils was a whole new strategy in the Celestial War. No wonder Asmodeus was pissed. How could Hell counter that?

Get up, Ashleigh urged. *We've got to get out of here before dawn. If anyone finds us walking around LA dressed like this, we've got a fifty-fifty chance of winding up dead in a dumpster.*

That shook Lorelei enough to get her moving. She held her hands out and shuffled forward until she found a wall. The fiends had climbed out of the drain using rungs set into cement. Those were somewhere overhead. She'd have to really jump to catch the lowest one, then drag herself up. Life was so much easier when she'd had wings.

Shebniel ascended the last few feet of the church's vacant stairwell and put his wings away as he walked into the old office. A bandana bound his wavy black hair away from his face. "I don't understand how the succubus fit into your plan."

Aza chuckled bitterly. What he'd done had infected even this moment of peace. He set aside his brush and sat back to gaze at the still-unfinished fresco. Would he ever have time to finish his prayer?

"It would be easier for us to stand with you if we understood what you were thinking," Shebniel prompted.

"I was thinking that Ashleigh never had a chance to become pure. She was too young to choose wisely, and then too ill. In her way, Lorelei was also innocent. She never recognized that she had a choice."

Shebniel considered that long enough that Aza picked up his brush again. Finally, he said, "I'd never thought you were delusional, Brother."

"I'm not," Aza countered. "Merely optimistic."

"It's worse than optimism to think that any creature born of Hell has any choice but to do Satan's will. They're not truly alive," Shebniel argued, "not really. They're manufactured like machinery in a factory, expressly fashioned to doom humanity. None of his minions would show a moment's mercy if an underling didn't advance the War."

"I left Lorelei alone in my cell," Aza answered. "Asmodeus visited her, recommending that she leave me alone. She could have acquiesced without consequence. Instead, Lorelei chose to follow me here."

"Then she chose to kick you down this stairway," Shebniel pointed out.

Muriel manifested on the scene abruptly. "That was an ugly bit of foreshadowing, wasn't it?"

Aza would have shrugged, but the pain in his shoulder prevented him. The interruption was so in character that it didn't particularly irk him.

Still, he didn't have to address her. "When Muriel led you to attack," Aza told Shebniel, "you can imagine how Lorelei felt. All creatures fight to survive."

Shebniel shook his head. "Delusional."

"At least the stink of her is starting to leave this place," Muriel remarked. "Thanks to Rafael for that."

Aza looked down at the brush in his hand. The mood of gratitude had entirely left him now. He collected his paints and retreated to the bathroom to clean his brushes. The fresco would have to wait for a time when Muriel was far away.

Lorelei kept to the back streets, but most dead-ended at industrial courts. Although they were close to several run-down neighborhoods, Lorelei couldn't bring herself to knock on a door and ask for help. There were too many questions she couldn't answer.

Look, Ashleigh bitched, *you're gonna have to let me take over.*

Lorelei wondered if it might be possible to become disconnected from her flesh. She envisioned Ashleigh living a new life in Lorelei's body. The more time passed, the less the thought frightened her. Maybe she could roam the world as a ghost and escape her looming punishment.

We're wandering around here like a fly banging against a window, Ashleigh observed. *You're obviously not used to walking in this town.*

Fuck it, Lorelei decided. Let the dead girl deal with the grief. She folded her thoughts and receded.

Fully in control, the first thing Ashleigh did was to orient herself to the growl of the freeway. Once she started toward it, she became aware how much her foot truly hurt. Whatever Ashleigh thought of Lorelei, the devil could definitely work around pain.

She crouched to examine the cut. Even in the dim light, it looked bad. A slice curved just behind the ball of her foot. The only thing keeping her from bleeding like a stuck pig was god-knows how much yuck from the storm drain packed into the wound. The skin around the cut burned. The Emergency Room seemed like a better alternative than hiking half-naked and barefoot through LA in the middle of the night.

No hospitals! Lorelei shrieked, pushing herself forward.

Ashleigh held her back more easily than expected. "Look," she said, "a lot of the places close to downtown have a backdoor policy of, like, Tylenol and Band-Aids for runaways."

Lorelei sounded worn out when she answered. *How do you plan to explain where your clothes are, or how you got the claw wounds on your back? You tell them a quarter of what really happened and they'll have you on a three-day psych hold faster than you can spell your name.*

Ashleigh couldn't argue with that. As she started toward the sound of the freeway, the cut throbbed. She needed to focus on the pain, use it, but really, like the rest of this evening, she just wanted it to go away.

While her first inclination was to head to the nearby road bridging the river, she couldn't risk it. The only other option to cross the water was an elevated pipeline that spanned the water about fifty yards away. The pipe had to be a good four feet around, held up by suspension towers that made it look like some miniature Golden Gate Bridge. She'd spent enough time hanging out down by the river to know there'd be a gate meant to keep taggers off. Even at this distance, she could see the marshmallow-soft letters that proved how ineffective it had been.

Navigating the pipe hadn't been easy with a gashed-up foot, but the last of Ashleigh's confidence drained away when she reached the freeway. A fifteen-foot soundproofing wall stretched as far as she could see in both directions. She pounded her fist against it, then pushed her anger aside. They had to have doorways in these walls.

She limped to her right. When she finally found an opening, it was a slot punched through by an out-of-control semi. Picking her way across the broken concrete, Ashleigh peered out.

To her amazement, the freeway held its breath. The next knot of traffic lurked some distance away. Ashleigh watched the half-dozen vehicles approach. The glare of their headlights transmuted almost instantly into the red glow of receding taillights.

She pulled herself through the hole and sprinted for the center divider. She angled toward a smashed couch, fallen off of some luckless movers' pickup.

Scrunching down as small as possible, she felt the next wave of vehicles thunder past. A vortex of sharp grit blasted her. Ashleigh felt the tail of the suit coat sucked up.

She had to laugh. If there was anything worse than cowering naked in a sewer tempted by a demon, it was being stuck in the middle of the Golden State Freeway, mooning traffic.

Like the anger before it, she shut the laughter down.

She heard a lull on the opposite side of the concrete divider. Ashleigh sprang over the barrier, landing hard on one knee. Another scrape to add to her injuries. Headlights burned in the distance, so she pushed herself up and started to run.

Halfway across the asphalt, the headlights loomed, almost upon her. Lorelei rushed up to take control, freezing before the oncoming lights and pulling open her jacket. Brakes locked up. Two vehicles collided with a deep bass thud. Then the traffic passed with an explosion of wind that hurled hair across her face and almost knocked her from her feet.

Lorelei flung her hair back as once again steel met steel. Her heart hammered in her chest. This is *so* cool, she thought. She wondered if anyone had been killed outright. That was the sort of thing she would've known, if she'd been herself.

Run! Ashleigh commanded. *We're standing in the middle of the freeway and causing accidents.*

"What's the matter, Ashes?" Lorelei teased. "Don't you like having a body that'll stop traffic?"

People are getting hurt because of us, Ashleigh hissed. *Why do you have to be such a cunt?*

Lorelei laughed.

The adrenaline kick faded suddenly, marooning her on the brink of nausea. She had to get away fast. If anyone *had* been killed in the accident, someone would be along to claim the souls. Lorelei couldn't think of anyone she wanted to see her in this condition.

She loped off the highway, then worked her way into the oleander bushes on the shoulder. Making her way down the slope in the semi-darkness, she blundered blindly into a chain-link fence.

It's supposed to keep people off the freeway, Ashleigh explained. *Look what you accomplished standing there for five seconds.*

Lorelei snarled at her, too irritated to find words. She prowled along the fence, growing more agitated with every step. For ages she'd studied human quarry and never grown bored, but her new life was like being inside a maze for which no one had bothered to find an exit. Pretty well summed up the hours since she'd met the angel.

Ashleigh had been right: Lorelei never walked in LA. There'd invariably been a limo or a cab or a victim to offer her a ride. In addition, Lorelei couldn't remember ever having been alone for so long in her life—there'd always been prey or others of her kind around. She'd been unfailingly confident what her next step would be. She realized that now, if it hadn't been for Ashleigh, she would have been worse than lost. Her need for the smug little girl infuriated her.

Lorelei kicked the fence. A white flash of pain dropped her into the dirt. The cut on her foot opened, spilling blood hot against her dirty skin. Lorelei cursed methodically in Russian, cradling her foot in her hands. She had no idea what to do next. Ashleigh's oblivion tempted her more and more.

You're gonna have to let me take over, Ashleigh urged, very gently. *Let me help.*

Scrubbing angrily at her tears, Lorelei nodded. She had next to nothing left to lose.

Hoisting herself up on the fence, Ashleigh nearly slit her throat on the jagged Y's of chain-link at the top. She dropped back down. Looking over both shoulders, she shrugged out of the fiend's jacket and flung it across the fence. The wire still poked at her as she shimmied over, but it would've been much worse on bare flesh.

Landing awkwardly on one foot, she reached up to tug the jacket loose. It tore in several places before coming down. She hoped that Lorelei would be the one to return the fucked-up Armani to the fiend.

Jeez. She couldn't believe she was thinking like *her* now.

She staggered over behind a nearby mail drop-box. Bloody footprints marked her passage. Crouching in the box's shadow, Ashleigh turned the fiend's jacket inside out. Change rang down on the sidewalk.

Grab it! Lorelei directed. *We can call Floria to come get us.*

Snapping Lorelei's nails off against the concrete, Ashleigh snatched up all the coins she could find.

Do you see a phone anywhere?

"About a hundred yards away." Ashleigh stacked the coins beside her, then began to tear out the coat's lining.

You are not going to tear up this jacket! Do you know what these things cost?

"It's already too far gone," Ashleigh argued. "Look, I'm on my way out of this body, so I don't care. But trust me, blood poisoning is an *ugly* way to die." She tore a bandage and wrapped her foot.

Lorelei knew when to compromise. *We are not giving this jacket back.*

Ashleigh chuckled. She shouldered into the jacket again and gathered the coins. Every step felt like being cut afresh, but she managed to reach the pay phone.

"Let me," Lorelei said. The transfer of personalities was almost effortless now. She opened her fist in the light. Stirring the coins around on her palm, she found a dinar, one pound sterling, 25 yen, a buffalo nickel, and a couple of coins she didn't recognize. Some of them were very old.

Just feed them in, Ashleigh encouraged. *Maybe something will work.*

Lorelei punched in Floria's number and pumped the coins in. The nickel didn't come back, but the rest clattered into the coin return. Lorelei fished them out to drop in again. Something else caught. She thought it was one of the ones she hadn't recognized, something blackened by time. Probably the fiend's lucky piece: something else she'd owe him for.

Floria's number rang and rang. The nausea rose in Lorelei again. Then her sister snatched the phone up. Even as Lorelei opened her mouth to speak, Floria said, "Hi, Lorelei. Knew you'd call. You're on your own this evening, Sister. I'm taking Tuan up to the hospital to have that nasty bite looked at. Maybe we'll see you there?"

The voicemail switched off without allowing Lorelei to leave a message.

She dropped the receiver, not bothering to hang it up. Such an aching chill filled her that she barely registered sirens approaching on the freeway. Move, she thought, lumbering further into the shadows.

Why are you going back there? Ashleigh wondered. *Floria doesn't care about you.*

"She doesn't slap me around the way your boyfriend used to do you," Lorelei growled.

I stayed with him because taking a beating now and then was better than being on the street and maybe getting killed.

"Bad company is better than no company, isn't it, Ashes?"

Ashleigh tried again. *I have friends who could help us.*

"Your friends wouldn't recognize you now," Lorelei pointed out. "If you told them you are a ghost possessing a succubus, they would think I was some actress who couldn't manage her E and got tossed out of a limo."

There are places we could get help. We could get some decent clothes and some hot food and medicine for your foot, a safe place to sleep…

"There is no discussing this," Lorelei snapped. "I am not a runaway. There *is* no running away. I belong to Hell. All I can do is go back to Floria's and wait for the exorcist." She trudged onward, then asked, "How do you think Floria knew to be outside the church waiting for us? Before that, when I was chained up in Aza's cell, Asmodeus came to taunt me. They're not human, Ashleigh. They can always find me. If my prince wants me to walk across LA as some kind of punishment, I walk. If I don't, whatever happens will be three times more unpleasant."

Ashleigh marveled, *This is worse than the Mafia.*

"What do you think the Mafia is based on?"

You have to do what they want, or else you die and go to Hell?

"No matter what I do, I will die and go to Hell," Lorelei corrected. "I have a soul that's already damned."

There must be some kind of hope?

"If I'm lucky, Asmodeus will get pissed off enough to devour me instead. Or when Aza gets around to rescuing you, maybe he'll do it."

She jerked to a halt beneath a streetlight. Every muscle trembled. Lorelei turned very slowly, to find herself alone inside the circle of light.

What? Ashleigh quavered.

Eyes on the sidewalk, Lorelei raised her right hand in the symbol of the horns. "Bloody Hell," she muttered.

What?

"I have a shadow."

So? You and everybody else.

"I'm not everybody," Lorelei protested. "I'm a... I'm supposed to be a spirit."

I know, Ashleigh countered. *I saw you: wings and horns and long pretty tail, looking like you should be selling X-rated fireworks. You're one of us now. Get used to it.*

Aza stood on the overpass, watching the emergency lights flash below. Crumpled vehicles lay scattered across the highway like a spoiled child's toys. A newspaper delivery truck rested on its side. Pages of the *LA Times* fluttered across the asphalt like carrion birds.

Crews of several ambulances treated the injured while highway patrol officers tried to establish how the accident began. Barbelo moved amongst the crowd, soothing everyone with her calm presence.

Lorelei had caused this, Aza knew. He could smell a faint trace of her perfume, but the night air was heavy with the stink of fiends, tempters, harpies, and Asmodeus. That odor Aza remembered distinctly from the hallway outside his cell, when the demon visited Lorelei in her captivity.

Tracked across the highway, moving into the oleanders and office park beyond, were Lorelei's bloody footprints. The path she'd taken burned before Aza's eyes.

They'd hurt her. They'd terrified her. And still, despite her encounter with LA's fierce prince, Lorelei and Ashleigh were together, limping away into the night. Aza ached to go after them, to rescue them if he could. Unfortunately, he had scarcely protected himself from Muriel's wrath. If he found his girls, he could do little more than sacrifice his life in their defense.

Rafael clasped Aza's good shoulder. "Leave them be for now."

Aza turned toward the archangel, breathing a sigh of relief. "Come to give me a good word or two?"

Rafael shook his head. "They have more to endure tonight that none of us can prevent." He offered a reassuring smile. "If it eases your mind, Brother, know that your prayers are being heard. You might want to take a moment and pray to give them strength."

The archangel moved away to leave Aza alone.

Aza lowered his head. Ashleigh and Lorelei had more to undergo? He wished he could suffer in their places. He'd hoped somehow that the sacrifice of his wings, his acceptance of the laming might somehow buy them indulgence—as if that old concept meant anything in these latter days.

He thought about his decision to step into the jaws of Hell the night he'd gone into Lost Angels after Lorelei. At the time, he'd felt the old sensations of direction and encouragement, wordless as they ever were in his exile here. The impressions had strengthened his resolve and lightened his heart.

Once he'd finally met the succubus, she was so alien—so infernal—that he'd lost his nerve and fled, leaving her helpless prey to his doom. As he'd walked back to his cell, Aza struggled with a crushing sense of failure that led him to vow that if ever their paths crossed again, he would work harder to befriend Lorelei, to find some common ground where their romance might work.

Of course, the soulless devil recognized only two forms of relationships: the abject subservience she offered her master and the dominance and subjugation with which she dealt with her prey. By adding Ashleigh's soul to the mix, Aza had hoped to teach Lorelei about the whole spectrum of friendship and affection and, if possible, love.

So he clasped his hands, fingers turning the simple gold band on his ring finger out of ancient habit. Then he spoke the words that brimmed in his heart. "May You grant Lorelei the strength to see this night through, that she might work Your Will in the world. May You grant Ashleigh the strength to guide Lorelei to the light of Your love. May the good for which I hoped yet come out of this darkness and uncertainty. But, as ever, Thy Will be done."

CHAPTER 9: TEMPTATION

Darkness pooled in the hollows amidst the hills north of downtown. The cool wet grass of Elysian Park almost made up for the torturous barefoot walk uphill to reach it. The post-bar-closing atmosphere was frighteningly still. It seemed that someone ran interference for them, keeping traffic away.

At the back of Ashleigh's thoughts, Lorelei wondered, *Where are we?*

"Up by Dodger Stadium, sort of, and the Police Academy."

Ahead, bathed in cool light, a fake adobe building stood beside swing sets and jungle gyms. The building looked for all the world like a twenty-four-hour taco stand. Ashleigh guessed it was a public restroom.

Limping over, she caught her reflection in a polished steel mirror mounted over the drinking fountain. Lorelei's thick hair hung raggedly around her face. Despite the tattered Armani jacket, the succubus' human form still looked damn attractive—in a wanton, Sophia Loren-as-hooker way.

Honestly, Ashes. You are so sweet, Lorelei said.

Women hated women that looked like Lorelei, Ashleigh realized. Had devils set that up to keep humans chewing on each other?

As Ashleigh drank from the fountain, she heard a strange dragging creak. She turned the tap off, but the sound continued. It came from around the building. Cautiously stepping out of the half-circle of light, she made out the big swing set. The blond fan of Damia's hair was silhouetted against the sky. The harpy crouched on the crossbar. Standing in a swing, Keisha rocked below in big, dangerous arcs. The swing stopped dead at the bottom of the pendulum. "Lookin' good, Ashes."

"Hey, Lorelei. What are the odds?" Damia stepped off the top of the swing set.

Not wanting to see her hit the ground, Ashleigh dodged back around the building, totally creeped out.

You maligned my friends, Lorelei reminded.

"I didn't realize they really were *from* Hell." Ashleigh struggled to feel as tough as her words.

Don't run, Lorelei advised. *I'll try to think of something.*

Ashleigh backed up against the building. Her heart raced.

Up on the roadway, a stretch limousine glided to a stop.

Father of Lies, Lorelei prayed, *look with favor on the least of your daughters. Protect me in my hour of need...*

"It's okay," Ashleigh interrupted. "This is LA. It's just some producer getting a blowjob."

The limousine jumped the curb. It continued up the sidewalk, gliding easily around the trees, until it pulled up in front of the restrooms.

One of the rear windows eased down. A delicate feminine hand beckoned Ashleigh. Heavy gold bracelets jangled as it receded.

Unceremoniously, Lorelei shoved Ashleigh's spirit aside. "Let me handle her, Ashleigh. Please."

Lorelei sauntered to the limo without limping. Damia and Keisha strolled into the light behind her, closing off that avenue of escape.

The limo door opened. Lorelei climbed inside, closing the door after her. The window hummed shut as she did. The car smelled of clove smoke.

She blinked in the darkness, expecting to hear the automatic locks. Instead, she heard the pop of a champagne cork. The limo's opera lights blazed to life, confirming what she already suspected. Thin as a lingerie model, exotic as a James Bond villainess, Yasmina sat on the opposite seat. Her face was a long oval with large, cinnamon-colored eyes.

"Congratulations, Lorelei. You've reached the top of the hill. Halfway home." Yasmina wore a long metallic evening gown, its design a Rorschach of blood- and copper-colored splotches. She had her legs curled up beside her on the car seat. She poured two glasses of Cristal and handed Lorelei one.

"Is this façade for me?" Lorelei asked.

"It didn't seem fair; you being stuck as a mortal."

Yasmina unfolded a copy of *Variety* onto the seat next to her. She patted it for Lorelei to put her injured foot up onto it.

Ashleigh urged, *I don't care what you think of this person; we really should get that foot up.*

Grimacing at how filthy it was, Lorelei consented. Where was Aza when she needed someone to wash her feet?

Yasmina tsked.

Turning toward the window, Lorelei summoned Ashleigh to the fore long enough that the girl could observe what was hidden to mortal eyes. Albeit vaguely, Yasmina's reflection revealed that her beautiful features were cruel, angular, almost reptilian.

She's not so much, Ashleigh said bravely.

Yasmina regarded them over her beaded flute of Cristal. Lorelei suspected that the elder devil could sense the communion between them, the way Aza and Asmodeus had. "Lorelei," Yasmina said, "I'm going to have a word with your little passenger. You can listen, but I'd prefer you didn't interrupt." As the temptress reached for them, her nails extruded inhumanly.

Ashleigh felt Lorelei's presence shoved so deeply into her breast that it seemed the succubus ceased to exist.

"I understand Prince Asmodeus asked you about your lover." Yasmina's smile radiated smugness. "Did you enjoy Azaziel? I understand him to be relatively skilled. Not that I've partaken of him personally, but I've had detailed accounts from those who have. Anah, for instance."

Ashleigh pulled her foot back from the seat. Yasmina snatched her ankle, caressing it, and eyed the girl carefully.

Ashleigh grimaced, still clinging to the belief that devils were incapable of the whole truth. "What do I care about Anah? She was supposed to have been his wife a long time ago."

"She was also my sister. You should be envious of her, of the way Azaziel took her to his bed with shameful frequency, especially after he discovered she was barren. She craved it, whorish little animal that she was. Loved having an untiring celestial husband with an insatiable appetite and the patience for her inept seductions."

"He must have loved her very much," Ashleigh shot back, not caring that she defended a woman gone so long that she might as well be a myth.

Yasmina raised an eyebrow, enjoying Ashleigh's reaction. "Just because I've never bedded Azaziel, don't think I haven't seduced my share of the Children of Heaven."

"I guess Anah wasn't the only whorish one?" Ashleigh asked, emboldened by ignorance. Lorelei applauded the stupid kid's style.

Yasmina sniffed. "You make it sound like something to be ashamed of. The shame is that Anah didn't use the opportunity to better herself."

"I don't know. Marrying an angel seems like a pretty good deal."

"Bringing about the downfall of several angels is much, much better. I never had to belong to anyone."

"What about Asmodeus?"

"Oh, child, that's a business relationship."

Lorelei laughed. No way she was letting that go unreported.

Yasmina's eyes narrowed, but she continued the story. "Back in the old days, there were many fewer mortals on the earth and more of *them*.

It wasn't so much a manifestation of angels as an infestation. Before they started falling, Heaven was teeming. I think the great I AM sent angels to Earth just to get them out from under foot. Mortals couldn't set up a shepherd's camp without angels poking around. Initially, they courted four of my six sisters. They thought we should be honored by their favors, the worthless festival tricks they passed off as knowledge. We deserved so much more."

Ashleigh asked, "What made you so special?"

"Our patriarch was Cain, the first mortal to protest the inequity of God's favor. Make no mistake, little one: Abel was a sycophant of the first order. You know what that means, Honey?"

Ashleigh shook her head.

"You know what a publicist is? Same thing, except Uncle Abel worked for a living."

Despite herself, Ashleigh laughed. She sipped the champagne. Lorelei wished she could spill the glass. They were weakened, wounded, and this was going down on an empty stomach. Ashleigh, ex-junkie that she was, should know better.

"Just so I'm not getting ahead of myself," Yasmina asked, "you *do* know the story of Cain and Abel?"

"Yeah. They were Adam's kids. They both offered up stuff they grew, right? When God liked Abel's better, Cain got mad and killed him."

Yasmina drank from her own glass. "You grasp the concept. But things were said, aspersions cast... Grandfather did what he had to."

Ashleigh opened her mouth, but Yasmina cut her off. "Before you say, 'You were descended from the first murderer, so what?'—consider the opprobrium his progeny bore. While most saw it as a burden," she huffed, "some of us accepted it as a legacy. Don't you see? Before my family, God created and God destroyed. Cain committed murder, then fathered children. He created life. If that didn't make us God's equals, it did at least make our family junior partners."

Drowsy from the single sip of wine, Ashleigh wondered, "What does this have to do with Aza?"

"I'm glad you asked. We had the same abilities as God: create, destroy, affect the land on which we lived, sustain ourselves without anyone's help, and suddenly, here come the Watcher angels. Sure, they're not bad to look at, but while angels can destroy, they are forbidden to procreate amongst themselves. That makes them inferior creatures. These 'Grigori' taught us cooking and how to make up our faces. After they passed on their 'wisdom,' they filled the bellies of my sisters with monsters that killed them. My sisters were not the only victims. I can't tell you how many women died delivering angelic bastards. Then the angels moved on, leaving the nephilim to roam the land."

"I never heard any of this," Ashleigh protested.

"It's in the Bible, child."

"Where?"

"In the story of the Flood. You remember that one?"

"God did that to get rid of all the wicked people."

Yasmina rolled her eyes. "The *only* good people in the whole wide world were on a first-name-basis with Noah?"

Ashleigh opened her mouth and closed it again.

Yasmina said, "You see my point."

"Wait a minute. How did you survive the Flood?"

"That's where my sister Anah and Asmodeus come in. Oh, yes, *and* Azaziel. In the months before the Flood, while the nephilim were performing atrocities, more angels showed up. Among them was Azaziel, who seduced my little sister Anah. She was just thirteen. But you know how men are, divine or otherwise, when it comes to pretty young things. That same golden tongue talked you into bed. After Azaziel persuaded my sister that there would be no repercussions for becoming his concubine, God decided the angels were too busy slaking their lust to sort things out on Earth. So He sent the Flood."

"That's when Aza took her away?"

"Exactly. I never saw my sister again. Azaziel left the rest of us behind to drown."

"But Asmodeus rescued you?"

"I summoned him. Of course, he was without form back then." Realizing that Lorelei was still listening, Yasmina added, "They all were. They didn't need them."

Go ahead, cover your tracks! Lorelei shouted defiantly. *I'm not forgetting a single detail of your blasphemy.*

Yasmina's brow knitted briefly.

Ashleigh said, "So you're mad at Aza because he saved your sister from drowning?"

"There's more to it than that. We met a few hundred years later in Judea, and believe me, Azaziel was shocked to find me grown so powerful. He said he couldn't kill me because of the love he bore my late sister." Yasmina's smile became unpleasantly ironic. "Because we know how God feels about killing *family*."

"Wait a minute," Ashleigh protested. "Humans can't become devils!"

"Of course they can. Only very special people, ones with the will and the purpose to do so. Back when I shed my first skin, Hell barely had a half-score of sinners to its name. They were more colonists than convicts, wondering why the afterlife was warmer than the land they'd left behind. The original tenants have all become members of the tribe, as it were."

Ashleigh fumbled with her champagne flute, looking for a place to set it down. "This can't be true," she murmured to Lorelei.

Yasmina refilled the glass from her own and pressed it back on the girl. "I'll let you in on the real lie, Ashleigh: humans can't become angels. There will never be any more of them than God made in the beginning."

She made a gesture and Lorelei found herself smothered. She struggled to fight her way out, railing at Ashleigh to be cautious.

Yasmina scooted closer to Ashleigh and nudged the girl's champagne flute toward her lips. "Contrary to what the other side will tell you, most of us joined Hell because it was the best alternative. I'm here to make you an offer."

Ashleigh echoed, "Offer?"

From the void of isolation within her own flesh, Lorelei railed, *Don't bargain with her!*

Ashleigh sensed a momentary stir within her chest, like a single irregular heartbeat. She heard nothing.

"It occurs to me that, other than oblivion, nobody has offered you any way out of this ordeal. Prince Asmodeus is galled that Azaziel cost him a valued representative. It's only fair that Hell be recompensed."

"She didn't mean to be—"

A single opaled nail drawn across her lips silenced Ashleigh. "Hssshhh. Yasmina is speaking."

"I just wanna go home to bed," Ashleigh said uncertainly.

"Hear me out. Then decide if you want to go back to Floria." Yasmina smiled. "It's a shame Lorelei got you off to a rough start with her. Floria's not a bad kid, but she holds a grudge a long time."

"Anyway...?" Ashleigh prompted.

"My point is you've never gotten a fair shake, have you? Family and boy so-called friend, then that lech Azaziel. He still wants you. You want him, yes? This can be worked out."

"How?"

All the champagne Ashleigh had drunk hit Lorelei. Under the wave of inebriation lay a needle of pure panic. She was fucked. She was well and truly fucked.

"Smart girl. It's time for you to be a player instead of a pawn." Yasmina patted Ashleigh's hand.

Ashleigh's vision transformed. She saw everything in gradations of color she could not name. Her body became hyper-attuned, caressed by the Armani jacket floating across her breasts. She curled her toes into the limo's thick carpet. Under her bare bottom, the leather upholstery was luxuriantly soft. In her loins a sweet fire ignited, a hunger that inspired her to smile.

"Become one of us," Yasmina purred. She leaned across Ashleigh to open the limo door. The car hadn't moved. It remained parked on the grass outside the public restroom. Tendrils of cool air summoned Ashleigh into the night.

As Ashleigh climbed out of the car, she saw that her skin had taken on the hell-red color of Lorelei's devil form. She turned back toward the limo. In the window, the reflection had Ashleigh's face, but much, much better. More than selling fireworks, Ashleigh felt like she could start fires with her smile.

Part of me should be panicking, Ashleigh thought.

Part of you is panicking, Lorelei moaned.

Ashleigh felt a tug at the base of her spine. Yasmina's be-ringed hand grasped her tail. Ashleigh flexed muscles she'd never had before and snapped her tail sideways, out of reach. That reminded her. She lifted her new wings experimentally, testing the breeze.

"That's my one condition," Yasmina said. "You don't fly until we strike a deal."

The temptress followed her out of the limo. Ashleigh learned something else about the unflinching clarity of her new eyes. She saw Yasmina as she truly was. Beneath coils of obsidian hair, slitted pupils bisected Yasmina's almond eyes. Below the waist, her bronze skin blended into scales the same copper-and-blood pattern as her dress.

"What deal?" Ashleigh asked.

Yasmina inclined her head toward the restroom. "I have a present for you, dear."

Ashleigh's nostrils twitched. She smelled a whole range of things, some not as unpleasant as might be expected. Amongst them she noticed scents that seemed out of place: gasoline, rubber, steel.

Damia and Keisha dropped from the air. They wore their true forms, more birds than women, ragged feathers black as vultures'. Their faces remained familiar above their bare breasts. Damia still had her piercings. The chaotic swirls of Keisha's tattoos reminded Ashleigh of the Satanic alphabet she'd seen earlier.

Damia flung open the restroom door. One-handed, she hauled out a crumpled Ninja motorcycle.

Keisha opened the other door and yanked out a boy in torn riding leathers. She pulled off his helmet, clacking his teeth together as the chinstrap broke. Bloody and dazed, Deion gaped at Ashleigh. She tasted his terror in the air.

She stared at the boy she'd fallen in love with, the one who'd given her that first line of speed. His warm brown skin had a chalky undertone now, as if he was on the verge of being terribly sick. He gaped at her new curves as if seeing her for the first time.

"He doesn't recognize me?" Ashleigh asked.

"Not in this form," Yasmina mocked.

Ashleigh stalked down the sidewalk. When Keisha let go, Deion collapsed to his knees. Ashleigh bent over him, locking her gaze on his. "See what happened after you put me out, Deion?" Ashleigh taunted. "I died and went to Hell. And it's *all* your fault."

He whimpered her name. Some part of him thought he should tell her that he was sorry, but she could see that he wasn't, not really. Ashleigh thrashed her tail, enjoying the novelty of the sensation.

He wanted her. She could sense it. The hunger she'd felt inside the limo was tremendous, a craving for sex like she'd never felt before. She licked her lips. She couldn't remember any of her old affection for her ex-boyfriend. Now he was just meat.

"What?" Ashleigh wondered aloud. "You wanna watch me fuck him?"

"If you like." Yasmina slithered up. "Rotten as it is, his soul is yours for the taking."

"*This* is our deal?" Ashleigh's tone sounded like her old voice, like a scared little girl. Keisha sniggered.

"Send him to Hell," Yasmina suggested. "You know how much he deserves it. Revenge is yours now."

Ashleigh's hand trembled as she reached out. She touched Deion's cheek with the back of her fingers so she wouldn't cut him with her talons. "I forgave him. Before Aza took my soul."

"There's a way around damning him," Yasmina answered smoothly. "Just put your lips over his, suck out his soul, and devour it."

Damia sneered, "You've had worse things in your mouth."

"You save him from Hell," Keisha pointed out, "you join the team, and we eat. It's a win-win-win situation."

"How do I start?"

"You might want to fuck him and loosen things up," Damia recommended. "Once they're drained, they don't thrash around so much."

Like you'd know, bitch-ass wannabe, Lorelei taunted.

Ashleigh ran her talons up Deion from knee to throat. His riding leathers parted like cheap latex. She flung her leg over his hips and slid down onto him, swallowing his groan with a kiss. Though it was tempting to finish him quickly, it felt too good. She slowed her rhythm, working her hips against his, marveling at every nuance of sensation. Her first orgasm caught her by surprise. More surprising, she didn't want to stop. Too frightened to enjoy any part of it, Deion clung to her.

His crying rekindled the connection between them. Ashleigh remembered the screaming nightmares he used to have, the ones that woke them both. She knew he'd had just as fucked-up a childhood as her own. While that didn't excuse the sort of person he let himself become, she couldn't deny him his demons—which, she supposed, now included her. She had to get this over with quickly, for his sake.

She forced them both into a climax that was more sensation than pleasure. Dragging him up into her arms, she covered his lips with hers. She could at least spare him an eternity of Hell. The better part of nineteen years had been enough.

She inhaled, but nothing happened. She remembered how Aza had taken her soul away from its pain, how gratefully she'd flowed out of her dying body into the angel. She tilted her head, slipped her tongue between Deion's lips, and tried again. Still, nothing. She clambered off of him, confused.

"Oh, I forgot," Yasmina said. "You've already got one extra soul inside you. Hm." She tapped one nail against a curved incisor. Her gaze dropped to Ashleigh's chest. "I believe we'll have to get rid of Lorelei first."

Yasmina affected a helpless 'there's no other way' shrug. The harpies mimicked her perfectly.

Ashleigh felt queasy. Despite all that had happened, it seemed she was back in the club crowd, low dog in the pack, her only real choice 'go along to get along.' What had Lorelei implied about the Mob being Hell's invention? Fuck that, they'd probably come up with cliques first.

Yasmina swayed above her. "You don't owe her anything," the temptress soothed. "Let me help. All I need is your consent, then you can be one of us."

Yasmina's kiss melted the girl's insides.

Lorelei knew, surer that she'd ever known anything, that she was doomed. There was no reason why Ashleigh should refuse Yasmina's offer. To be eternally young, ever on the prowl for sex and souls, luring people to their damnation: there was no finer life in creation than that.

Yet Ashleigh drew back.

Yasmina caught Ashleigh's hair and pulled her into another kiss.

Lorelei had seen enough humans, at the ends of their miserable lives, making promises and offerings, begging for another chance. Nothing ever withheld fate. Despite that, Lorelei couldn't surrender. She fought the force of Yasmina's will, seeking hidey-holes against the whirlwind. She wondered if all the souls she had ever taken had known similar terror. Oh, God, she thought, her despair complete, she did not want to die yet. Not without seeing Aza one final time.

Ashleigh struggled. She felt Yasmina's mouth open against hers, too wide to be natural. When she shrank away, something sharp pierced her cheeks. Molten pain jolted her. Ashleigh wrenched her head back and felt her flesh tear on Yasmina's fangs.

Was that was venom in her mouth? It tasted like ozone and steel. Ashleigh spat blood onto the sidewalk.

"It's not my soul to give up," she protested. "Talk to Lorelei."

Deion shrieked, shrill as a child tortured in a dream. The scream choked off in an abrupt wet noise. Ashleigh flung herself around to see a pale gray-green mist rise from the red slick of his entrails. Damia and Keisha wrestled over the soul, tearing it apart and inhaling the shreds. The glow disappeared down their throats. Gore smeared Keisha's grin.

Ashleigh gathered her wings and leapt toward the sky.

Yasmina caught her ankle with a loop of tail and flung her back into the limo.

CHAPTER 10: THE DOTTED LINE

When she landed against the leather upholstery, Lorelei was back in command of her mortal form.

Yasmina resumed her place on the seat opposite, once more the very picture of Beverly Hills rich bitch, all Palm Springs suntan and Paloma Picasso jewelry.

Yasmina sighed as the limo started up. "That could have gone better."

When Lorelei reached for the door this time, the locks clunked into place.

"Wherever you're going," the succubus said, "I don't need to come along. Just let me out and nothing needs to be said to anyone."

"Be reasonable, Lorelei. Do you think Asmodeus would care?"

"Reasonable?" she spat. "You tried to devour me! You not only tempted a mortal with the offer to elevate her to an undeserved infernal state, but your lackeys killed another mortal before his time and devoured a soul meant for damnation. Since when are you entitled to murder them?"

Yasmina rolled her eyes as if the subject were already stale. "Now that you've been cast out of Hell until this predicament is behind you, have you given any thought to how you're going to survive alone in the big, bad world?"

"I have Floria," Lorelei said confidently.

"Of course you do," Yasmina agreed in amusement, "and good thing, too. A girl in your position needs a patroness. Since you're too proud to accept me, who better than the soon-to-be temptress who's replaced you in the plans of our prince?"

"Knock it off, Yasmina. My drama quotient is maxed. Straight up, no bullshit: what do you want?"

Yasmina purred smoothly, "If you'd picked another angel, we wouldn't be in this position."

"He's mine," Lorelei vowed.

"You'll be sorry," Yasmina assured.

And the lights went out.

Lorelei opened her eyes to a dirty concrete floor. She sprawled across a rough wooden table, chin overhanging its edge. Her breasts felt squashed beneath her. The cold air on her backside confirmed that she was naked. She wondered if she should remember who had had his way with her.

"What'd I miss while I was out?"

Ashleigh didn't answer.

Lorelei's wrists and ankles burned as if she'd been tied down. She rubbed one smarting arm. Touching it magnified the pain. Instead of the anticipated rope burn, she saw it was ringed by a tattoo. The broken handcuff was gone.

Both her wrists and ankles had been inked with cuffs sketched in feathers. The tattoos were a mix of blue and dove gray. Her neck stung too. That scared her the most.

She sat up to take in her surroundings. It appeared to be another of Aza's warehouses. Cobwebs festooned the rafters.

Aza strode in, trench coat over his arm. "Finally." He seemed amused, and not in a good way.

Lorelei demanded, "Have I been out long?"

"Long enough for the purpose at hand."

Was he talking about the exorcism? Lorelei frowned. "Where's Ashleigh now?"

"Gone." That sounded very final.

"And the story behind these?" She held up one tattooed wrist.

"A precaution. Regrettable, I'll grant you, but necessary."

Lorelei chewed her lip, trying to guess what the tattoos were a precaution against. "Is this your latest attempt to bind me, Aza?" Hosting a soul had merely vexed her. Magical restraints had their limits as well. "Let's test them, shall we?"

Aza shifted uncomfortably. He didn't seem to think that was a good idea, but why? Lorelei couldn't wait to manifest her true form.

As she squatted on the tabletop, she reveled in the unfolding of her tail. A single beat of her wings should propel her with lethal force at this distance. A screech of joyous fury rolled from the bottom of her chest as she leapt.

The angel made no effort to sidestep her. Her rage wavered as she realized she still saw him with mortal eyes. Her voice was a pale echo of her hunting cry.

Still, her impact against his chest sent him reeling. When she reached up to rip out his throat, she saw that her hands, beyond the tattoo line, were all too human.

Stealing a glance to the side, Lorelei saw the leathery tip of her wing dip past.

Aza twisted her hand. The pain flared enough that she lost her grip. He tossed her backward.

Landing in a crouch, Lorelei sprang toward the rafters. Although she could still fly, gaining a purchase on the beam was difficult without the articulations of her natural feet. A panicked grab at a crossbeam prevented her from falling.

This was as bad as being spiritually divided. Closing her eyes, Lorelei attempted to smash the binding by force of will. She was rewarded by an exquisite sense of strength in her fingers and toes. When she opened her eyes, it was like being delivered from the brink of blindness.

Everything was reversed. She might as well have been wearing taloned gloves and socks: the line of demarcation was that clear. A fifth tattoo must encircle her throat. She could have been some human bitch made up as a devil. Lorelei gnashed her fangs in frustration.

The hard vibration of a bared weapon thrummed through the sluggish air. Sword drawn, Aza held his free hand up to her.

"You're joking," Lorelei growled.

With a sigh, Aza leaped upward. Unfurling wings a darker gray than she remembered, he joined her in the rafters. "You think that hosting a mortal soul was anguish? This half-existence will be hell." He chuckled. "A temptress who can't fully conceal her nature, a devil with soft human flesh: vulnerable doesn't begin to describe you now."

Holding onto a support beam, he swung toward her in a lazy arc, more predatory than she could've imagined. His sword clove her beam neatly. She clawed for another refuge, but he slammed into her in midair. Swooping into a tight turn, he flung Lorelei down across the table.

"You wanted me fallen. You required my lust." His hands fastened hard on her shoulders. "Come on, my love. Bring back that hellwhore body for me. In return, I'll grant what you bargained so hard for."

Lorelei shook her head fearfully.

With a raffish grin, the angel bent over her. He enclosed her lips with his own, summoning her long fierce tongue into his mouth.

Defiantly, she reached down to tear at his trousers. As he entered her, the transition happened instinctively. Her breasts swelled beneath his hands as the delicate arches of her human feet molded to the backs of his thighs.

"What finally made you come over?" she panted.

He stopped thrusting to stare at her. "Asmodeus gave you to me, on the condition that I surrender Ashleigh's soul."

She grimaced, trying to remember her part in that.

"I fell because of you, Lorelei. I fell *for* you." Aza laughed as he grabbed her hair and yanked her head back to lick the raw tattoo across her throat. "By the deal I struck, that makes you mine seven times seven, times seven, times seven, times seven."

She tried to concentrate, to add it up, but kept losing track of the sum as he pounded into her. "That's...?"

"Sixteen millennia, give or take." He flipped her over, pulling hard on her wings. "Lose these," he hissed.

Lorelei transformed into her human body. Aza grabbed her horns, using the hold to take her savagely from behind. She longed for the compassion she'd felt from him when he fucked her before, the sense that he treasured her responses, that they fed his own.

"Aza, please..."

He slapped her head down against the table. "New rule: never use my name again, slut, because I'm forgetting yours."

Any reply stuck in her throat.

"You couldn't abide love. Now you can endure being nothing more than property."

The force of his fury scalded her infernal senses. Intuition told her it would only get worse. He hated her now that he'd lost Heaven. She might have delivered an angel to her prince, but Asmodeus sold her out as a slave. She didn't have her life back. She didn't have love. The only thing she could count on was being fucked slowly to death over sixteen thousand years. Give or take.

The realization tore her from the fugue and sent her reeling back into Yasmina's arms. Lorelei struggled, dimly aware of Ashleigh's whimpers. What Asmodeus had started, the arch-temptress seemed intent on finishing.

"If Azaziel falls through your agency," Yasmina whispered against Lorelei's sweat-wreathed brow, "it will happen exactly as you've seen. Your only hope is to land him at my feet. If I get the credit, I will protect you."

Lorelei tried to reply, only to have the words pressed back by Yasmina's be-ringed fingers.

"Don't argue. Don't promise. Don't fail."

The limo glided to a halt. The locked door thumped behind Lorelei's back. She spun around to claw at the door handle. When she scuttled out of the car, she discovered it was double-parked outside Tuan's.

"Pleasant dreams, Lorelei."

The door closed smoothly as the limo slid away.

That was fucked, Ashleigh whispered.

"Yep," Lorelei agreed. "If they have their way, you get 'et'. I get enslaved. We've got to find us another way to get that angel in our corner, 'cause I'm sure as shit not letting that bitch lay a finger on him."

Stripping off an oversized earring with her free hand, Yasmina reached forward to answer the limo's phone. "Yes?"

"Success?" Jequon asked.

Yasmina sighed. "Hard to say. She's stubborn."

"That's why Lorelei has been good at what she does."

"I suppose." The temptress lit a clove cigarette and leaned back against the leather upholstery, blowing out a long plume of smoke. "I just hate using tools that could turn in my hand and bite me."

"No biting her first," Jequon cautioned. "You know how our prince feels about having his toys marked up."

"You should see what he's already done to her." Yasmina chuckled. "Her days as one of his favorites are clearly numbered." Yasmina took another drag and changed the subject. "The girl protected Lorelei."

"Really?"

"And Lorelei's first thought was not her own discomfort, but the girl's."

Jequon hissed.

"I'm not sure what stunt Azaziel planned to pull, but it's a safe bet he's succeeded in ruining Lorelei. Our prince should be scraping her off his shoe in no time."

"Then you'll be able to use her freely."

"I love it when angels create the implements of their own destruction," Yasmina purred.

There was a pause on the phone, long enough for a chill to spread. Then Jequon remarked, "I'd be careful whom you said that to."

Yasmina pulled her legs up onto the seat beside her and made her voice warm. "Present company excepted, of course."

"Of course." The fallen angel added, "I was thinking about tools that bite."

She gave him a sultry laugh. "You know I'd never use my teeth on you."

"I'll hold you to that. Are you coming over?"

"I'm on my way now."

"Why don't you stop on the way and get us someone to eat? I'm feeling peckish."

"As you like." Yasmina pressed the intercom button to give her driver new directions.

The sky had paled toward dawn. Lorelei's pierced back ached. The least Yasmina could have done was let Ashleigh's transformation work its infernal magic and heal Lorelei's abused flesh, but of course the kindness was beneath that arrogant bitch. Lorelei was too numb to do anything but drag herself toward the security box. If, out of spite, Floria had changed the code...

Lorelei didn't dare finish the thought. She punched the numbers into the box.

The gate buzzed. She yanked it open, shouldered through the door into the building, and staggered through the lobby toward the elevator. She wondered if anyone would be coming down for an early morning jog. She didn't have enough strength to be glad when the elevator doors opened on an empty car.

Ashleigh kept silent the whole ride up.

Standing in front of the penthouse door, Lorelei realized her key was in her purse, back at the angel's lair. If she'd been herself, the locked door would have presented no problem. Now, it was insurmountable. She slumped down in front of it, too worn out to cry. She let her head fall forward against the door.

After a moment, the deadbolt snapped back. The door swung inward to the extent of its chain. Lorelei expected to hear Floria's laugh. Instead, the door slammed shut, the chain rattled, and Tuan stood over her, naked but for a blue silk dressing gown and the gun in his hand.

Lorelei held her hands up to him. He tucked the Ruger into the sash of his dressing gown and pulled her to her feet. She leaned against him, inhaling his scent of Marlboros and CK and sweet young man. "Can you help me get into the shower?" she asked. "Floria will kill me if I track up your house."

He knew she'd been called to report to her boss. He could see it hadn't gone well. She felt fear pounding in his chest as he carried her into the bathroom.

He propped her against the sink and filled the bath. Apparently, he'd decided she was too weak to take care of herself. Lorelei wondered if she'd have the strength to get out of the water. Maybe she'd just sleep in the tub.

She tried to slip out of the ruined Armani jacket, but the wounds in her back had opened during the long walk home. Blood had scabbed into the fabric.

"I need your help with this, too," she said weakly.

Tuan tore the jacket away from her back with a hiss. Lorelei felt the blood flow again. She twisted to survey the damage in the mirror. Claw marks scored her white skin, leaking bright crimson blood.

Jesus, Ashleigh thought.

"Hush that," Lorelei murmured. She asked Tuan, "Where's Floria?"

"She went out after we got back from the hospital."

"You waiting up?"

"Too wired to sleep," he corrected. "I was screwin' around with the PlayStation."

He supported her as she eased down into the water. Goosebumps shivered up over her skin, but it wasn't too cold. She thought he'd go back to his videogame, but instead he sat on the toilet lid. She was grateful for the company. She wondered what to say to him.

What'd the doctor say? Ashleigh prompted. Lorelei echoed her.

"Seventeen stitches. But that wasn't as bad as all the antiseptic they poured over it. And the shots they gave me, and the pills I have to take. You messed me up good."

Lorelei struggled with the sodden fabric knotted around her foot. When she finally wrestled the makeshift bandage off, the skin beneath was smooth and unmarked. Yasmina must have healed it. Was that bribe meant to buy her silence?

"Why?" Tuan asked.

She wasn't sure what he meant. *Biting him*, Ashleigh reminded.

Oh, yeah. "Because I needed to taste blood," Lorelei guessed. It had seemed important at the time. She'd been a completely different creature then.

"You might've just asked," Tuan said.

"I'm sorry, Tuan. I really, really am."

It was stupid and cruel, Ashleigh added. Lorelei repeated that as well.

He laughed. "Never thought I'd hear that from any of you."

Lorelei leaned her head back against the rim of the tub and let her heavy eyelids drop. "Bet you never expected to see any of us like this either."

After a long pause while he fought his curiosity, he asked, "Can I make you some pho?"

"Could you just help me wash? I'm too exhausted to do it."

He rolled back the sleeves of his robe and knelt beside the tub. Lorelei pushed herself to sit up again. It was a challenge. What she really wanted to do was to let her head slip beneath the surface and never come up.

Pink tinged the bath water. Would she be scarred for life now, like the ones cast out after the War with Heaven? She thought of Asmodeus's limp, the half-feathered wings, the faces and bodies marred forever by angelic weapons. At least those wounds were badges of honor, gained in combat with the Enemy. She'd been disfigured by her own kind.

Tuan soaped his hands and caressed the bubbles over her back. It felt good to be touched so gently. Lorelei remembered Aza washing her feet. Would she take pleasure from those hands ever again?

Tuan washed her arms and legs, before gathering the courage to wash her breasts. Lorelei lay back and closed her eyes again.

He took no liberties. Lorelei wasn't sure if she felt insulted. Then his fingers traced the bruise on her chest. "Did I do that?"

"Paybacks are Hell, aren't they, Lover?" she answered.

He changed the subject. "Stand up and I'll dry you off."

She yawned. "I thought I might just sleep right here."

"Those...cuts...on your back won't heal if you soak too long." He pulled a towel from the rack. "Come on, Lorelei. You need to go to bed."

Hauling herself to her feet was an arduous process. Tuan patted her with the towel, then sat her on the toilet lid. "I'm gonna put some Neosporin on those..."

"Claw marks," Lorelei supplied.

"Did they do that to you because you got kidnapped?"

She shook her head. "Because I fucked up so bad with the guy that kidnapped me."

He smeared some goo into her wounds. Lorelei endured it. Eventually, she voiced what she'd been thinking. "I don't deserve it, I know, but...could I sleep with you?"

"You'll get blood on Floria's sheets," he hedged.

"It won't be the first," Lorelei teased, "but say no, if that's what you mean." She held up her left hand. "I swear I won't bite you again."

"You just want to sleep?"

Lorelei grinned over her shoulder at him. "I'll give you the best hand-job of your life first," she promised.

Whenever she had a break in her duties, Muriel liked to tag along with Samael. Although his work never ended, he did it gladly, always ready to terminate lives at the behest of the Lord.

Perhaps if she'd been created a seraph rather than a member of the choir, Muriel might hope to be promoted to a position like Samael's. Instead, she knew she would never be anything more than what she was. It was a hard lesson to take, when creatures like Azaziel still walked the earth. Sometimes Muriel dreamed about what it would be like, being commanded to use her sword to cut the cords of life every day, rather than the occasional mortal she was allowed to take.

Samael didn't comment on her train of thought as he glided down, his pinions black as space against the blue morning sky. Muriel followed uncertainly. She didn't sense a living soul on the hillside.

The angel of death strode down the slope in steps so large that Muriel had to use her wings for balance as she hurried after him. They angled toward a large tan boulder amidst the dry grass. Draped around the stone was a broken motorcycle.

As if he'd been thrown clear in the collision, the rider's corpse lay some distance downhill. Samael used the butt of his javelin to roll the body onto its back.

The boy's riding leathers had been torn open from collar to crotch. He'd been molested before his death. Muriel wrinkled her nose at the smell. "Lorelei."

Samael's voice was a low rumble. "Azaziel's harlot?"

"The same." Muriel stared into the boy's entrails, blackening in the warm morning. Only belatedly did she think to look up to his face. The skull peered through shreds of flesh. "Who is this?"

"His name was Deion Gutierrez. This is wrong," Samael said abruptly. "It wasn't his time yet."

"Did she kill him?"

Samael gestured toward his cheek, where talons had torn the skin. "Harpies."

"We'd better report it," Muriel said. "I'll tell Rafael."

Aza knew that walking the streets wouldn't solve anything. Lorelei was bound to be hiding amongst her own kind. He prayed that Ashleigh was still safely hidden inside the succubus. All he wanted to do was release the girl, but he couldn't bring himself to disobey and search them out. However, if they crossed his path…

The ache that burned along his back was nothing compared to the pain within his heart. Love or hate, loyalty or betrayal, God-given joy, even desolate sorrow: he could tolerate those with ease. But not loss, the physical displacement of something so valued it could not be replaced. He needed Lorelei, needed to know she was okay. His arms ached to encircle her.

Taking shelter from the sun beneath an overpass, Aza placed his palms against the concrete wall and pushed his head against the hard surface.

The realization was like a blow: he loved for himself again.

He thought of the other girl, so long ago. It no longer helped to think of her as his wife. That had been another world, a reality as fragile as any dream, one that lived in him alone now.

He remembered her sun-browned skin, the curve of her lips, her gleaming teak eyes when she stole her first glance at him. That moment connected something between them. Azaziel, sent to teach Man, discovered a knowledge he had not been prepared for: that it was possible to love one above all others. Anah was that one.

A blast of wind hit him like a slap: part rebuke, part reminder. The Almighty barely appreciated it then and probably less now, since Aza dared to repeat the transgression with one born of Perdition. Yet he knew that he had bent rather than breaking the rules. Loving a devil was something for which no rules had been stated.

Still, to circumvent The Word twice in one existence was not prudent for one who remained an angel purely on sufferance. Being lamed was surely just the beginning. Even a grain of sand could be crushed to a finer powder...and he was no grain. He was of the created, anointed hosts. Divine punishment, when it came, would likely be very pointed, with a sharp-edged justification he would be powerless to refute. Any delay in his fate indicated his growing insignificance in the scheme of time.

"You created us to love!" he protested.

"I smell romantic self-pity," a friendly voice drawled at his back. "Must be Azazi-El."

A hand clapped his shoulder hard enough to make him wince. The hand belonged to a large man with piercing pale green eyes and red hair that seemed to bristle with static electricity. A ruby wreathed with black thorns crested his lapel.

Aza didn't recognize the face. He thought he should have some memory of the entity who spoke so familiarly to him, especially one who referred to him in the old way.

Taking the angel's hand, the stranger pumped it with a politician's ease. The friction of his touch revealed him to be quite infernal. "Name's Mastema. We've never actually met, but I expect we'll be working together very soon."

Aza ground his teeth against nausea. He'd been thinking about judgment and who should appear but the very demon responsible for administrating the fallen host on earth? Angels never met Mastema until it was too late. Was this proof that his thoughts were now open to Lucifer?

Mastema steered Aza down the sidewalk, his arm pressed forcefully against the angel's wounds. "Does this hurt, Azazi-El?"

Aza nodded. The demon only pressed harder.

"Good. We're going to have to find your pain before we can bring you into the fold. Some sort of mutilation is usually in order... A protocol, if you will." Glancing about confidentially, he whispered in the angel's ear, "Between you and I, Nebiros wants your face cut off. I get to make the final recommendation."

Aza's thoughts swept back to the calamity of the Fall. When protesting rebels crowded Heaven's precipice, Nebiros held his ground. His cohorts tumbled past him on either side. Proud and vain even as he faced banishment, Nebiros's eyes searched Aza's when they found themselves measured against one another.

Turning his beauty toward the watching light above, Nebiros pleaded, "Master, send me Micha-El, send Zadki-El, anyone but my friend..."

In a heartbeat, all the thunder of Judgment condensed within Aza's fists. They surged forward in blows that shattered Nebiros's beautiful features and sent him hurtling down.

Even now, Aza's hands throbbed, remembering the power with which they had been invested. That brought tears of pain with no connection to his wounds.

Mastema abruptly released his hold on Aza.

The recollection and its pain evaporated with the broken contact. Had the memory been the demon's conjuring?

"So we are quite clear on this and you have nothing to deny?" Mastema fixed his gaze on Aza's tear-dimmed eyes. "You smacked up your brother and liked it. Even with all the Almighty's power behind you, it was your choice to strike."

Aza hadn't thought about Nebiros since that time. He had been friends with so many of the fallen host, all of whom were lost to him. He wondered if he loved mortals to justify turning against his brothers.

"All this talk of falling and mutilation can be put aside for now." Mastema rubbed his hands together vigorously. "Time to give you a few good reasons for the deal."

"There's no deal. I refuse to accept this fate." Aza stepped away from his Fallen comrade, off the curb into the path of an approaching bus. The metal bumper scraped painfully by his knee.

Mastema applauded from the curbside. "Steel-belted heavy-traction treads: that would be some creative mutilation."

The bus's doors gasped as Aza pulled them open. Grimacing at his tormentor, Aza clambered into the bus, emptying his pocket of silver as he passed the fare box. Rushing to the rear seat as the bus leapt away down the street, he watched the dwindling figure of Mastema wave from the bus stop.

The Almighty often did work in mysterious ways; an angel's fall, once precipitated, could be as arcing and indirect as the path of a feather. *Was he right?* Aza wondered. *Am I about to fall?*

Barbelo pulled him down to the seat beside her. "You tell me, Aza. Did what he said make any sense?"

"No."

Mastema had said that following the directions of The Word was a choice. He implied that falling in love had been a choice. Aza had never felt a choice, only a growing realization that he did as he must. If to choose were to fall, then he could only wait, praying for guidance.

"That was a little frightening," he confided in his sister. "I wish you'd come sooner."

Barbelo gave his hand a friendly squeeze. "You can only do so much with the buses in this town."

CHAPTER 11: PAYMENT PLANS

When Lorelei woke up, Floria stood bare-chested above her. The semi-transparent wrap skirt slung at Floria's hips gave the impression of something casually thrown on that could be just as easily thrown off. "Get out of that bed," Floria ordered. "Work's been piling up while you've been lying there."

Lorelei rubbed her eyes and heard the handcuff jingle.

Tuan jerked awake at Lorelei's side. He crept off of the bed and slunk wordlessly out of the room. Floria followed, fastening an expensive embroidered bustier as she went.

While the boy got his instructions and caught a shower, Lorelei poked around in the closet and found a black crocheted sundress she'd forgotten she'd loaned to her sister. She pulled it on, relieved to see that the wounds on her back had finally closed. If only the bruise on her chest would go away.

She nicked a black velvet thong out of Floria's underwear drawer and a matching pair of mules out of the closet. They'd do if she wasn't scheduled for any more cross-country hikes. Stretching out on the floor, she felt around under the bed until her hand landed on a red lacquer box. Inside hid a jumble of flashy jewelry. Lorelei stirred it around until she found a matched set of ruby earrings. Behind the stones flashed the glyph for her prince's name. The way things were going, it wouldn't be a bad idea to display her ownership again.

After slipping the earrings on, she dumped the rest of the jewelry back into the box and shoved it back under the bed. Okay. She was ready to face the outside world.

When she turned, her gaze caught on Floria's angora dress, lying in a heap on the floor as if thrown there by the fiends. Had they been in the room while she was sleeping? Lorelei shuddered.

As Lorelei reached for the doorknob, Ashleigh finally spoke up. *Who was that bitch last night?*

"One of Asmodeus's favorites." Lorelei moved back to sit on the empty bed. "I knew they went way back, but I didn't realize she was antediluvian."

What's that mean?

"Before the Flood. That's when a lot of things changed for Hell." Lorelei didn't remember as much of her history lessons as she supposed she ought to, but it had never mattered before.

Why should we care about Aza's first wife?

"I think her point was that I'm over my head this time. Between you and me, hadn't we already figured that out? Yasmina's got some kind of Queen Bitch jones on for our angel. I don't know about you, but the whole ordeal was enough to make me swear that I'll do everything in my power to keep him out of her hands."

Good, Ashleigh said. *What can I do to help?*

"Let's start by reporting our adventure to the boss. It might not protect us, but it could help us out down the road. I'd like nothing better than to see that bitch get what's been so long in coming to her."

Ashleigh wondered what else the snake woman had done to piss Lorelei off, but didn't ask. If it was as bad as last night, she didn't really want to know.

When Lorelei left the bedroom, Floria was nowhere to be seen. Instead, a young Vietnamese man huddled on the living room floor in front of the TV, putting Lara Croft through her paces. Lorelei never understood the fun in video games. At the moment, she empathized too closely with the game's heroine.

"You remember Hai?" Floria asked from somewhere in the apartment.

Hai's whole body swayed as he ducked an imaginary blow. Lara's attacker sent her over a cliff. "Fuck!" He tossed the game controller down on the rug and turned toward Lorelei.

"Hi, Tiger." Lorelei smiled at the boy. His body twitched in response. Studiously cool in black leather jeans, cowboy boots, and faded hair, Hai was all of eighteen. He was Tuan's second-in-command. She'd done him a couple of times, as a favor, when Floria first consolidated the gang. Guessing that he wouldn't live long without constant supervision, Lorelei hadn't bothered to offer him a contract. Why buy souls when you could get them for free? He'd gotten a little taller since she'd screwed him last, but Lorelei didn't mention it.

"Haven't seen you in a long time," Hai drawled.

"Too long," Lorelei teased. "Where you boys off to today?"

"We need to run over to the lab in Downey. We'll prolly be out all day."

"Pity."

The shower shut off in the other room. Hai switched off the TV and shoved the PlayStation into the black-lacquered entertainment center. Floria grinned, satisfied to see such order in her house. She picked up the phone and retreated into the bedroom with it.

After the boys were gone, Lorelei tore a blank page out of the back of Floria's Day-Runner and settled down to compose a note.

She hadn't reached the end of the block when a Mercedes sedan pulled over in front of her. Its passenger door swung open to obstruct her path. *Run!* Ashleigh encouraged.

"Are you kidding?" Lorelei sauntered up alongside the car, tracing her fingertips along the gold-fleck paint job. "This is our ride." Hands on her thighs to give the clearest view down her dress, Lorelei leaned down to talk.

"Where do you think you're going?" the fiend inside growled. The boss's sigil flashed on his tie tack.

"To get somethin' to eat. Wanna come?"

"Get in."

Are you sure? Ashleigh wondered. Lorelei ignored her, sliding into the front seat. Compliance wasn't optional.

"I haven't been to a decent restaurant in *days*," Lorelei said, putting some flirt into her voice. "Know anyplace good?"

The fiend grunted noncommittally.

"Why don't we go wherever you took the boss last?" she suggested.

"You got money?"

She laughed, playing the sound for maximum flattery. "Let's expense it."

"Think the boss will clear that?"

That was blunter speech than she expected from a fiend. In answer, she laid the letter on his thigh. He could see Asmodeus's sigil. The fiend glanced sidelong at her and tucked the letter into his suit coat.

"Collecting in advance," she said.

They rode in silence until the fiend's phone rang. He picked it up off the dashboard. "Yeah, she's here. Yeah." He chuckled like bone ground against stone. "She's got a letter for the boss. Didn't say."

He listened for a moment. Lorelei strained her ears, but heard only silence on the other end.

The fiend returned the phone to the dashboard, offering no comment on the conversation.

Smug *and* silent. Of all Hell's minions, fiends irritated her the most. They were too stupid to recognize a bargain when offered one. While she'd been bred for sex, fiends were created for obedience, to get things done. If most weren't smart enough to protect themselves when their masters ordered them into danger, there were plenty more where they came from.

This one stopped at the next traffic light and fished her letter out of his jacket. After a glance in the rearview mirror, he slid his window down and held the envelope out. Lorelei opened her mouth to protest. Then a bike messenger snatched the letter, pedaling furiously past.

The light changed. Cars crept forward. Dodging and swooping on his bike, the imp zipped through traffic. His oversized duffel coat flapped around his narrow ass.

Lorelei hoped he was going straight to Asmodeus, not by way of Yasmina. Her flesh crawled at the thought.

"You like seafood?" the fiend rumbled.

"Any food," Lorelei answered.

He turned left across two lanes of traffic, deaf to the car horns blaring behind them.

The restaurant, two floors up, would be invisible from the street. The décor was all chrome and deep blue leather, which gave the place an underwater ambiance. The fiend ignored the pretty hostess and chose a table in the corner where the windows met, where he could watch both the room and the street below. Lorelei sat across from him with her back to the restaurant. She didn't like it.

A Japanese waiter arrived. Before the menus reached the tabletop, the fiend growled, "I was here for a private party Sunday night. Bring lunch from that menu."

"I'll see if that's available," the waiter sniffed.

The fiend favored him with a slow smile. The man gulped and bumped into an empty table as he scurried back to the kitchen.

The pause stretched out. Lorelei watched people on the street below: unaware ants. She realized, "I don't know your name."

"Thodos."

She radiated a smile. "Worked for the boss long, Thodos?"

"Decade or so."

"Really?" She looked him over: slicked-back hair, immaculate black Gucci suit, ruby cufflinks, the boss's sigil on his crimson silk tie. He was playing it carefully, hoping to be promoted to archfiend, and none too pleased about chaperoning a succubus who didn't keep away from angels.

A different waiter brought hot sake. Lorelei filled the tiny cups, raised hers, and said, "*Kampai.*" The fiend didn't drink. She tossed her sake back and set the cup carefully on the table. In Japanese etiquette, it would be rude for her to refill her glass until she filled his as well. Which was good. She didn't need to drink much of this stuff on an empty stomach. The single cupful left her flushed.

"What's the letter about?" he asked.

"Yasmina."

His eyes flickered red, before he caught it. Yet another person who didn't like the temptress. Lorelei grinned.

"Dancing shrimp," the waiter announced. He set down two bowls, each half-full of clear liquid. The waiter's assistant held a goldfish bowl full of large shrimp. The waiter caught one with his chopsticks and deposited it on its back in Lorelei's bowl.

Immediately the shrimp thrashed its little legs, struggling to right itself as it drowned in the sake.

What's it doing? Ashleigh wondered.

Without waiting until the shrimp was dead, Lorelei picked up her chopsticks and peeled off its shell.

The meat inside was succulent, delicately pickled by the alcohol. Thodos ate his shrimp whole, starting with its head and crunching down to its tail. Lifting the bowl in one hand, he drained the sake. After that, he picked up the cup Lorelei had poured for him and said, "*Kampai.*"

She refilled both cups, but didn't pick hers up again.

"Lobster sashimi." The waiter slid a platter onto the table. As Lorelei reached forward with her chopsticks, the lobster scurried away. Thodos caught its larger claw in his left fist. He pinned the tail with his chopsticks. From the slit in its carapace, Lorelei plucked out a morsel of meat and set it on Thodos's plate. She chose a bite for herself, which left a large hole inside the lobster's body. It continued to struggle.

"See its spinal cord?" Thodos asked.

A thick black thread ran through the lobster's flesh. She caught the nerve in her chopsticks and snapped it.

Thodos released the tail and retrieved his napkin from the floor to wipe his hand.

Is all the food here alive when you eat it? Ashleigh quavered. *That's just sick. How can this place exist?*

Lorelei ignored the voice in her head and popped the morsel of lobster into her mouth. It didn't have the flaky texture of boiled lobster, but resisted her teeth. She savored it, eyes closed.

Don't push me forward, Ashleigh warned. *I'm gonna puke.*

Lorelei enjoyed her second bite every bit as much as the first.

Had the fiend been directed to bring her here? Was this a test of Ashleigh's influence over her? A test to see if her new soul made her squeamish?

Lorelei matched the fiend bite for bite and drank her sake when he downed his. Under her hair, her ears burned. She hoped he couldn't see how drunk she was getting.

As a waiter cleared the lobster shell away, Lorelei said, "*Kocha o kudasai.*" He nodded sharply.

His assistant quickly brought out a pair of pottery cups and a cast-iron teapot, which he placed on a cork trivet.

The main course came next. Translucent slips of white flesh were arranged in a chrysanthemum pattern on a black pottery platter. "Fugu," the waiter announced.

"I haven't had this in a long time," Lorelei sighed. She had several bites of the fish before the tingling crept into her lips. After several more, her tongue felt swollen.

Stop eating, Ashleigh begged. *I think they're poisoning you!*

They were, of course. That was the point. Haitians used poison from a relative of fugu to turn healthy men into zombies. Only the Japanese raised preparation of the blowfish, with most of its poison removed by a master chef, to a delicacy.

Lorelei poured herself some tea and drained it between numb lips.

"What do you think?" Thodos asked.

"This is a real treat." Her voice sounded slurred. She hoped he'd think it was the sake. "Worth fasting for. Thank you."

He observed, "It's knocked some of the flirt out of your voice."

"Disappointed?"

"Surprised," he said. "I didn't think anything cooled you slits off."

Lorelei shrugged. "I miss home."

"You haven't been home in years," he corrected.

Caught him. He'd been briefed on her, so their meeting hadn't been accidental.

A smile split his face and Lorelei's stomach flip-flopped. "You don't have any clue what you've gotten yourself into, do you?"

"How is today different than any other day?" Lorelei countered.

"You know who your boyfriend's nemesis is?"

Lorelei shook her head. She hadn't thought beyond the situation at hand.

"Nebiros."

The General of Hell's Army. Lorelei looked for the last of the sake, but they'd already drunk it. How had Aza survived so long, with enemies like that? She hoped Nebiros would be kept busy in Palestine for a good while longer.

The wait staff cleared the dishes away. Lorelei noticed how deftly they avoided looking up from the tabletop.

The fiend slipped a billfold out of his jacket and laid the corporate card on the table without asking for the check.

Rather than send the valet after the car, Thodos retrieved his keys—with the aid of a bill whose denomination Lorelei couldn't read—and went into the garage after it. Lorelei followed nervously. Her heels rang in the concrete parking structure.

To get a conversation going, she asked, "How'd you get stuck babysitting me?"

His gaze met hers. "I volunteered when I lent you my jacket last night."

Ice raced up Lorelei's spine. "That was you?"

"We all look the same in the dark, don't we?"

Her mouth was a desert. Damn, she thought. Ashleigh had made an expensive mistake.

"You drop my jacket at the cleaner's?" he continued.

"It didn't make it home in one piece," Lorelei admitted. "Will you let me make it up to you?"

He swiveled toward her, huge and menacing in the empty garage. Lorelei was sick to death of cowering, of being off-guard and afraid. She stared up at him. At her show of defiance, a slow grin split his face. It *was* scary.

Goosebumps shivered up over her skin, but Lorelei stood her ground. His hand streaked out to snatch her elbow and yank her along. In the far corner of the garage, the Mercedes was parked behind a large square pillar, somewhat secluded from the rest of the cars.

Clueing in belatedly, Ashleigh remarked, *I don't like this.*

Lorelei had hoped to get him back to Tuan's or someplace else a human might walk in on them, so the fiend would have to restrain himself. She had hoped to have enough time to seduce him, or to buy him somehow if seduction failed, so that he would be careful with her. Here, she had no safeguards and little possibility of rescue.

Thodos shoved her toward the hood. Lorelei spun as quickly as she could, but caught her heel and lost her balance. Thodos snatched her back before she stumbled into the car.

"Don't scratch the paint," he advised, voice a low rumble.

Lorelei wrapped her fingers in the collar of his suit coat and pulled herself close against him. He smelled like the jacket she'd worn last night.

He disengaged one of her hands and thrust it toward his crotch. As scared as she was, Lorelei was also curious. Fiends were notoriously shortchanged when it came to anatomy. While still in the boss's harem, she'd worked some who had only nubs or nodules too small to insert. They took pleasure in other ways, inventive in their substitutions.

Thodos's sex was solid beneath her fingers, compact and hard, about the size and shape of her fist. Lorelei's heart sank. It was going to be tricky to satisfy him without the ability to shift her anatomy to accommodate his.

Thodos shoved her back against the car, rocking it as he engulfed her with his embrace. Desperate to keep her legs from being mashed by the fiend, Lorelei scrambled up to sit on the hood.

Thodos wrenched her head back by the hair. "Don't scratch the paint."

"I remember." Lorelei shrugged the strap off her shoulder, sliding the dress down to catch on the swell of her breast. Thodos bent to lick her bruise.

She worked the clasp on his trousers, opening things up enough that she could get her hands inside. Was it pressure that would work for him? Clawing him with her nails? Lorelei tried both.

He let her get away with more than she expected, before— trembling—he shoved her away. Lorelei hoped that meant they were finished, but the glint in his eye told her no.

"What's that spirit think about all of this?"

"I don't care." Lorelei reached for him.

"I never had a human girl before." He flashed her that razor grin.

No, Lorelei, please, really I'll do anything...

Lorelei shoved the girl forward. It was the only way she knew they could communicate without the fiend overhearing. *If you're gonna beg, beg him. He'll get off on it.*

"No!" Ashleigh protested. "Omigod, I —"

He clapped a meaty hand over her mouth before she could scream. The fiend licked his sharp teeth. "So you're the little ghost?"

Ashleigh nodded.

"Ever fuck a devil before?"

She shook her head as vigorously as he'd permit.

"You never forget your first." He smoothed her hair back with his free hand, studying her face for every minute change in expression.

Lorelei directed, *Go along with him. Do whatever he says. I promise I will protect you as much as I can.*

"Probably nothing like fucking an angel," Thodos continued. "How many times you do that?" He removed his hand so she could answer.

"Once."

"I heard it was twice."

"Just once," Ashleigh repeated. "Aza —"

"No names." The fiend laid his finger against her lips. "Lorelei ever fuck that angel alone?"

Ashleigh shook her head. "She's still pissed about it."

"Maybe she'll think twice before she dogs anyone else with feathers." Thodos grasped her chin, holding her in place as he forced her lips open with his tongue. When Ashleigh shrank away, his teeth cut her lips. A big hand clamped down on the back of her neck as he sucked at her blood. Then he started to peel the thong down over her thighs.

Ashleigh drew breath to scream. Thodos whispered into her ear, "Scream all you want. We own these people. I gave the valet enough money to forget he ever saw Lorelei here. But don't scream in my ear. I hate that shit. You'll pay for it."

Ashleigh began to cry.

Smirking, the fiend licked up her tears.

He skinned the dress up over her head and threw it in a heap on the hood of the car. Then he pushed Ashleigh onto her stomach. His rough fingers traced the marks from the claws last night. "Damn," he said admiringly. "They worked her over good."

Ashleigh wormed her way away from him. *Don't scratch the paint,* Lorelei reminded. *When we switch, I want you to coach me. I want to know when you would scream. I want to know how you would beg. I want to make every little whimper you would make. Fiends aren't very sensitive and I seriously doubt that he can tell the two of us apart, but I want to be good enough to win an award. Nod if you understand me.*

Eyes squinched shut, Ashleigh nodded. "Oh my god. I can't... I can't... Oh, Mama..."

That's good. I can take it from here. Lorelei switched their positions in mid-sob. Concentrating as hard as she could, Lorelei thought, *Can you hear me? Yes.*

Good, Lorelei thought back. *We can communicate without talking now. Don't be scared. We can get through this, just like we did with Yasmina.*

Thodos dragged her across the hood of the car to meet his hips.

Hang on, Baby, Lorelei soothed. *It'll be over before you know it.*

Lorelei took Thodos's first thrust with an infuriated scream that echoed around the cement garage.

CHAPTER 12: A DAY AT THE OFFICE

The bus let Aza off in Sherman Oaks, on a street of lawns that never lost their drought scruff. Uneven palm trees jostled for room with scrub oak and shade elms.

Muriel awaited him. Aza recognized her blazing white tennis shoes from half a block away.

As he neared her, Muriel started in. "The police haven't been to see the mother yet. Though I made sure they found the boy's body this morning, it took them time to identify him. It had been made to appear that he'd lost control of his motorcycle and coyotes mutilated his corpse." She trembled with disgust. "Typical Hellish sport, rendering him unrecognizable. The harpies didn't leave much of his face."

"Two young harpies were set to take Ashleigh's soul," Aza reported. "I stole her away from them."

"So you're to blame for this, too."

Aza shoved his hands deep into his trouser pockets, gazing down the street. He wished he could be walking to any other house. It rang true that this boy's death was related to Ashleigh. Poor girl. "Perhaps Deion was used as an inducement to her temptation."

"What does it matter?" Muriel snapped. "That girl and all who've come into contact with you are affected for the worse by these events. It must end here."

"The girl needed saving," he started defensively. "More importantly, so does Lorelei."

Muriel shook her head. "I don't care to hear your blasphemy. Deion's mother needs you here. Her son's moment has come and gone, but hers is at hand. Go inside and attempt to help her."

He climbed the wooden steps, ignoring the flaking paint. Muriel followed close behind.

"I can do this alone," Aza said.

"Indulge me."

The house was clean inside. An elaborate cross built of Popsicle sticks hung alone on one wall. Dolores Gutierrez's life had started here when

117

she'd married in 1998 and delivered her only child. Collage frames held moments out of context that spoke of a life no longer recorded once it went wrong. There was no picture of Deion after his ninth birthday. That year his father went to prison, taking Deion's childhood with him.

Dolores twisted the thin gold wedding band around her finger. A tiny gold cross hung at her throat. She still wore her uniform from the car rental office. An unshakable sense that something was wrong sent her home early from her shift at the Burbank airport.

She looked uncertainly up at the angels coming into her house, less distressed by the intrusion than she might have been. "If you're looking for Deion, he was just here yesterday. I'm not sure when he'll be coming by again."

"We haven't come to ask after your son, Dolores, but to bring you tidings of him," Muriel said. "He will not come home again. We are sorry for your pain."

Aza looked up in surprise at the rote way Muriel spoke.

Not yet forty-five, Dolores made every effort to look efficient and youthful, wearing a short, layered haircut, frosted at the bangs. Her face suddenly gained every moment of the nineteen years she'd held at bay since her son's birth.

She stepped back as if trying to find the couch behind her. Her sister Rae reached up to guide her down.

"It was the police? They picked him up?"

Muriel shook her head emphatically.

"A gang? Some of those boys from the Eighteenth…"

Aza reached for her. Mrs. Gutierrez drew away abruptly.

"He's dead," she said flatly. The acceptance gave her insight into her visitors. Mrs. Gutierrez looked to her sister, who evidently wasn't surprised at her nephew's fate. "Did you take him?" Dolores asked, clearly hoping.

"He died out of the Almighty's hands," Muriel said, more sorrowful for what that boded for God than what it meant to Deion.

Dolores's eyes flashed with a mother's ferocity. "He would've turned his life around, if he hadn't taken up with that girl off the street. She got him all messed up with drugs…"

Aza felt his heart sink at the woman's pronouncement. He knew there was no point in saying that Deion had started selling drugs for his dad even before the marriage fell apart. Aza had done this countless times: led mortals to the threshold of acceptance and rejection, in order to let them choose. It was an unfairly loaded situation, a spontaneous test of faith.

"I was meant to deliver this to your son," Aza said, unfolding

Ashleigh's farewell note. He handed it to Dolores and watched her read, hearing in her thoughts the echoes of Ashleigh's words of love and forgiveness.

At length Mrs. Gutierrez put aside the note, tears coming at last. Her sister placed loving arms around her. Truth overcame denial in Dolores's thoughts. She tried to find the right words to say in the presence of angels bearing her sorrow.

Aza took Dolores's hands in his own. "All I know of your son was the love others held for him."

"When did she write this?" Dolores asked.

"The day she died."

"My son is gone." Her voice broke as she spoke the words aloud, crossing herself. "God watch over them both."

Instinctively, Aza's arms went around Dolores. Accepting his compassion with a tear-laden sigh, she gathered the angel in a hug.

Muriel at her elbow, Rae pulled aside the curtain. "Police are here."

"I should go and meet them." Dolores stood, using Aza for support without realizing it. He had already faded from her consciousness.

"Are you going to tell them that you know?" Rae asked.

Dolores shook her head, joining her sister at the window. "No point in that. They'll have been working up to break this news to me." She wiped her eyes. "The best thing I can do for them is bear it well, let them know it was God's will."

Aza smiled. For the first time in days, he actually felt like an angel. He looked for Muriel to share his joy, but she had already left.

Lorelei rode in silence as Thodos attended to the boss's errands around town. The fiend apparently had no desire for music, which might have made him miss the ring of his phone.

Lorelei shifted on the leather upholstery, irritated and uncomfortable. She would've liked to know the gossip from the boss's place or at least the purpose of the meeting Thodos had attended Sunday night. Unfortunately, since he was a fiend, he'd only divulge what he was told to. He'd already sampled the only thing she might have bribed him with—and she definitely wasn't ready to go another round with him yet.

She was relieved when the car finally pulled into the private lot behind the boss's club. Walking into Lost Angels was like coming home. Lorelei was surprised how comfortable it felt, even toting an extra soul. Hell wasn't much of a presence at the moment, but the crowd was pretty good for after-work. Since it was rockabilly night, things would take a while to warm up.

One of the mortals tended bar. Lorelei didn't bother to give him a peek down her dress. Not his taste. "Hey, Mando. Floria here?"

"She's around."

"She being a cunt?"

Mando grinned but held his tongue. "Cranberry and Absolut, right?"

"You're good," she flirted. "What've you got that tastes nasty for my date?" She nodded toward Thodos, looming over her shoulder.

"After-Shock," Thodos rumbled. Lorelei faked a shudder.

"Rocks or water?" Mando asked.

The fiend ignored him.

"Straight up," Lorelei interpreted. She leaned forward to whisper in the bartender's ear, "But spit in the glass first, would ya?"

Mando laughed as he took the bottle down from the bar back.

Lorelei scanned the club, looking for Floria. Mastema sat over in one shadowy corner, surrounded by a trio of young succubi.

"This going on your tab?" Mando asked as he set the glasses on the bar.

"He's paying." Lorelei picked up both drinks and sipped hers, watching Thodos. He surprised her by pulling out the company credit card.

She spat into his glass while his back was turned.

He let her choose a table near the dance floor and settled his bulk into a chair in such a way that he could watch the greater part of the room. Lorelei grabbed a chair, pulled it close, and snuggled against him. He ignored her. She let the music make her sway and tried to imagine the fiend dancing. Should've ordered two drinks if they weren't going to talk.

Can't we just get out of here? Ashleigh whined.

Where would we go? Lorelei answered. *I'm over walking home.*

Floria glided through the crowd, brushing too close to the dancers she passed. Lorelei watched the expressions change in Floria's wake and grinned. Her sister was dressed for the evening as Norma Jean Baker, beauty mark and all.

The fiend watched through slitted eyes.

Hands gripping the back of the opposite chair, Floria took the fiend's measure. "Who's this?"

"Don't you know each other?" Lorelei had assumed her sister requested the chaperone.

"Haven't had the pleasure yet," Floria said.

Thodos regarded her, face impassive.

How interesting, Lorelei thought. She tapped Floria's chair with her foot, so her sister would feel the vibrations in her hands. "Join us, why don't you?"

Floria pulled out the chair and perched on it. "Jenna's looking for you."

Lorelei rolled her eyes. "Tuan couldn't set her up?"

"I think she's gonna kick it tonight." Floria leaned forward to grasp Lorelei's wrist in one feverish hand. "You want me to take over?"

Lorelei forced a smile. "I can handle it."

Floria studied her, her smile insincere.

Tuan arrived with an armload of drinks. Lorelei selected out her cranberry juice and vodka but set it aside. "Where's Hai tonight?"

Tuan shrugged. "Prolly sleeping."

Lorelei laughed at him. "No rest for the wicked, Sugar."

Floria nudged the boy with her elbow. He jumped, then glanced at Thodos.

"He's one of us," Lorelei said.

Tuan slipped an envelope out of his coat, under the table, and onto Lorelei's lap in one slick gesture.

"For Jenna?" Lorelei tucked it under her thigh.

Floria nodded. "And some extra for you. You know how she is."

When they sipped their drinks, the thumping of a coffin bass filled the pause. Lorelei watched the dancers and wondered what she was going to do with Jenna. Her death wasn't unexpected, but Lorelei wasn't exactly prepared to handle it tonight. She hoped she could put it off.

"You wanna dance?" Lorelei asked Floria. "I got too much energy to sit still."

Floria's gaze slid toward the fiend.

"Don't stray too far," he grumbled.

"Okay, Daddy." Lorelei pecked his cheek as she stood, holding her hand out to Floria.

Jenna came swooping down on her. "I've been looking for you everywhere!"

Lorelei accepted an air kiss as Floria sank, smirking, back onto her chair.

"Well, Honey, I've been right here," Lorelei cooed.

"Got my medicine?" Jenna demanded, eyes too bright.

"Sure."

"Can we play-test it right now?"

"Sure, Honey, sure." Lorelei retrieved the envelope from her chair. "You'll excuse us while we go powder our noses."

No! Ashleigh shrieked. *Not speed, Lorelei. Please don't make me!*

Lorelei pasted on a smile, tucked the envelope under her elbow, and allowed Jenna to drag her toward the ladies room. What would Thodos make of all this? She wondered if he was even now rising to follow her. Or if Floria was pumping him for information. Lorelei didn't turn back to see.

Jenna pulled her into the little hallway to the restrooms. Two women waited ahead of them.

"Damn!" Jenna's fingers twisted together. "I have had *such* a day," she blurted. "I think Mrs. Kim suspects there is more going on in the office than script development. I want to tell Mr. Kim to chill until his wife calms down, at least until their anniversary, but he's the boss. How do I tell him to back off and keep my job? And I had to go to the gynecologist again. I missed another period. The pregnancy test was still negative, but I'm sure this time. I mean, I must be pregnant. I've missed three periods in four months. What else could it mean?"

Tell her she's missing her periods because she's doing too much speed, Ashleigh pleaded. *She's losing too much weight and her body's shutting down on her. Ask her the last time she finished a meal.*

What Ashleigh couldn't see was the condition of Jenna's heart. Even Lorelei could tell that Floria's estimation was on target. The flighty little secretary *was* close to the end. If this dose didn't do it, the next one would. Since Jenna was here and so was Lorelei, it would be tonight.

Lorelei was tempted to ask the last time Jenna prayed.

They got their turn at the toilet. Jenna dragged Lorelei in and locked the door.

"You always get the best stuff," Jenna gushed. She pawed through her purse for some carefully folded bills. Inside Tuan's envelope, Lorelei found a handful of packets filled with white crystals.

"You wanna go first?" Jenna placed a new syringe and a little bottle of bleach on the counter behind the sink. "Please? The only time I see you is when we get off together."

"This shit is strong," Lorelei warned. "You want to be careful with it."

Please, Lorelei, anything, Ashleigh begged. *Anything you want, anything at all, oh please don't make me shoot speed again.*

Lorelei looked into the mirror, over Jenna's shoulder, and flashed a savage grin as she untied the scarf around the strap of Jenna's purse.

Jenna caught sight down Lorelei's dress at her bruised chest. "Oh, my god!" Jenna blurted. "What happened?"

"A trick got rough," Lorelei said.

"You've got to quit going out with anybody who asks," Jenna warned. "You're a beautiful girl, Lorelei. You're worth more than that. And that creep you're with tonight? He's *too* scary."

The succubus shrugged. "I do what I have to in order to get by. Just like you do."

That sounded weird even to her ears. Jenna was past the point of getting by. Strangely enough, it occurred to Lorelei to tell the girl how close she was to death, but Jenna broke open a new syringe, fixated already. The time to talk her out of this would've been three months ago. Now, it was beyond too late.

The white flash burned itself out until Lorelei could open her eyes. Her heart rattled triple time in her chest. She found herself on the floor between the toilet and the wall, legs sprawled in front of her. She'd lost a shoe. Jenna knelt beside her. "Oh, Honey, I thought you were dead."

"I'll wish I was dead once I look at this floor," Lorelei slurred. She let Jenna help her to her feet. Getting her mule back on was a challenge. Her whole body vibrated. "Son of a bitch, this shit is pure."

Jenna looked at the crusty brown sink on which she'd laid the syringe. "I hate this," she said.

"No, you don't," Lorelei commiserated. "That's the problem."

"I've just gotta get through tomorrow," Jenna explained. She took the scarf from Lorelei and wrapped it tight around her own bicep. "There's a big meeting with these Korean investors. I can clean up over the weekend."

She ran bleach through the syringe and rinsed it out thoroughly in the filthy sink. Then she set up her own shot, flicking the syringe with one manicured nail.

"Go easy," Lorelei reminded. "That floor is disgusting."

Jenna leaned against the wall to take the shot. As the plunger sank, her breath came out in a long sigh. Lorelei took the syringe from Jenna's arm and set it aside.

Jenna rubbed her chest and looked at Lorelei with vague horror. "My heart is…"

Lorelei stroked the blond hair back from the girl's face, noting her roots.

Jenna clutched her. "Oh God, Lorelei. I feel really sick—"

"Breathe normally, Jenna. It's just speed. You know how it comes on."

Jenna convulsed, clinging to Lorelei. "I think I did too much," she said in a very quiet voice. "I think I need a doctor."

"I warned you." Lorelei tried to step away, but Jenna's terror made her strong. "Let's walk out and get some air."

She convulsed again, coughing up vomit that splattered on the floor.

The smell singed the air.

Dammit. Not for the first time, Lorelei thought that free will made them idiots and rationalizations made them fools. Ashleigh screamed for Lorelei to get help, get a doctor, call 911, but it was too late. Nothing would save Jenna's abused heart. She'd chosen the death she'd wanted, pursued it singlemindedly. All Lorelei could do was to claim her for Hell. Gluttony was still mortal, even if the hunger was chemical.

Lorelei kicked over Jenna's purse and stirred the contents with her toe until she found a compact. Lorelei struggled to reach it, fighting the last of Jenna's strength. Then she raised the compact in front of Jenna's face and opened it to catch the girl's reflection. Jenna's soul flowed out a moment later, swirling into the glass.

You killed her, Ashleigh accused.

Lorelei pushed the corpse away. "She killed herself," Lorelei answered, "same as you did. You all kill yourselves, in your various ways, or you kill each other. We're forbidden to harm you. That's why what Yasmina did to your Deion was so wrong, and one of the reasons I turned her in. As long as I don't kill anyone, I'm beneath Heaven's notice." After she wiped her hands on her skirt, she took Jenna's purse and bent to collect its contents.

"Only angels are allowed to kill," Lorelei continued. "If they find out Yasmina is taking matters into her own hands, they'll stop her. If they wanted to, they could make war over it."

Something heavy thudded down against the door. "Just a minute!" Lorelei called. Her gaze caught on the dead girl. "Shit."

Any other time, she'd just escape unseen, a spirit flowing out into the club, leaving the dead junkie alone behind a locked door. But now, trapped by Ashleigh in her flesh, Lorelei had to walk out the door same as anyone else. Fuck. What was she going to do? There was nowhere in the small room to stuff a body. No closet. No window. Even the trashcan was too small...

"Open it, Lorelei, or I'll take it down."

Thodos. Her savior. Lorelei fixed her lipstick in the mirror, then twisted back the deadbolt.

The fiend took in the scene with a glance. He squeezed through the door into the bathroom, locked the door behind him, and asked, "She damned?"

Lorelei handed him the compact. "You'll have to deliver her for me."

With a sharp nod, he slipped the compact into his trousers pocket. In the same movement, he drew his cell phone out. "Ladies' room needs cleaning," he grunted at whoever answered. "Yeah." He smiled as he turned the phone off.

Someone knocked, more delicately.

"Pipe's busted," Lorelei shouted. "Use the men's!"

She looked at the fiend. "Something else I'm gonna owe you?"

He patted the pocket where he'd stashed Jenna's soul. "You paid for this one."

Next time someone pounded on the door, the fist fell as heavily as Thodos's. The fiend opened the door to a pair of imps pushing a trashcan on wheels. Thodos helped them lift the girl's body into the can. One of the imps cinched the garbage bag closed over her head. They rolled the can back out into the hallway.

Lorelei hung back for a moment, looking at the vomit tracked all over the floor. Was that all that remained of Jenna's existence on earth?

Before she came to any grand conclusions, the speed washed over her again. She tucked Jenna's purse under her elbow and hustled out into the club.

Tuan sat alone at the table when she returned to it. Lorelei sank down into the chair across from him and flung the envelope of speed back into his lap.

"Is she dead?" the boy demanded, his voice deep with disapproval.

Lorelei nodded. Her hand trembled as she reached out for the sweating glass of vodka and cranberry juice. Tuan watched her, blank-faced, calculating. Lorelei closed her eyes against him and drank deeply, looking for the sort of oblivion that mortals found at the bottom of a glass.

"You take your hit before or after you killed her?" Tuan asked.

"First. She insisted." Lorelei misjudged the distance to the table and set the glass down with a loud crack. "And she fixed herself."

"Ever occur to you to talk her out of it?"

"Yeah." Lorelei tilted her glass, hoping to find some vodka she'd missed.

"Getting drunk won't bring her back."

Lorelei met his eyes. "You had a choice about signing Floria's contract, boy. I am Hell's slave."

"Finished?" A waitress reached down to take the empty glass out of Lorelei's hand.

To Lorelei's surprise, this was one of the mortal waitresses. Usually, the live girls had more sense than to walk into the middle of an argument.

"Bring another," Lorelei said.

"She's had enough," Tuan corrected. He pushed his chair back from the table and stood. "C'mon, Lorelei. I'll take you home."

She tilted her head back, trying to focus on his face through the dazzling lights and the chemicals in her blood. "Can we leave?" she wondered.

"You've done enough damage for one night."

Lorelei worked her way unsteadily to her feet. She suspected that, before very long, the vodka/speed combination was going to seem like a bad idea. Now she was disoriented and preternaturally jittery.

"I mean," she said with exaggerated care, "is it okay with Floria if we bail?"

Tuan took her elbow and aimed her toward the stairs. "Floria didn't leave me any orders when she disappeared this time, so let's get out of here before she remembers."

CHAPTER 13: REASSESSMENTS

Lorelei came to with her heart battering her breastbone. It hurt even to draw breath. She wondered if Ashleigh had been in charge, maybe talking to Tuan, or if she'd also been passed out. Had there been something stronger than vodka in her drink? If so, who'd dosed her: Floria, to keep her from seducing Tuan—or Thodos, on orders from the boss?

No time to worry about that now. Tuan continued to slow the BMW. Lorelei focused her eyes and recognized the 5, not far from where she'd crossed under the freeway earlier in the week with Aza. Tuan was cursing—or praying—too low for her to understand.

Adrenaline flooded her bloodstream, to compete with the toxins already in place. "What's wrong?"

"I don't know. I wasn't speeding. Get the registration out of the glove box."

When Lorelei opened it, Tuan's pistol tumbled out to strike her knee. The pain sobered her a little. She kicked the gun under the seat and sorted through the scraps of paper. They were mostly delivery addresses. When Tuan went down, he was taking a crowd with him. That should've amused her, but it didn't. Lorelei asked, "How much are you holding?"

"Enough. All divided for sale." Tuan coasted to a stop, put the BMW into park. He slid both windows down and cut the engine.

Red light flared and flickered through Tuan's car. Lorelei wished desperately she could calm down. Felt like she was next in line for heart failure. Ashleigh had no advice on the subject. There'd be no exorcism for her, if Lorelei kicked it right here.

"Fuck! They're LAPD." Tuan angled the rearview mirror back at the police car. "Why are they pullin' us over on the highway?"

Lorelei found an official-looking piece of paper with Tuan's name and the make of car on it. "This what I'm looking for?"

"Yeah." Tuan took it from her fingers. "Thanks."

Shadows strode up on either side of the BMW. A blade of white light stabbed into Lorelei's eyes. She flinched, fighting a headache as sudden as an ice pick.

The light played down her body, highlighting the pallor of her skin beneath the crocheted dress. Lorelei knew she had to get her shit together enough to work it, but her stomach twisted mutinously. She was *so* not in the mood.

A semi blasted past in the next lane, rocking the car.

"That your girlfriend?"

Lorelei's head whipped around at the slick sound of an infernal accent. A young tempter leaned in Tuan's window. The devil's eyes were invisible behind mirrored glasses, but what Lorelei could see of his uniform was immaculate and crisply pressed. On his badge blazed the number 216—six times six times six. A devil with a subtle sense of humor.

The tempter pushed Tuan's license and registration back into the car. "How about it, kid?"

"My girlfriend's sister," Tuan answered warily.

"That's a shame," the tempter drawled. "If she was your girlfriend, we might've been able to come to an arrangement."

"What kind of arrangement?"

That provoked a laugh from the mortal cop on Lorelei's side of the car.

"Since she's not your girlfriend," the tempter said, "you don't know if she gives good head."

The human cop laughed. "Pretty Boy here looks like he knows a thing or two about givin' it."

Tuan tensed.

"I don't think he's her sister's boyfriend at all," the human continued. "I think he's her pimp. Look at this car! How do you think some teenage gook can afford a Beemer?"

Tuan flushed with fury.

The tempter shone his flashlight on the butt of Tuan's gun, where Lorelei hadn't shoved it far enough under the seat. "Make a move," he invited with cheerful menace. "Whadaya say, kid?"

What was the tempter up to? Lorelei didn't recognize him. He wasn't wearing the sigil of his allegiance where she could see it, even though hers burned in her earrings. The mortal was already damned; he stank of selfish ambition. Why hadn't the tempter steered the man to his death and gone on? What was the point of harassing her and Tuan?

"Suspects killed in the exchange," the human cop gloated.

Lorelei's heart sank. *Ashleigh, if you have any suggestions on how to get us out of this, I'd love to hear them.*

The girl didn't pipe up.

The tempter told Tuan, "If you have a counter-bargain, now's the time."

Tuan surprised Lorelei by looking to her for his answer. No way could he seriously think he could shoot his way out of this.

"Don't do anything stupid," she advised.

"Get out." The tempter drew his own gun and stepped back.

Tuan unhooked his seatbelt and opened the door. Waves of fear spilled off him so strongly that even Lorelei could taste it. As long as he didn't dodge out into traffic, Lorelei told herself, he'd be okay.

The human cop played his light over her like he'd be happy humping her corpse. He was clearly getting hard over this power game, feeding on her fear as much as any devil. Lorelei clenched her fists. A week ago, she'd never felt fear or remorse or nausea. She was over being human. If she could manifest for even a few seconds, she'd work that hard-on until it popped.

Her eyes must have flashed red. He stepped away from the window, thumbing back the hammer on his Beretta.

Lorelei's world narrowed down to the mouth of the gun. She'd fucked up now. They'd both be killed and never see Aza again. *Oh, Ashleigh,* she thought, *I'm so sorry.*

A pair of headlights spotlit the tableau. Two motorcycles rumbled to a stop behind the BMW. Lorelei watched the gun. Maybe the tempter had just led this cop to the brink. She wondered if she'd get a kickback out of her assistance.

"Not a word," the tempter ordered, pointing a warning claw at Tuan, before straightening to face the new arrivals.

Lorelei twisted to see her saviors. A pair of California Highway Patrol officers dismounted from their bikes. As they stepped in front of their headlights, Lorelei saw them for what they were. Angels.

"Doesn't look like a routine traffic stop to me," one of the angels remarked. As he strolled closer, Lorelei's heart skipped a beat. The power pouring off him dazzled her eyes. This angel came straight from Heaven, without centuries of exile in the mortal plane to dull his glory. He stood straight and stern, eyes like granite, every inch a warrior. When he lifted off his motorcycle helmet, the headlights shone from his shaven pate. His skin was the color of mahogany polished by generations of hands. His nameplate read simply, "Michael."

She swallowed hard. She'd been wrong when she'd thought things couldn't get worse.

Without so much as a backward glance, the tempter leapt to perch on the rear step of a truck speeding past.

"What do we have here?" the second angel asked amiably.

"Possession of...of..." the human cop stuttered. He gestured awkwardly with his gun.

The archangel took the gun away. At the slight contact of the angel's hand on his, the cop looked about to cry.

"You're a rotten soul, John," Michael said matter-of-factly. "So what you're going to do is drive up toward the next exit, with my brother following. When you get below that underpass, he's going to sort you out."

Glancing up the freeway to where his death waited, John stumbled back to his car. He wheeled slowly out into traffic, crawling to the underpass.

"Give him a shot at contrition at least," Michael called. His partner made an affirmative wave as he ambled back to his bike, clearly not worried the cop would run.

Returning to the business at hand, Michael's gaze commanded Lorelei's. She felt him reading her, judging her. As much as she longed to, she could not flinch away.

She prepared to feel Ashleigh torn from her. Dammit, after the day they'd had, the two of them deserved to have shared Aza's kiss one final time.

The archangel smiled. Someone else who could read her thoughts, Lorelei realized. "I won't use it against you," he promised. "But I need to speak with Ashleigh now, if you don't mind."

Lorelei nodded miserably and effected the change.

Ashleigh realized she could no longer hear the traffic passing. It was as if she sat alone before the mahogany angel, outside of time.

"Are you here to take me now?" she asked cautiously.

The angel smiled. "Are you ready to go?"

"I don't know," the girl said. "I'm ready to be away from this place, wherever I end up going, but I have a responsibility to Lorelei. She wouldn't be in this position if it wasn't for me."

"Actually," Michael corrected, "she wouldn't be in this position, except for Azaziel."

Ashleigh couldn't argue with that. "What will you do to her, once I am gone?"

"Nothing," the angel said.

Ashleigh wondered again whether angels could lie. "You wouldn't destroy her for chasing Aza, trying to seduce him?"

"Should I punish her for serving the purpose for which she was created? Whether Azaziel survives the temptation she represents is not my concern. His fate lies in his own heart, not in any temptation a succubus might offer."

Ashleigh puzzled over that. Finally, she asked, "Why are you here?"

"Because you needed us."

"People need angels lots of times," Ashleigh countered.

"When it's appropriate to the greater scheme, we appear." The angel ruffled her hair as if she were a child. Even with Ashleigh up front, Lorelei felt his touch clear to her toes. The sensation was the direct opposite of the shame Aza had shown her in the alley.

The angel looked out across the highway. Ashleigh wasn't sure if she heard a gunshot. Then Michael focused on her again and she saw nothing else. "Azaziel believes Lorelei can be saved. Do you?"

Ashleigh felt the weight of her responsibility. She chose her words carefully. "Lorelei has changed already. She protects me. She feels guilty for what they make her do. But she's afraid of what they'll do to her if she doesn't do what they say. Asmodeus said he would destroy her rather than let your side have her."

The angel laughed.

That made Ashleigh shiver. "It all works out for the best, right?"

The angel shrugged. "It depends on whose definition of best you use."

"You're the good guys," Ashleigh hoped.

"God's on our side."

"So you know how it all works out."

"Pretty much. You'll know soon enough."

Even if all he'd given her was a nicely phrased "maybe," Ashleigh didn't feel he was kidding. Her chest swelled with a burst of elated hope.

"Just out of curiosity," the archangel asked, "do you want to come with me now?"

Ashleigh smiled up at him, still riding the buzz of confidence. "Not yet. I do think Lorelei can be saved. I want to help her, if I can."

Michael's grin said it all: *Good answer.*

Time unfroze. Lorelei was back in control of her body. Ashleigh thought she could be saved and was working on that even now. Nausea washed through the devil girl. She considered being sick on the archangel's boots.

Tuan stood trembling in the BMW's headlights. "Can we go?" he quavered.

"Go home, son," the archangel ordered. "The standard line here is 'Go and sin no more,' but I'll be satisfied if you count your blessings tonight."

Michael turned to Lorelei, lifting one hand in benediction. "You girls, try to stay out of trouble."

It was a command, not a suggestion. Lorelei's mouth felt parched. The angel speared her with his gaze until she nodded.

When he turned away, she was panting so fast, she felt lightheaded. He was going to let her go? He was going to allow her to leave with Tuan's contracted soul and Ashleigh inside her? And either she let Ashleigh save her or live in dread of Hell's next attempt on her life?

The archangel kicked over the engine of his motorcycle and accelerated into traffic with a roar.

Tuan slid back behind the wheel. The keys jingled in his shaking fingers as he started the engine.

Lorelei pushed in the cigarette lighter on the dash and fished the pack of Kools out of Jenna's purse. She slipped two between her lips, lit them both, and handed one to Tuan.

He sucked hard on it, but didn't speak until he'd merged. The silence only magnified Lorelei's discomfort. She inhaled her cigarette in record time and pushed the lighter back down.

She realized Ashleigh hadn't spoken to her directly since Jenna's death. Silence was an isolating pressure that once again made her heart race.

As if she heard her name in Lorelei's thoughts, Ashleigh prompted, *Ask Tuan if he's okay.*

Lorelei breathed deep, feeling a hitch loosen in her chest. "Did he hurt you?" she asked.

"Other than fuckin' scarin' me half to death?"

"Yeah. Other than that."

"It was bad enough when they were pigs. Bad enough that they pulled me over outside their jurisdiction. Bad enough that I got a car full of drugs and money and guns and a succubus dressed like a hundred-dollar whore, but then I seen in the mirror that one of 'em's got horns... What the fuck was up with that, Lorelei? Friend of yours?"

"No." She stubbed out her second cigarette and moved to light a third. "I don't know him. I didn't see anything that said he was working for the boss." She changed the subject. "You have anything to drink in here?"

His laugh was mean. "You're not riding with Hai."

"Sorry."

He changed the subject back. "You didn't recognize that...monster?"

"No."

"I can't believe he picked us by accident."

"I don't know what to tell you, Tuan. I'm not exactly high on the list these days. I really fucked up with that angel I'm after..." There, she'd admitted it.

"That guy really was an angel?"

"Yeah. That guy who chained me to his bed is an angel. And those two CHP, they were angels, too. What's more, I think they were sent to save us from being killed just now."

She noticed how conservatively Tuan was driving, trying hard to blend in with traffic. Finally, he said, "This is some serious shit you're in, huh?" He looked at her like she was contagious. "It *is* just you, right? I mean, I just happened to be in the wrong place?"

"Yeah. It's just me. I crossed Yasmina over my would-be boyfriend. You've probably heard Floria mention her."

"*Stupid bitch*," Tuan piped, in a scarily dead-on impression of her sister. Clearly, someone paid attention around the house.

"The very one." Solving this piece of the puzzle didn't make Lorelei feel better. "You know who your soul belongs to," she reminded. "You were safe just now unless you did something suicidal, because Floria wasn't here to claim you. Anyone who crosses Floria—even Yasmina—is gonna be fuckin' sorry."

Tuan slid his gaze over to Lorelei, but didn't react the way she expected. "Hai was packin' blunts on the ride down this morning. Why'n't you see if there's still one up on the visor?"

She tipped the sun visor. Down tumbled an aluminum sunglasses case. Lorelei was amazed it hadn't fallen out on its own during the traffic stop. Tucked inside were a fat joint and a disposable lighter. *Yeah, that's what you need*, Ashleigh bitched. *One drug to balance the next 'til you feel normal or OD.*

The voice of experience? Lorelei shot back as she tilted the paper down into the flame. She asked Tuan, "You gonna smoke it with me?"

"Fuck, yes." Tuan accepted the joint from her and sucked contemplatively before handing it back. "The thing about you is," he said, breathing out a long plume of smoke, "I can't figure you out. Floria's a bitch nonstop. She's all about how to get ahead: how to get more money, how to do more business, how to impress the Prince of LA. Somehow, I'm part of her plan. I get that. But...she's *supposed* to serve me. It's in that damn contract, so she does what she can to make me happy. It may be the *last* thing she thinks of, but at least she thinks of it. But you..."

Lorelei handed the blunt back, not sure she wanted to hear the boy's summation of herself. "You think I look like a cheap whore."

Tuan looked at her blankly before remembering what he'd said. "A hundred bucks ain't cheap, Lorelei. Twenty dollars is cheap. But you sure as shit don't look like no two-K call girl in your transparent dress with your bruised chest. You look like your pimp beat you."

Lorelei agreed, "Every day for a week." The pot swam around inside her head. For the first time in a long time, she felt disconnected from her flesh, free of gravity. She waved at him when he tried to pass back the joint. He stubbed it out in the ashtray.

"All in all," Lorelei said, "this experience has sucked."

"Was he worth it?"

Lorelei closed her eyes and thought about Aza. Details of their one lovemaking rose in her mind: the flavor of his shockingly compassionate kisses, the feel of him inside her when she regained control of her flesh. It had been marvelous. The realization filled her with fierce joy, rather than the sorrow that had nibbled at her for two days. She had experienced something that few—if any—of her sisters ever survived. She might have been possessed, a prisoner in her own flesh, and unable to fuck him the way she truly wanted, but she had been screwed by an angel. In the end, it had been heavenly.

"Yes?" Tuan prompted, grinning.

"Yes," Lorelei agreed. "I'd do it again in a second. But tell Floria that and I'll say you've been smokin' crack."

Tuan laughed. Lorelei sank into her seat, surprised by the smile on her face. She felt as if—like Ashleigh predicted—all the drugs in her system had balanced each other out and she'd attained normalcy. She was surprised to discover how much she liked Tuan. She'd never bothered to form much of an opinion about him before. He was Floria's, so more or less beneath notice. Lorelei had manipulated him, when occasion called for it, but hadn't considered him as emotional or autonomous, not really. She understood that the gang followed him because he was basically a decent person, even-handed and fair to them, generous even when he couldn't afford to be. He might even have been saved, if he hadn't fallen for Floria's contract in a moment of weakness.

"What was it you were gonna say about me?" she asked.

"When?"

"When you said that Floria was driven, but me…?"

"You'll laugh," he said.

He pulled the car into the garage. Lorelei hoped they'd beaten Floria home. It would be nice to ride this buzz a while longer.

Tuan turned toward her in the dim car. "I always kinda admired you," he said. "You seemed like such a free spirit. You knew when to relax and how to make things fun."

"How could I not have fun?" Lorelei asked. "Succubus is the best job in existence. But it sucks being human. Once I get exorcised, I wouldn't go back to *that* on a dare."

Lorelei fluffed her hair in the visor mirror, practicing a humbled expression. "I've learned my lesson."

Yeah, yeah, Ashleigh commented. *Come the exorcism, we'll just see what you've learned.*

CHAPTER 14: THE EXORCIST

Lorelei woke to the sound of voices in the living room. Ah, shit, she thought. *Since I'm awake, it must be time for the next horrific thing to happen to me.*

Bearing in mind that we were wasted twice yesterday, Ashleigh said, *is there any chance that stuff didn't really happen?*

No, Lorelei told her. *It's a miracle we're still here.*

The light creeping in around the blinds was bright with afternoon. Floria must have been busy, to let her sleep all day.

The sound of a popping champagne cork roused Lorelei. Her sister stood in the doorway, holding a bottle and two champagne flutes. Lorelei took a glass warily. "What's this for?"

"Still being alive," Floria said. She rang her glass against Lorelei's. "I heard that bitch is on the warpath."

Champagne. Lorelei smiled. Breakfast of champions. This was shaping up to be a good day.

"*That bitch* has some sort of family tie to my angel. I guess it was okay that he was walking around unfallen until somebody else got busy on the project."

"Is she protecting him?" Floria wondered.

"She just doesn't have the balls to do the job," Lorelei said. "She's trying to terrorize me into doing the work for her."

"Rather than for our prince?"

"Yeah. Creepy, huh?" Lorelei sipped the champagne. "This is good. Did Tuan buy it?"

"Asmodeus sent it over, along with his congratulations for making it home safe last night."

Sure as shit, somebody had gotten her note. As Lorelei rubbed the goosebumps down on her arms, the handcuff rattled on her wrist. She changed the subject before Floria could comment. "Did you hear about the archangel?"

Floria slopped champagne on the white carpet. "What?"

"Michael," Lorelei said casually. "The one who threw away the

Morningstar's key."

"I know who he is," Floria snapped.

"He was really hot."

Floria shuddered. "Did he touch you? I wondered what that weird stink was in here."

Lorelei pulled a handful of hair across her face and smelled Michael's touch. It made her think of sunshine and lilies.

Floria moved back to a safe distance. "You're in some serious shit, Sister."

"Getting more entertaining day by day," Lorelei remarked.

"Well, today's fun is waiting in the next room. The exorcist is here."

Lorelei's flesh turned cold. "Are we gonna do it now?"

"He's not convinced he's going to do it at all," Floria answered. "It's up to you to make up his mind."

Lorelei stretched, trying to work the adrenaline out of her system. She looked down at Tuan, passed out on his stomach beside her, his mouth open. "What does one wear to sway an exorcist?" Lorelei wondered.

"Come as you are," Floria teased. "That's sure to impress."

Lorelei slipped out from under the bedclothes. Her gaze fell on Tuan's dressing gown, hung on the corner of the closet door. The midnight blue silk was a kid's affectation. Lorelei pulled it around her and knotted the sash as she came into the living room.

A barrel-chested older man clutched a glass of whiskey like a rosary. Lorelei offered the defrocked priest her best smile. "What a pleasure to meet you, Father."

"Joseph," he corrected. "Just Joseph now."

She took his hand and looked up at him with eyes as warm and irresistible as she could manage in this form. "Joey," she purred, unwilling to pronounce the holy name, "did my sister tell you how *much* I need your help?"

He didn't try to withdraw from her grip, although she would've let him go. He sucked unsteadily at the whiskey. Lorelei led him to the sofa and sat him down, then perched with her knees touching his. Floria set a bottle of Talisker on the coffee table, along with a glass for Lorelei, then withdrew to rouse Tuan.

Joseph ran a finger inside the collar of his turtleneck, as if the memory of his clerical collar tightened around his throat. "I understand you want me to perform an exorcism."

"That's right." She refreshed his drink and poured herself one. "Except that the soul you are to cast out is human. I am not."

"Succubus," he guessed.

She clinked her glass against his, then sipped her whiskey. It burned down her throat like liquid smoke. She closed her eyes to savor.

"How did you become possessed?" he asked.

"Through no choice of my own," she assured him. "Being what I am, though, you'll need to speak the Latin backwards."

"That won't be a problem."

Ah. He'd performed the Black Mass. Hail Satan. She wondered how Floria had found him, who was responsible for his downfall.

"Let's discuss your compensation," Lorelei said. "Of course, the things I can offer you are limited until after the ceremony."

"I won't sign your contract," he said.

Lorelei kept herself from shrugging. Why would he need to sell his soul? He was a fallen priest, three-quarters damned already. Maybe he hoped that a deathbed confession would save him. The delusions of mortals never ceased to amuse her.

"Your choice," she agreed. "Take your time to decide how I can satisfy you best."

He let the silence rest, then said, "Tell me about the spirit that possesses you."

"Would you like to speak to her?"

"May I?"

Lorelei sank backward and let Ashleigh take over. The priest watched closely. Lorelei wondered what he hoped to see in her face.

Ashleigh moved away from the old man and pulled Tuan's robe over her knees.

"The ceremony's been set for tomorrow at midnight," Joseph said. "I take it you're not possessing her by choice?"

Ashleigh frowned. "It was only supposed to be for one night."

"What happened?" the priest asked.

"The other angels attacked before I could get out."

The priest sighed. "I've always wanted to see an angel. Are they beautiful?"

Lorelei said, *I'll let you handle this, Ashes, but be careful. You know Floria is eavesdropping.*

Ashleigh swallowed. "One of them was."

The priest surprised her with a fatherly smile, one touched by sadness. "If you were about to do a favor for a succubus," he asked, "what would you ask her for?"

Ashleigh shook her head. "I didn't ask her for this. And Lorelei didn't give her permission. The angel said I was only going to use Lorelei's body for one awesome night. Now I'm trapped in it. Anything anyone offers you is a trap. On either side."

"I know."

"So figure out what you want," she continued, "and ask for that. Be specific. I'll help if I can. Is there anything *I* can get for you?"

He looked at her long and hard. Ashleigh wished he could really see her, instead of being dazzled by Lorelei's appearance.

"How old are you?" he asked gently.

"I was seventeen when I died."

"Were you a good girl?"

"No," she said simply. Ashleigh dropped her gaze. If what he wanted was her, she would do it, but she wasn't about to seduce an ex-priest who was older than her dad for Lorelei's sake.

He reached out and patted her hand. "That's okay, child. If these were other circumstances, I'd offer to hear your confession."

Lorelei swam back into control. She crawled over to the priest, making sure to show plenty of inner thigh, and whispered into his ear, "Don't talk like that, Joey. I'm in enough trouble as it is."

She was sure Floria had come back into the room, but didn't check. Lorelei wound her arms around the priest's neck and pressed herself against him. He shifted uncomfortably, but didn't push her away. She traced a slow, wet kiss under the curve of his jaw and felt that twitch inside her that said she was making contact. Good. She'd need that later.

She settled back, straddling his knee, but didn't drop her arms. The dressing gown slipped, revealing more young flesh than he'd probably seen in a long while. "Do you have a car, Joey?"

The non sequitur flustered him. "What?"

"I left my favorite shoes someplace and I need a man of the cloth to get me back in the door."

Floria interrupted. "With that bitch out for blood, Tuan's boys better go along."

Lorelei smiled at Joseph, trying to enlist his complicity. Then she wiped her expression and turned toward Floria, who was calmly setting out lines on the far side of the glass-topped coffee table. "If you think an honor guard will help. I think the place we're going is still holy."

"Where are you going, then?"

"Back to his lair. It's over in the warehouse district someplace. My purse is there, and my favorite lipstick, and those black Ferragamo pumps."

"The boys could get them for you." Floria waved a rolled fifty-dollar bill toward Lorelei and the priest.

Lorelei climbed out of his lap and knelt beside Floria. She took the bill in her right hand, pinched one nostril closed, and bent over the table. Floria swept Lorelei's hair up before it could drag through the drugs. Lorelei inhaled one line and rocked back on her heels, blinking back tears. The powder felt like ground glass inside her nose. White light slammed into her brain, followed by a drop in her stomach like a sucker punch. "I was expecting coke," she said.

"I thought Ashleigh might be missing her speed," Floria said, innocently enough.

Twice in two days? They were working on the girl's addictions, clearly not trusting Lorelei to feed them herself. "Thank you," Lorelei said, mimicking the timbre her voice took on when Ashleigh used it.

Ashleigh herself was very quiet.

Floria leaned over the table and inhaled a line of her own. She sat back, grinning to show sharp teeth. She dipped two fingers into Lorelei's glass, then inhaled the whiskey up her nose.

"It's not like I could tell them where the place is," Lorelei argued. "I didn't see the address, or even which street it was on. We came and went through the back, from the old train tracks. I'm gonna have to retrace my steps."

"What's so important about a pair of shoes?"

"I want to look nice for the exorcism. Besides, my datebook is still there. I don't want that in the wrong hands."

"What makes you think it isn't already?"

Lorelei took her glass back and sipped the whiskey to balance out the jitters. She let the robe slip casually off one shoulder when she shrugged. "If it's gone, maybe the priest can help me figure out whose ass I'm going to have to kick to get it back."

Floria did her second line.

"Remember that party we worked," Lorelei said, "given by that rock star of yours? That night when we cut the coke on his breastbone? His blood made the coke go down so easily."

"Those were the days," Floria agreed.

"Back when you didn't feel you had to fucking babysit me." Lorelei coiled her hair around itself and pushed it over her shoulder.

Floria rubbed her nose, sniffling a little. "Don't push it, Sister. You know the boss told me…"

"I know." Lorelei took the fifty back. "I just wanted you to remember what it was like to trust me."

She leaned over the table, positioned the rolled-up bill, and thrust Ashleigh forward.

"No!" the girl protested.

Before she could straighten away from the table, Floria pounced on her with a strength that was more than human.

Do it, Lorelei ordered.

"No," Ashleigh whimpered. "No. Not again. Not anymore. I don't want to."

"Yes, you do," Floria soothed, stroking her arm. "One for the road, Ashes. Might be the last speed you'll ever see."

Don't lie to her, Lorelei instructed. *She knows you want it. She can feel it as strong as I can. Just do it and let's go get my shoes.*

Tears dropped from her eyes as Ashleigh bent over the table. She did want it. She could feel the familiar sick anticipation, the dread and the joy, that speed used to give her. This was pure crystal, not cut with any of that powdery baby laxative shit that Deion sometimes brought home. Shaking with self-loathing, Ashleigh inhaled the last line. They'd left the longest one for her.

It took a while to organize the boys and the ride. Standing in front of the closet, Lorelei debated her wardrobe options. The dressing gown wasn't much protection from the outside world, but it could serve other purposes. She left it on and retrieved Ashleigh's boots from behind the toilet. Good thing Tuan hadn't had time to clean up yet this week. If she had to walk down those railroad tracks again, she wanted something more substantial than mules on her feet.

Lorelei had just about finished making herself up when Floria appeared over her shoulder in the bathroom mirror. Lorelei smiled at her sister's reflection.

Floria lifted an eyebrow. "I'm not sure the robe/boots thing is working. You gonna wear that out in public?"

Lorelei tugged the neckline open a little more and said, "Easy on, easy off."

"Careful with that priest," Floria advised. "It takes a lot of groundwork to get one into his position."

"Hell, yes, I'll go easy on the old man," Lorelei promised. "He's her ticket out of here. The boys ready to leave?"

"Amped and ready to rock," Floria answered.

Lorelei trailed her sister back into the living room. Several young Vietnamese men leaned together in a huddle on the floor, doing lines off the coffee table. In the corner of the sofa, Joseph was determinedly getting drunk.

"Hi, Tiger." Lorelei smiled at Hai. He'd dressed up for her today, wearing a skintight black T-shirt and black Levis that left nothing to the imagination. Lorelei licked her lips.

"Be careful," Floria warned them all.

"Now more than ever," Lorelei promised. She took the priest's hand and pulled him toward the door.

A shiny new RAV4 with tinted windows waited at the curb. Even from the sidewalk, Lorelei could hear the bass pounding. Inside the truck, the music was going to be a physical assault. Ideal.

Hai opened the RAV4's door, ushering Joseph and Lorelei into the back. Hai himself rode shotgun. Sammy already waited behind the wheel. He was the gang's enforcer, the one who saw to it that debts got paid. It didn't hurt that he'd grown up in the juvie and had no loyalty except to the other boys. He'd bulked up in city custody, a big ugly mass of muscle that Hai liked to have at his back.

The rest of the pack climbed onto brightly colored Japanese motorcycles, kicking the engines over with a roar of noise. Why such a force? Lorelei wondered. Simply to protect the priest?

Joseph huddled miserably against the far door. Lorelei would've felt much better if he'd asked her for something, even something small. The last thing she wanted to do was piss him off by offering the wrong thing. Step One was to win him over.

"Put your seatbelt on, Father," she suggested. "Can't afford to have anything happen to you."

The truck swung around in a tight U-turn. Lorelei leaned back in the seat. Her heart fluttered in her chest. She really hadn't needed that second line.

Over the music, the priest shouted, "Why force the girl to do drugs?"

Lorelei twisted a lock of hair around her fingers, just to feel the tug. She was tired of explaining things that ought to be obvious. She scooted over next to him, so she wouldn't have to yell. "Look, *Father*. I'm in a difficult situation here. Just because Ashleigh chose to inhabit me, my people—all my people—have doubts about me. Try for a minute to imagine what that's like." She sighed. "Floria and I have been together a long time. I know what she's capable of—and *she's* the closest thing I have to a friend in Hell."

You promised to stop tempting me, Ashleigh sulked.

Lorelei continued, "Did it hurt the girl to give her what she craved? No. If there's any real damage done, it's my body. Ashleigh got one last high and we got out of Floria's house. That was worth a few jitters."

Besides, Ashleigh and her speed could be put to use. The priest had offered to listen. A little bonding between the two might serve Lorelei in the end.

She snuggled against the priest. He turned away rigidly, but she said into his ear, "Look, Joey. I know you've been defrocked. You can't grant absolution, right?" She waited for him to nod. "I don't want you handing out acts of contrition. No 'Hail Whatsernames.' But if it would do the kid good to make her confession, I'll allow it. It's got to be done quickly and quietly, and I'm gonna stay close enough to the surface that I can give the boys directions. Agreed?"

"Why are you doing this?" Joseph pulled far enough away from her that he could see her eyes. He clearly didn't trust her. That was fine, as long as he would help Ashleigh.

"Because she saved my life."

Why are *you doing this?* Ashleigh echoed.

Lorelei sank backward. *Time is short, Miss Crank.*

Ashleigh leaned over against the old man. He reeked of whiskey. "I wasn't Catholic," she said. "I don't know what to do."

The priest put his arm awkwardly over her shoulders and held her close enough that he could whisper, "Bless me, Father, for I have sinned," into her ear.

Ashleigh repeated the words and began.

Lorelei found it tricky to ignore Ashleigh's pathetic confession while trying to imagine what she'd seen from the air. She asked the boys to start at Lost Angels, then circle outward.

Surprisingly, it didn't take long to find the place where she'd joined Aza walking down the train tracks. The boys drove as close to the warehouse as Lorelei could get them. Then they abandoned the vehicles to search on foot.

Removing helmets and checking weaponry was a big production. Lorelei huddled in the dressing gown, wishing she'd borrowed a coat. She hadn't realized it was going to cool off when the sun started to go down. Being cold was the worst part of being human, she decided. All the other discomforts she could handle, but feeling cold was miserable.

Hai made an elaborate exhibition of folding a match around the outside of the matchbook and striking fire without first tearing it out. He lit his cigarette, then looked up to see Lorelei watching him.

"I'm not supposed to let you out of sight," he said.

She reached out slowly to take the cigarette from his mouth. Her eyes slid closed as she sucked hard on it. Turning her palm toward Hai, she offered the cigarette back, filter first. His lips lingered against her fingers before he took the cigarette from her.

Lorelei breathed out a long plume of smoke. "Can I borrow your matches, Tiger? You're gonna need some light if you're gonna watch me."

He grinned at that and held up the matchbook. Lorelei palmed it.

"Sammy, stay with the truck," Hai ordered. "Vin, keep him

company."

The other boys formed rough ranks with the priest in the middle. Lorelei led them down the overgrown tracks, avoiding the broken bottles, the rusting hammer. They reached the warehouse without seeing another soul.

The metal door was still rolled upward. Claw marks scarred the metal. The boys and the priest paused to stare, but Lorelei recognized them as her own and continued up the hallway.

Aza's cell stood open. Lorelei struck a match and looked inside. Her pumps waited at the end of the futon, lined up, heels and toes together. Her purse lay bottom up, its contents strewn around it. Her money clip was gone. *Enjoy your poison,* she wished the thief philosophically. *See you in Hell.*

"Joey!" she called. Her voice echoed through the warehouse, sharper than necessary. The boys clustered together, nervously herding the old man toward her. "This is where I need your help, Baby." She tossed the match down and lit another so he could have a look.

He peered into the room as if he expected to see carnage.

"Step over the threshold and call me in," she urged.

"That's all?"

"For now."

"What's in there?"

"Nothing." Focusing everything she had left, she smiled at him. "You can trust me on that, Joe. I don't dare put you in any danger, 'cause without you, there's no party tomorrow night."

"Why can't you cross the threshold?"

That was more than she'd wanted to admit. She sighed. "The guy who held me here said he spoke an abjuration. I thought I left because I chose to, but now I'm not sure. If he barred me, I need someone else to invite me back. That would be you."

She watched him wonder why she didn't just send one of the boys in, but he didn't ask. She handed him the matchbook. "Why don't you light one of those candles?"

He squared his shoulders before stepping into the room. Nothing happened. The first match wouldn't catch. He set it on the shelf between the candles and tried another. Lorelei realized she wasn't the only one holding her breath. "Relax, Joe. Anything that's gonna happen will happen to me."

The match sparked. He transferred the flame to a candle. Light flared from the mirrored sunburst glued to the wall. Joseph jumped.

"What was that?" Hai demanded.

"Nothing," Lorelei hoped. "You okay, Joe?"

When he turned, she glimpsed what he must have been when he was young, before his faith shattered. He'd lost something, she realized, a loss he couldn't forgive. He'd begged for a miracle and been denied.

"Joe?" she repeated.

"Enter, Lorelei." It was a command, not a request.

As the toe of her boot crossed the threshold, goosebumps shivered over her skin. That hadn't happened before. There *was* something to this abjuration business after all.

Even if Aza had thrown her out, Lorelei knew she'd gone after him by her own choice. She had broken her attack by choice. Had she been operating under free will all along, despite everything she'd ever been taught about being a devil? *That* was a troubling thought.

Lorelei took the matchbook back from Joseph. When she touched a match to the wick of the outermost candle, nothing catastrophic happened. As she lit each candle, she whispered, "Azaziel." She continued until the room flickered with firelight.

"What're you doin'?" Hai demanded.

She nodded over her shoulder at the futon. "I thought Joey and I might have ourselves a party."

"Crazy bitch," one of the boys muttered in Vietnamese.

Lorelei pulled the loose end of the sash so that Tuan's dressing gown fell open as she turned. "What do you think, Joe?"

"You're mad."

"That's not what I'm asking." She advanced on him, slipping the dressing gown backward off her shoulders.

"This is not the reward I want."

"I know." She dropped the robe, but not the sash. One of the boys giggled. Lorelei concentrated on the priest. "This will probably be the last time Hell lets me off the leash. I need help to do this. It can be yours, or the boys'. It's all the same to me."

She backed Joseph against the wall beside the futon and pressed herself against him. He held his hands up, away from her.

She grinned. "You don't have to be afraid of me, Joey," she purred. "You're so much bigger than I am, and the boys are right here... Or is that the problem?"

Leave him alone, Ashleigh begged. *We need him. You need him.*

Raising herself up on tiptoe enough that she could catch his earlobe in her teeth, Lorelei quickly knotted the sash around the pipe at the head of the futon. Their bodies shielded her hands from the boys. Joseph was too distracted to do anything but hope that she didn't bite him. Lorelei tugged surreptitiously on the satin, hard enough to set the knot. The slipknot on the other end was already prepared. She hoped one of the boys had a knife. She hoped Aza's abjuration was strong enough to protect the room from devilish intervention. She hoped that the priest was frightened enough of his infernal masters that he'd do whatever was necessary. Most of all, she hoped her sacrifice would be enough for the task.

What are you up to? Ashleigh wondered.

Lorelei stepped up on the futon and pulled the noose over her head. In the same motion, she fell to her knees and dropped face forward.

"Dear God!" the priest shouted. He staggered onto the futon beside her, fumbling at the satin sash. Every tug tightened the noose around her throat. *Damn, being throttled hurt.*

The boys boiled into the room, getting in each other's way.

Lorelei fixed her eyes on the starburst Aza had glued to the eastern wall. "I need you," she managed before darkness claimed her.

CHAPTER 15: TREADING THE EDGE

Shoving the boys aside, Joseph pulled frantically at the broken mirror on the wall. As a curved shard came loose, it slashed his hand.

The old man stumbled back across the room to saw unevenly through the sash. Lorelei collapsed face down onto the futon. The priest rolled her over and gently opened one eye to check her pupil.

The smell of his blood brought her back to her senses. Lorelei tried to resolve details from the gray fog obscuring her vision. The priest knelt over her. Concern etched his face. A pair of Tuan's boys stood to one side, butterfly knives open in nerveless fingers. Good thing she hadn't relied on them.

Footsteps rang hollowly in the empty warehouse. Turning her head, Lorelei saw Aza framed in the doorway. The rumpled shirt he wore shone bright white. Another archangel and that blond bitch from the church flanked him. Lorelei's heart sank. She'd expected him to come with an escort, but the bitch was a bad omen.

She leaned painfully up onto her elbows. Inside, Ashleigh all but pushed her aside, trying to get closer to Aza. What we have here, Lorelei thought wryly, is a triangle.

Something was off about his posture, a slight stoop. That might have been to allow the archangel to rest his hand on Aza's lowered shoulder, but the stoop remained after the hand was taken away. Had her kick injured Aza that badly? The thought made her wet.

"Give us a moment alone?" Aza asked Hai.

Hai's cigarette shifted to one side of his mouth. He blew a stream of smoke against Aza's face. "No way."

The smoke parted neatly before reaching the angel. Aza murmured, "Kids," before gently shouldering past.

Hai's Glock was out, canted sideways, muzzle pressed to the back of Aza's neck.

"Shoot Lorelei with it," the female suggested, redirecting the barrel with her fingers.

Instead, Hai fumbled with the gun. Lorelei hadn't realized she was holding her breath.

Like the CHP angel last night, the unfamiliar male of the trio seemed to have come straight from God. Power flowed off of him in shimmering waves. He was tanned and angular, with a smile to match his snow-white hair. His gaze followed the trail of blood across the floor to the bit of sash wound around Joseph's hand in an unconscious bandage.

"Good work there, Father. Fast thinking." The angel's tone was jovial, like a cruise ship entertainment director.

In fact, he seemed to be choosing his words as a segue in a show. "Hey now, boys. He said give him a moment, okay? You know what they say: God loves a cheerful giver."

Lorelei clapped her hands over her ears just as the archangel belted out a children's hymn. "Oh, God loves a cheerful giver. Give it all you've got. He loves to hear you laughing when you're in an awkward spot. If the odds seem up against you, it's time to stop and sing. Thank God. To praise him is a glorious thing!"

When he finished, Lorelei uncovered her ears. Beneath the surface of his voice lurked power, as if a change of pitch could make eardrums bleed.

She wanted Aza to reach down to her, to bring her into his arms and heal her aches. Instead he squatted down and cupped her cheek. Not quite as nice, but his smooth hand felt sweet against her flushed face. Lorelei gave him a genuine smile.

He didn't return it. "That was foolish." He slipped the sash, suddenly unknotted, from her throat.

"It worked," she countered hoarsely. "You're here."

"Let me speak with Ashleigh."

"Dammit!" Lorelei struggled to sit up. "Aza, I—"

He touched his palm to her sternum and brought Ashleigh forward. Smoothing her hair, Aza said, "My brave girl."

"Can we come with you?" Ashleigh asked.

Aza looked hopefully at Rafael.

"I am expressly forbidden to interfere with the succubus and the girl," the archangel explained. "It must take its course."

"Not yet," Aza translated, grimacing as if the words tasted bitter. "Are you all right?" he asked, knowing perfectly well that she wasn't.

Ashleigh shrugged. "She's stopped tempting me. Now she just sets up these ordeals and forces me to go through them. She's stopped giving me any choice." Ashleigh added, "She is the most selfish person I ever met."

Aza shook his head in sympathy. "Does she hurt you?"

Ashleigh stopped to consider. "No. She only hurts herself. I think she likes it."

Aza touched his fingertip outside the bruise Tuan left. "I wish I could heal that for you."

Ashleigh realized she was naked in public again. Blushing, she curled up, trying to cover her body with her arms and legs.

The change in position revealed the scars on Lorelei's back. Aza rested one hand gently over them.

"They were going to kill her," Ashleigh explained. "So she told them she needed more time to bring you down."

Thanks for sharing that, Lorelei sniped.

Aza looked at her more sharply. "You two can communicate directly?"

Yes, Lorelei replied.

Ashleigh echoed her aloud. "Yes. If we concentrate real hard."

"How long have you been able to do that?"

"Since Lorelei kicked you down the stairwell."

Since you slammed her back into me, Lorelei corrected. *After your 'friends' attacked.*

"Something happened when you put me back," Ashleigh explained. "She has a soul of her own now. And Asmo—"

Aza stopped her with a finger on her lips. "Her prince knows she has a soul?"

Across the room, Aza's custodians seemed to prick up their ears. Ashleigh nodded.

Great, Lorelei groused. *Tell everyone. They are the enemy, Ashes.*

"She arranged for Father Joseph to hear my confession," Ashleigh told him. "But he said he couldn't forgive my sins, 'cause he's not a real priest anymore. Can you do it?"

Aza shook his head and hugged her closer to him, mindful of her injuries. He placed the kiss of compassion on her brow and one, more passionate, on her lips. Ashleigh clutched him in her arms.

Aza smiled. "Know that I love you, Ashleigh."

She blinked back tears and nodded.

Before she could say more, Aza called Lorelei to come forward.

"I don't know why I should," she snapped, pushing out of his lap. Here she was putting herself in mortal danger and all she got was Ashleigh's sloppy seconds. Her heart was as pierced as if he'd run a dagger through it. "Give me my robe."

The archangel retrieved it from the floor and held it out at arm's length. Lorelei snatched it, whirling it around her shoulders in a wave of blue silk.

"Why did you lure us here?" the female angel demanded.

Lorelei wrapped the dressing gown closed, then remembered who had the longer piece of the sash. She held out her hand to Joseph.

"Can you be trusted with it?" he wondered.

"If I hang myself again, I promise to do it in another room full of people."

He held up his hand. The purple sash binding it was full of blood. Lorelei sighed and measured the length Aza had removed from her throat.

The flash of the broken handcuff, still encircling her wrist, caught Aza's eyes. His head jerked up sharply. Lorelei met his gaze.

Before her misery betrayed her, she said, "I called you here to tell you this: tomorrow night, Joey will perform an exorcism. Come rescue your beloved Ashleigh."

"And you, Lorelei."

"I belong to Hell, Aza. Body *and* soul, thanks to you."

"I won't leave you behind," he promised. That had the flavor of steely determination.

Carefully, so that all the angels would understand her, she said, "My prince has sworn my destruction if I ever think of leaving him, but the girl is yours. Take her and may you be happy together. Leave me to the fate you made for me."

Aza stood suddenly, startling her. He swept her into his arms, crushing her hard against his chest. She felt the connection in her body hum like a bowstring. Contrary to her nature—and her desires—Lorelei forced herself to hang limp.

She had to do this. She had to let Ashleigh go. The girl deserved her deliverance for all she'd done for Lorelei. The succubus was certain it was the right thing to do. Why did Aza have to make this any more difficult than it already was? It's not like she could choose to go with him and expect to survive the night. The archangel said she wasn't welcome, anyway.

That powerful angel pulled Aza away. Letting him go was the most difficult thing she'd ever done. Lorelei swayed, fingers cramping with the desire to hold Aza. He gazed at her, his green eyes damp with tears.

Gazing at the mismatched trio, Joseph wondered, "Who are they?"

Lorelei watched Aza collect the casket of ritual implements from the altar. Her heart ached worse than all her injuries. "That is the noble angel Azaziel."

"Angel?" Joseph repeated.

Business, Lorelei reminded herself. Pitching her voice to ring from the concrete walls, she commanded, "Wait."

At the doorway, the angels turned back.

"One thing you must do to protect the soul I give you."

They watched her with the full spectrum of expressions. The revulsion in the female angel's face amused Lorelei. The archangel forgave Aza's attraction to her. Aza himself gazed at her as if his heart was breaking.

"What was spoken here must be secret," Lorelei said, "or I won't see tomorrow dawn." She nodded toward the boys.

The archangel made a gesture, complex and arcane.

As he cast his spell, Lorelei knelt to retrieve the things spilled from her purse. From the corner of her eye, she watched Aza kiss the first two fingers of his right hand and hold them up in a benediction. Then he was gone.

She closed her eyes and shuddered.

The bottle of lighter fluid was unbroken. Lorelei slipped that into the pocket of her robe. The antique gold cigarette case and its matching lighter seemed to be gone the way of her money clip, but she found the Tramp-colored lipstick, her Bruise eye shadow, her compact, and her little black book. Life could resume with those things alone.

When she straightened from the floor, her head spun. She might have fainted, if the priest hadn't reached out to steady her. She leaned against him and willed her vision to clear.

"Okay?" he asked. His fingers lifted tentatively toward the bruise around her throat.

Damnation. She'd forgotten about that. She'd have to bullshit some plausible explanation before Floria saw the bruise.

She raised the old man's fingers to her lips and kissed them. He snatched his hand away.

He loves me, Ashleigh sighed to herself.

So the girl remembered seeing her angel? Hell's bells, yet another complication. Hopefully, Ashleigh would have enough sense to keep from thinking of it in mixed company.

Turning her back on the priest, Lorelei muttered, "Of course he loves you, Ashes. You're the agent of my destruction."

I'm sorry I said you were selfish, Ashleigh whispered. *Thank you.*

"Don't make me regret it." Lorelei's voice felt tight in her throat, as if it had turned sideways.

She handed Hai her pumps and Joey her purse. Opening the bottle of lighter fluid, she cast its contents in an arc across Aza's lair, splashing the futon generously. She tipped the last candle in line onto the puddle. Flame roared up in response. Hopefully, that would cover the traces of the archangel's presence in the room. She hoped she wouldn't be running into any more of them before her possession was over.

She would've stood in the doorway to watch the cell burn, but Hai pulled her away.

As they walked away down the railroad tracks, Aza mused over the last time he'd passed this way. Then Lorelei had been ridiculous and realized it, tottering over the railroad ties in her stiletto heels. The memory of her exaggerated sway brought a smile to his lips.

Muriel looked like she'd smelled something bad. "She's using you, Brother."

Aza laughed. He felt better than he had in days. "Using me? What does that matter? Everyone uses us. Isn't that what we exist for?"

Muriel shot a significant glance at Rafael while Aza pressed on.

"What other purpose do we serve for those who need us? We are agents of hope and mercy."

"No amount of truth in your words can justify their intent," Muriel warned. "We don't question, we don't debate, we simply act. We are messengers from the Word. Not the same thing as being used. Not at all."

Rafael's fingers brushed Aza's shoulder. "All we're counseling is caution when it comes to these two."

"*Caution?* A soul is in jeopardy!" Aza felt fierce electricity build at the back of his throat, tinged with rebellion. Of their own volition, his thoughts found a path to his lips. "We're talking two souls, now: one mortal and another new-formed and created by my experiment. Why should any of us hesitate to serve that new soul?"

Muriel spat, "She was born to be damned."

"Lorelei had no choice in the creation of her soul. I love her. Should I revel in her damnation? And if she's sent to Perdition, what happens to the mortal spirit coupled to her flesh? I don't know about either of you, but I've not been directed to choose one above the other."

"You love her?" Rafael's last vestige of joviality faded like daylight before a storm. "Careful, Brother."

Muriel exploded. "Careful? How can you continue to caution him? He's speaking rebellion before an Archangel of the Lord! Why don't you split the earth and send him to his doom?"

Aza turned on her. "If you feel that strongly, why didn't you take Ashleigh just now? You could have killed them all, just to save the girl's soul."

"I would have destroyed them both!" Muriel shouted. "Unclean, unnatural, and surrounded by sinners. The vile flavor won't leave my tongue. They all should have perished in a cleansing fire, and you amongst them."

Aza's heart pounded fiercely. He felt himself rushing to a moral precipice with no sign of stopping. "It seems to me that the only true rebellion would be to set myself as judge over Lorelei's chance at salvation. This has never happened before. It may well never happen again. To save her and Ashleigh both, I would willingly damn myself."

There. It was said. Now that the words were out, Aza straightened.

The lightning did not come, nor the ground yawn open at his feet. Aza actually felt a measure of certainty, of peace. What Muriel refused to see was how changed Lorelei had become. Aza recognized it as soon as the succubus met his eyes. She'd looked on him without lust and seen how he had been punished for consorting with her. She'd pitied him. Pity from a devil: that was a new thing in the history of Creation. Most importantly, through her eyes gazed a soul she had not had before, a soul with a yearning toward the Light that Lorelei would never be allowed to satisfy. Hell would undoubtedly devour her, unless Aza could prevent it.

He vowed silently to rescue her from Hell—or perish in the attempt. The Almighty did not contradict that decision in his heart.

Rafael gazed at him, waiting, and Aza gazed back, drawing strength from his conviction. Muriel might turn her nose up at the tang of Lorelei's musky perfume, but she had heard from Ashleigh herself how the devil had ceased to tempt her. Aza began to phrase his defense.

"I believe that it was easily within Lorelei's power to damn Ashleigh, if she chose to," he said quietly. "You heard for yourselves that Lorelei has ceased tempting the girl. She encouraged Ashleigh to make confession. She allowed Ashleigh to ask forgiveness of her sins…"

"Granted," Muriel snapped, "but confession was made to a fallen priest, a man in Hell's employ. Ashleigh asked forgiveness from one not empowered to give it."

Aza looked upward. The others followed his gaze and were silent.

"All right," Rafael said at last, joviality returned. "Your faith is persuasive. But you don't believe—in all honesty—that *you* created Lorelei's soul?"

Aza shook his head, profoundly embarrassed by that slip of the tongue. "No. I must have had divine aid. Who else could create a soul?" His gaze dropped back to the pavement. "That alone justifies any sacrifice I am called upon to make."

"If you go into the mouth of Hell to retrieve the soul of a devil," Muriel cursed, "may you never return."

Aza stood fast in the face of Muriel's deep and holy anger. "I will go where I am bidden."

He remembered that when he'd touched Lorelei's face, her smile—stripped of artifice—was as beautiful as any painter's Madonna. She was radiant, compared to Muriel.

Shaking his head, Rafael grabbed Aza and Muriel by the scruffs of

their necks and leapt upward. He flung his blazing wings open as they
rose.

CHAPTER 16: VERBAL CONTRACT

Lorelei and her honor guard returned to the vehicles. When Hai asked what was up, Sammy offered nothing out of the ordinary. They hadn't noticed the angels. That was a relief.

She huddled into her corner of the back seat, chin resting on her chest. Tuan's robe smelled like Aza now, like myrrh and sadness. He'd hugged her only briefly, but his scent marked her as surely as if she'd fucked him. She couldn't possibly go back to Floria, reeking of her would-be boyfriend.

Probably his compassionate kiss burned on her brow, too, for those who had eyes to see. These complications were endless. Every time she thought she had a grip, something else slipped from her control.

Leaning up into the front seat, Lorelei told Hai, "I don't know what your orders are regarding the priest. Is there any reason we can't just return him home?"

"Floria said to leave a guard with him."

Lorelei nodded. "What'd she tell you about me?"

Hai flashed her a grin that was meant to be scary. "Ignore you if you talk to yourself."

Lorelei flashed her own scary grin and watched the boy flinch. He forced out a laugh and flung himself back around in his seat.

"What'd you say to him?" Joseph asked.

"We're gonna run you home," she answered. "Tell them where you're staying."

The priest's directions led to a nondescript apartment building on East Wilshire. The boys parked their motorcycles close to the RAV4, clustering together for courage. This was Little Korea. They might be shot on sight.

As he rounded the truck, the priest asked, "Would you come up for a moment?"

"Wanna talk business?" Lorelei hoped.

Joseph nodded.

"Hai has to come," she said. "He's under orders not to let me out of his sight."

"Does he know what you are?" Joseph asked.

Lorelei cautioned him with her smile. "No."

As she closed the RAV's door, she saw the glowing cherry of a cigar across the street. Someone stood in the darkened window of one of the tacky 1960s apartments. Red eyes burned above the cigar. While Lorelei watched, several other pairs of eyes appeared beside the first.

It was hard to turn her back without knowing whose fiends they were. Lorelei was grateful when Hai wrapped an arm around her waist and steered her up the stairs behind the priest. Billy and T.N. came up behind them.

Hai and the boys searched the apartment before they'd let Joseph and Lorelei inside. Lorelei would have conducted her own investigation, but these days she'd probably miss as much as the boys did. Hopefully, Heaven would leave the priest alone, now that she'd cut Ashleigh's deal, but Yasmina might fuck with the old man out of spite. The boys could do nothing about that. Lorelei simply hoped Asmodeus looked forward to the exorcism enough to protect the priest.

The boys settled into the cramped living room. A nubby brown sofa sagged in the dim light thrown by a cheap pole lamp. After this was over, Lorelei promised herself a better class of prey.

She would've liked to see Joey's bedroom. To all appearances, the priest hadn't matured beyond appetites of the flesh. She wondered what reading material he kept under the bed. That might give her a clue what to offer him.

She trailed him into the kitchenette and sat on the split plastic cushion of the only kitchen chair. Hai leaned just outside the doorframe, giving her a minimum of privacy to make her deal. She appreciated the boy's restraint.

Despite what she'd told Joseph, Lorelei couldn't afford to give him time to get complicated in his demands. Without the otherworldly sharpness of her senses, she'd have to fall back on sympathy to create the link she needed. "How did you start performing the black mass?"

He sighed. "When I left the Church..."

"You were desperate to know that everything you'd heard was not a lie," Lorelei guessed.

"I contacted several organizations until I found one that wanted to summon a demon."

"Who did they call?"

"Beelzebub."

Lorelei nodded. He'd been in charge of LA before her boss staged his coup d'état. "So you received confirmation that we exist."

"One or another of you has been after me ever since," he said.

"Another man might embrace his faith again," Lorelei answered.

"Faith in what?" Joseph snapped. "If God is dead, faith is a lie."

The blasphemy horrified Lorelei. Some devils used similar arguments on their prey, but Lorelei's seductions had been more straightforward. The existence of the Enemy was too close to philosophy—and philosophy was not for a devil who did her best thinking in bed.

"What destroyed your faith?"

"The Church. The bureaucracy."

Yasmina had made much of her reputation in the seduction of holy men. Anything that bitch had done, Lorelei avoided. Now, she wondered: if she'd seduced a bishop or two, would she have had the skills to accomplish what she intended with Aza?

Anger quivered in the priest's voice. "My parish was poor. The congregation was elderly. The neighborhood changed as those who could afford to moved away and immigrants took their places. I tried to perform missionary work in the community. I tried to reach out to the children. But they were like your boys here, seduced by sex and the glamour of easy money. I couldn't tempt them with what the Church offered. Rather than supporting my work, the diocese looked at the bottom line."

"They closed your church?"

"I prayed that my faith would be a beacon to illuminate God's works on earth. I begged for a miracle. Instead, someone set the church on fire one night."

Lorelei remembered her first glimpse of Aza's refuge, the church silhouetted by the dazzling sunlight. She remembered the ghosts of smoke across its façade.

"There had been no money to keep the parish functioning, so of course there was no money to repair the damage. The diocese salvaged what they could loot away and left the boarded-up building until such time as they could find a buyer for the lot." Joseph sighed. "This city has a very pragmatic cardinal."

Lorelei laughed. "He's working for us, you know."

She saw a flicker of belief in Joseph's eyes and her heart sank. Was his faith shaken enough to believe so blatant a lie? That she could taunt him so easily gave her no pleasure.

Still, business was business and they had better make a deal tonight.

She needed him in her corner, or else he might really fuck her up when the time came. "What will be your reward for helping me?" she asked the priest. "Have you decided?"

"I think so."

Joseph took a bottle of Old Times from the scarred wood-veneer cabinet. He poured himself a tall glass of whiskey, but didn't offer one to Lorelei.

If she'd been herself, she would have known what he wanted. She would have been able to use the lure as a bartering point. Now, she was forced to wait. He stared down into his glass. The pause stretched on long enough that Lorelei was tempted to ask for a drink. Finally, Joseph said, "You've seen angels."

He'd forgotten that he had, too. Good. Cautiously, she said, "Yes."

Joseph continued. "Are they beautiful?"

He'd asked Ashleigh that question already. "The angel that Ashleigh told you was beautiful was the one who possessed me with her," Lorelei hedged. "She's hardly impartial."

"I'm not asking her. I'm asking you."

"Why do you want to know?"

"I want to see an angel," Joseph blurted. "In its glory. With wings and a halo."

A shudder coursed through Lorelei. The coincidence with the arrangement she'd already made was uncanny. She took a deep breath. "You don't know what you're asking, Joe. Can you imagine what an angel would do to a fallen priest?"

"No."

"There are agonies that never consume. Perhaps they'd visit you with a plague of weeping sores, like they did Job. Or they might crystallize you to salt one molecule at a time, like they did to Lot's wife…"

"Hell is waiting for me anyway," Joseph said. "Isn't it? There'll be agony enough for me there."

"The certainty of Hell for their victims never impeded the Inquisition," Lorelei answered.

Joseph's hand trembled as he raised the whiskey to his lips. "If I set this as a condition of your exorcism, you will be beholden to me until you fulfill it."

"Yes," Lorelei admitted.

Why don't you tell…?

Lorelei spoke louder than the voice in her head. "What if I can't arrange it before tomorrow night?"

"Then you will serve me afterwards." The way he said it, she understood that she wouldn't enjoy serving him very much. He'd probably have her dishing slop in a soup kitchen.

Her voice quavered. It was only partially forced. "Would a fallen angel suffice?"

"No. I want evidence of the divine."

Lorelei shivered. "I don't know if I can help you, Father. There aren't any celestial angels at my beck and call."

"Even Azaziel?"

She winced at the name, even though she knew Joseph had heard it in Ashleigh's confession. "Especially him, Father. I just set his cell on fire."

"Is that where we were?"

"Yes."

She watched him puzzle over his incomplete memories, but then he downed the last of his drink and rapped the glass on the countertop. "Agree, or there will be no exorcism."

"Do you know what my prince will do if he discovers I arranged for you to see our enemy?"

Joseph's tight smile was worthy of any of Hell's advocates. "Why should I care, harlot?"

"Because, without an exorcism, Ashleigh Johnson continues her half-life in my flesh. She forfeits all hope of Heaven." Lorelei kept the smile off her face, but she had him. She saw it in his eyes. Lorelei congratulated herself. Allowing the girl to give her confession had been a stroke of genius. The old man felt responsible for Ashleigh now.

Lorelei reminded him, "I know you're not doing the exorcism for me, Father. You'll do it for Ashleigh. All the same, I will do what I can to fulfill your request. A deal is a deal."

He relaxed visibly.

"Generally, at this point, I would draw us up an agreement," Lorelei continued. "This is one I'd rather not have floating around in written form, you understand?"

"Wouldn't want this contract to fall into the wrong hands."

"Exactly. Could we just shake on it?"

Joseph took a chipped glass from the cupboard and poured them each a slug of whiskey. He tipped his glass against hers and they both drank. Lorelei shuddered at the taste: nothing worse than cheap whiskey.

Joseph asked, "Would you swear on a Bible?"

Lorelei felt goosebumps creep over her again. She reminded herself that having Ashleigh along provided her a measure of protection. "Do you have one?"

"Not any more. I'd have to borrow it from the neighbors."

She realized that he'd been teasing. Lorelei forced a laugh. "If you won't take my word, even knowing how grateful I am to you, would you accept Ashleigh's?"

Without waiting for his answer, she pushed the girl forward. *Watch what you say*, Lorelei cautioned. *The walls may have ears.*

The priest watched Ashleigh tug the neckline of the bathrobe together.

"Can I trust her in this?" he asked.

"She takes her promises very seriously."

"You warned me before that everything they give you is a trick. Where's the trick in arranging for me to see an angel?"

Careful, Lorelei reminded.

"Once they know what you want, they'll use it against you. I'd distrust any angel you see until you're sure he's Heavenly."

"Thank you for the warning."

Hai stepped into the kitchen before anything else could be said. "Let's go, Lorelei. I don't wanna leave the boys outside too long."

Lorelei swam back into control, shifting so that the hem of the robe slipped to reveal her thighs. "My business is done," she said.

Hai told the priest, "Two of the boys stay with you 'til tomorrow night."

Joseph sputtered, "Nothing was said about this before."

"I got orders, old man."

Joseph looked to Lorelei.

"I can't contradict my sister, Joey. Sorry. It's for your own protection."

He stared at her: broken handcuff on her wrist, bruises on her throat and chest, wrapped in a dressing gown. Lorelei let him look, trying to remain confident in her appearance.

"What sort of danger am I in?" he asked.

"Probably nothing. There were three fiends across the street when we pulled up. They're probably working for my boss…"

"Fiends?" Joseph echoed. Clearly he knew what that meant.

The doorbell preempted Lorelei's reassurance.

"You 'spectin' anyone?" Hai demanded.

"No. But it's not a complete surprise. The neighbors watch out for each other here. I'm sure they saw you come in."

Following Hai's lead, the boys checked their guns.

"That's not necessary." Joseph hurried over to the door. Raising his voice, he called, "Who's there?"

"Kyle."

"He's a neighbor," Joseph explained. He looked to Lorelei, begging, "Please. I *will* help you. I'll *be* careful. But I have to continue to live here."

The man outside called, "Is everything all right, Joseph?"

"Yes. Just a minute. I've got company." Dropping his voice, Joseph repeated, "Please, Lorelei."

"All right. Billy, look out and see if he's alone. The rest of you: stay alert, but hide the guns, okay?"

Billy peered out the peephole. "He's alone," he reported. "He looks like Chow Yun-Fat."

"That's Kyle."

Lorelei was impressed that the priest knew who Chow Yun-Fat was. Whoever was really at the door, he wasn't big enough to be a fiend. She watched Joseph reach for the locks and wondered if her life should be passing before her eyes.

A square-jawed Chinese man in a charcoal gray suit stood in the hallway.

"Sorry to have kept you waiting," Joseph said, extending his hand. "It's just…I have a houseful. Kids from the old parish," he extemporized. Lorelei liked the flavor of the lie.

When the man stepped into the room, the atmosphere changed. Tension drained out of the boys. Kyle made the rounds, shaking each boy's hand. They gave him their names as if seeking his approval.

Lorelei watched from halfway behind Hai. The man's eyes lit up when he reached for her. Hai stepped out of the way, leaving her no protection. Lorelei flashed a smile that left no doubt about her purpose in life, but dropped it as soon as he caught her hand.

He was an angel. One of the Fallen.

"Enchanted." Kyle clasped her hand hard enough that she didn't dare yank it away. For her ears only, he murmured, "Leave Joseph's protection to me, Little Sister."

"I need him," Lorelei whispered.

"So I understand. Your sister Floria and I have already reached an agreement regarding his participation. It's his soul that interests me."

"You're welcome to that," Lorelei assured.

"Just so we understand each other."

He raised her hand, lingering over her knuckles with his lips. She saw the ruby ring flash on his pinky. Asmodeus's glyph simmered inside the stone.

When he straightened, he touched his forefinger to her forehead, to the place where Aza kissed her. "Tell Azaziel that his brother Barakiel compliments his taste, would you?"

"If I see him," Lorelei lied, "I'll tell him."

She looped her arm through Hai's and said, "C'mon, Tiger. We shouldn't leave the boys outside too long."

"Everything's okay here?" Hai asked.

"Yeah."

The fallen angel turned back to the priest and the remaining boys. "Since there'll be four of us," Barakiel said, "let's play bridge."

"They were all just leaving," Joseph corrected.

Lorelei shook her head. "The boys *really* need a place to stay tonight, Father."

He couldn't lose face in front of his friend, so he gave in. Lorelei rose up on tiptoe to brush her lips across the rough stubble of his cheek. "Thank you, Joe."

Behind her, Billy asked, "What's bridge?"

"It's a card game. We'll play a couple of hands open, 'til you get the hang of it," the fallen angel promised.

Lorelei didn't like leaving the boys behind, but they weren't hers to worry about. If Floria had made a deal with Barakiel—payable in souls— it was one more debt Lorelei would be called on to make good.

After the door had closed behind them and Joseph re-fastened the locks, Ashleigh demanded, *How can you trust him?*

"What choice do I have?"

Hai halted in mid-step, then realized she was talking to herself, as he'd been warned. Lorelei shrugged, patted his arm, and said, "Sorry. Conference with the possessing ghost. Ignore us."

"Just don't go off in front of the boys, Lorelei. You'll weird them out."

I'm serious, Ashleigh interrupted. *I'm scared. Didn't you hear what Yasmina said about all the angels she fucked into falling? What if that creepy guy is one of hers?*

What can I do about it, Ashes? He's got a deal with Floria.

What kind of monster is he?

It's kind of a long story. Lorelei sighed. *When the War began in Heaven, a whole lot of angels—including some of the most powerful ones—followed Lucifer's banner. Most of them were mutilated as they were vanquished. No longer beautiful but with their powers intact, they shifted the War against the Angels to Earth. You people have always been the chips in the games they played.*

Barakiel and those like him—the Fallen—are angels who were cast out of Heaven after the battle moved to Earth. Sometimes, if they strike powerful bargains, they are elevated to demons. Usually, though, they work in a kind of middle ground, sometimes aiding one side, sometimes the other. They do things for their own reasons. Because of that, sometimes you can trust them when you can't trust anyone else.

Puzzled by Lorelei's silence, Hai adjusted the gun in his waistband and took her arm, hauling her down the nondescript hallway. Lorelei felt eyes peering out peepholes at them.

"What's this talk about angels?" Hai demanded.

"Eavesdropping?" Lorelei scolded.

"Gotta report to Floria," he reminded with a grimace.

Against Hai's, her word wasn't worth its weight in shit. And once Floria knew how she was paying the priest, the boss would know, and Lorelei's ass was back into the fire. She had to think quickly.

The thing Hai craved more than anything else was prestige. He adored Tuan because the gang leader had gotten him this far. If he thought something else would get him farther...

"I'm gonna try to summon an angel," she lied. "That's what the priest wants in trade for getting me exorcised."

"Are angels for real?"

Lorelei stopped him, so she could hold his gaze. "Yeah, Baby. Angels are real. Dangerous as fuck, but real. I know you have to report to Floria, but if you could keep that part out of it, I'd do anything."

She traced her hand up his fly, giving him some idea what that "anything" might include. "You know how Floria is: she doesn't mind using magic to do business, but she never looks beyond the next C-note. Summoning an angel: that's heavy."

"Can I help?" he asked eagerly.

"I hope so. Floria didn't tell you we had to come straight back, did she?"

His eyes narrowed. "Where do you want to go?"

"Someplace we can party."

"Just you and me?"

Lorelei gazed at him, making him the center of her universe. "I'm yours all night, Tiger."

Hai practically skipped down the stairs. When they reached the front door, Lorelei buzzed it as Hai pulled it open.

A hugely muscled figure stood in the shadows beyond the stoop. "Call me in, Lorelei," he rumbled, stepping forward into the light. She recognized the sharp-toothed fiend from the boss's limo the other night.

"Come in, Brother."

Hai gawked at the fiend, marveling at the ugly man's size.

The fiend crossed the threshold and shoved between her and Hai on his way toward the stairs.

"You here to keep an eye on the priest?" Lorelei called after him.

He nodded. Then, turning, he fixed her with beady eyes. In the infernal tongue, he said, "You stink like angels."

Lorelei gulped down the lump in her throat. Answering in Hellspeak, she said, "It's that friend of Joey's," and rubbed her hand on the robe.

The fiend's smile was mean. Then he resumed climbing the stairs.

Lorelei grabbed Hai and pulled him after her. The sooner they got on the road, the better. She had no doubt that Barakiel had seen Aza's burning kiss. The fiend was too low in level—she hoped—to see the evidence for himself. She needed to get Aza's scent off her right away, before any more of Hell's staff caught a whiff of her.

CHAPTER 17: PISS AND VINEGAR

Hai ordered Sammy to take one of the spare motorcycles and see the other boys safely home, then climbed behind the wheel of his RAV4. He gave Lorelei a look like he wanted to eat her right then and there. When he started the truck's engine, the music rushed up, full volume. Fine. She was relieved he didn't want to talk.

Lorelei sank into the passenger seat and closed her eyes. Aza's myrrh-like scent choked her in the enclosed space. Heaviness lodged in her chest where her heart should beat.

What did she want? It was a question Lorelei had never asked herself before. She'd always done what was required of her, more than what was expected of her, and taken pride in her accomplishments. Since she'd met Aza, she'd only taken down Steve the Stockbroker and poor Jenna. The last, she'd done grudgingly. She had to get back to work, ushering souls to their damnation. If she did not, what purpose did she serve?

Serving Creation was the last thing she wanted right now. It was hard not to long for the feel of Aza's sweet smooth hand cupping her cheek, or the sparkle of his green/gold eyes, or the wonderful flavor of his kisses. She brushed her fingertips across her lips, remembering his mouth on hers.

Of course, he'd been kissing Ashleigh then.

Molten tears flooded in under her closed lids. Lorelei forced her eyes open, staring hard at the road. Her eyes felt weighted and hot, more like stones than flesh.

Why had Aza done this to her? Was damning devils really the newest gambit in the Celestial War? Or had he done it for more personal reasons? If he'd wanted to fuck the girl, he could've done it at any time before Ashleigh died. He could've healed her, if he'd wanted to. Saved her life. But he hadn't: he needed her spirit to possess Lorelei, because it was Lorelei he wanted. Because he loved her as she was, but felt he had to change her, render her harmless, in order to justify his passion before his god?

Lorelei ground her teeth. How fucking dare he? Maybe she would have changed on her own, given time and enough attention. But his god had allowed her creation for the sole purpose of luring his mortal pawns into damnation. She had a purpose to serve, for which Aza tried to pollute her by instructing her on compassion, forgiveness, mercy, and love.

She had to bring him down. It was the only way she'd ever be sure that he'd quit doing his job and commit to her. The only way she could be certain she could continue doing the best job in Creation.

Lorelei ran one finger around inside the broken handcuff. Aza'd said she could remove the cuff when she left him, but the seduction wasn't ended by their separation. In fact, she wanted him more now than ever. How could she ever pry him away from his chaperones?

Hai turned the music down a notch. He nodded at her fingers, still inside the cuff. "Who was he?"

Lorelei shook her head. As she did, a tear escaped to roll down her face. She brushed it away angrily.

Hai smacked her hard with the back of his hand. "You're fucked up," he accused. "I never seen you like this before."

Lorelei found that to answer would splinter the fragile composure she still maintained. She wanted to fling open the truck's door, spread wide her wings, and flee into the night. But she couldn't. She had no wings now, trapped by Ashleigh in her mortal form. Trapped by the speed of Hai's driving. Trapped by Asmodeus's threats, and Yasmina's.

"What the hell did he do to you?" Hai insisted. There was a nakedly possessive anger in his voice.

Without Ashleigh and the angel, Lorelei would never have felt this giddy, desperate yearning—not just for Aza's body, but for his company as well. She could not name this feeling desire or arousal or any sensation she had known in her unsullied succubus days. This complex, agonizing sensation might possibly be love.

She hated the feeling. She would have renounced it, but she had no idea how to do so.

She was broken. Aza had broken her. And he hadn't spared any thought for what that would mean for her life, once he washed his hands of her. Grief overwhelmed her and she shattered, sobbing. She wrapped her arms around her waist and rocked, keening for the loss of her innocence.

Hai stared straight ahead, so unbelievably pissed that his fingers went white on the steering wheel. What the fuck was wrong with her? The Lorelei he remembered had been one nonstop party, not this sniffling, wailing bitch. This was too close to why he'd left home, unable to deal with his mother's bawling. Yeah, life sucked. Yeah, bills were due and there wasn't any money coming in after her hours got cut at Vons. Yeah, the cops had been by looking for him again, but, shit… He was glad to be Tuan's soldier, because with the boys he didn't have to deal with any fucking drama. And here he was, babysitting some whore having a breakdown over a trick. He'd throw her out of his truck to find her own way home, except that Floria would take it out of his hide later.

Goddammit. Lorelei had better pull her shit together enough to give him the fuck she'd promised.

Ashleigh took over when Lorelei seemed unable to calm herself down. She'd watched Deion's rages build too many times. Clearly Hai was so insulted that he was going to have to prove his masculinity by beating some sense into the succubus before long. Lorelei might not care if a thrashing was coming her way, but Ashleigh would just as soon get off the planet without enduring another one.

She stripped off Tuan's robe and used it to wipe her face. "You have anything to drink?" she asked as she let the robe flutter out the window.

Hai shot her a glance, aware that something had changed but not sure what. "Bottle of Cuervo. Under the seat."

Ashleigh fished it out, downed a heavy slug. "We going back to your place?"

"Got any better ideas?"

"Anywhere that's not Floria's is good by me."

He laughed at that.

Thanks, Ashleigh.

The girl faded back and let Lorelei regain control. "Let's go up in the hills," she suggested. "I know a turnout on Mulholland with a great view."

She scooted across the seat to snuggle against his shoulder, casually dropping one hand in his lap. "Just keep your eyes on the road, Tiger. I'm gonna make it all worth your while."

Okay, Lorelei thought, caressing the button fly of Hai's jeans, *here's our cover story. I seduced Joey and did him on the futon. The robe's sash got tangled around my throat. You don't know how it happened. I'd be dead if Hai hadn't cut me down. Then I set the place on fire and we bailed.*

Why do we need a cover story? the girl asked.

Because Floria's been charged by the boss to look after me. She's known me long enough to know she can't trust me. She'll think that you'll spill easily, since you're mortal.

Ashleigh quivered at the thought of being interrogated—if not outright tortured—by Floria.

Relax, Lorelei instructed. *You'll be out of me tomorrow, one way or another. But, basically, there was no guarantee that Asmodeus wouldn't destroy you out of spite afterward. I asked Aza to make sure that doesn't happen. I set this up for you, Ashes. It's the first time I've tried to get someone off the hook ever. You gonna help me cover my ass?* Lorelei didn't wait for an answer. *Think about the cover story. Imagine it. Embellish it. Live it. Because it really happened—got it?—or Floria will know.*

Ashleigh asked, *Won't Aza be in danger when he comes for me?*

Bitch, bitch, bitch. Lorelei sighed. *I can't protect him. I've done a shitty job of protecting us. And anyway, he's still my would-be boyfriend, 'cause you're dead.*

Ashleigh changed the subject. *What are we doing here now?*

Aza held me in his arms. The smell of what he is lingers on my skin. I might've been able to explain it away if he hadn't kissed you. I need Hai to help me rub Aza's kiss off.

Without much hope, Ashleigh asked, *Can't you just wash?*

Remember how Floria smelled the archangel's touch in my hair, even after we'd rolled around with Tuan? This will be a lot more fun.

For you.

Yeah. Lorelei grinned. *About time I had some fun.*

Lorelei crawled into the back seat. It was less spacious than she might have liked, but there was room to work. "How do you want me, Tiger?"

"Hands and knees. I don't want you biting me like you did Tuan."

As she complied, Ashleigh whimpered. *Relax*, Lorelei told her. *He's just a kid. It'll be over so quick, you won't believe it.* She heard the faint rip of a condom foil and wiggled in anticipation.

She let Hai use her. If she'd been in her true form, she would've savored the conversion of his anger into lust. If she'd merely been garbed in mortal form, she would've fed his fury, not fearing the consequences. Now, trapped by Ashleigh, Lorelei was reduced to pleasures of the flesh. Her life as a succubus had prepared her well enough for those.

His breath rang raggedly in her ear. Lorelei licked the length of his forearm, drawing his attention up from his loins. "What's your hurry, Tiger?" she whispered in Vietnamese.

"You *are* crazy, you know?" He thrust into her a few more strokes. "I'm tryin' to rape you here."

She twisted her head sideways and stopped his mouth with a kiss. He forgot about moving his hips.

When she let him breathe again, he rested his cheek against her shoulder and gazed at her with an eighteen-year-old's infatuation. "Why'd you stop comin' to see me?"

"The boss sent me off on business."

That wasn't exactly true. Lorelei had business to handle, sure, but the schedule had been more or less up to her. She'd done what she'd needed to ensure Hai's allegiance to Floria, then left without looking back. Now she wondered if she might've swung an arrangement like Floria had, contracted herself a home and a willing servant. Probably not without some sort of subservience to Floria, she realized. Ick.

Hai, she knew, would be damned with or without her attention. For the time being, he was serving his purpose in getting Aza's smell off of her. She had to get the boy off and get back to Floria's before she was missed. She rocked her hips in a rhythm that elicited a groaning orgasm from him. *That* made her come, too.

Hai collapsed onto her. Lorelei twisted sideways enough that she could guide his lips to kiss her forehead.

"Don't rest too long, Tiger," Lorelei purred. "I've got a few more tricks I'd like to show you."

When the headlights hit the RAV, Hai froze. Lorelei humped him a little longer, but fear finished him before she could. Hellfire. Lorelei hoped it was just the neighborhood patrol, not more minions of Yasmina's.

Floria's laugh rang through the night. She stepped out of the car as Tuan shut off the BMW's engine. "Sorry to interrupt your party."

"Wish you'd given me a few more minutes," Lorelei answered. She climbed unsteadily out of the truck, knees quivering with exertion. Yet another unpleasant new sensation.

"Where's the priest?" Floria demanded.

"We took him home," Hai answered. "Billy and T.N. are watching the place. Like you said."

Floria glanced back at Tuan. He pulled out his cell phone and started dialing.

Floria grabbed Lorelei's shoulder and turned her to face the headlights. "What happened to your neck?"

"Is it bad?" Lorelei raised her hand to the bruise. "I'm gonna be one big black-and-blue mark if I don't get unpossessed pretty damn soon."

"What happened?" Floria repeated.

"Something went wrong at the angel's place. I was working the priest and got tangled up in Tuan's robe.... I'd be dead, if it hadn't been for Hai."

Floria turned to him. "Wha'd you do?"

He looked at her blankly.

"Don't you remember?" Floria pressed.

Lorelei shivered. It was only half-faked. "You cut Tuan's sash from my neck with a knife. You don't remember?"

He shook his head. "All I remember is you setting the place on fire."

"We got the hell out," Lorelei agreed.

"You don't remember anything before that?" Floria asked again.

"Sorry, Floria." Fear flashed through Hai's eyes. "I really don't."

Lorelei imagined the scene as it might have been and shivered again. "The whole thing was really creepy," she said. "We should've just gotten my stuff and split, but I wanted to fuck the place up so the angel couldn't use it again."

"I'm just glad you're okay," Floria lied.

"Better now, thanks to Hai." Lorelei stretched. "Actually," she confided to Floria, "you won't believe it, but I'm kind of worn out. This mortal body is shit for stamina. I'm ready for bed."

"Sucks for you. I want to talk to Hai, then we can all go home."

"I was hoping maybe he would put me to bed."

Floria bitched, "You want to get off, get your own boys. This was a school night and he had work to do. You cost me a bundle in sales."

"Relax, Sister," Lorelei teased. "Not everything is about business."

Floria's hand snapped out. Without thinking, Lorelei caught her wrist. "Don't hit me in front of the boys."

Floria twitched her hand free. "They're not yours."

"Of course not." Lorelei felt sweat creep down the back of her neck. She should've taken the slap. Now things would be worse. More contritely, she said, "I thought I was giving you and Tuan a little private time."

"How very sweet of you." Floria lit a cigarette, sucked on it, and ate the smoke. Lorelei kept her amusement off her face. Whatever else Floria could do, she didn't think fast on her feet. Finally, she reached a decision. "You're comin' back with us. Fuck-toy can tag along, if he's not used up."

Hai's eyes flashed, stung, just as Floria wanted him to be.

All she had to do, Lorelei instructed herself, was keep her head down until the exorcism. Then she'd have her old life back. Maybe she could convince the boss to reassign her to another city. Everything would be fine if she kept from pissing Floria off until then. It would be easier if Floria wasn't determined to be such a cunt. Had she always been this bad?

"Get in the fucking car already."

Her pumps—the ostensible excuse for this whole excursion—were still in the RAV4. She hoped Hai would remember to bring them up for her.

Tuan opened the BMW's door for her. Lorelei crawled into the car's back seat and curled onto her side. Tuan closed the door after her.

Drowsily, Lorelei opened her eyes in the back of the car. Tuan had thrown a Tijuana blanket over her. She snuggled into it.

"What happened to her neck?" Tuan asked.

"No one remembers, except Lorelei, and she's lying about it." Floria paused to drag on her cigarette. "Looks to me like she's got a collar to match that cuff she wears."

"You think she's working for the angel who took her prisoner?" Tuan asked skeptically.

"Yeah, right. I know how badly he fucked her up. Still, she's up to something, that's for damn sure." Floria twisted to look around the headrest. "What are you up to, Sister?"

Lorelei grinned sleepily. "I'm always up to something."

"What is it this time?"

"Yasmina…"

"That bitch," Floria interjected.

Lorelei smiled. "Yasmina, that bitch, told me to kill Aza or arrange for his brethren to do it. But I still think it would be much more enjoyable to drag him in chains through the streets of Pandemonium."

"You really think he'll fall?" Anxiety creased Floria's brow. How far ahead of the game would that catapult Lorelei?

Lorelei raised her arm and made the handcuff flash in the headlights behind them. "I may not understand what guilt is, but I know how to use it."

"Did he mark your throat too?"

"Indirectly," Lorelei said. "I thought the priest had nullified the abjuration, but I guess not."

"Are you suggesting that's what wiped the boys' memories too?" Floria asked, not believing it for a moment.

Lorelei yawned, still tasting condom. "It won't matter after tomorrow night," she promised.

CHAPTER 18: DEFINING THE TERMS

Lorelei woke with Hai wound around her body, clutching her even in his sleep. Last night they'd made a nest of blankets on the living room floor and collapsed into sleep without much more than a goodnight kiss. Now she raised her cuffed hand to pet the velvet stubble of his hair. Hai's blunt features weren't pretty like Tuan's—his nose was wide and flat, his eyes set too deep beneath his brow. Only his generous mouth was beautiful. Lorelei traced her fingers across his lips, too gently to wake him.

The tenderness she felt surprised her. He was a greedy child, eager for money and status, quick to take offense. Floria had insulted him last night, but he was so enchanted by Lorelei that he'd come to her bed anyway.

Perhaps he'd been trying to assert ownership of her. She'd know if she were herself, but then, of course, she wouldn't care. She knew Hai was damned for lust and damned for greed. She had a burst of desire to spare him an eternity bathed in filth, but that would mean first depriving him of the shiny RAV4, the new clothes, the drugs and money and excitement of his chosen lifestyle. She had no doubt that Hai would die before willingly giving any of it up.

Tuan appeared in the hallway. His dark eyes met Lorelei's across Hai's bare shoulders. She had the impression Tuan understood her second thoughts, but he ruined it by bitching, "We got work to do."

Hai mumbled something.

Lorelei nipped his ear. The boy responded with a gratifying ardor.

"Clock is tickin'," Tuan said, subconsciously mimicking Floria.

"Can we have a minute?" Hai huffed over his shoulder.

Lorelei grinned at Tuan. "Is Floria out already?"

"Yes," Tuan sighed. "Make it quick." He went back toward his room.

"Clock is tickin'," Lorelei teased.

Hai crawled over to paw through his leather jacket after another condom.

To her amusement, Hai's passion was more mental than physical. Lorelei played with it as best she could, but they were both sore. She couldn't get used to being raw the morning after sex. It was going to make the exorcism tonight that much more arduous.

Hai finished before Lorelei did, but she let him go with a kiss he would feel for the rest of the day.

While he caught a shower, Lorelei went to the bedroom to see about getting dressed. Tuan was riffling dispiritedly through a stack of bills.

"When's Floria gonna be back?" Lorelei asked.

Tuan flung his checkbook down on the bed. "I don't know where she is. I don't know what she's doing. I don't know when she'll be back."

Lorelei held up her hands. "Sorry."

The shower shut off.

"If Floria didn't leave me a list of stuff to do," Lorelei said carefully, "can I borrow your phone? I'd like to set something up with the priest."

Not placated, Tuan handed her the iPhone out of his jeans pocket. "Hit redial," he said. "I just checked with the boys there."

Lorelei balanced the little phone in her hand, puzzling out which button to press.

Someone on the other end drawled, "Yeah?"

"This is Lorelei," she answered. "Can I talk to Joey?"

"Minute."

Before that long had passed, Joseph asked, "Hello?"

"Hi, Joe. I've been thinking about our agreement. Got time to discuss it with me before tonight?"

"I wanted to go up to the old parish today," he said. "I told that boy Tuan I didn't need his gang following me around."

"That's still between you and my sister, Joey. Tuan can't rescind her orders, either." She understood a little of Tuan's mood: the priest had serious petulance in his voice. "Look, Joe, we need to speak in person. I want to give you an update on my progress."

"You've made progress?"

Ah, good. That tone was more hopeful. "Yes," Lorelei hissed. "Can you meet me at Tuan's today?"

"I'll be there."

"Great." She had a stroke of inspiration and added, "If you're in the mood to discuss the existence of the divine, ask your pal Kyle."

"I'm an idiot." Fury constricted the priest's voice as he recognized what had been in front of him all along. "He's fallen, of course."

"I'm breaking his confidence here, Joey. I'd appreciate it if you keep my name out of your conversation."

"I will."

"We'll discuss the other matter when we're together, okay?"

"Thank you, Lorelei."

After she hung up, Tuan said, "You just gonna hang out with the priest all afternoon?"

Lorelei had forgotten he was still in the room. She shrugged as she returned the phone. "A girl needs her rest before her big night. Are you coming?"

He sighed. "Don't see how I can miss it."

Hai appeared in the doorway, flushed from his shower. He wore last night's rumpled clothing. His eyes lit up when they found Lorelei, still nude.

Tuan shook his head, ever the big brother. "You wanna go by your place and change?"

"S'pose I better." Hai grabbed Lorelei into his arms, kissing her hard as he sneaked in one last grope. Then he trailed Tuan out the door.

After they were gone, Lorelei wandered around the penthouse, not sure what to do with herself.

Take a shower, Ashleigh suggested. *When was the last time you had one?*

"Wanna hot tub?" Lorelei asked. "We deserve it." She stepped through the door-wall onto the roof and pulled the cover off the Jacuzzi. She hoped the water would heat up quickly.

She turned slowly, surveying the brownish haze over the valley. She'd worked in LA for almost fifty years, much of that with Floria at her side. Funny how quickly that friendship crashed and burned. She wasn't as sorry as she expected.

Lorelei combed her fingers through her tangled hair. The bruise on her chest ached. Good thing she'd be out of this form soon.

Why don't you see if there's anything to eat? Ashleigh suggested. *I can't remember if we've eaten anything since we were out with that fiend.*

"And you whined about *that* meal," Lorelei reminded. Still, she went back into the apartment. Not surprisingly, the cupboards were bare. Not even a box of dried pasta lingered on the shelves.

Do a line, prompted a voice in her head. *It'll take the edge off.*

Worst of all, Lorelei realized the thought was her own. She and Ashleigh had been together much too long.

Instead, she opened the refrigerator. Someone had actually remembered to fill the ice tray for a change and there was a pitcher half-full of sangria. Lorelei swirled it, watching blood cling to the glass. Yum, the real stuff. She wondered whom Floria had been entertaining.

Lorelei poured herself a glass and carried it out onto the roof. She slipped down into the hot tub, trying to simply luxuriate in the hot water.

If she'd been herself, she would know if anyone from the surrounding buildings was getting off on her girlie show. Without that knowledge, she felt totally alone. The realization solidified that soon she would be rid of Ashleigh.

Will you miss me? Ashleigh wondered.

Lorelei admitted, "I think I will."

Who will you have to talk to?

"Prey," Lorelei answered. That didn't require any thought. Would she ever be able to talk to Floria again?

You have to get out of this life, Ashleigh told her.

"Define 'getting out'?" Lorelei asked. "Devils will always come after me."

Except to Heaven.

"I don't expect to be invited there."

She sank down until the water rose up to her chin. It was too hot to be comfortable, but she wasn't ready to admit that. She wanted something to dispel the cold core where her heart was.

"If Aza won't be with me," Lorelei said softly, "then all this suffering is wasted."

There must be some way for you to be together, Ashleigh insisted.

Lorelei had known from the first how much Ashleigh adored their angel. She felt an awful twist inside her and knew what it cost the girl to step aside, to hope that the others would continue their relationship once she was gone.

If—in the face of death—they were finally going to talk honestly, Lorelei hoped she could get some answers. "You've known him longer than I have," she began cautiously. "Did he give you any indication why he picked me?"

Ashleigh measured Lorelei's sincerity and answered it with her own: *Because he loves you.*

Lorelei answered hopelessly, "I don't know what that means."

It means that he saw you, that he watched you—I don't know how long—and that he liked you. That he wants to be with you.

"Be with me, how?"

You should ask him.

"I'm afraid to. How can we possibly be together?"

Ashleigh didn't have an answer for that. Maybe it was too painful for her to guess. Instead, she changed the subject. *Have you ever been in love before?*

A shiver ran through them both. "I'm not in love," Lorelei protested.

Yes, you are, Ashleigh argued. *I know how it feels. I felt it last night when we were in the truck with Hai. You've been in love with that angel since I've been with you.*

"Then how do I make it stop?" Lorelei asked softly. "It's crazy. We can't be together, unless he falls. And for all my bullshit to Floria last night, that's the last thing in the world I want. They'd never let us be together. They'd use him against me. I want him to safe and happy and far, far away from Hell's grasp."

That's what love is, Ashleigh assured, *putting the other person's well-being above your own. Doing anything, giving up anything, to make them happy. And you don't make it stop. All you can do is wait until it stops hurting so much.*

"One more fucked-up gift from the Enemy," Lorelei bitched.

"Talking to Ashleigh?" Father Joseph asked.

Lorelei sloshed around in the tub. Joseph stood behind her with the sliding door in his hand. "I didn't know you were there," Lorelei said.

He didn't apologize.

Lorelei reached for her sangria and gulped it, trying to get a grip. If Floria had crept up—or Asmodeus overheard her—her souls would be sliding down someone's gullet right about now.

She licked blood from her lips and asked, "Want to join us?"

Joseph came over to sit on the chaise longue beside the hot tub. He realized she was naked under the water and stared down at his interwoven fingers. "What have you learned about being mortal?"

Lorelei fished an ice cube out of her glass and ran it across the back of her neck. "It fuckin' sucks. I could've told you that last week."

"Any insights you're gonna take back into your diabolical existence?"

"Joey, what do you want me to tell you? That I'm gonna cut people slack? I'm not gonna cut anyone any slack. Fuck you all." She sucked down the last of the sangria, purposefully letting some of it trickle from the corner of her mouth and roll down her throat into the hot water. She saw that he recognized it for what it was. "I didn't ask to be possessed. With Hell's help, we're going to correct that. You are going to do the exorcism flawlessly."

The priest smiled grimly. "I'm glad you have such confidence in me."

"Confidence has nothing to do with it, Joey. If you chase me out of my flesh and leave that little girl in charge, you'll never see your heart's desire. No angels will come to rescue *my* tarnished soul."

Fury inserted steel into his spine and she caught another glimpse of the man he'd once been. "What was it you called me here to tell me?" he snapped.

"Let's not talk here." She stood, letting water sheet down her body. He turned his head, but she knew he'd seen her. She padded into the apartment, unsurprised to see Billy and T.N. cutting lines on the coffee table. Billy smirked at her like he expected to get lucky for sitting there.

"Hi, boys," Lorelei purred. "Do you have wheels?"

"Hai left us his truck," Billy answered.

"Good boy. I'd like to go up to the observatory. Give me a minute to get dressed and we'll get out of here." She wished a plan would come to her.

Under the level of the music blaring from the front seat, Joseph asked, "I know you've seen angels." He snared her with his gaze. "Have you seen God?"

"No." Cold spilled over inside Lorelei and she shuddered from head to foot. "I don't ever plan to."

"Why?"

"Because…whatever else happens to me, Joey, even if Hell rejects me, I was born a succubus. I don't want to meet the Enemy of everything I hold dear."

"But you know He exists."

Even though it wasn't spoken as a question, Lorelei heard Joseph's need for confirmation. Before she could formulate a response, Joseph said abruptly, "The world, the way it is now, angels seduced by devils," he groaned. "Why does a just god allow that?"

"If Ashleigh gave you the impression that I seduced Azaziel, she was mistaken. I tried to seduce him, Father. I failed. Instead, he put her soul into me against my will and made love to her. I could only watch. He says he was trying to make me understand about love, by showing me an example of what love is, but what I experienced was closer to rape."

"But you can feel Ashleigh's love for him, can't you? You understand how it feels now."

Lorelei stared at him, unable to answer, even in her thoughts. Was this the trap Asmodeus had set for her?

The priest saw something in her face that led him to ask, "Now that you've felt love, can you come to love him?"

If Joseph knew that a devil could love, would he see that as the divine evidence he required? Lorelei took a deep breath, wondering how perfectly she could lie.

Ashleigh had a better idea. *Tell him about your soul*, she said.

Not a bad plan. Lorelei just might see a way out of this. She turned away from the old man and stared out the window, trying to organize her argument.

The boys made no pretense of hiding the joint Billy'd found tucked up on the driver's side visor. As they puffed it, Lorelei took Joseph's hand.

She led him around the observatory onto the balcony cantilevered out over the cliff. She never tired of seeing the city stretched out at her feet.

"Did you have a chance to speak with Kyle?" Lorelei asked.

"Barakiel, you mean?" Joseph snapped. "He asked which of you outed him."

"What'd you say?"

"I kept your secret. I told him I watched him play cards with the boys last night and guessed." The old man grimaced. "I don't know why it wasn't obvious to me before."

"Not all of us are as easy to spot as I am."

"You're not as obvious as you might be," Joseph said. "This week has been hard on you, hasn't it?"

Lorelei laughed ruefully. "Do I look that awful?"

"I don't think it's possible for you to look awful," he said, more honestly than he meant to. "You just look... I don't know. More human."

"Great." Lorelei walked a little farther along the balcony, then leaned back against the railing, posing to show off her legs beneath Floria's little black dress. "That's one of the things I wanted to talk to you about."

"What's that?" Joseph stopped beside her, staring out at the city arrayed below them. He clasped his worn hands together unconsciously.

Lorelei faced the view as well. "I'm more human than I would like to be."

"Because of Ashleigh."

"Because of Aza."

The priest shot her a startled glance. "Because of what happened between the two of you?"

"It all went wrong from the start." Lorelei sighed. "There was something between us, I could feel it. But he wouldn't touch me. And when we kissed... Father, were you ever in love?"

"No," Joseph lied. Before she could follow that up, he repeated, "*Are you in love with the angel?*"

Lorelei glared at the city below. She wondered how much of the conversation he'd overheard while she was in the hot tub. It was grueling to reveal herself without certainty of the outcome. Finally, she hedged, "Ashleigh thinks so."

"Can your kind love?"

Lorelei smiled at that. How had the priest worked so long in Hell's employ while loathing them so much? "I think the worst of it is: I'm not my kind any more."

His gaze snapped around to her. "What do you mean?"

He had to know, she'd decided. When he cast out Ashleigh's spirit, he had to be able to differentiate between their two essences. "I have a soul," Lorelei whispered. "I think it was an accident. But I'm completely changed now. I'm...I'm not sure I can do my job any more." She couldn't look at the priest as she confessed. "Asmodeus has threatened to devour my soul himself before he lets the enemy have it. And I don't know what Aza's initial plan was for us, but he put me out as soon as the other angels discovered us. I don't think he can protect me."

"You have a soul?" Joseph echoed. "How is that possible?"

"I don't know." She turned to him, clasped his hands in hers. "Look, Joseph, this is important. Terribly important. You know that only beings created by divine inspiration have souls, right? Do you still believe that?"

"I...I hadn't thought about it in a long time."

"Devils are produced without souls: succubi, fiends, tempters, all of us. Every devil fashioned in Hell is soulless. Just as all angels contain the divine essence. That means the Fallen still have a spark of divinity, and so do the demons. They're not divine anymore, but the Creator made them in the beginning. No matter what trouble they cause, that divinity still burns inside them. But I existed without a soul until Aza got hold of me. And now my soul is damned because of all the things I've done in the past. I want you to destroy it, Joseph. I don't know how, but when you cast Ashleigh out of me, my soul will undoubtedly come, too. I want you to annihilate it before Asmodeus or anyone else can."

"I can't kill you, Lorelei. I may not accept all the doctrine any more, but I still cling to 'Thou Shalt Not Kill.'"

"You won't be killing me," Lorelei argued softly. "I existed before my flesh was inhabited by the souls. I will continue to exist after the souls are gone."

"You're guessing," Joseph sputtered. "You can't possibly know that."

"No one knows. I don't think there's ever been a creature like me before: a succubus with a soul. But you know that as long as Hell owns me, I will be forced to tempt mortals into damnation. If I ever waver, one of my fellows will arrange for me to walk out in front of a car or slip in the tub or choke on a chicken bone and my soul will have centuries of sin to atone for. Please, Joey, please. You can save me from torment, but only *if* you choose to."

He stared at her. If he accepted that the succubus had a soul, he had the evidence of divine intervention in the world he'd asked her to provide. He struggled with it. In the end, it was easier for him to decide that she was lying than to make the leap of faith.

He pulled his hands out of hers and took a step backward. His voice was cold. "You're good."

Blinded by tears, Lorelei watched him stride away. She had to go after him; he was much too important. But how could she dig herself out of this one?

A female voice interrupted her thoughts. "Are you ready to give the girl up?" The voice shimmered on the air.

Lorelei stared around in panic until she caught sight of an angel far away on the path winding below the observatory. With her mortal eyes, Lorelei could barely pick the figure out of the haze. Still, there was a luminance about her, an odd hard flicker that hurt Lorelei's eyes like someone flashing a mirror. The halo's owner was unmistakable.

If she couldn't cough Ashleigh up, the blond bitch clearly had no qualms about killing Lorelei for sullying her brother. In that angel's eyes, Lorelei's murder would solve everything: Ashleigh would be freed, Lorelei sent to her just damnation, and Aza would survive, unfallen, to carry the guilt of daring to love a devil.

"No," Lorelei moaned so low in her throat that none of the tourists nearby noticed. "No, no, no, no, please."

Nowhere to run. No weapons. No chance. Aza was nowhere near to protect her this time.

"Maybe I'll do instead?" another female offered.

Lorelei turned so fast that she lost her balance. The second angel's hand closed on Lorelei's shoulder before the succubus' mortal eyes registered the movement. Having people around was clearly no hindrance to these creatures, Lorelei realized. The laws of nature did not apply to them.

"She'll damn you if you run," the new angel said evenly, like she'd been asked her opinion about a dress.

Despite her parched tongue, Lorelei managed, "How do I avoid having you damn me?"

"I'm not here to damn you," the brunette said. "I'm your ride home." She gestured back toward the parking lot.

Lorelei recognized this angel as another of the three who'd come across the playground at her. Cloaked now in mortal seeming, the angel's curly brown hair was held back with a blue scarf shot through with silver. She looked like she should be walking barefoot at Venice Beach. Wholesome, Lorelei pegged it.

"Thank you." The angel smiled. "You can call me Barb. I'm a friend of Aza's. Shall we go?"

"To see him?" Lorelei hoped.

"I thought you had plans for later tonight," Barb answered, maneuvering herself between Lorelei and the blond angel.

"If I live that long," Lorelei said.

"I thought long life wasn't on your list of priorities any more."

"I'm tired," Lorelei admitted. "I'm tired of being so fragile, so scared. I liked it better when I didn't know any better."

"Everyone always does."

There was a Veteran's cab waiting at the curb beyond the art deco statue of the astronomers.

Beyond it, Thodos charged across the parking lot, sweeping tourists aside with his pitchfork. Wailing rose up behind him but he ignored it, too focused on his mission to enjoy the anguish caused by his passing.

"I have to go," Lorelei said hurriedly.

"He can't protect you from Muriel," the angel warned.

"But you can." Lorelei turned toward her and forced a smile. "I thank you for Aza's sake."

Barb smiled back. "For Aza's sake, you're welcome."

Lorelei sprinted toward the fiend, not even glancing over her shoulder to see how the angels would work it out. Thodos greeted her with a fist to her temple. Even as she blacked out, he flung her over his shoulder and ran back the way he'd come.

CHAPTER 19: BURNING BRIDGES

Through the ringing in her head, Lorelei let herself indulge in a good dream, the first she'd ever had.

Aza was asleep when Lorelei crawled into bed beside him. She leaned close enough to breathe gently into his ear, "Just a dream, Lover."

A slight smile curved his lips. She watched to see if he'd wake, but his eyelids didn't even quiver.

Moving as fluidly as possible, Lorelei slipped the sash from her robe and tied a slipknot at each end. There was much less fabric to work with after the fiasco in his lair, but that made the job easier.

She caught his right wrist and pulled the knot tight as she threw her weight down on his left arm. Aza woke up, automatically tensing to fight. Lorelei wrapped the sash twice around the railing at the head of the bed and snagged his left wrist. His first instinct—to ball his fist and strike at her—tightened the knot before she could do it herself.

"This will never hold me," he promised.

She flung the coverlet off of him and licked her lips. "It's not meant to, Angel," she said, sliding her body down the length of his. She grabbed his sex in her left hand and hung on as he thrashed, ducking her head down to place a kiss on the shaft. Aza froze, waiting for the bite sure to follow. Instead, Lorelei opened her mouth and swallowed him. Aza made a noise something between a groan and a sigh that melted Lorelei's insides.

A new idea occurred to her and—without removing her mouth from him—she crawled up onto all fours. She swung her left knee over his shoulder and knelt above his chest, shifting her hips back until she was inches from his face. He could choose not to look. In fact, she hoped he'd be horrified when confronted with the reality of her being—but he wouldn't be able to ignore the scent of how aroused she'd gotten, performing this simple act on him.

Lorelei took up a rhythm, using her other hand as an extension of her mouth.

She jumped when he touched her, light as a feather. Lorelei stared over her shoulder, to meet a grin fierce as any devil's. His hands were still tied, at least for the moment. She adjusted her weight to crawl back a little more, so he wouldn't have to strain his neck, and Aza obliged her with another lick that drew a shuddering moan from her. It made him laugh.

She applied her attention to his sex with new determination. He mirrored her, dragging her perilously close to the brink of orgasm and drawing back, teasing her with a skill that reminded her of Asmodeus's intention to add Aza to his staff.

Lorelei wriggled around to face Aza, licking her own wetness from his lips, tasting herself and angel too. She straddled him and rubbed the source of that wetness down his length. His eyes rolled so sweetly closed that love swelled in her chest.

"Say you want me," Lorelei prompted.

His eyes flashed open. Aza gave her a hard glare.

"Or don't," she allowed. "Kiss me and I'll go."

She rocked her hips down against his, pulling away as soon as she felt him thrust, so that he realized he had followed her.

"You know that I do," he admitted, sinking back onto the bed.

"Do what?" she asked, rewarding him with another slow glide against his hardness.

He clenched his teeth, unwilling to say.

"I want you, Azaziel," she purred. "I want to feel you inside me. I want you to make me come. I want to fuck you so hard that you'd break Heaven's chains just to cling to me."

As much as the words aroused her, she could feel the tension gathering in him. She changed her angle just a fraction and slid down around him, then held still. That caught him off guard. He didn't relax completely, but he seemed more inclined to wait and see, rather than attack. She kissed him with the softest brush of her lips. No louder than a breath, she whispered, "I love you, Azaziel. Like I've never loved anyone."

"Love?" he echoed hoarsely.

"Love," she repeated, sealing the word with another kiss.

His hips shifted beneath her. Lorelei followed his motion slowly, prolonging the exquisite sensation.

"Devils don't love," Aza told her.

"And angels don't lust," she answered. "So what's become of us?"

His answer was to push up against her, filling her more completely than was possible as long as he had resisted her. Lorelei continued her gentle kisses. She felt herself sliding toward orgasm and hoped she could coax him along after her. How would it feel to have an angel come inside her?

A shift of weight beside her frightened her out of the dream. Lorelei opened her eyes to find herself sprawled across Floria's bed.

Eyes aflame, Floria stared down at her in her full aspect: feral, inhuman, and absolutely terrifying.

Lorelei was completely disoriented. She'd remembered seeing the angels at the observatory and now she was here. How long had she been out?

Floria grabbed Lorelei's chin and demanded, "Your dream or hers?"

"Hers." But Lorelei heard the lie in her voice. "Mine," she admitted, cringing. "I want him so badly I can taste it."

"Who did you fuck in the angel's lair?" Floria asked.

"The priest," Lorelei said. That lie was more practiced. It sounded almost true.

"Why did the boys forget?" Floria pressed. "Why doesn't the priest remember?"

"I don't know," Lorelei said. She lay frozen on her back, unable to move for fear of sparking Floria's rage.

"I know you're lying to me," Floria told her. "I think the angel was there. I wonder how long you'll stick to your story when our prince asks you tonight." Floria's smile implied that she would make it her business to see that he asked.

Lorelei's heart sank.

"Oh, yeah. Your case has piqued a lot of interest back home. People are betting on which side you'll worm over to in the end."

Before Lorelei could answer, Floria thrust her hand under the covers, between Lorelei's thighs. She stroked Lorelei once, hard, and brought her fingers up slicked and wet. "Love?" Floria demanded. "What's the difference between this and sex?"

Lorelei pushed herself to sit up. She licked her own essence from her sister's elongated fingers. Floria grimaced at her, baring sharpened canines.

Lorelei let her hands rove across the hard muscles of Floria's thighs, the crimson skin sleek and hot beneath Lorelei's human palms. The infernal heat of her sister's flesh wasn't a sensation she'd explored with mortal senses. Her heart beat faster.

Floria wrapped her free hand across the back of Lorelei's head. Sharpened talons caressed both of Lorelei's ears at once, thumb on one side, middle finger on the other. Lorelei wondered how Floria intended the threat. Floria removed the fingers of her other hand from Lorelei's mouth gently, tracing the pad of her index finger across Lorelei's lips.

Floria thrust her pointed tongue between Lorelei's lips. Lorelei let

Floria shove her back down into the pillows—anything, so long as she didn't break the kiss. She tasted like hot copper and cinnamon.

Lorelei pressed her thumbs up along the insides of Floria's thighs. Her sister parted her legs enough to invite. At first Lorelei confined herself to the sweet full outer curves of Floria's sex, feeling them grow fuller with anticipation. When she chanced upon slick wetness, Lorelei followed it back to its source, slipping just the tip of her forefinger inside. She waited for the impatient catch of Floria's breath before thrusting in the rest of her hand.

Lorelei pushed her tongue into Floria's mouth, raking it hard against the succubus' feline teeth. She felt Floria smile against her lips, as she tasted the blood. Floria's orgasm was effortless for them both.

Pulling herself away from Lorelei's hands, Floria sat back on her heels. "You taste different now," she observed. "Not quite like family."

Lorelei watched the avid hunger flickering in her sister's eyes. "Like prey?"

"Better than prey."

Lorelei tasted her own blood. It seemed no different to her. "Do you want to stop?" she asked cautiously. Lorelei could satisfy the arousal lingering from her dream herself, but this seemed an opportunity better shared.

Floria regarded Lorelei with smoky amber eyes. "What are you up to?"

Lorelei lifted her sister's thumb to her lips and kissed it, sucking it between her lips. She smiled. "You always think I'm up to something."

"You always are."

"What could I be up to now? You can read my lust. Tell me." Lorelei stretched to full effect, toes pointed, fingers splayed, back arched.

Inspired by her sister's arousal, Floria sighed. "What do you want to do?"

Lorelei met her gaze. "Take your human form. Let me show you what I can do with my right hand."

"Why human form?"

"Because you'll exhaust me too quickly otherwise," Lorelei said reasonably. She rolled onto her side and rested her head on Floria's thigh. "Come on, Sister. I'll make it worth your while."

"Is this a bargain?"

Lorelei shrugged. "Gratitude."

Floria traced her talons up Lorelei's ribs, coming to cup her breast, feeling its mortal weight. "What have you got to be grateful for, Sister?"

"Everyone else has turned their backs on me." Lorelei felt Floria tense up. She kept her gaze downcast, running her nails firmly up the back of

Floria's calf. "Oh, Floria, I know you've been ordered to keep an eye on me. I know you might choose differently, if you were allowed any choice at all. But since you're forced to extend your hospitality, you might as well take some pleasure in it."

"What are you offering?"

"Relax for a change. Pretend I'm a talented mortal."

"You'd have to be pretty damn talented."

"You know I never back down from a dare."

Floria pinched Lorelei's nipple between the pads of her fingers, just to see it crinkle in response. Lorelei wondered if her sister could relax enough to allow herself to be serviced. Perhaps not. As much pleasure as the succubi took from their work, they were trained from the time they were imps that no mere mortal lover was worth surrendering control to.

"I don't intend to surrender to you."

"I don't expect you to," Lorelei agreed.

The change was instantaneous. Floria's flesh cooled as it became a pale shell-pink. Her mound was still shaven, the way she preferred it. She raised Lorelei's head to meet her eyes. "You give, I take. That's it? No catches?"

Lorelei grinned. "Stop me when you've had enough."

Floria moved her knees apart, pulling Lorelei's face toward her sex.

This was work that she loved to do, work for which she'd been born: giving pleasure to humans. In the centuries they'd worked together, Lorelei had explored Floria's human shapes as attentively as she had her own, studying Floria's likes, teaching them to their prey. She and Floria never troubled to pleasure each other, unless they'd lured a mortal into their web. Now Lorelei drew on all that she'd learned, using tongue and fingers and even the sounds she made to bring Floria as much stimulation as a girl could stand.

When Floria breathlessly pulled Lorelei up into a kiss, Lorelei continued to touch her sister, swallowing her moans and riding her tremors. She allowed her hands to be pushed away, but replaced them with her thigh, holding it hard in place, using it to grant another orgasm. Floria clung to her.

After her body stopped thrashing, Floria wondered, "Why?" Her voice was husky.

Lorelei licked the sweat from Floria's temple. "You asked me the difference between sex and love," she reminded. She traced her fingers up inside the sweet folds of Floria's labia, rubbing slow hard circles across her clit.

"This is just sex," Floria said, shifting her hips to take best advantage of Lorelei's touch.

"And that's all it will ever be for you," Lorelei whispered. "You can see Tuan's love, but you can't feel it. I felt the angel's love."

Shuddering in revulsion, Floria shoved away with a strength that was more than human. "Let's not do this again," she snapped, stumbling toward the closet door.

Lorelei raised her fingers to lick them clean.

Floria yanked dresses from their hangers, looking for something to shield her body from Lorelei's touch. "You'd fuck him again right now, would you?" she accused.

"Well, we only had the once in the church, before you rescued me, and we were interrupted. That wasn't when I felt him love me. It was before, on our first morning together. He loved me when he saw me, wings and tail and horns, as I flew to attack. He loved the devil I am. And his fall began at that moment."

"I don't know which of you fucked the other up worse," Floria said, words tumbling over each other in her fury. "Bottom line: you are *not* the succubus I knew."

"The succubus you knew never gave a thought to thanking you for being her friend," Lorelei said.

"Don't you get it? I'm not your friend. I never have been." Floria tugged a gold lamé dress over her head. "Do you think you've taught me a lesson here? Do you expect for one second that I'll protect you from Hell's fury once they see what you've become?"

Lorelei gazed at her sister and said, as honestly as she'd ever spoken in her life, "No. I don't expect you to do anything for me, Floria. You never have before. Just as I'd never done anything for you."

Floria shoved her feet into a pair of gold pumps and stalked toward the door. "Clean yourself up," she demanded. "I don't want *my* Prince to smell me on you."

Lorelei watched her go, waited until the apartment door slammed shut behind her. "What about my scent on you, Sister?" Lorelei called after her.

Deep masculine laughter echoed from the next room. Lorelei's heart thudded hard inside her chest. How long had they been there?

Ashleigh finally worked up her nerve enough to ask, *Who is that?*

"Fiends," Lorelei answered. "They must have come in with Floria."

Wonder where she's been all day, Ashleigh commented as Lorelei left the bedroom, still naked. Two fiends sat in the living room, watching a video. Floria had left lines of speed laid out on the glass coffee table, along with a tableau of candle, spoon, and hypodermic syringe. Lorelei walked past it without a second glance. Ashleigh didn't want it and Lorelei didn't need it. Lorelei ignored the sound of her own moaning in the porno and walked over to the door wall.

A fiend stood at each corner of the roof, guarding the cardinal points, gargoyles in Hugo Boss. No chance of Aza dropping by before the exorcism. Not that she honestly expected him to do anything other than follow directions.

Should we take a shower? Ashleigh quavered. *I don't want to set Floria off later tonight.*

Lorelei faded back and pushed the girl to take over. *You want a shower, you do it. I've got to think.*

"I don't like the sound of that," Ashleigh bitched. To her surprise, Lorelei didn't answer.

Of course there was no lock on the bathroom door. The sheer number of fiends in the apartment made her flesh crawl. Ashleigh wondered if she should have taken the angels up on their offers of safety.

While she waited for the water to warm up, Ashleigh caught sight of herself in the mirror. She could no longer see the cute, accessible party girl that so dazzled her in the mirror at the church. She didn't need imagination to see Lorelei's sharp teeth and horns. This was probably what the angels saw—the devil beneath the skin—whenever they looked at the succubus.

Lorelei believed that she had the best job in the world, seducing humans into damnation. Ashleigh hadn't seen any evidence yet that the succubus's love for Aza would put an end to that. Even so, Ashleigh fervently prayed that the succubus and the angel could end up together. They'd just have to work out some kind of two-career-couple arrangement. Aza would have to stop trying to change her and be honest that he loved her just the way she was.

For a second, Ashleigh wished she'd be around to see how it all came out, but with any luck at all, she'd be erased from Creation before the credits rolled.

Azaziel had been walking for hours when he arrived at Hollywood Boulevard. Not being able to fly changed his perspective on getting around LA. Humbled, he understood what faced mortal Angelenos who lost their accustomed transport. Though he'd comforted many in that position over the years, he only now grasped the enormity of their difficulties.

Was that all part of some greater plan?

Aza eyed the diffused glare overhead, wondering at his own train of thought. Celestial angels mostly thought of the Almighty, of the whole of Creation and how to serve it. Watchers were different: once earthbound, many picked up the mortal habit of pondering their own existence. The practice put them on a closer footing with those they walked amongst, but perhaps it taught them to rationalize, too.

Aza turned himself to the Eternal and tried to remember the feel of a sun untouched by any cloud, cool air never sullied. In his heart, he still knew the place of every star in existence, however hidden from earthbound eyes. Unfortunately, he felt pressed to recall any but the closest. The problem was Lorelei.

His eyes still saw her, as she had been in sky above the alleyway downtown. Dark and lethal, she'd been a strange mix of sinewy voluptuousness. He'd never touched infernal flesh before. Never expected to crave it afterwards. Despite the eons of his existence, his desire for her mystified him.

She'd seemed so determined to be shut of him when they met in his warehouse. She'd risked her life to pass the invitation to the exorcism along to him, just so he could rescue Ashleigh. He'd been right to think there was something special about Lorelei. She was helping him do something completely good. She might not have meant or wanted to, but she had changed. She was showing Ashleigh mercy.

Shaking himself, he focused on the mortals who passed without recognizing salvation's messenger in their midst. Every soul spoke to him, wordless and revealing.

Unusual for the Boulevard, precious few infernals lurked around. The truths and aspects of those that he saw were monotonous in their petty cruelties.

That made him more aware than ever of the spark that set Lorelei apart from the others. She wasn't an eating, fucking automaton like them. She actually took an interest in her prey. It didn't change the outcome, but Lorelei focused on the individuals she damned and remembered them after they were gone. He hoped that interest would extend into the realm of compassion even after Ashleigh had left her.

About to cross the street, he caught wind of paltry wickedness about to transpire. Lorelei's sister devils were working their wiles just ahead.

He bore to his left, strolling beneath the El Capitan's jewel-like marquee. Aza shouldered past a couple of succubi waiting patiently for their companion to seduce a father away from his family.

The family were tourists from Kentucky. The excuse the father had just been inspired to fabricate was perfectly reasonable: while the mother took the children to see *Peter Pan*, Dad would go down the street for a drink at Musso & Frank's, like the hero in the Hollywood detective novels he loved.

Aza watched the man pay his family's admission, winning them over. The succubus made a show of talking—into a switched-off cell phone—

about meeting her husband at the bar. Her smile held such cheerful contempt that the angel wondered how thick mortals could be when it came to sex.

Aza barged over to the ticket kiosk before the man's wallet closed. "Mister, you got three or four bucks to spare? I only got a couple and Hamburger Hamlet don't sell nothin' for less than six..." Absurd and brassy, it was utterly unsympathetic. "Out with the family, huh? That's great! You can get both them kids in an' her and still have some cash left over."

Aza thrust his hand out expectantly, envisioning it as dirtier, his clothes more ragged than they were. This had to be played carefully. Too much and the man would bolt; too little and he might actually cave in and give over his cash, then flee to the bar with just his credit card and the devil girls.

"Can we get a manager out here?" the cell phone seductress growled, losing charm.

The man stammered about having only enough cash for his family, a minor lie, as he bought his own ticket as well. He paused to empty his pocket silver into Aza's hand before retreating to the sanctuary of the lobby, with his family and soul secure.

The pair of succubi burst into laughter as the family vanished. The jilted devil bared her teeth in a nasty smile.

"No hard feelings, Darlin'?" Aza reached out to her. The girl scuttled back on her heels as if his hand were truly filth-encrusted.

Unlike Lorelei, they weren't the least bit appealing. Aza found some relief in that.

Whistling happily, Aza headed across the street to the Red Line station. The pocket change jingled in his hand. Why walk to his date when he could ride? The subway couldn't take him all the way to his destination, but it was good to support mass transit.

Once on the train, Aza watched the station walls slide by, filled with typical LA ads: bank loans, cell phones, lingerie, dating services, total fitness gyms: all with liberal doses of sex. There was even a billboard for an adult film studio.

Crimson clad and voluptuous, one of the succubi he'd just left behind smiled from the poster. Bright horns poked from her curls as she advertised *Devilgirls IV: Damned and Loving It.*

He thought again of his own devil girl. There *was* something special about Lorelei. The mortal-seeming flesh she'd chosen to clothe herself in had a certain appeal—but her Hell-flesh pulled at his thoughts. Creatures like Lorelei could be anything they wanted, saving their true form for their greatest power. Yet when she'd dove to attack him, the succubus had chosen to take on her familiar mortal shape. Why? Did she think he would prove susceptible to the weaker-seeming flesh?

The fact was she simply didn't, couldn't, know how much he wanted to hold her as she was. The truth shook him more deeply than he expected.

The centuries of loneliness, of barely touching, being a scant whisper against so many souls that he could scarcely help, let alone save… It led him to this. Mortals were all but forbidden anymore, only for kissing and caring for. He couldn't take a lover among his own kind again. The business between his brethren and Sophia had proven the futility of that, long ago.

Never had there been a specific prohibition against what he'd done: to love another spirit not bound by the finite realities of Creation, those that made dust of mortal lovers and devils of celestial ones.

Love couldn't be wrong. In his deepest heart, Azaziel prayed that he and Lorelei were part of some greater purpose of the Almighty's to prove that very thing.

It reaffirmed his determination to take her away from Lost Angels, if at all possible.

The train rumbled soft and smooth into the North Hollywood station. As he got out, Muriel waited by the escalator, arms crossed. "Nice work with that family at the theater. It's good to see you can still do something right," she said. "I wonder how you'll fare once you enter the Mouth of Hell."

CHAPTER 20: LAST CHANCES

Wrapped in a towel, Ashleigh walked purposefully past the fiends to Floria's bedroom. She'd find something to wear and she'd put on some makeup. By then, Lorelei *had* to be done thinking and would keep her company again.

It felt weird rummaging around in another woman's dresser. Ashleigh had never been one to snoop. Even with Lorelei's permission, this felt more like theft than borrowing. Floria would surely see it that way, if the mood struck her.

Of course, Floria didn't own anything that would actually cover her ass. Well, nothing that would cover her ass and crotch simultaneously. Ashleigh finally settled on a black velvet thong as the piece that provided halfway decent coverage. One good gust of wind, though, and she was gonna get arrested.

After she wrestled it on, she sat at Floria's vanity. Even with wet hair and no makeup, Lorelei looked stunning, especially her unnaturally violet-blue eyes. Ashleigh saw a twinkle in them that let her know that Lorelei had surfaced again. "What have you been thinking about?" Ashleigh asked the reflection.

Lorelei swept back into possession of her herself and dodged the question. "That's our dress."

A black lycra sheath hung on the back of the bedroom door. Someone clearly meant it to replace the one Aza had destroyed in the alley.

This version of the dress represented Floria's taste more than Lorelei's. Instead of sleeves, which would've hidden the broken handcuff, it had spaghetti straps. The plunging neckline accented the magenta bruise on her chest. At the very least, she could hide the plum-colored bruise around her throat. Lorelei took one of Floria's crimson scarves and tied it around her neck.

She rolled on some of Floria's black stockings and straightened the seams, then made up her face.

Not long after she finished, a fiend shoved the door open and pitched her purse in with an underhanded toss. "Let's go."

As the phalanx of fiends escorted her out of Tuan's building, the driver straightened from buffing a limo at the curb. She sauntered over to open the back door.

Lorelei got a good look at her. Her mouth had been fused shut into a perfunctory groove, like a badly molded doll's mouth. Her coarse white hair hung in a stark, uneven pageboy. The brim of her chauffeur's cap shaded big sweet brown eyes. They gazed straight ahead, so used to the shock her appearance prompted that she no longer watched for it.

Her long black velvet coat hung open. Purple-red scar tissue swirled flame-like across her scrawny white torso. Her breasts were gone. The scars continued down, disappearing into a featureless juncture between her grooved thighs.

Lorelei stooped past her into the limo. Joseph already huddled inside. The blood drained from his face as the driver closed the door.

"What is that?"

"Her name is Jezebel."

"A lost soul?" he wondered.

"Worse. She was a succubus once, but now... She's a warning." Lorelei wondered if Jezebel had left her coat unbelted on orders from Yasmina. Arms wound tight around herself, Lorelei could feel Jezebel's misery radiating from the front of the car. Deprived of sex, of sustenance, slowly starving to death while forced to serve the elder temptress... Destruction would be a blessing.

Sifting her memory, Lorelei tried to recall the infraction that merited Jezebel's punishment. If she had ever known, Lorelei had forgotten it now.

If only she could do the same for that night in the park. Too many memories crowded the back of this limo, though she'd only ridden in it once. What if she and Joseph were never going to the club? What if she was already locked in some chamber of torment in Hell, reliving this excruciating moment unto insanity?

Lorelei rocked herself, fighting back tears. Realizing that Joseph watched her, she twisted away, biting her lips. Was it possible she didn't always enjoy being watched?

Tentatively, the priest touched her shoulder.

Lorelei let him turn her around, gather her against his chest. She clutched him, shaking.

He began to struggle as she unfastened his trousers, but Lorelei was fighting for her life now and wasn't about to hear no.

"Lorelei..." he pleaded. "Ashleigh, please, this won't help anything."

"You're defrocked. I'm damned. What does it matter?" The words tumbled over each other. "Jezebel crossed Yasmina once and look what happened. What if that's going to be me?"

Genuine tears rolled down her cheeks, streaking her makeup. "Joey, I can't wind up like that. Please, I need this more than you need me not to."

Taking his face in her hands, Lorelei filled his eyes with her desperation, wondering if this was what sincerity felt like. "I'm helping you save Ashleigh. Isn't that worth a favor?"

"No." He tried pushing her away, but she had him off-balance. Sandwiched into the corner of the back seat, he had nowhere to run. "No!" he repeated more strenuously, as she yanked his trousers down to reveal dingy white y-fronts and his arousal beneath them.

"Yes." In the same pounce, she straddled his hips and caught his arms. She wasn't as strong as she should be, but she had surprise on her side. "Forgive me, Father, because I'm sure as Hell going to sin right now."

Stop, Ashleigh begged, *please, please stop. We need him.*

"He'll do the exorcism now, or he'll be killed," Lorelei answered, staring hard at Joseph. "He passed the point of backing out when he came to Floria's apartment."

"I passed the point of backing out a long time ago," Joseph said wearily.

Lorelei felt a stab of pity for him, but thrust it down. "You knew what I am from the moment you saw me. And you wanted me. So don't lie to me, Joey."

The bright red shame that suffused his face was as sweet as an orgasm. "I—" He swallowed hard and began again. "I don't want you, Lorelei. Not at all. You have a soul now. You have free will. This sin will damn you more certainly than anything you ever did in Hell's service, because now you know you have a choice."

This isn't fair, Ashleigh whined. *He's done nothing but help you. You're not proving anything by raping him.*

"Shut up," Lorelei muttered.

Raping him isn't going to stop Yasmina from tormenting you. It's not going to help you win Aza's love. This poor man is helpless. Aza would be as disgusted as I am.

Lorelei shrieked, "Shut up!"

Leave Joseph alone and I will.

Clasping her head, nails pressed hard against her scalp, Lorelei peeled her eyes open to stare at the old man. "Do you want to stop?"

"Yes," he panted.

"Fine." She pulled herself off of him and settled back on the seat. She smoothed the spandex dress down over her hips. Bending forward, she straightened her stockings.

Catching his breath, Joseph reassembled his own clothing.

Lorelei found the compact in her purse and fixed her face. "You can thank Ashleigh for your blue balls," she snarled.

"Thank you, Ashleigh." He sounded as if he really meant it.

Yasmina wasn't the only devil slipping, Lorelei decided. She would ask the first angel she came across to kill her and end this humiliating ordeal before she degenerated any further.

"And thank you, Lorelei, for listening to her."

"Fuck you," Lorelei snapped. Frustrated by the tears that started up in her eyes and threatened to ruin her makeup all over again, Lorelei retreated and left Ashleigh to take over. This might be the last time she had that luxury.

Ashleigh closed the compact and slipped it back into Lorelei's purse. "Did she hurt you?" the girl asked shyly.

A shudder ran through the priest, but he said, "No."

"Sex is the only comfort she has," Ashleigh explained. "It's the only way she knows how to connect with people." She chuckled, half to herself. "I think I'm the only friend she's ever had that she could fuck with, but she couldn't fuck. Excuse my language."

He wiped his face with a pocket-handkerchief. "Is she trying to give me a reason to kill her soul tonight?"

Before Ashleigh could answer, the limo door abruptly opened. Whatever stood outside, they were large.

When Muriel escorted Aza from the subway, Michael and Rafael were waiting. "Thank you, Muriel," Rafael said. "We'll take it from here."

She strode off into the crowd around the subway station's mouth.

The pair of archangels walked Aza away from the bustle of mortals. The sounds of the world muted.

"I remember Anah," Rafael said meditatively. "I remember how, when she gazed at you, her soul praised God that you existed."

Aza's heart panged with loss that the millennia muffled, but could not bury.

"She always saw you as the messenger of God's grace," Rafael said. "Through you, she glimpsed the Divine. She would have submitted to the floodwaters or joined Noah's family on the ark, but you took her away from her destiny. Did she forgive you for doing what you both sensed was outside God's plan?"

Aza bowed his head. "She prayed that the Word would excuse me.

She offered herself up to buy my absolution. She called Samael, and Azrael, and all the other angels of death to undo what I had done and— when none of them came—she forgave me."

"Have you forgiven yourself?" Michael asked.

"Saving Anah from the Flood did not save her from old age or death. I think I knew that, even before the rains began. Ever since, I've endured the knowledge that I'm a fool. And yet, I trust that I'm made as I am for a reason." Aza straightened. "As Muriel is so fond of pointing out, so many of the Watchers of my generation fell. I've long wondered if they fell because they did not see the Word's reflection in their loved ones, if they forgot to praise the Almighty as they practiced the sacraments of love, or if they forgave themselves too quickly for becoming distracted from their heavenly purposes."

"And what was your heavenly purpose in regard to the succubus and the girl?" Michael wondered.

"I don't know if I had any clue," Aza admitted. "I wanted to refine Ashleigh's soul and save her from the harpies with whom she'd fallen in. I wondered if Lorelei could return love."

"So it's not every succubus you wish to bed?" Rafael asked.

Aza's lips twisted apologetically. "No. Only one."

"That's a relief," Rafael said. "Hell would have to make war over *that*."

"And I didn't intend to make love to her flesh," Aza protested. "I wanted her to feel what Ashleigh felt, what Anah felt. I wanted Lorelei to know the joy that love can bring when it confirms the holy love that comes from above. Unfortunately, the only way to reach past her defenses, to speak to her spirit, was to connect with her in the flesh." He added quickly, "I know it was wrong, but it wasn't forbidden."

"Not yet," Michael commented dryly. "The jury's still out, but Rafael's point is a good one."

"I'll remember," Aza promised.

"Do you intend to make this succubus an honest woman?" Rafael asked. Michael chuckled.

"I am in God's hands," Aza said simply. "As is Lorelei."

Ashleigh followed the priest out of the car, expecting to see Thodos or Floria. Instead, three unfamiliar fiends crowded around. Big as pro wrestlers, they were dressed alike in nondescript black slacks and black silk tour jackets. One of them had a headset wound in front of his mouth. "They're here," he growled. "No trouble."

The head fiend unclipped the red velvet rope. Ashleigh tottered forward, awkward and uncomfortable in Lorelei's too-short skirt. She felt like a little girl walking into a grown-up party where the adults would mock her with cruel smiles. Where was Lorelei? Ashleigh prayed the devil wouldn't sulk until the exorcism. Fear rattled her flesh.

The heel of her shoe caught in the grate between the sidewalk and the doorway. Ashleigh toppled. Before she broke her ankle, Joseph grabbed her. One of the fiends yanked his hands back as soon as he realized that to touch her would be to touch the priest.

That's interesting, Lorelei noted. *They're afraid of the priest.*

"I'm okay," Ashleigh told Joseph. "Thanks."

A fiend retrieved her shoe and handed it back. Hanging onto the priest's sleeve for balance, Ashleigh slipped the pump onto her foot.

Do you want me to come back? Lorelei asked.

"Yes." Ashleigh heard the hiss in her voice and flinched.

Then don't question my actions again.

Lorelei stalked into the club, using the height of her heels to accentuate the sway of her hips. Joseph sensed the change almost immediately and withdrew his hand from her elbow. Whatever. Chalk up one priest she couldn't seduce beside the angel she couldn't seduce and count them against all her successes. Lorelei hoped the boss had enjoyed her letter. She hoped he'd remember how eager she had always been to do anything he required. She'd go back to working in his private harem. She'd go back to serving in Hell. She'd even go, without complaint, back to being an imp: anything, so long as it kept her out of Yasmina's clutches.

"T'Ain't What You Do" came booming over the speakers as the DJ kicked the sound system up another notch.

Hai sat at the main bar with Tuan and Sammy. His face lit up when he saw Lorelei coming down the stairs. She worked up her best smile—for everyone who might be watching this exchange—but her heart wasn't really in it. She deserved this year's Academy Award for Best Actress.

All around the room, heads turned, followed by hands raised to shield snide whispers. The club wasn't very full yet, but its usual ratio was reversed. Rather than a smattering of devils amidst a sea of mortals, Hell was widely represented tonight. Several knots of her sisters had apparently shown up to see what came of screwing angels. Charming, Lorelei thought: she'd already been reduced to an object lesson, just like Jezebel. Lorelei recognized Ruby, with whom she'd worked in Atlanta, and Carmilla, whom she hadn't seen since Paris. *Bitch.* Surprised no one had stabbed *her* in the back yet, Lorelei's smile grew mean. Enemies, too, had come to see Lorelei slapped back into her place. Sasha was still pissed about having laughed off Joe Stalin as a wannabe, leaving Lorelei to scoop up the glory. Sasha'd put her money on Kirov and, boom, two days later, bullet in the head.

Floria wasn't with her boys, which was strange. Not like her to leave property out for anyone to play with. That meant she was off kissing ass.

"Not that I should be surprised," Joseph grumbled, "but it's hot in here."

"Makes people drink faster," Lorelei answered by rote. How many nights had she had this same conversation? Lorelei found it hard not to get nostalgic. However the evening turned out, she doubted she'd be allowed to freelance in here again.

"I thought it was just to make your kind more comfortable."

"If you knew how many of my 'kind' were here tonight, you wouldn't joke. This doesn't look good for our heroine."

"Ashleigh?"

He hadn't meant to be cruel, she saw. Lorelei caught his gaze and made him understand her promise. "She's taken care of, old man."

You're scared? Ashleigh asked.

Lorelei didn't answer, even in her thoughts. She continued across the dance floor, then turned. "Do me a favor and at least pretend to be with me," she whispered to Joseph.

For your safety or his? Ashleigh wondered.

No one else dared to be seen speaking to her. Everyone moved out of her way, clearing a path to the bar.

"We thought you were already here," Hai shouted over the music. He caught her hand and pulled her over for a kiss, his tongue slipping between her lips even as his hand squeezed her ass.

When Hai let her up, Tuan explained, "Somebody's got our tab."

"You know that ain't Floria," Sammy drawled.

Tuan shrugged it off.

The bartender set down a glass of whiskey on the rocks. Lorelei was shocked to see Barakiel tending bar.

"Since I've been outed, I was invited to work tonight," he snarled. "Hello, Joseph."

"Barakiel."

Lorelei picked up the whiskey before Joseph could touch it. "Am I on the boss's tab, too?" she asked.

Barakiel inclined his head.

"I'd like a bottle of Evian, please."

That cracked Barakiel's anger. "I'm not sure we even have that here."

"It's under the counter." Lorelei pointed at the large pink and white box.

"And what, exactly, do you intend to do with bottled water?"

"If you must know," Lorelei sniped back, mimicking Barakiel's tone, "we do not fix with LA tap water."

That produced the desired effect: a bottle of Evian was procured. Lorelei broke the seal and took a deep swallow, leaving a dark ring of lipstick around the bottle's neck. She offered the bottle to the priest. "Just water," Lorelei said. "Don't drink anything else anyone gives you."

Joseph's eyes narrowed. Lorelei realized that he wasn't entirely sure which one of them he was talking to. That was the scariest thing of this evening yet. Lorelei shuddered to think she could pass for Ashleigh.

"Were you teasin' about shootin' up?" Hai demanded.

"Don't be disappointed, Tiger." Lorelei patted his thigh with her free hand. "This won't be your last chance."

Joseph accepted the bottle and its cap from her. "Thank you, Lorelei."

How she was coming to hate that three-word combination. She sipped the whiskey—too chilled for her tastes—and said, "It might amuse everyone else to get you fucked up enough to botch it tonight, but I'd rather you stayed sober and got through this as smoothly as possible."

She leaned against Hai. He twisted on his barstool so she could stand between his knees and rest her weight back against his chest. He puffed up with such pride, basking in her presence. Lorelei knew she ought to distance herself from him—for his protection—but really, this moment made him happy. This might be the last happiness she could give him. She craved his solidity, the realness of his flesh against hers, more than she wanted to protect him. That, at least, had not changed.

CHAPTER 21: FEATURED ACT

"Go with God, Brother." Rafael placed his palm over Azaziel's heart. A wave of confidence smoothed away Aza's fears. The healing grace of the archangel's touch also erased the pain of Aza's lamed wing, fully repairing the damage Muriel had inflicted.

"You'll likely have need of those tonight," Rafael said.

"Bless you," Aza answered. The healing ensured he could go forth, undistracted by the pain that had colored every thought for the last several days.

Aza blinked hard, eyes barely able to contain the tears of gratitude that silvered them. Rafael brushed a single drop aside with his thumb. His touch filled Aza's senses with the scent of honey. With that touch, the archangel gathered the regret from the outcast angel, pulling it away. Angelic love was no less powerful when bestowed upon their own.

Aza joined the hopefuls waiting in a line that stretched down the sidewalk bordering 'Lost Angels.' While he waited, Aza glanced across the street at the throng gathered at the bus stop. Compared to the humanity cozying around him, Rafael couldn't have been more conspicuous if he'd spread his wings.

The line inched forward. Aza noticed phrases set into each square of sidewalk beneath his feet. "It's good to get out of your spouse's hair for the night," soothed one. "Thanks for pumping some revenue into downtown," applauded another. A third counseled, "You're no good to anyone if you don't unwind now and then."

Aza turned away to read the souls around him. Each carried its own mantle of color: saved, damned, truly damned, looking bad but salvageable, way too far gone. What would Lorelei's look like when he saw her again?

The black leather curtain to the back room swung back and a trio of fiends stepped out. Three pairs of eyes swiveled toward Lorelei, flashing red briefly before the fiends began their inexorable process across the floor.

Lorelei grasped Joseph's wrist. "Stay with the boys," she ordered. "Don't go anywhere until the boss commands it. Insist on that."

"I wouldn't recognize Asmodeus from Beelzebub."

"Don't say anything like that again, if you plan to walk out of here tonight."

"I don't expect to be walking out of here tonight."

"Should've let me fuck you then."

Lorelei pulled Hai's head toward her. She focused all her affection for him into her kiss, feeding on his response. It assured her that she wasn't a failed succubus after all. She still had her uses. The boss had to recognize that.

One of the fiends closed a big hand around her bicep. They marched her across the dance floor, nothing like subtle. The few mortals in the crowd stopped dancing to watch her, wondered if they should recognize her. Beneath the manic music, the room was eerily silent.

The fiends parted the curtains and stepped out of her way. The room inside was full of darkness, a wall of it so thick that the light from the club did not penetrate.

You don't have to tell me to keep quiet, Ashleigh promised.

Lorelei nodded. She had other things to worry about. She stepped up and let the darkness engulf her.

The smell inside was complex: cloyingly rotten like durian, rancid as week-old fish, heady as opium. Lorelei continued forward, head held up and arms at her sides. They wouldn't trip her. The test would be more elaborate than that.

She caught a sudden breath of blood and crushed grapes. Without hesitation, Lorelei sank to her knees.

Asmodeus caught her head before she could prostrate herself. He pressed her cheek against the shaggy fur of his hip.

Lorelei took him into her mouth. Her mortal form seriously hindered the task, with her inability to unhinge her jaw or retract her teeth. Still, she did the best she could, hoping enthusiasm and expertise would compensate for physical limitations.

Accepting her attentions silently, Asmodeus stroked the hair back from her face. Lorelei worked until her jaw cramped and knew he was no closer to release than when she'd started. It didn't matter. She was his to command.

Spindly fingers grabbed her hips and guided her back onto her feet. The short lycra skirt was rolled out of the way. Feverish hands caressed the tender flesh above her stockings.

"Smells like priest," a tenor voice carped.

A chorus laughed: some female, some making no pretense at humanity.

"Good," Asmodeus purred. He stroked Lorelei's jaw, erasing some of the pain. "The old man's loyalties were not entirely cemented."

Whoever had been examining her thrust into her now. If he hadn't been holding her hips, Lorelei would've stumbled right off her pumps. Asmodeus held her head in place, using her hard. Tears of frustration burned in her eyes as she fought the urge to choke, to bite down, to pull away. All she could do was to hold still, let them take their pleasure. She understood her place all too well—possession, plaything—but she wanted desperately to participate, to help, to take her own pleasure as well.

At least screwing Thodos had prepared Ashleigh to take it and not interfere.

Her hands were pulled away from Asmodeus to be variously filled and inserted. The demon behind her was replaced by someone else, and someone else after that. Lorelei lost track of the changes of flesh to leather to fur to scales beneath her fingers, across her lips. Only a few were demons. Some, she guessed, were fiends or tempters or succubi in Asmodeus's employ. She thought she recognized Thodos. The others were a blur and a mystery.

She drank what she was given, moved however she was guided, but not one of them allowed her release. The tension in her body descended into torment. Asmodeus did not move to take the pain away again. Lorelei held the agony, studied it, suffered it—because that was required of her. Eventually she found a way to dissolve into the pain, to float away on it. She felt herself beginning to come apart.

Ashleigh began to tell a story. *Once there was an angel who saw a devil and fell in love. But he couldn't have her the way she was, the way that he wanted her. Because they were so different, they couldn't connect, like the ends of magnets. So he found a soul who would help him, a soul who was willing. And he made the most beautiful love to that soul in the devil's body, because that was the only way he could imagine to make a devil feel love.*

Released by her tormenters, Lorelei collapsed onto the floor.

"Bravo, little Ashleigh." Asmodeus applauded. "Well told."

Thodos scooped her from the floor and carried her across the room. A faint glow, brown with old blood, burned up from the floor. Lorelei blinked a couple of times to focus her eyes. The septagram resolved as the fiend carried her around and in at its gate. He laid her on the bier and stepped away. Asmodeus traced the outer circle with his cane, sealing her inside.

They were alone.

Are you all right?

Lorelei took a deep breath. Quite honestly, she ached. "I'll live."

What were they trying to do to you?

"Remind me what I am and to whom I belong."

What happened to no being as easy to say as yes?

"One does not say no in Hell. That's lesson #1."

We're not in Hell, Ashleigh argued.

"We might as well be," Lorelei pointed out. "This is Hell's embassy."

You have a soul of your own and they're afraid of it. They weren't punishing you because you haven't been doing what they wanted. They were punishing you because you've been doing exactly what they wanted. I think if you stood up for yourself, they might leave you alone.

"The universe doesn't work that way, Ashes."

Who told you that? Ashleigh demanded. *You're going to believe the Prince of Lies?*

"You're speaking blasphemy," Lorelei said, forcing herself to sit up. "I'm exhausted. Let's not fight."

With clumsy fingers, she picked at the knot in Floria's scarf and used the silk to wipe her face. She spat on a corner of the scarf and rubbed the mascara out from under her eyes. She washed her hands and between her legs as well as she could. Of course, the smell would remain on her skin. Without a doubt, Aza would know she belonged to Hell.

Strange, but she no longer had the strength to cry. She lay back on the bier and crossed her feet at the ankles.

Looking upward, she discovered a skylight in the ceiling. Moonlight flowed in, blue and cold. If she'd been herself, she could have savored the caress of the light on her skin.

She expected to see Aza peering down at her, in position to snatch Ashleigh once she was freed. If he smashed through the glass and swooped down, wings unfurled, Joseph would have the vision of divinity he craved. Lorelei too desired to see Aza in all his celestial glory, pinions flashing, inner light shining. She'd cowered the first time he'd revealed himself. Before she died, she wanted a good long look.

"When you see him?" Lorelei murmured. "Give him a message, as soon as you can? Tell him…he's made powerful enemies, too many to fight. He should leave town as soon as he can."

I'll tell him, Ashleigh promised.

Lorelei closed her eyes and thought she might sleep, but Ashleigh wasn't done yet. *Why are you doing all this for me?*

"Because you got me home from the river that night. Because you didn't abandon me to Yasmina. Because you've been the first real friend I've ever had." Lorelei smiled, hoping Ashleigh could feel it. "Thank you, Ashleigh. I hope you go to Heaven and live forever in bliss. But let me sleep now, if I can. We're going to need my strength to get through the rest of the night."

"You, Feathers! Step on up!" one of the security guards shouted. "Hey, you deaf or somethin'?"

The pudgy hands of a decidedly human bouncer yanked Aza out of line. The silky fabric of the man's tour jacket hissed and sang between the creases of his overpadded torso. Aza controlled his reaction so he didn't reflexively hurt the not-quite-damned bouncer. The man's aftershave was familiar from the angel's last visit inside this club. He was a regular in Hell's employ.

Two fiends at the door unclipped the velvet ropes. Aza was shoved forward hard. He struck the revolving door and found himself face to face with a brass plaque bearing the legend: "I'd turn back if I were you."

"Too late for that now." Taking care not to touch angelic flesh, the fiend tending door rubberstamped a blurred image of Baphomet on Aza's hand. The ink glowed accusingly. Aza found himself moved forcibly through the doorway.

Heat blasted him as he entered the foyer, drying his tongue. Tobacco, brimstone, alcohol, and perfume swirled around arousal, bitterness, fear, and anger. It formed an overwhelming incense that dared the senses to adapt or succumb.

The mortal bouncer stayed outside. The last thing Aza saw of him was a look of disgust and pity. Perhaps a reason to be saved yet, Aza thought, taking what comfort he could.

Just beyond the bar ahead of him, he saw the stairway down into the interior. The club scarcely looked like the place he'd visited a week ago. The bars, bandstand, and dance floor were altered; the clientele was now more infernal than mortal. Aza spotted the trio of succubi he'd met outside the El Capitan. Behind the downstairs bar hunched Barakiel, another Grigori. Aza wondered how many other Fallen brothers might be here tonight.

Some of the boys who'd escorted Lorelei to his cell were drinking at the bar with Father Joseph. Aza wondered what he could say to the priest to spur him on tonight, for Ashleigh's sake. Would he get the chance? One of Lorelei's laughing sisters perched in a boy's lap. She certainly looked settled in.

Instead of the earlier lonely stereo, the music now came from a full-on swing band, fronted by a lean, zoot-suited tempter with a gleaming pompadour. His single displaced curl twitched in time with the beat. The chorus was something about "the maddest kind of love." He winked at

Aza.

"What's goin' on?" Sammy wondered.

Floria twisted on Tuan's lap to follow the boys' gazes. At the platform just inside the doorway stood an angel. His human form wasn't much to look at: blond, green-eyed, much too white-bread for her taste. He wore a nondescript brown leather jacket over a white button-down shirt and blue jeans. Nice to see he'd dressed up for his big night out, Floria thought acidly, like he'd ridden into town to look after the little missy.

Four fiends converged on the stairway in addition to the pair who'd followed the angel into the club. Trouble brewing, all right. Leave it to Sammy to pick up on it.

"That's Lorelei's fiancé," Floria sniped. She smiled at the fury that lit Hai's eyes.

Trying to soften the blow, Tuan asked. "The one that kidnapped her?"

"The one who cuffed her to his bed and fucked every ounce of common sense out of her head." Floria continued, "The one she probably fucked that night the boys were supposed to be guarding her and the priest." She watched the old man struggle to remember, but nothing came to him either. Whoever had blanked their memories was good. That pissed Floria off all the more.

"The one who put that bruise around her throat?" Hai demanded. "The one she's all crazy over?"

"Must have a big dick," Sammy guessed. Hai's laugh was mean.

"I'll go find out." Floria slithered off Tuan's lap to intercept the angel.

Behind her, she heard Sammy say, "Don't know what either of you sees in those bitches."

Aza tried to push past a pair of fiends. A nauseating jolt ran through him, leaving something vile on his tongue. He reflexively wiped a hand across his dry lips.

The fiends didn't care for whatever happened either. Probably, as far as they'd been told, they were to keep the angel from moving until told otherwise. Maybe the brighter of them now suspected that they were components in a temporary ward, that it was in their best interests to see this angel stayed put.

Somewhere a clock chimed eleven. Crossing the dance floor, Barakiel made an elaborate show of checking his pocket watch as he passed through the dancers. His gaze traveled to Aza to make sure he had an audience. The fallen angel paused to kiss a mortal customer on the cheek and whisper in her ear. The woman, who should know better than to be in a place like this, shrugged and turned away.

Barakiel signaled a waitress over to meet the angel, then whispered to the customer again, slipping her a business card. A brittle smile replaced her brief, incredulous look of anger. Whatever he'd told her seemed to satisfy some personal requirement. Twirling the watch on its chain, Barakiel moved toward the angel and his guards.

Even as Azaziel watched the woman over Barakiel's shoulder, some critical aspect of her fell. The fallen angel felt it too. He rolled his eyes with a theatrical smile.

The waitress hustled over to Aza. Unlike the other girls working the crowd, she was mortal. Too frail, coppery complexion with a gray undertone, she looked strained and anxious, but managed a smile that was a fair approximation of her infernal coworkers'.

"Evening. I'm Dora. You gents like something from the bar?" she asked Aza and company. The fiends shook their heads, as did the angel.

Something sank just behind her eyes. Aza saw what to her had been a potential five-way tip vanish.

"You sure?" she continued gamely. "First one's free at Lost Angels."

"They're sure, Dora. Why don't you call it a night?" Barakiel arrived at her shoulder, easing the tray from her hands and the checkbook from her apron pocket.

"But I just got on an hou—"

"And now you're off again, for the rest of your life."

She gaped at him. "But…"

Barakiel shook his head, mocking and sad. "Can't give a drink to a thirsty angel? You're no use to the boss. Boys, show her what she's won."

Aza felt her mind working fiercely, trying to comprehend what had occurred. The fiend in front of Aza took Dora firmly in hand, hauling her through the swinging doors behind the bar. Dora looked back in confusion before the doors closed on her.

Shaking his head, Barakiel faced Aza. "If I were you, I'd not make waves. You never know what consequences will befall whom otherwise."

As Barakiel faded back toward the bar, Aza caught a whiff of Lorelei. The succubus he'd seen with Lorelei's boys glided past the fiends and wrapped herself around him. Her sex pressed insistently against his thigh even as one of her hands groped the front of his trousers. Despite her scent, she was entirely infernal. Aza shoved her away hard. She left patches of heat where her flesh had touched his clothing.

She caught herself on her spike-heeled pumps and rocked back to her balance. Her hair was honey blond, complimenting a gold lamé dress left less to the imagination than anything he'd seen Lorelei wear.

"Not my type, Floria."

He saw that naming her like that unnerved her. Hell's fury flamed undisguised in her eyes. "Haven't had the pleasure," she flirted, flashing him a tight kewpie doll smile.

"You won't."

Aza realized that she didn't smell like Lorelei so much as of her. He regretted whatever Ashleigh must have suffered at this creature's hands.

"It's not just any of us you want to corrupt?" the succubus demanded.

"Corrupt?" Aza echoed.

She phrased it another way: "Why Lorelei?"

"Because she has the capacity for compassion," he began.

The succubus cut him off with a bitter cackle. "Among other things, Lorelei took credit for the Soviet purges. She brought millions of souls to Hell. You couldn't have chosen a more damnable devil on which to inflict a soul."

Wincing at the reminder of Lorelei's past, Aza asserted, "Souls can be saved."

The succubus glanced beyond him, then transfixed him with her gaze. *There* was a genuine smile, although it looked like it had been cut into her face with a knife. "Can't help noticing the Celestial Army isn't backing you up on this one, sweetheart."

He saw that she was rubbing the hand that had touched him against her hip, as if to wipe off his taint. He nodded toward it. "Want to wash that, do you?"

"What I want is your heart on a plate," she snapped. Aza saw the fiends crack a smile. She continued, "I wanted to know why she's obsessed with *fucking* you."

"Aza has always had a way with the ladies," a smooth, deep voice remarked.

Aza recognized the long thin angel standing outside the ring of fiends. A scarlet silk blouse played up the darkness of his skin. Last time they'd met, Jequon had been wearing a pasha's robes. He'd still been overdressed and out of place. "It's been a long time," Aza said.

"I told you I'd see you again," Jequon agreed with a feline smile.

Pitching her voice flirtatiously, the succubus wondered, "You know each other well?"

"We used to discuss the aesthetic merits of various human females while sitting on the Celestial Steps."

The succubus unsuccessfully suppressed a shudder.

"I never," Jequon taunted, "*never* in a million years, suspected you'd fall for a succubus, Brother."

"Who are you calling Fallen?" Aza asked with false congeniality.

"Yet here you are." Jequon's shrug was eloquent.

"I'll let the two of you catch up," Lorelei's sister said, trying to extract herself from the conversation.

"Actually," Jequon said, catching her before she could slip away, "I've come to let you know it's time for the old man to suit up. The boss wants you to take over with him."

She licked her lips. "My pleasure."

Aza pitied the priest as the succubus sashayed off.

"No need to worry about getting you a good table. That has been arranged." Jequon took Azaziel's elbow, guiding him through the club. "I apologize for you having to wait on line, but I'm sure it was instructional. No lack of doomed souls there for your examination."

The angel looked around, taking stock as they wove through the crowd. "Plenty still that will evade Hell's grasp."

Jequon halted his smooth glide, tugging Azaziel back to face him. "Yes. That might be a problem." The fallen angel's entire being radiated a chill that caused other patrons to shiver and step back.

Azaziel shrugged his arm free, his own fingers tensing. "Their problem, not ours."

"You've got concerns of your own now."

As if on cue, one of the infernal waitresses pressed a highball glass into Aza's hand. She disappeared back into the crowd, leaving him with nowhere to set it down.

Jequon gestured him forward, up a short flight of steps. Two silent fiends kept mortals from investigating the private party beyond. Behind them, a black leather curtain swallowed all sound of the festivities within. Aza steeled himself, prepared to face the torments of the damned if need be, for the sakes of Ashleigh and Lorelei.

CHAPTER 22: RINGSIDE

Azaziel sat stiffly, patience stretched nearly to breaking. Ever since Jequon escorted him to the demon's side, Asmodeus had completely ignored him.

Yasmina arrived, all studied elegance and expensive jewelry, to take her place beside her master. Aglow in the red light of the candle burning at the table's center, Yasmina watched Asmodeus intently. It appeared rapt sycophancy, but Aza knew better. She was worried.

He'd despised her for so long the feeling had almost lost its meaning. He wondered what would have transpired if he'd wooed her instead of Anah. The thought was as inconceivable as loving someone born in Hell should have been.

Lorelei lay motionless on the altar in the center of the room. She was nude again, except for her stockings and shoes. Her torn dress had been discarded in a heap on the floor. Her purse made a makeshift pillow. The broken handcuff twinkled on her wrist like a bracelet. Her beauty was wasted and meaningless here, merely decorative. He recognized that she wasn't the bait in this trap, simply another victim. Aza wished the exorcism would begin, so they could leave this place.

Noticing the ice in his drink had melted, he set the untasted glass aside. Then a theory occurred to him. Lifting the glass to his lips, he sipped the diluted Crown Royal.

Asmodeus focused on Aza with warmth that—while only a shadow of his former angelic glory—gave every appearance of sincerity. "That's better. Now that you've decided to accept my hospitality, we can be friends again, Brother."

"I'm not here to be friends," Aza said. "You know what I came for."

"In good time," Asmodeus promised. "For the present, let's get you a fresh drink."

Asmodeus signaled a waitress over. The succubus was over-generously poured into a little French maid's costume. Aza ignored her as she switched his barely touched glass for a fresh one.

Asmodeus didn't have to leave the table to work the room, since the room seemed intent on circulating around to him. The demon introduced Aza to every succubus at the party. Aza catalogued their names and reactions to him, uncertain how that information would ever become useful. All of them paled in comparison to Lorelei.

He'd accepted her invitation to this event, trusting that love and faith would see him through the evening. Now, surrounded by Asmodeus's heavily armed fiends, he realized the demon in charge of Los Angeles anticipated violence. One-sixth of the exorcism's audience was comprised of the entourage of Beelzebub, former prince of the city who'd been unseated in a coup. Aza wasn't sure if the two demons had shared a civil word since the exchange of power. The Hellish office responsible for the oversight of succubi was well represented, along with the Home Office, reporting directly to Lucifer himself. The pressure on Asmodeus must be intense, but the demon gave no sign of it. He greeted each guest with amused disdain. All this seemed a game to him.

A game in which Aza was the prize to be won. How long had Hell been trying to set him up? The answer burned clear in Aza's mind: he'd sought Lorelei, spied on her, put himself in her path once he was certain she couldn't resist the challenge he presented. No one was more responsible for his presence here tonight than he himself.

By the time Floria reached the office, three of the lesser girls—Lulu, Deirdre, and Maris—had backed Joseph into a corner. Each brandished a garment bag or shoebox, prancing and mincing, baring flesh in ways that, while fine for eroding willpower in a strip club, were totally ineffective for getting the old man out of his clothing.

Floria ground her teeth. Was this indicative of hell's current litter, barely out of imp flesh? "The boss wants you dressed. Just put on the damn clothes before you screw up tonight's timetable."

"I can dress myself," Joseph growled.

Floria held out a hand for the garment bag. "Knock off the girly show."

Lulu pursed her lips, considering refusal, before she surrendered the bag.

"Good call." Floria smiled icily, nodding for Maris to leave the shoebox on the desk.

The would-be seductresses glowered at Joseph, no longer concerned with pleasing him. Now the priest was a black mark against them.

"Bitches, leave." Floria angled an overlong nail toward the door.

As the girls sulked past, Floria divested Deirdre of the small red velvet cufflink box she'd conveniently 'forgotten' in her ample cleavage.

"I may see about getting you three a situation where you can learn while you work," Floria suggested, her tone full of sweet poison.

Joseph was tired and the night had barely begun. Usually he was in bed at this hour, shaking his head over the late-night news, trying after all these years to ease himself to sleep without prayer.

Floria smoothed the garment bag across the desktop. "If you don't want to be pampered, fine. Whatever you like, Joe."

"I don't want to be accompanied," he snapped.

"You've made that clear," she answered amiably.

"Or watched."

Floria shrugged and turned her back.

Joseph tore the paper wrapping from the shirt. He was unfamiliar with the Borelli name on the label, but the black cotton was smooth under his rough fingertips, the weave as fine as silk. He pulled the turtleneck he was wearing over his head and folded it carefully, surprised to see how frayed the cuffs were. He stuck his arms into the new shirt and wished he'd worn an undershirt. The fabric felt too luxurious against his skin. Decadent.

Conversationally, Floria wondered, "Has Lorelei paid you yet?"

He was caught off-guard by the question. It meant that Floria didn't know the terms he'd set. "Not yet."

The succubus wasn't put off that easily. "She gonna be working for you when this is over?"

"I doubt it."

"Was she good to you in the limo?"

The abrupt switch in topics caught him again. His fingers stumbled on the shirt buttons. He realized Floria was tapping her fingers on her crossed arms, waiting for an answer. "Lorelei's always done her best for me," he said carefully.

"But you don't want to tie yourself down?"

She got the tone of voice just right: flirty, with a heavy dose of 'you can trust me.' This one was quite an actress. Joseph was glad she had her back to him and couldn't dazzle him with those warm amber eyes.

Changing the subject had worked for her. He wondered if Floria would let him get away with it too. "I thought Lorelei had a contract with that boy Hai."

"We don't go signing binding documents with just anyone," Floria answered. That tone wasn't as well camouflaged. It held a hint of something—huffiness, rather than flattery?

"You've got one with Tuan," he guessed. "For what: money? The penthouse? Your company?"

"Everything he wanted," she bragged.

"Except his freedom."

She laughed. It was a very good laugh: throaty, conspiratorial. A shiver trickled down Joseph's spine. "Freedom's overrated," the succubus said. "Lorelei's didn't get her what she wanted. She would've been happier with Hai."

Joseph slipped the new trousers off their hanger, bemused by the hint of flash in the fabric's nap. For clothing that was going to be hidden beneath a robe, Hell had gone to a lot of trouble to dress him. He recognized the bribe, feeling only an emptiness they'd meant to fill with covetousness. They couldn't grasp that he had no desire for material things. When he saw the expensive clothing, all he could think about was the good the money could've done for his parishioners: food on their tables, debts eased. He wished Hell would offer a bribe that might mean something to him. This was such a waste.

As he unbuttoned his trousers, he realized the succubus was watching him after all. His gaze met hers in the chromed frame of the Coop poster behind the desk. Floria smiled, showing her teeth.

"Was that Lorelei's angel out in the club?"

Floria swallowed her smile. "Yes."

"He wasn't what I expected."

"Not much to look at," Floria agreed.

"It's not that." Joseph turned his back on her to step out of his pants and into the new ones. "It's that he looked so normal, so human. All of you look artificial to me now, even the fiends. You're too shiny, too young, too attractive. He looked...like he'd really lived. Like time had marked him."

"Exile, too," Floria confided. "Wonder how bad one of them has to fuck up to be cast out of Heaven and *not* be allowed into Hell."

"Then he's not a celestial angel?" The disappointment in his voice was raw as a new bruise.

"Cast out," Floria clarified. "He's got a jones for mortal pussy."

Joseph tucked his shirttails in and thought about that. What must it be like to be certain of Heaven and forbidden it? What kind of torment was exile in a hellhole like LA, surrounded by the half-naked flesh of your desire? How had the angel withstood Lorelei? And why was he here tonight? How could he walk into this corner of the Inferno and expect to survive with any of his divinity intact?

"What kind of god would allow this to happen?" Joseph wondered aloud.

"One sick fuck," Floria answered. "Can I turn around now?"

She did anyway, plucking the tie off the desktop. He looped it around his neck, but his hands were shaking so badly that she tied the knot for him. He wished Lorelei hadn't taken away his whiskey earlier.

He staggered back to sit on the edge of the desk. Floria knelt at his feet and stripped off his socks. She cradled each foot in her lap as she replaced its sock with something smooth and cool. She rubbed his feet, hinting that the pleasures she could offer didn't need to be sexual. Then she laced on new leather shoes. The shoes fit like a dream, conforming to his bunions and the broken toe he'd never had set.

"God is dead," Joseph said.

Floria rapped on the mahogany desk with her knuckles. "I can't imagine the Enemy would condone what's happened to my sister and that mortal girl."

"Maybe we're in the Final Days," Joseph suggested.

"You mortals always think you're in the Final Days," Floria answered. "Face it, Joe: you, for one, are *not* that lucky."

She was busy threading ruby cufflinks into the black shirt, so he couldn't read her face.

"Say whatever you want," Joseph said, forcing the issue. "I know your purpose is to torment me."

She laughed again, meaning it this time. "Your church, your cardinal, your *god* did that, Joe. Now you're someone else's account. The only reason I'm dressing you is because the boss wanted me to."

She unzipped the garment bag and lifted out a robe. It smoldered a deep reddish black, the color of blood spilled in shadow. Spun gold embroidery snaked around the collar and sleeves. Floria held it up reverently, head bowed.

It was pretty, but unimpressive. Joseph held his arms out. Floria draped the robe around him. Goosebumps shivered up over his skin and didn't fade. He felt like he'd been soaked to the skin with icy water.

As the succubus fussed over the way the robe hung on him, he could see her true appearance. Her skin was red as raw flesh. A pair of black bat's wings folded against her shoulders. Bone spurs at her elbows echoed the horns peeping up through her hair. She was at least truly blond. Joseph found himself gaping at the way her charms threatened to spill from her little gold dress.

Floria dropped to one knee, muttering, "Adoring your darkness, greater than any light."

"Why the sudden deference?" Joseph wondered.

"It's for the *robe*," she snapped. "You feel that cold? That's power, old man. Not that you'd recognize it, but your cardinal would feel right at home in this."

He hesitated to imagine what evil had been done in this garment to affect it this way.

She handed him the stole. He lifted it halfway to his lips before he realized that habit had taken over. The devil hadn't missed the gesture. She flashed her teeth at him.

He shook the stole out and settled it over his shoulders. Almost showtime.

Behemoth waddled into the room. Stopping to hold court with various infernals along the way, he cast glances at Asmodeus's table to make certain the Prince of LA noticed his important new guest.

"Someone," Yasmina sniped, "appears miffed at being a guest and not the host. Then again, Lorelei wasn't his girl, was she?"

Asmodeus turned away, letting her know that she'd just crossed a line. "Meaning what: it does him no honor to be seen at this affair? Or that it's his host's misfortune to have such incompetent help?" The demon's benign tone belied the way he twisted her words.

Azaziel looked at her almost pityingly before saying a blessing over his new glass. Something fizzed unpleasantly, making him wonder what he'd just found and, hopefully, destroyed. The first drink had been fine, he was certain of it. This was just another reminder to keep on his toes.

Jequon returned, leaning over Yasmina to run his fingers along her throat. Together they rated the present succubi.

Sasha and Ruby stirred up trouble at the entrance, each coming up with outrageous reasons why one should be admitted and the other denied. Aza tried not to listen, but that became impossible once Lorelei's name was bandied about.

Yasmina whispered to Jequon about Sasha's grudge against Lorelei. Jequon made a sign to the fiend at the ropes. Sasha was permitted both true form and entry, while Ruby lost her dress and was handed a tray crowded with champagne flutes.

Jequon pulled Yasmina closer, teasing her ear with both tongue and words. Then he hissed, "Nebiros is here," loudly enough that Aza would overhear. "Guess that conflict in the Holy Land is on hold for the evening."

"How does he look?" Yasmina murmured.

"Messy. Having no teeth on one side makes it damned difficult for him to do anything neatly." Jequon gave Aza his most feline smile.

Tuning out the rest of the conversation, Aza located the General of

Hell's Army. Nebiros's table stood straight across the room from Asmodeus's, behind the bier where Aza couldn't watch the demon general directly. Still, the point was clear enough: if Aza made a grab for Lorelei and Ashleigh, Nebiros would pounce. He'd been awaiting odds in his favor since Aza drove him from Heaven's precipice. How could Aza get the girls out now? If Nebiros recognized their importance to the angel, their time on earth was already counting down.

When the procurer moved on, Yasmina refocused her attention on Aza, smirking. "You're being impolitely quiet, Azaziel. Trying to decide which of your darlings you'll miss more?

He stared at the tabletop.

Nails caressing the air over his forearm, she worked up the nerve to actually touch him. He could do nothing to her here, safe at her prince's side.

With a hissed intake of breath, Yasmina brought her hand down atop the angel's. Nothing sizzled or ached. His skin was cool under her fingertips.

She leaned close. Her lips brushed the hair above his ear, tasting him without touching. The sluts Lorelei and Floria had been there. Also, there was the scent of what she guessed must be an archangel. Didn't he ever bathe? Beneath it all lay his own familiar scent: clear as cold night air, a hint of desert, palm oil, and myrrh.

Some small part of her shivered at the recollection of her lost humanity. She hoped vainly that Asmodeus hadn't noticed.

The thought of times past inspired her to press on. Splitting her finger on the jagged rubies set into one of her rings, Yasmina spread a gemspot of blood onto the back of Azaziel's knuckles.

The angel stole a glance at her hand on his, her perfect skin showing webs of old henna. He felt the faintest pulse of Anah in that touch.

"You've been so alone for so long, an eternity among the noisome fools in this valley," Yasmina whispered in the old tongue.

He fought to ignore her words, feeling as vulnerable as any mortal he'd ever defended. Anah was gone. This was only the blood speaking to him.

"It's no great secret what you really want, Azaziel, what your heart desires, what you've always needed. If one considers the situation, Brother-in-law, we've never been closer. Between us is a bond closer than any between you and those born or created after me. Why not talk as family?"

Immensely interested, Asmodeus leaned forward. "Have you nothing to say to your sister, Azaziel?"

"Where is thy brother Abel?" he murmured into his drink, letting the hollowness within the highball glass carry the words back to her.

Yasmina drew her fingers back sharply, irises dilating. "My lord, should I see to the consecration of the sacrifice?"

Asmodeus nodded and waved her off with a distracted flick of his ring finger.

Almost out of earshot, Yasmina remarked, "Well done. You could take to our ranks just fine."

"Is that the reason for this ordeal?" Aza asked.

The demon sighed, as if Yasmina talked too much. Asmodeus folded his hands on the edge of the table and leaned forward. "You arrived of your own free will, Brother. I didn't invite you."

Aza wondered if that was true. When he'd walked into the bar, he'd been certain that Lorelei told him of the exorcism out of good will. Now he knew he'd staked his existence on the belief that the succubus was acting out of compassion for the first time in her life. Had her invitation come at her master's decree?

Either way, Aza knew that Asmodeus was a creature of his word. He did not bind himself with promises without the intention of carrying them out. Perhaps he could arrange for the girls to survive, even if Aza could not join them himself.

"I don't know what you see in them," Asmodeus said, nodding toward the bier. "Mortal flesh never held any appeal for me."

Recognizing the demon's lie, Aza saw no reason to justify himself.

"It withers too quickly."

That was so obvious as to require no comment.

"Her immortality is within your grasp," Asmodeus said.

Aza looked down into the new glass. "Whose?"

"That depends on your taste. One flesh, two very different spirits. If your preferences run to vanilla, you could own Ashleigh in Lorelei's immortal flesh." Asmodeus suggested soothingly, "Fold your wings and just let go."

"What would happen to Lorelei?"

"Hell is deep and always hungry."

"She never agreed to this," Aza protested.

"If I may quote: 'Do whatever it is you want to me.' That's a fair approximation of a verbal contract." Asmodeus tilted his glass against the angel's. "Well done, Brother."

Aza tasted the shame he'd inflicted on Lorelei in the alley. He hadn't coerced the words out of her, but he'd twisted her consent, ignored its meaning.

The demon lifted his glass, savoring his cognac's aroma. "There *is* a place for you on my staff, Brother," he continued. "You're good with misdirection. I understand that you know what you're doing in bed. Think of all the mortal girls you could enjoy on their way to damnation." Asmodeus sipped his cognac, nodding in the direction Yasmina had taken. The menace in his tone explained Yasmina's anxiety as he said, "I expect to have an opening shortly."

Pushing his glass away, Aza wondered what line Yasmina had crossed.

"If you prefer, we could arrange to send little Ashleigh to her deserved reward—and you can fuck the succubus of your dreams guilt-free. In fact, Lorelei could work for you. You could start a staff of your own."

"What would that cost me? Eternity under your heel?"

Asmodeus gave an easy laugh. "We both know how long eternity is, Brother. I'm sure we can agree upon a reasonable term of service."

Aza could no more resign Lorelei to damnation than he could conscience her continued slavery to Hell. Still, he would not buy Lorelei's soul at the price of Ashleigh's freedom.

Behemoth finally reached Asmodeus's table. His tuxedo strained around his bulk. Aza looked up briefly into the demon's eyes, then cast his glance away, not so much out of respect as sorrow. He remembered when the bloated monstrosity had been an angel of beauty, lively and iridescent as a beam of light.

"Welcome, Brother," Asmodeus said, without rising. "You honor us by attending tonight."

With a grin nearly swallowed by his many chins, Behemoth said, "Perhaps we ought to hold these get-togethers more often. Any other girls of yours you'd like to see afflicted with souls?" He winked at Aza.

"Let's discuss it next week," Asmodeus said brusquely. "I promise you won't have to wedge into the elevator if I know you're coming." He looked past the demon to the entrance of the room. "Ah. The main event is finally about to begin. You'll excuse me, I'm sure."

Behemoth laid a sweaty paw on Aza's shoulder. "If you and Asmodeus can't come to an agreement, Brother, please discuss your needs with me."

Azaziel downed his drink in a brief, hungry gulp. His nostrils twitched from the sweat-stink that Behemoth's hand left on his shoulder. His former brother filled with him pity. He didn't dare wonder for whom. Asmodeus would be quick to leap on that, echoing Mastema's promises of pride preserved and falling without undue mutilation.

Aza recognized the blond succubus, Lorelei's jealous sister, escorting the priest. Dismay swept over him. All the angels knew of Joseph's break from the Church. By an angel's reckoning of time, that was barely yesterday, but the span of years had all but crushed the old man.

Asmodeus stood to grip the priest's hands. "Welcome, Father. You know Azaziel."

The priest stared uncomprehendingly at the angel. Aza was certain, from something in the old man's face, that he saw the angel for what he was. The vision deeply disappointed him.

"We haven't met," Joseph said.

"Don't you remember, Father? Last night in Azaziel's cell, just before Lorelei burned the place down? Let's see, Brother, you were there with Rafael and that sweet and flinty Muriel. Isn't that right?"

Asmodeus grinned down at Aza, daring him to lie in the midst of Hell's company.

Aza couldn't admit that Lorelei had asked the angels to blank the priest's mind for her own protection. Misdirection, half-truths: was that how his fall began? "We met yesterday, Father, but you don't remember."

Joseph stared at him, trying to force the memory. Nothing about this angel—not the pearly wings, not his green eyes—looked the least bit familiar. He didn't emanate peace or strength or heavenly grace, just weariness. If there was an angel of melancholy, this was surely he.

"Since you saw an archangel last night, Father," Asmodeus continued smoothly, "Lorelei's debt to you has been paid in full."

"Another satisfied customer," Floria ground out, furious that Lorelei had deceived her so well.

Joseph stared at the angel, hoping for him to do something, anything. When Azaziel didn't move, Joseph turned his back in frustration. There was no God. There was clearly no goodness left.

Lorelei lay on the dais in front of him, naked and alone except for the soul possessing her. Joseph felt strength return, along with his determination. Evidently, he alone could set Ashleigh free: a good deed, snatched from the jaws of Hell. It was up to a human to do what angels could not.

Asmodeus laid a comforting hand on Joseph's shoulder and leaned close. "For what it's worth, Father, that's the way it's always been. Now, if you'd be so kind as to separate the milk from the honey…"

Aza looked up at the empty skylight. The dirty glass above reflected the candle flames below, creating an artificial field of stars surrounding

Lorelei's mirror image. Beyond the reflection, he saw no hint familiar faces, not so much as a wingtip. Aza thought of his own wings. Even if he stormed out right now, left the club and all this temptation, he'd still be stuck in Los Angeles, grieving the latest creatures he'd loved. He would never be able to forgive himself.

Asmodeus licked his lips. This was starting to taste like despair.

The demon felt a sudden stab of revelation. It rang so true, so coldly accurate in its ability to put his wayward brother on the spot, it had to have come from the very core of Hell, where the all-knowing ever-watching Father of Lies struggled against his chains.

"You're in love with her." Asmodeus chuckled wonderingly. "Truly and hopelessly, you love our chattel Lorelei." His eyes glowed above a fang-framed smile. "Having seen how well you've handled that singular emotion in the past, I don't think it's so much a matter of waiting for you to come over as wondering how you'll subvert God's will this time. You think He'll let you get away with that twice in one existence?"

Azaziel glanced sharply at the demon. There was nothing he could say.

"I don't say this often—at least, not with sincerity—but you poor *bastard*." Asmodeus chuckled with genuine warmth. He raised two fingers for a waitress.

Without delay, three made their way through the crowd. The succubus with the grudge against Lorelei arrived first to place another round of drinks on the table.

"Ask me about Atlanta sometime," Ruby offered. "Lorelei and I set that town on fire."

"Drink up," Asmodeus encouraged, pleased with the girl's obvious lack of respect for privacy. "I hear you can really put it away. Then again, if I had your taste in women, I'd drink heavily too."

CHAPTER 23: ON WITH THE SHOW

Lorelei jolted awake from a fantasy of rising from the bier, taking Aza's hand, and going away with him. That thought was dangerous. With all the demons in the club, Aza would be blessed indeed to survive the night, even without a succubus on his arm, slowing him down.

"What'd I miss while I was out?" Lorelei asked, then shivered. Was this the déjà vu mortals described?

"Must not be anything on TV tonight," Ashleigh said bravely. "We drew a crowd."

Lorelei twisted to look. Little round tables crammed the room, each lit by a candle flickering inside a red globe. Every chair was full. Shadows swarmed in the back. She recognized a who's who of Hell's hierarchy in Southern California: elephantine Behemoth, ebony-skinned Beelzebub in his pin-striped suit, flame-haired Mastema—Hell's liaison with the Fallen Angels—and skeletal, twisted Nebiros, General of Hell's Armies. Thodos had said Nebiros was Aza's nemesis. Weapons snarled and hummed from Nebiros's section of the room. Death, formerly hypothetical, looked certain. The best she could hope for was to have her soul drunk by one of those blades. Maybe the same weapon would swallow Aza. Wasn't there a song like that: 'to die by your side is such a heavenly way to die'?

The fluid swish of drapery caught her attention. Robed in power, Joseph stood at the bottom of the steps, flanked by Yasmina and Floria. As Lorelei flinched, Yasmina's cruel laughter sparkled around them like broken mirror. Lorelei's eyes met Floria's and she watched Floria think: *Bitch*.

The trio circled the ward around the bier in ritual formation. Yasmina carried a chalice grimed with centuries of use. Floria balanced a time-blackened platter holding a small brown cake. Joseph brought up the rear, dressed for a funeral. After three anti-clockwise rotations, they marched up the steps. Yasmina caught Lorelei's hand, tracing her nails lightly up the wrist, lingering over the veins. Lorelei lay back, breathing as slowly as she could. Floria took her other hand. Joseph stood just beyond her feet.

This wasn't right. Assuming the priest's invocations separated them, there were no precautions to protect Ashleigh from being consumed. Either Floria or Yasmina could snatch the girl's soul up. Where was that cursed angel? They'd relied on him to come charging to the rescue.

Yasmina's voice razored her skin. "He's here at your invitation, then?"

He's here? Ashleigh echoed. She had no idea of the danger she was in, Lorelei thought. Lucky for her.

Yasmina's cinnamon-colored gaze pierced Lorelei. "I told you to break him, Little Sister. Not invite him to a party."

Lorelei remembered Yasmina's case of tattoo needles. She would count herself fortunate if she dodged Jezebel's disfigurement to be sold to the angel.

Hopelessly, Lorelei turned her gaze to Floria. Her sister was still following orders, same as ever. When she laced her fingers through Lorelei's and smiled, Lorelei wasn't comforted.

"Shall we begin?" Joseph asked.

When he'd called her into Aza's cell, she'd glimpsed the power inside the tired old drunk. Now it blazed from him. He'd been robed in a gown the color of clotting blood, but its power paled beside the authority of the man. His eyes flashed with an intensity that riveted her gaze. Either he'd gone mad, or Asmodeus had somehow inspired him.

Joseph drew a black-bladed knife from the sleeve of his robe and pricked the top of her right foot. Walking to her right, he pushed the tip of the knife into her wrist. She felt blood trickle from her flesh as he moved up behind her head. He touched the point to her forehead, then the hollow of her throat. The blade was so sharp it stung like a needle. He pierced her left wrist and returned to prick her other foot.

"*Nema,*" he pronounced, the palms of his hands crossed over her feet. "*Sutcnas sutirips te ailif, airtap enimon ni...*"

Lorelei forced herself to relax under the familiar words. How many times had she served as the altar at Black Masses? She'd never heard the denial spoken with such force, such a dare to the Enemy.

At either side of her, Floria and Yasmina shimmered out of their mortal appearances, glowing with their true beauty. Lorelei's own flesh crawled, yearning to regain its infernal form. When Joseph ended the prayer, Lorelei looked out to see her rapt audience had reverted to their Hellish shapes.

Now that all glamours had been cleared, she saw Aza at last. Seated beside Asmodeus at the table directly in front of the bier, Azaziel shone with silvery light like sun behind a storm cloud. What was he doing there beside her boss? Had he been captured? Had he come over after all? Aza seemed quite comfortable, as if he'd resigned himself to whatever might happen.

The angel's green gaze met hers. She'd seen love in enough faces to recognize it. She shuddered. Love was not going to fend off their enemies.

Asmodeus leaned toward Aza. "If you don't choose, I'll choose for you, Brother. Inaction, while not a sin, does no good for anyone."

With effort, Aza broke Lorelei's fascination. "How can I persuade you to give both of them a chance?"

"Them?" Asmodeus scoffed. "There is no them. Choose one: either Ashleigh the tarnished innocent or Lorelei the burnished whore."

The demon nodded toward the stage where the chanting had begun in earnest. "Choose, Brother, and be quick about it."

Aza tried one last approach. "If I were to promise I'll raise no hand against anyone in this room? You will not have brought any guests to their doom tonight."

The table linens bunched under Asmodeus's nails. His expression darkened beyond theatricality. "Is that a threat? However veiled, it insults my hospitality. Anyway, I'd just as soon you do me the service tonight of eliminating some of our hierarchy's useless chaff." Asmodeus surveyed the room. "None of them would mourn if you cut my heart out here and now."

"I've brought no weapon with me," Aza countered.

Asmodeus favored the angel with a pointed grin. "There you have it: your good conduct is practically guaranteed. Reiterating said promise does nothing to increase its value."

After a long pause, Aza said, "I came here to retrieve Ashleigh's soul."

"In light of all I've laid before you, you're rejecting the position I offer?"

"I reject it."

"You're rejecting the gift I'd make of your heart's desire?"

"It's not yours to tender," Aza argued.

"You're rejecting the chance to send a succubus to eternal torment, knowing she will persist in luring souls to damnation?"

"What Lorelei does remains to be seen," Aza said.

"She'll do what she's told," the demon answered.

Aza decided to push it. "If she chooses to come with me after the exorcism is complete?"

Asmodeus waved a languid hand at the assembly. "You are my guest," he reminded. "Would you steal from your host?"

"Her *choice*," Aza repeated.

The demon's smile was as gentle as the rebuke in his tone. "If you think Lorelei would choose to walk out on Hell's protection, you don't know her as well as you think. She's made her share of enemies on her ascent in my service."

"I could protect her."

"An angel recently lamed by his own kind? Who's going to protect you, my friend?" The demon's smile edged toward malice. "That's what you need to consider."

Yasmina forced Lorelei to sit up; Floria tilted the chalice against her lips. Lorelei closed her eyes and drank deep of the innocent blood. Joseph's words became gibberish as she listened to them through the filter of Ashleigh's senses. Floria and Yasmina finished the blood, then nestled the chalice upside down between Lorelei's thighs. Then Floria embraced her as Yasmina broke the brown cake. Lorelei swallowed without chewing, unwilling to oppress the girl's spirit with the knowledge of what they ate.

Joseph wrapped up the Mass and segued smoothly into the exorcism. "I cast you out, Ashleigh Johnson. Be gone and stay far away from this creature of Satan. For it is He who commands you, first created of all living things. It is He who commands you, who was flung headlong from the heights of Heaven into the depths of Hell. It is He who commands you, who led the first of our mothers into temptation. Hearken, therefore, and tremble in fear, Ashleigh, before the foe of the human race, the corrupter of justice, the root of all vice, seducer of men, author of pain and sorrow. How, then, do you stand and resist?"

"Boy, can he talk," Yasmina marveled. "I could listen to this all night."

Floria shot her a look so sulfurous that any other creature would have shriveled.

Asmodeus snapped his fingers and a succubus hurried over. Facing Aza, she leaned over so the boss could whisper in her ear. Her ample cleavage practically leapt out of her dress. Then she scurried off to fulfill her master's wishes.

The exorcism was working. Lorelei felt a dreadful tearing in her chest, like the agony a cell feels as it divides.

Joseph watched her closely. He raised his hands to shoulder height, palms facing her, and began to pray. "Satan, Father of Lies, Author of Evil, look in pity on this your servant, now caught up in the coils of this human spirit. Unravel this angelic labyrinth, break asunder these snares and traps, put this childish ghost to flight. By this sign,"—he drew an upside cross—"let your servant be protected. Keep watch over the inmost recesses of her heart, rule over her emotions, strengthen her will. Let vanish from her flesh the temptations of this human child. As we call on your name, O Satan, allow this child to retreat in grace and in peace, so that this servant of yours may sincerely and steadfastly render you the service which is your due."

The agony spiraled beyond anything Lorelei had previously imagined. The more she tried to shove aside Ashleigh's ghost, the more of her own spirit she felt ripped away. Her flesh had turned to stone, galvanized by lightning. She convulsed and arced and struggled, breathing out a steady tormented moan.

The waitress returned with a chromed martini shaker on her tray. Asmodeus twisted off the shaker's cap to examine the cup, confirming it was brilliantly polished inside and out.

He screwed the cap back down. The waitress ferried it up to the edge of magical circle. Yasmina reached over Lorelei and nudged Floria to retrieve the shaker.

Scowling, Floria did as bidden, snatching the martini shaker across the barrier. As soon as her fingers closed on the hot chrome, she realized what it was intended for. She returned to stand at Lorelei's left hand. Smirking, Yasmina swiped the shaker from her. Floria swallowed her anger, consoling herself that no matter what else, it was Lorelei on the table instead of her.

Joseph grasped Lorelei's ankles, holding her down to the bier. He burned with a holy radiance. Perhaps he had lost his faith, but he'd continued to live by its tenets, persisting in poverty, celibacy, and service to his fellows. He might be calling on Satan now, but he was doing God's work. It was terrible to see.

"Light shines in the darkness," Joseph told her, "and darkness cannot lay hold of it. The light is love. The angel Azaziel so loved the devil Lorelei that he blessed her with the company of a mortal soul. Come out now, Ashleigh Johnson, thy work is done. You have suffered long enough in the name of love. Come out and take your rest."

With a final excruciating rip, both souls burst free of Lorelei's throat, riding the last of her breath. The body slumped. Lorelei looked down at it tenderly, but no trace of animation remained. They had killed her.

Floria twisted the remaining handcuff between her long fingers. The metal snapped. She pulled the pieces free and flung them at Azaziel. His hand shot up and caught them from the air.

As Lorelei examined Ashleigh's spirit, she looked every bit as frail as when Lorelei saw her in the flesh. Ashleigh's ghost spun slowly like a tethered balloon, scanning the crowd. Being out of body in front of Asmodeus down in the storm drain had been unpleasant. This was a moment no mortal in Creation had ever seen: the most infernal faces in LA turned her way, scrutinizing the impertinent soul who had sent a shock through their realm. They blamed Ashleigh, even if it hadn't been her idea.

Ashleigh tried to say something, probably Azaziel's name. Lorelei wondered what prevented Aza from rescuing the girl, if he'd somehow lost his nerve, or faith, or cut a deal... chosen Lorelei instead?

A single ripple of something powerful gripped them both. Ashleigh stared around in confusion as a sudden invocation, close by and undeniable, condensed her essence into the silver ribbon that bound her to the dead flesh below. A roar from the audience greeted the terror on her face.

Ashleigh's ribbon unraveled from Lorelei's, guided away from the body into the vessel in Yasmina's outstretched hand. Ashleigh understood how helpless water felt whirling down a drain. The temptress struck a pose appropriate to a magician's assistant. Her wildly triumphant grin blazed in a way that made it clear that there was a bigger trick yet to come.

Lorelei couldn't help but wonder what the girl had expected: a shaft of golden light to guide her to safety? This dark and hostile room was Hell's VIP entrance. Ashleigh Johnson knew she was gate-listed.

True to his word, Joseph put his knife away, determined not to kill Lorelei's soul. The succubus decided not to wait around to see what would happen next. She dove back through the loosening coils that had bound her to the mortal girl. She hit the body with a shudder. Instantly her chest smoldered with pain. Hell's heat ranged over her skin, transmuting mortal substance to infernal. This was nothing like the dreamlike transition with which Yasmina had tempted Ashleigh. This was painful rebirth, using dead flesh as womb and fuel.

The first sound she could make was a strangled scream. Her talons raked the altar as she writhed there, unnoticed and no longer needed. She hurt, she had a soul and was therefore damned—but she was whole again.

She thought she heard Azaziel's voice. Formless words of love and need tugged at her.

It took all of Lorelei's will to turn her head toward him. He was on his feet, something glinting in his outstretched hand. She couldn't focus her vision, but obviously he must be holding up a mirror of his own, intent on capturing Ashleigh's spirit for himself. His choice had been made.

Floria rolled her eyes. The angel was waving the handcuff around like some sort of memento that sealed their engagement. She looked down to see Lorelei's response. Her sister lay still, her eyes closed, resigned to her fate. Perfect.

Asmodeus pushed Azaziel's hand down against the tabletop. "I've been thinking about what you said, about giving both of them a chance. I'll make you one final offer, in which there is something to please everyone."

He vaulted up onto the table. A bright white spotlight snapped onto him. "Friends, noble assemblage of the great and fearsome hosts of Hell, guests—" he gestured expansively with both arms "—and family, welcome to Lost Angels. Many of you know our long-estranged, soon-to-be-reunited, brother Azaziel."

A variety of hisses and catcalls greeted the name. Someone in the back yelled, "Chicken hawk!" which garnered a round of applause.

Across the room, someone else shrilled, "Flesh junkie!"

A third voice, deeper in pitch, jeered, "Soul daddy!"

Asmodeus gestured for them to settle down. Without intervention, the lesser wits of Hell would be up all night, trying to top each other. "What you may not know is that we have Azaziel to thank for bringing us together tonight. If he hadn't gotten the hots for the pathetic wisp of a mortal soul he cached within our servant Lorelei …"

"Kill her!" some high-pitched voice screamed. "Kill the abomination!"

Lorelei shuddered, remembering her first nightmare. Had it been a premonition?

"One thing at a time," Asmodeus soothed. "Others thought that perhaps we ought to keep the two of them around as a freak for our pleasure."

Several fiends whistled.

"But we couldn't do that any more than we could press an undamned mortal soul into infernal bondage. I've even heard that some advocated elevating the mortal girl to a station she didn't deserve." He waggled a scolding finger at Yasmina.

There was a gasp when the assembly realized he was serious. Yasmina's eyes went black. She set the martini shaker down on the altar and receded out of the spotlight.

Asmodeus had not finished. He hauled Aza up onto the table beside him. Displeasure rumbled through the crowd. It was one thing to have an angel amongst them, quite another to have him sharing the spotlight. A liquid growl rose from Nebiros's table.

The angel ignored the audience, fixing his eyes on the martini shaker.

Asmodeus leaned over to ask, "What's that, Angel? You ask, 'Didn't I mention a deal?'"

He was interrupted by the scrape of claws on tabletops, the gnashing of teeth, angry shouts.

Inside the protection of his robe, Joseph blanched. This is what the fury of Hell sounded like. Now, as final proof of God's absence from the world, he would have to watch this angel torn to pieces, if Azaziel didn't accept the demon's bargain.

Asmodeus curled a finger at Floria, who swept up the martini shaker. She crooked her arm around Joseph and brought both of them to her master.

Rather than having a quieting effect, the gesture brought the room into gleeful pandemonium that forced Asmodeus to throw a fiery sigil of silence into the air before him.

The only sound to break the silence was the slither of scales as Yasmina left the room.

Asmodeus placed a conciliatory hand on the angel's shoulder. "Since after this you will never be trusted to shepherd another soul, you might as well develop a taste for them." He took the martini shaker from Floria and pressed it against Aza's chest. "Drink her down, Brother. It's time for communion."

CHAPTER 24: HEX VEX SEX

The entire room shifted in impatient exultation, waiting for the sigil of silence to burn out so they could express their enthusiasm. Asmodeus cast a glance at the skylights above Lorelei's catafalque, wondering if they'd survive the force of the roar. Oh well, glass lived to be shattered. It wasn't like it would be falling on his head.

The sigil flickered out and the clamor began. Raw unholy joy, ravenous excitement, and a single voice of maddened rage shattered the silence. From Nebiros's table there came a crash as an unhallowed weapon glowed purple in the darkness.

With calm that completely contradicted the situation, Aza thrust the martini shaker toward the priest. "Take care of her, Joseph."

He turned back to the room, unwilling to face a mutilating initiation without a fight. Then the real roar went up and the windows, as expected, splintered.

Lorelei flung her fists over her face, taking the falling glass with her forearms. Despite the screams and curses filling the room, she could hear each shard plinking down around her. What a blessing to have her infernal senses back! She grinned, despite and because of the pain. The chaos around her might provide cover for her escape.

With a joyful shout, Barbelo and Shebniel dove inward, swooping into the gathering melee.

The room exploded in a cacophony of shouts and the ring of weapons. Accusatory cries rose loudest, directed at Asmodeus. "This was supposed to be a safe place!" Behemoth protested, as his retinue upended their tables to use as shields.

"Betrayer!" Beelzebub yelled. "He brought us here as prey for angels!"

Sauntering back toward the public half of the club, Asmodeus sneered, "What are you all afraid of?" His bodyguard of fiends shoved everyone with whom they came into contact toward the fight. "It's only three angels. Two and a half, if you count that one." He jabbed a finger in Aza's direction.

"And you!" he shouted toward Nebiros. "What are *you* waiting for? Here is your enemy delivered unto you, with cause to destroy and the means to do it."

Nebiros's head snapped toward Aza with a painful crackling of vertebrae.

"If I've brought you anything tonight," Asmodeus added, "it is the chance for glory and revenge. Never let it be said that Asmodeus is anything but a generous host!"

That is what I call spin control, Floria thought, awed, as she slipped neatly into Yasmina's vacant place. Grinning, she accompanied her prince's retinue past the leather curtain. The boys appeared to have gone from Barakiel's bar. She wondered if Tuan had had the sense to get himself and the other boys out safely, or if she'd be looking for a new place to live come morning. Either way was fine with her.

Out on the dance floor, heads turned as Asmodeus passed the leather curtain. Just what kind of good time were they having in the back room? Still, the swing band didn't stop playing. If anything, they stepped up the volume to compete with the racket in the back. In the public area, the party continued unimpeded.

Aza faced the hosts of Hell unarmed. Thodos bulled forward from amidst Asmodeus's staff, seemingly determined to take the angel out of the spotlight. Aza swatted him away with a backhand that knocked him against the base of the catafalque.

Most infernals of note quickly found their ways out of the ballroom by whatever means, magical or mundane. Other than Nebiros's entourage, only cannon fodder remained behind to secure their masters' escapes.

Shebniel's halberd arced toward a snarling fiend whose ratted fur pooched out from beneath his three-piece ensemble. From the smell he carried, he was one of Behemoth's enforcers. Even without an archangel's unsullied grace behind the blow, the slender battle-axe cleaved through and beyond, severing the leg of the succubus from Atlanta on its way to the floor.

Screaming, Ruby toppled. Azaziel silenced her with a blow of his fist that crumpled her skull into her shoulders.

Even as the gore melted from his hand, Azaziel found himself swarmed by a trio of toad-headed devils. Their bodies were slimed with venom that foamed from beneath their clothing. Rather than touch them, he slipped out of his leather jacket, wrapping it around a bare fist before he launched into them. This would make two coats he'd lost this week.

Muriel touched down on the roof beside the pair of archangels, who watched the scuffle through the skylight. "How can Azaziel *still* be unfallen?" she demanded.

"That decision is for none of us to make," Rafael reminded.

Below them, Barbelo's lance was a blur of gold and blue as she speared a pair of devils who had the misfortune to be at the rear of their retreating pack. Shebniel stood wing to wing with Aza, who defended himself barehanded. Beside the bier, Nebiros hacked through fleeing devils, trying to reach his nemesis.

Michael said, "You wanted an opportunity to use your sword."

"Not in Azaziel's defense," Muriel argued. "He got himself into this mare's nest. Let him fight his way out."

"Azaziel's temptations vex him only while he's embodied. If his flesh is destroyed, there's nothing to prevent his spirit from cleaving forever to his succubus. Think of the Enemy's triumph then." Michael gripped her shoulder. "You, Muriel, can prevent this."

Grinning, Muriel dove to the attack. The murderous holiness in her eyes flared brighter than the flames of her sword.

Entirely forgotten amidst the eternal battle, Joseph hugged the martini shaker to his chest. As it touched the robe, the cup burned intolerably hot. His senses filled with a sweet young girl moaning in deepest terror. The robe might be powerful, but it wouldn't allow him to comfort a child. Never releasing the cup, he shrugged out of the robe and let it cascade to the floor.

A bright new angel descended through the skylight to land beside Azaziel. This immaculate creature didn't so much have a halo as blaze. A thatch of white hair shone above vivid blue eyes. His wings were huge, easily twenty-five feet in span, and feathered in shimmering silver.

Heart full of wonder, Joseph fell to his knees.

The archangel pressed a sword into Azaziel's hands. "This is all the help I can give you, Brother."

"It's probably more than I deserve," Aza said quietly. Brandishing the blade, he turned to engage Hell's host.

The archangel came to lift Joseph to his feet. "Father, I'm Rafael."

The scales dropped from Joseph's eyes. He recognized the angel from Azaziel's cell who praised his quick thinking. "I remember you now."

"This is no place for you and the young lady, Father. Shall we go?"

Joseph wanted to thank Lorelei for giving him everything he'd asked, but the bier was empty.

Behind the altar, Lorelei huddled on the floor, miserable and terrified, desperate to disappear.

The friendly angel from the observatory rounded the catafalque. At the sight of Lorelei, the angel's lance dematerialized. Barbelo held an empty hand down to the succubus.

Lorelei relaxed only marginally. "Are you my ride home again?" she asked, pleased that she managed to sound more skeptical than terrified.

"Do you have a home?" Barb wondered.

"I doubt it."

"Let's get out of here, anyway," Barb said. "You don't have to go home, but you can't stay here."

Lorelei grinned, surprised to find the angel had a sense of humor. She trailed Barb across the back side of the room. Angelic invisibility certainly had its benefits. Another leather curtain shielded a nondescript door. Barb opened it as if it wasn't even locked.

Lorelei slipped into the storeroom and locked the door behind her, shutting in the darkness in with them. Behind the Absolut cases waited a freight elevator to the alley above. The succubus was relieved to have her night vision back.

Barb fiddled with the elevator controls in the blackness. As the machinery clanked to life, Lorelei bounded onto the lift platform. While it rose, Barbelo reached overhead and shoved open the steel doors to the street. The bolt sheared off. She sprang out, lance in hand, and made sure the coast was clear before she gestured to Lorelei to proceed.

Leaping upward, glorying in having her true form back at last, Lorelei said, "Thank you for not just dragging me out of here."

"There isn't room for both of us to open our wings," Barb explained. "Now, let's get out of here."

Lorelei turned back toward the nightclub. "What about Aza?"

"He has what aid our fellows can give him," Barbelo said. "While you're here, you can be used against him. Shall we go before someone sees us together?"

Enraged and refusing to be cowed by the archangel's sword, Nebiros and his cadre finally surged toward the trio of angels who held the center of the dance floor. Shebniel screamed as a chainwhip found his ankles and dragged him down under a hail of claws and flailing hooves. Aza batted two of the fiends aside with Rafael's sword. Nebiros caught Aza's next strike against his scimitar and forced the angel to retreat.

A pair of fiends howled as they dragged the halberd from Shebniel's grip. Their hands smoked and melted where they'd touched the holy weapon.

Muriel hacked her way toward Shebniel, oblivious to the weapons that sliced the air around her. She stayed low, finding openings where she could. She inflicted terrible injuries, then moved on, letting the fallen hosts accumulate around her in such a way that any who tried to attack found themselves compelled to hack through their own wounded.

Aza closed with Nebiros, thrusting deeply past the General's defenses, but without lasting effect. His adversary threw a vicious swing with the serpent he carried as rank of office. The creature's fangs scored a bloody sweep over Aza's chest. Thin licks of fire fed off angel's blood.

Nebiros's misshapen lips curled into a grin. "Don't worry, Brother. You won't bear the mark long. I'll see it lost in myriad disfigurements."

Bleeding from a hundred wounds, Shebniel dragged himself away from his attackers and flung himself awkwardly up toward the rafters. Streams of his angelic blood spattered the devils that leapt up to yank him back down.

He hit the floor with a crash that rattled everything in the room. Devils piled atop him, each hungry for a handful of angel's flesh. When Muriel finally drove them back, nothing of Shebniel remained by a heap of bloodied feathers.

"That's more like it," Nebiros cheered. "One down, two more to go."

Aza remembered Shebniel from the old days, when there were few enough women that the childbed angels could gather to oversee each birth. Shebniel had always loved infants, standing for hours rocking their cradles, watching over them with love burning in his eyes.

He'd adored Barbelo after her unique birth. Of all the angels, Barbelo had been born of a mother, rather than created directly by the Word. Shebniel held her, as he'd held the mortal infants, rocking her in his arms and singing.

Shock at Shebniel's destruction ran cold through Aza's body, locking him into place. He too would have fallen to Nebiros's scimitar, had Muriel not screamed his name and brought him around.

Lowering Rafael's weapon to the floor, Aza feinted. He released his grip on the holy blade and sprang barehanded onto the demon before him.

Not expecting to be attacked by faith alone, the General overcut his attack. The curving blade of his weapon found only empty floorboards. The scimitar jammed fast, setting the floor around it ablaze. The flames made it dangerous for Aza to retreat from the advantage he'd gained.

Fire lapping at his wingtips, Aza hurled a blow from inside of Nebiros's guard and connected with his misshapen jaw.

Shebniel's song echoed through the burning club, shimmering with joy. Now that he'd been rendered discorporate, he could see the glow of Heaven's gates opening before him. Self-sacrifice had paved his way home.

Azaziel had no illusions that the death of his own flesh would open any doors for him. He was doomed to this mortal plane forever, it seemed.

All around them, devils writhed and moaned, tormented by the voice of the formless angel. Aza shook himself, retrieved the archangel's sword, and swung it toward his nemesis. Eyes blurred with tears, Aza traded blows with the General of Hell's Army. Their weapons threw glowing motes that burned everyone close by.

Muriel quite happily made it her business to avenge Shebniel. Her features froze in a grin as terrifying as anything dreamed of in Hell. She slaughtered everything within reach.

Aza grabbed double handfuls of Nebiros's jacket. The demon's breath felt as corrosive on his skin as the fire had on his feathers. Shouting to the glory of Heaven, Aza leapt toward the skylights. His stiff wings snatched the clamor-filled air. Nebiros felt the lurch and fought it, taloned feet biting into the scarred dance floor. The boards screeched and snapped like a horse having its limbs broken.

Unable to drag the demon aloft, Aza braced his knees to spring clear. Muriel reached up as he sailed past to slap him down. Aza crashed down atop a table, flipping it crazily off balance.

Muriel realized her mistake as Nebiros pounced on Aza in a roar of stinking breath, serpent in hand. Muriel's leap to aid Aza was interrupted by the demon's coterie, who compelled her to see to her own skin.

Aza heard the whipcrack of the serpent and felt a terrible rip as its fangs took hold, hauling him upright. He snatched back over his shoulders at the source of fiery torment.

Expecting that the snakebite was prelude to a deathblow, his thoughts raced with dizzying precision: Asking forgiveness of God. Granting absolution to Muriel. Declaring love for his Lorelei.

The blow never came. A half-dozen of Nebiros's servants dragged the General backward, yammering in panic about there being no time left.

To prove their words, Michael and Rafael closed from opposite sides of the ballroom. Both were unmistakably fierce in purpose.

Someone in Nebiros's company threw a hasty sigil on the back wall, conjuring a portal to safety. The General, still not realizing he was the last demon in the club, spat and swore, rending the flesh of his would-be rescuers.

One of the fiends holding Muriel loosed his smoking grip on her. Waving his burned, weaponless hands in a mollifying gesture, he came off like a carny magician about to produce her underwear.

"Truce, Sweet Wings. We just wanna get the General out of here. Lemme point out, we didn't so much as scratch you."

"That's gotta be worth somethin'," the second fiend chimed in as he released her arm. He glanced nervously toward the flickering portal, now filled with a writhing mass of devil flesh. Nebiros's charges succeeded at last in pulling their infuriated master to safety.

Incensed they'd dared to lay hands on her, Muriel took the fiends' heads with a single blow. Ichor spilled over her. She reached down to tear the scimitar out of the floorboards. Then she flung it, spinning, into the infernal escape hatch.

The portal in the wall solidified and the General was gone, leaving his serpent firmly attached to Aza's shoulder. The creature shuddered, hollowing into ashes that clung to the angel's back in a smoldering trail.

The screams of the maimed and dying bled into an onrushing wail of mortal sirens. As the fire spread, panic shrieked from the public portion of the club.

Retrieving his sword, Rafael assisted Aza through the skylight. The other angels joined them on the roof. Muriel shook the blood from her sword and turned to re-enter the club.

"If you go in, it must be to save mortals, not to cleanse with fire and sword," Rafael cautioned her.

"Why not both?"

"None of us have been set up to judge here, Little One," he reminded, his tone gentle. The hold he took of her shoulder was less so. Aza exchanged a concerned look with imperturbable Michael. Lines, it seemed, were being drawn and crossed everywhere amongst their kind.

"There are times for harder actions," Rafael admitted, trying to smooth Muriel into a hug. "The Rebellion, the Fall...but not now. These are times to move with the heart, instead of the hand."

"Look where that's gotten one of us," Muriel spat, leaping skyward.

"What did I just say about judging?" Rafael sighed to the other angels as he took to the night skies.

The fiends abandoned their post at the door of the private ballroom once the fire spread into the public area. They kept busy blocking the exits so that the damned would perish inside. As a perk, the barricade trapped many questionable souls as well. The fiends caught what they could of those and gobbled them up.

No one stood to oppose Samael when he burst open the revolving door and strode into the building. One fiend he beheaded with a swipe of his javelin. The other he skewered and flung down off the balcony onto the dance floor below.

Struggling mortals clogged the stair up to him. Some had been trampled. Still others were succumbing to the smoke. When those still living saw him with his glory revealed, a moan rose above the coughing and screams, the crackle of flames and the noises the building muttered in its death throes.

Here and there burned a pale white light as a soul, in honest terror, repented its sins and begged forgiveness. Samael moved to aid those first, walking over other mortals as necessary. He pulled the survivors from the flames or debris that confined them and helped them into the night above. They left the dance club with unshakeable faith that their survival was miraculous, a sign that they were meant to work God's will in the world.

But those he rescued were few. Mostly amongst the mortal survivors Samael found the truly damned. Those souls he swept up with the hem of his robe to be disposed of later.

A few devils continued to feed on the unsaved, flailing after the dying in an orgy of gluttony. Disgusted, Samael killed every devil he came across, casting them down to feed the flames.

Because of the venom in his wounds, the short flight from 'Lost Angels' to the neighborhood of the old church was rough on Aza. He settled to a landing at the corner market. Bracing himself against the payphone on the wall, he slowly gathered in his wings. Pain sang through him, bright as trumpets.

From down the block rang a lament for Shebniel in the voices of the other angels. Rafael loosened the side vent on a fire hydrant, then blessed the water as it fanned through his fingers into a healing mist. They cleansed themselves as they shared memories of their old friend.

Aza shut his eyes. He'd lost so many friends over the ages. At least Shebniel had gone home. Aza struggled not to envy him.

He thought of Ashleigh, trapped in that hellish martini shaker. Poor terrified child, who'd suffered so much in order to love and be loved. He hoped that Rafael had found her redeemed and released her soul to

Heaven, saving her further torment.

He thought he'd seen Joseph leave with Rafael, too. It would be a wonder if Lorelei had saved the priest when Heaven's emissaries failed. Surely that would count in her favor.

Where was she now, the devil he loved? He'd walked blindly into Asmodeus's embassy, trusting that faith and intention would rescue Lorelei. Once the fighting had begun, he'd been unable to spare a thought for her. Had she escaped? Had any of the angels offered her sanctuary? Had Asmodeus destroyed her, as promised?

Aza tried to reach out with his soul. Surely, if Lorelei was dead, he would know.

If she was dead, what reason did he have to continue living?

The thought was blasphemy. He rejected it immediately. He lived to serve. There could never be any doubt about that.

What was it the mortal writer Lewis had divined? After a man lay with a woman, however briefly, an eternal bond was forged between them. Once formed, such a bond had to be enjoyed or endured forever after.

Aza hadn't meant to lie with Lorelei. He'd meant only that she should understand love through the intercession of his mortal charge. While the ties of his heart to Ashleigh remained pure, it had been Lorelei's flesh he'd known. For better or worse, he'd unintentionally bound himself to the succubus.

A chill washed through Aza. He knew he should rejoin the others at the corner. However, a barrier seemed to exist between him and the other angels. He could almost visualize the sanctification of the air around them. What was this: hallucination? Premonition? If he drew near them, would the barrier slow his approach, burn his flesh?

Aza fought panic as he retreated around the corner, out of sight of the healing assembly.

A succubus stood atop the Nicolas Juareno's shuttered clothing shop. She was naked but for a pair of sheer black stockings, absurdly high heels, and Barbelo's blazer. Black bat wings folded back against her shoulders, ruffling a little as his gaze caressed her. A silver ring glinted from the bone spur atop one wing. Aza wondered what she'd done to be punished with a bone piercing. With a shiver that was half desire, he realized how little he knew about his personal devil.

Lorelei's voice drifted past Aza's senses to the core of him. "I never thought I'd be saying this, but should I come down to your level, Angel?" Despite the glib words, her tone was as full of hope and fear as his own heart.

"Let's meet in the middle," he offered, finding strength in the promise of her touch.

Lorelei stepped off as he leapt up. When they reached each other, his arms circled her waist as much for support as in longing. Her wings beat gently in time with his as they floated down to the asphalt.

"Kiss me," she suggested helpfully.

Aza tilted his face down to her. The strangest thing was he found compassion in her lips. She was undoubtedly a different creature than the one he'd felled with a kiss a week ago. Lorelei slid her hands up his back beneath his wings and held him tightly.

When at last she slipped from his arms, Lorelei said, "Here we are again, near where you fucked me. Wanna do it again?"

The rejuvenating effects of their kiss faded with the broken contact. Aza laid his cheek on her shoulder. "What a punishment this would be," he mused aloud, "to only feel alive and intact when kissing you."

"Oh?" Lorelei teased. "*Please* throw me in that briar patch."

To her surprise, the angel kissed her almost hungrily, as if trying to prove his point. Lorelei allowed herself a throaty moan.

Aza stepped back with a smile. "We can't talk here."

"Say the word and we'll fly."

Glancing toward the sky, Azaziel winced as if even *that* hurt. "I'm not up to it."

So there would be no romantic flying away to another plane. Disappointment stung Lorelei. Despite that, she kissed him again. He straightened a little; it didn't hurt her disposition either. Maybe there was something to this kissing and healing thing.

"How 'bout if I take hold of you and we glide somewhere?"

"If my brethren saw us, I'd be in trouble."

"Aren't you already?" she mocked.

"I'm not ashamed of you, just cautious. Just because we're happy to be together doesn't mean there's anyone from either side that feels the same. I'm not strong enough for a fight, if one comes up right now."

Lorelei glanced toward the voices of the angels around the corner. How many of them were there now? Maybe retreat was the smartest course of action at the moment. "Do you feel up to a little stroll? We can rest as often as you like."

Wrapping his hand around hers, the angel led her down the sidewalk and into the shadows. "Back to the church?" he asked.

"After the week I've had, it feels almost like neutral territory," Lorelei said.

Even injured, the angel's grip was fierce. It felt more possessive than restraining.

"I'm sorry I lost the handcuff," she said.

"Your sister…"

Lorelei laughed. "Yeah. There's gonna be Hell to pay over that. Still, the cuff meant something to me. I wanted to let you know that. I'm sorry it's gone."

"Maybe I can give you something nicer," he said.

She looked up at him, trying to read his expression. Had he just made a pass at her? "Well, you know, I'm not about collecting material things," Lorelei said, trying to pin him down. "It's not like I have a place to keep them."

"Not going home any time soon?" Aza observed.

She grimaced. "Are you?"

"We both know the answer to that, Lorelei."

"Stuck here with me? That's a shame."

The angel reached for her again. "I am what I am."

"As am I, Aza. But here I am, with you. What am I supposed to do, be your girlfriend until you figure out a way to get back into the Heavenly graces? Give up everything I know only to be stopped at the gate when you finally go in?"

Spreading his arms and, by reflex, wings as well, he asked, "Do you really think I could leave you?"

"No," she admitted. "Because you didn't leave that Anah chick. But that was way back in the day. Maybe you've wised up some. Will you make that same choice again, push come to shove, if some glad-handing archangel gives you the politician's pump and says, 'Drop the skirt and all's forgiven'?"

"Do you require a signed contract?" he asked sadly.

"No. Those things tend to get out of hand." She reached out as if to embrace him, but stopped achingly short. "Aza, I'm a succubus. There's no getting around that. All I know is sex and duplicity. Maybe a certain fucked-up kind of loyalty, too, but not much else."

"I know," he whispered.

"I just had to make that clear, 'cause if there's one thing I'm capable of being honest about, that's it. Usually, when I'm this honest, it's already too late."

"Not for us."

He smiled in a way that made Lorelei unsure whether this new heart of hers was soaring or breaking. Fucking angels.

"We'll figure something out," he promised, offering his hands. "Give me time, Lorelei. I have faith this can be made to work."

Lorelei launched herself into the angel's arms, wrapping every limb and even her tail around him. Not fallen, of course, but definitely hers.

ABOUT THE AUTHORS

Loren Rhoads is the author of *The Dangerous Type*, *Kill By Numbers*, and *No More Heroes*, the books of the *In the Wake of the Templars* trilogy. Her Lorelei stories have appeared in the books *Sins of the Sirens* and *Demon Lovers*.

Keep an eye on her at LorenRhoads.com.

Brian Thomas served a decade-long stint as a researcher at 20th Century Fox, specializing in religion, arcana, death, and creative violence. He contributed his expertise in matters celestial/infernal to such projects as *The X-Files*, *Millennium*, *Buffy the Vampire Slayer*, *Angel*, *The Order*, and *The Omen*. Brian also contributed to *Morbid Curiosity* magazine, *Jamie Foxx's Night Tales* website, and many uncredited script-doctoring assignments. He currently operates Rogue Research, a freelance research service for filmmakers, authors, and artists.

COMING IN NOVEMBER 2016
FROM AUTOMATISM PRESS

Angelus Rose – As Above, So Below: Book 2
by Loren Rhoads and Brian Thomas

CHAPTER 1: THE LONG GAME

Floria kept her gaze down while she served Asmodeus. He hadn't commented when she slipped into the limo between a pair of fiends last night. They left space for her at the prince's side, then ignored her, taking calls and reporting to the boss. Asmodeus pushed her head toward his lap and leaned back. This allowed the succubus to eavesdrop unapologetically.

The angels who had attacked them at Lost Angels, including the archangel Rafael, were playing in a broken hydrant outside their church. The choir Muriel, who'd done service for Hell once before, lingered amongst them. Back at Lost Angels, an angel of death hovered inside the burning nightclub, gathering souls from both sides.

"What?!" Asmodeus roared. "Stop the car!"

Whatever was driving the limo slammed on the brakes. The tires squealed, then a second car struck the limo from behind. A sickening lurch threw Floria to the floor. Asmodeus's limo continued sliding forward until its driver regained control.

The only thing to lighten Asmodeus's scowl was when he sent one of the fiends to collect the soul of the driver who'd crashed into them.

Grabbing the other fiend by his lapels, Asmodeus demanded, "Who's left at my club to oppose Samael?"

The fiend punched a number into his cell phone with a blackened claw. Then he reported, "Nebiros was the last demon to leave, when his cadre dragged him through a portal."

"What sort of spineless trash is working for us these days?" Asmodeus bellowed, tearing a handful from the fiend's suit.

Concern flickered over the fiend's angular face, but he continued, "None of us remain alive inside the club. Two angels are proselytizing the survivors. The fire rages out of control. All the mortals left inside are dead."

The other fiend climbed back into the limo. His gaze lingered on his brother's ruined suit as he handed his chromed cigar case to the boss. Asmodeus slipped it into his jacket without comment.

"Turn the car around," Asmodeus ordered. "We're going back."

The car traveled in silence back toward downtown. The demon prince of LA rolled his cane between his palms, intent on the silver mass of writhing bodies that crowned it. At length, he asked, "The seraph Azaziel?"

The fiend relayed the question over the phone in the same deliberate, grinding voice he'd used all night. Then he reported, "He's with Lorelei."

"Unfallen?"

"Not for long, if she knows what's good for her," the fiend promised.

"That remains to be seen," Floria muttered.

Asmodeus grasped Floria's shoulder, his talons just piercing her skin, and pulled her up onto the seat beside him. As if she were a doll, he smoothed the gold lamé dress over her curves. "I'm pleased with how you conducted yourself tonight, my girl. Well done with the invitations, too. I enjoyed seeing so many of the family at Lorelei's exorcism. We ought not to wait so long before we gather again."

The car pulled to a smooth stop. Asmodeus reached past Floria to open the limo door. He inhaled deeply. Acrid smoke with a pleasant tinge of burning flesh filled the morning outside. Flames engulfed the dance club in an inferno battled ineffectually by a quartet of fire trucks.

Involuntarily, Floria's gaze shot upward. She scanned the sky for the angel of death. Smoke would provide him the perfect cover.

"I'll give you credit for any sinners you harvest," Asmodeus told her. "Boys, go along and make sure that angel doesn't molest her."

He drew Floria to him for a kiss so deep it unhinged her limbs. With a grin, he shoved her away. "Come report when you've finished. The boys will call you a car."

Head swimming with confidence, Floria slipped out of her dress and pumps, rather than have them ruined by soot. She laid them on the car seat, then checked her small spangled clutch to make sure of her dagger and compact. Shifting into her true form, the succubus uncoiled her tail as her skin became as red as the fire before her. Both fiends tagged after her in silence as she walked into the inferno.

Morning dawned brown in Los Angeles, just the way Lorelei liked it. The air smelled of car exhaust and dust, underlaid a hint of charred flesh.

She wondered if her sister Floria had gotten out out of Lost Angels safely, if any of the nightclub still stood. If not, it could be a whole new world this morning. The succubus licked her lips.

Wearing her human form, Lorelei snuggled against her angel on the cement stoop of the shuttered bodega. Azaziel, also in mortal seeming, looked wan in the morning light. He'd lost his leather jacket during the fight at the nightclub. Angelic blood – mostly his – smeared his torn white button-down shirt. Dried ichor flaked off his blue jeans. She petted his blond hair back into place, but there was little she could do while sitting on this stoop to ease the exhaustion in his eyes.

"Look," she purred, "we both could use some shut-eye. If you don't want to take me back to your church, fine. I have a couple of places we could crash."

"We're not going back to your sister's den," Azaziel answered. "I met her last night. She didn't like me much."

Lorelei laughed. "Don't take it personally, Aza. Floria doesn't like anyone much. But I'm not in a hurry to link back up with her either. Things were done last week, aspersions were cast... She and I need some distance, if we're going to keep our friendship."

Azaziel chuckled. "I think that's true of my family as well."

"I don't doubt it." The succubus stood up and held her hands down to him. "Come on, Lover. The longer you sit, the harder it's going to be to get moving."

He rubbed his thumb over her long thin fingers to sneak in a caress as she pulled him to his feet. His tone was not as affectionate. "We're not going to put one of your projects out of his bed, either."

She smiled, letting the dawn sparkle in her lavender eyes. "Nice idea, Aza. Jealousy always works in my favor. But why invite complications? All I want is a bath and some clean sheets. Work can wait."

He wrapped his arm over her shoulder and held her close, even as he commented bitterly, "I thought you were still on the clock."

When they first met, she'd teased him that all the time she spent with him was in service of Hell, trying to tilt him into falling. She wasn't sure that was still true. She was too tired to invest much thought in the topic right now.

"First a bath," she promised. "We can debate philosophy afterward, if we're still awake."

She stepped out from under his arm to open her Louis Vuitton clutch and pull out an antique silver compact. A few quick strokes with her fingers touched up her makeup and smoothed her hair. Then she drew out a slip of shadow which slid up under the suit coat she'd borrowed from Azaziel's sister. The shadow quickly molded itself into a form-fitting dress that sheathed her from knees to wrists. She twisted to make certain the seams on her stockings were straight.

Azaziel watched the transformation with a bemused smile. She was glad to see him take some pleasure in the prize he'd won, after he'd marched into Hell's embassy to rescue her.

The angel surprised her with a rare flash of humor. "Now that you've got your armor on, ready to face the world?"

"One corner of it at a time," she teased back. "That's the secret of my success." She thrust up her right hand, hip slightly cocked toward the street, and waited.

Aza stared at her. She could tell by the crimp of his sandy eyebrows that confusion wasn't an emotion he was used to. He looked at mortals and knew what they were doing, why they were doing it, and how they justified the action to themselves. Now that Ashleigh's soul had been exorcised from her, Lorelei was once again infernal enough to be mystifying. If he were a shade less exhausted, that would probably intrigue him.

Luckily, he didn't have to wait long to decipher her pose. A Veteran's Cab pulled up to the curb. Lorelei leaned over to talk to the driver, a dried-up ex-soldier, old before his years, counting the days until he could jump this chickenshit world. Definitely something she could work with, if she didn't already have a date.

"I don't know what I'm doing in this neighborhood," the driver groused. "I never come out here."

"Chateau Marmont?" Lorelei asked sweetly. "Could you take us in the back way? I'd just as soon duck the paparazzi, you know?"

"Sure," he said, not at all sure.

"It's on Sunset Boulevard," she said helpfully.

"I know where it is," the driver snapped. "I just don't know where the back entrance is."

"No worries." She helped the wounded angel shift into the back of the cab, tucked her legs inside, and pulled the door shut after her. "I'll direct you."

"Chateau Marmont?" Aza asked, sotto voce.

Lorelei grinned. "The staff is very discreet."

"I can only imagine."

To be continued in *Angelus Rose*, available in November 2016.

www.ingramcontent.com/pod-product-compliance
Lightning Source LLC
Chambersburg PA
CBHW071144170626

46809CB00002B/763